BY JAMES LEO HERLIHY

Novels

ALL FALL DOWN

MIDNIGHT COWBOY

THE SEASON OF THE WITCH

Plays

BLUE DENIM (with William Noble)

CRAZY OCTOBER

STOP, YOU'RE KILLING ME

Stories

THE SLEEP OF BABY FILBERTSON AND OTHER STORIES

A STORY THAT ENDS WITH A SCREAM AND EIGHT OTHERS

SIMON AND SCHUSTER NEW YORK

THE SEASON

OF THE WITCH

JAMES LEO HERLIHY

The excerpt on page 171 is from *Demian* by Hermann Hesse, published by Harper & Row. Used by permission of the publisher.

First Printing

SNB 671-20905-1
Library of Congress Catalog Card Number: 73-151496
Designed by Jack Jaget
Manufactured in the United States of America
By The Book Press Inc., Brattleboro, Vt.

Special thanks to Evan Rhodes
for valuable help
in editing the manuscript.

J.L.H.

For DICK DUANE

THE SEASON OF THE WITCH

BELLE WOODS, MICHIGAN, IN MY BED, SEPTEMBER 2, 1969

Sometimes I think Mother hits it right on the nose when she calls me a cold cookie. I've just spent five full minutes eyeballing this room and telling myself all sorts of sad things like Oh dear, my princess doll will miss me, and Just think, Gloria, you'll never spend another night here, etc., etc.

But nothing happens. You might think I could squeeze out one teensy little tearlet just for form's sake, but my eyes are as dry as stones. All I feel is relief, anticipation, and enough excitement to keep me awake for the rest of my life.

Unless . . . !

There. That's better. I just found a roach in my bag and got two lovely tokes out of it. Thanks to the prez and his grass curtain on the Mexican border, we're suffering a ghastly marijuana famine this summer, so this is my first smoke in days. I'd almost forgotten how much I dig it. (Not really.)

———

Now, let us return to

Departure Blues, absence of

Back in the dark ages of my girlhood I used to think I'd have to get married to spring myself from this dainty quilted prison, but not a bit of it, my dears. John, my fellow fugitive, is homosexual. The first time we took LSD together, we observed our relationship. It couldn't be simpler: He's my guru, I'm his earth mother. Which means I'll be walking out of here tomorrow not in bondage but with a beautiful soul companion. No compromises, no strings, no bullshit, just two free souls (both Pisces!) dedicated to one another's purity and freedom, embarking together on their journey into reality.

Reality. Wow. And to think it starts *tomorrow!* If I weren't just faintly stoned, I'd probably faint and turn to stone.

This has been such a bleak summer, with John going to the mailbox every day expecting to find the Big Finger waiting for him, me trying to help him decide what to do, and neither of us able to come up with any answers.

And then suddenly, Friday morning, the waiting is over.

I hear John's voice from the yard next door, calling up to my window. I look out. He's leaning on the fence, waving an envelope in his hand. I know immediately what it is.

"When?" I ask.

"Monday, the twenty-second."

"How do you feel?"

"I've decided to split. Want to come?"

"Yes."

I loved my answering without a second's pause. I thought that had style. So did John. He told me so later.

Where to go?

We went to Delano's to discuss it, because Delano knows everything. He really does. I found *that* out when he was my lover.

John thought he'd like to try living underground for a while, right here in the States. If he had to, he could always go to Canada later on. So the only question was *where* in the States. I said what about New York, because that's where my real father lives and I've been dying to meet him ever since I was 12 and first heard of his existence.

Delano thought New York was sheer genius. He said it was the only place in the country where a person could get really lost. So that was it, the perfect place for both of us. There have been other miracles, too.

An hour ago for instance, while I was next door in John's basement going over our super-simple plans for the 99th time, Delano phoned to say he had a buyer for the Vespa. This is major news. It means we won't have to hitchhike, we'll have bus fare *plus*. We both know luck like this can't be just luck. It's much too spooky. Obviously our trip is being guided by higher beings. All John and I have to do is keep our heads straight, maintain a nice high, and *go with it*.

Tomorrow, we wake up whenever we feel like it, grab our bags, and head out on the Vespa in the direction of Aunt June's cottage. Then, at Jefferson Avenue, we turn right instead of left. The buyer for the scooter will be waiting at Delano's. From there, after relaxing for a couple of hours and stoking our beautiful heads on some of Delano's righteous hashish, we proceed downtown to catch the Greyhound at 4:30, never to be heard from again.

That's not true. We'll have to write occasionally. Otherwise we'll feel guilty.

Speaking of which, I'd better compose a little number right now to leave on the kitchen table.

Or.

Why don't I just put the Beatles on the stereo downstairs, let it play over and over again

She's leaving home
after living alone
for so many years.

But that wouldn't do, because when it got to the part about "she's meeting a man from the motor trade," mother'd say, "Ha, the little slut, she's run off with a used car dealer!"

Why am I chattering to myself like this? Avoiding something?

The note, of course. Okay. Here goes.

Dear Mother,
 I'm gone.

Stunning beginning. How obvious can you get?

Dear Mother,
 By the time you read this

That's an *improvement?*

Dear Mother,
 At first I wasn't going to leave a note, because you never believe anything anyway, but I feel I have to explain, even if you think it's all crap. To begin with, I'm not angry. I love you. I really do. I *was* angry, because you made me miss the Woodstock Festival, but I'm over that now. And yet, missing Woodstock is the reason I have to leave now instead of waiting till I'm 18, as agreed. This is hard to explain, maybe impossible. Woodstock wasn't just a festival, it's the future and I have to go out and meet it somewhere. No doubt it'll be muddy and crowded too, with not enough food and no place to pee, but there'll be love and peace wherever my compatriots are, and

that's why I have to go find them and live with them and try to make a real

It's no good. She'll never buy it. To her, love and peace is sex and drugs. Besides, who am I kidding when I say I'm not angry?

Dear Mother,

I'm getting out of here because I'm pissed off. I missed Woodstock but I'm not missing my life, no matter what you say. You and a hundred million mothers just like you are the reason there had to be a festival in the first place. It's urgent that the earth be saved from your lethal, uptight clutches before you succeed in hassling the life out of it altogether. I'm sick of living in this house pretending to be your daughter just because you gave birth to me. I saw very clearly under acid that *I'm your mother*, and you're a wicked, reckless, selfish brat. I'm fed up to the teeth with your blind, criminal, phony, aggressive, power-mad behavior, and I have decided to abandon you to shift for yourself in this plastic palace that means more to you than I ever could.

Okay, Gloria, now that the bile is out of your system, can't you write something sweet? *Try!*

Dear Mommy,

Your itty-bitty girl is running away from home because she's naughty. But she loves her mommy very much and she promises not to take any more nasty old drugs. So please don't worry about her. Her's a big girl now and if some dirty long-haired bum tries to stick his thing in her, she'll scream for the Green Berets to come and save her. Love and Kisses.

Gloria

Maybe I'll do better in the morning.

Good night, room. Good night, princess doll. Good night,

15

my girlhood, you poor wretch. Somehow I've managed to survive you.

Later

Can't sleep. My head won't quit.

Fantasy: The simple act of running away from home causes some miraculous change in my character! I become disciplined. I keep my journal faithfully, every single day. Starting tomorrow at 4:30, the minute the bus pulls out of Detroit, I record everything that happens to John and me, his adventures living like a fugitive to avoid becoming a hired killer in Uncle Sam's Army, and my first meeting with my real father. I write it all down, a simple flat report of the truth, no flourishes, no bullshit. To keep myself honest, I vow it's not for publication. Then, one day in New York, when I've got enough material to fill a good fat book, I lose the notebook on the subway. By chance, it gets found. By a reader for a publishing house, etc., etc. The Detroit *News* calls it the Most Fabulous Human Document of Our Time, *Time* magazine prints my picture. (On the cover?) Much success. Much money. We buy a strip of land in Central America, start a new nation dedicated to love and peace. Live happily ever after. End of fantasy

DEPARTURE DAY MORNING, SEPTEMBER 3, 1969

Dear Mother,

The reason I'm leaving is to put an end to the hassles. You and I have been hurting each other and I don't think either of us wants to. I won't make any promises about what I'll be doing, because the whole point of leaving home is to be free. But I can promise one thing. I'll be myself. I won't fake anything.

I've given some thought to whether or not I can truthfully say I love you, and I find that I can. I do love you, Mother, I truly do. But hardly ever when we're in the same room. *And I know you feel the same way about me.* I don't think we should blame each other for this. It's just life.

Love,

Gloria

This isn't much, but at least it's honest and not unkind. John says I should mail it special delivery instead of leaving it on the table because if she sees it before we leave town, we're fucked.

Late afternoon, on the bus

Another miracle. The bus fare was only $28.75 apiece, so if we don't make friends immediately in New York, we can spend a night or two in some hotel.

Back at the Greyhound station, I suffered a minor attack of paranoia. I was sure the clerk knew we were runaways and would call the police the minute we left the window. John quieted me down, which is a switch. Usually he has the paranoia and I do the soothing.

Then two minutes later, while I'm in the phone booth calling Mother to get my father's address, John has a little fit of his own. As I'm dialing the last digit, he slaps his hand down on the receiver cradle, severing the connection.

"Gloria, *think!* She'll know it's a local call, and if she's not too stupid, she'll send fuzz to all airports and bus stations."

"Who cares?" I said. "By then we'll be on the bus and gone!"

"All right, but be safe. Look." He took from his pocket a handful of ¼-inch brass washers with the holes in the middles stuffed to make them act like dimes in pay phones. "When she answers, don't say a word. Drop in five or six of these. Then the bells'll go ding ding ding and she'll think it's long distance."

I didn't stop to think it through, but it sounded reasonable. So I dialed again, and when mother hello-ed, I dropped in a few washers and made the bells go. Then I said, "Mother, this is Gloria. I'm phoning from a distant city."

"What are you talking about, Gloria? Gloria, where are you?" She was talking stiff-lipped, which painted the whole picture for me. I could see her lying on her chaise longue next to the phone with a mask of Sudden Beauty all over her triple-Virgo face.

18

"I'm in a distant city, Mother, and that's all I'm telling you."

"You're at Aunt June's cottage. Now stop this nonsense."

"If I'm calling from Aunt June's, why did I have to drop in seven dimes?"

"To deceive me. I don't know why yet. I suspect I'm about to be punished for something."

I covered the mouthpiece and whispered to John, "She didn't fall for it. Now what?"

"I don't know. Brazen it out." He crossed his fingers for me. Big help.

"You truly hate me, don't you, Gloria," Mother was saying. "And that's what all this *behavior* is about. All right, hate me if you must, but I'm still your mother and I demand the truth."

"All right then, we're at Kennedy airport in New York. John McFadden's with me. I can prove all this because he's right here and you can talk to him if you want to."

"First of all, young lady, you're lying. But if you're not, I'll die. . . . Oh, God! *Are* you telling the truth?"

"I can't talk forever, Mother. I don't have that many coins."

"Then give me the number and I'll call you back."

"No, thanks. I'm not getting into any big discussions. I've sent you a note, special delivery. All I want is my father's address."

"Your father's what? He's at the office, you know that."

"I didn't say my stepfather. I said my father. Hank Glyczwycz."

Pause.

"I beg your pardon, Gloria?"

"I don't expect you to understand this, Mother, but I've had a revelation, and I know I've got to meet my real father. That's what I've come to New York for."

"Gloria. Sweetheart. Have you taken LSD again?" She went into a cooing voice thing, like somebody luring a lunatic out of a treetop. "Mother's not angry, darling, she loves you very much, but you must be truthful. Are you tripping again, honey? You know you did promise Mother you'd never do it again, hmm?"

"I'm not tripping. I'm in a phone booth in New York and I'm asking you for Hank Glyczwycz's address. May I have it or not?"

After a loaded silence, she said, "I do not carry on conversations with cruel, evil young ladies."

"Okay then, I'll hang up. Shall I hang up?"

"I want to know where you are, immediately."

"We'll make a bargain. Give me the address and I'll tell you the whole truth."

John made a warning face and shook his head vigorously. I gave him an I-know-what-I'm-doing with my hand, but of course I was just playing the whole thing by ear.

"Gloria, I do not have the address you are requesting. I am not in contact with that person, and you know it."

"Yes, but I'm sure you have the address where he teaches, don't you?"

"Cruel cruel cruel."

"What's so cruel about a girl wanting to meet her own father?"

"Nothing. Nothing at all. No matter how much she makes her mother suffer. Anyway, I haven't the faintest idea how to reach him. Being a Communist, he's probably changed his name a dozen times by now. So there's simply nothing to go by."

"Do you mean to tell me *you* couldn't locate him if you wanted to?"

"Suppose you tell me how?"

"Let's skip it. I'll just hang up. Okay?"

"No, no. We won't skip it. I won't have you thinking I could lie to you. Now you just tell me, Gloria, how would I go about locating the man? You don't think City College of New York would hire a man who admitted to having once been a member of the Communist party, do you?" (Thank you, Mother dear! Until you blurted it out, I hadn't known it was City College!) "His name was in the papers and everything. Don't you suppose the FBI knows what it's doing? So of course he had to change his name. If he hasn't been deported altogether. Which is really quite likely. He's probably back in Poland somewhere by now. In fact, I'm sure he is. Yes, I'm sure he's been deported. So you see, darling, you're looking for a man who for all practical purposes has ceased to exist. That means you're not thinking very clearly, doesn't it? And do you know why? It's because your hostility toward your mother is clouding your brain. Truly, sweetheart, and I'm not angry either, I'm just pointing this out, because I know how you love candor."

I decided to play it her way. "Thanks, Mother. You're right. I do appreciate having things like that pointed out. But listen, and I know I'm probably not thinking too clearly, even now that you've straightened me out, but what if a person were to go to the History Department at City College, and just ask around? Don't you suppose she could gather some sort of a clue?"

There was a long silence on the Belle Woods end of the telephone, a silence my moon-in-Scorpio self bathed in luxuriously while Mrs. Random recovered her aplomb. And I knew exactly what she'd say. Her first words would be Very well, Gloria. And they were.

"Very well, Gloria." Her voice was dark with tragedy, pain, and assorted bullshit. "*Persist*," she said. "*Persist* in your hatred of your mother. *Look* up this man. *Stir* up the past. *Make* as much pain as you can for me. Perhaps that's

21

the kind of person you want to be. And if it is, I can't stop you. Just know that whatever you do, and however you hurt me, I'll still love you. You can't stand that, Gloria, can you? The hardest thing you have to bear in this world is that your mother really loves you. If it weren't for that, you'd be free to become just a wanton little bitch who takes her high IQ that God gave her and her wonderful flair for words, and uses them to cut people up with. Is that what you really want to be, Gloria?"

While Mother was delivering her neat little thumbnail portrait of me, John started tugging at my elbow. It was time to get on the bus. Somehow I managed to round out the phone call with a minimum of hassle and followed John to the departure gate. But all the while my mind was playing a movie for me:

I arrive in New York, trot right up to City College, sit in on one of Professor Glyczwycz's classes. At first glance, it's perfectly clear he's a Great Man, Turned On, Wise, Open, Terribly Big in the Movement. And for extras, he's got long- ish salt-and-pepper hair and a thick walrus mustache. After class I introduce myself. Big shock, much fainting. We hug. He thinks I'm terrific, just the kind of daughter he'd always hoped for. I go home with him, to this big, sort of empty bachelor's apartment and cook a meal for him. It turns out heaven, pure Julia Child. He's bowled over. Within a week, I become indispensable. John and I both move in and the three of us become a family, go to peace marches together, etc., etc.

———————

Something wonderful just happened. No one watching would have seen a thing, and yet it was spectacular. I just looked at John and really *saw* him. The whole thing, inside out, in the round. He's glorious. Every once in a while I get a blast like this, and it reminds me why I adore him so.

At the moment, he's scared. Sitting here next to the window pulling his eyebrows and biting his nails. No, I guess he's working on the cuticles, the nails are already gone. This trip is his first big manhood test thing and he's afraid he might blow it. My earth-mother urges are overwhelming. I want to hold him and say, Shoo shoo, baby, everything'll be great. But of course I wouldn't dare. And yet I can actually *see* him worrying and it touches me so I can hardly bear it. Everything about him does. Unfortunately we don't turn each other on sexually, not even when we're lying around naked together. I suppose that's just as well. No sex, no hangups. I shouldn't phrase it so negatively though, because the thing we have together is wildly positive. Between the two of us there's this colossal flow of soul energy that keeps us both super-UP, and we're both totally committed to the belief that we simply must as a matter of conscience stay high as much of the time as possible. John and I are convinced that people who go around *un*high are the ones who are crapping up the world. John is definitely not one of them. He is entirely sweet. He is pure light. Once when I was tripping I saw his aura, and it's just about 99 per cent angel-colored.

I function as the female principle in his life. When I look at him, I reflect him. He sees mirrored in me how totally marvelous he is in all ways. Gradually he'll come to know himself fully, and then his mind will stop over-amping. He's always worrying about things that will take care of themselves. For instance, right now he's trying to outsmart Manhattan before we even get there by memorizing the map Delano gave him. Delano drew directions all over it with magic markers, circling in Tompkins Square Park, Fillmore East, etc. John had all the north and south streets committed

23

to memory before we left Detroit, and now he's working on Greenwich Village.

Thinking about sex and hangups just now, I flashed on Delano. He's been an angel this week, helping John and me make our getaway. And he doesn't have that much time to spare either. Getting out an underground newspaper every two weeks is a full-time job, especially with the cops hassling him all the time and constant money problems, but he came through like a real brother. What I want to know is why he had to spoil it all by getting me excited. Ever since we "broke up" (stupid, infuriating phrase!), everything's been lovely and relaxed between us. I'm never uptight with him, and I don't make him uptight. We're just brothers. But this afternoon, he wanted to make love. I knew he did. He kept trying to turn me on with his eyes, deliberately looking at my neck in that lingering way that makes me want to faint. Also, there must be something aphrodisiac about having a newspaper office in the dining room of an old tumbledown house. I always have to remind myself not to get turned on by the smell of it. And of course when the editor and publisher happens to be not only a Leo but a lion with a beautiful tawny mane and enormous gentle hands . . .

Enough. *Later* for Delano. I'm on my way to New York, and right outside my window there's a glorious sunset.

John and I just had a conversation.

I said, "John, remember 'America,' that Simon and Garfunkel song? That's us, John. 'Michigan seems like a dream to me now.'"

"Oh, wow, you're not gonna believe this," he said. "But I've been hearing that exact song in my head, and look! There's the moon rising over an open field!"

It was. It was right there, rising over an open field. We both got enormous goose pimples from the magic of it, and then John said, "My God, there's a man with a gabardine suit; do you suppose he's a spy?" John and I can riff like this for hours, our heads are *always* in the same place.

Anyway, this whole Simon and Garfunkel thing makes me want desperately to cry, but I'm trying to wait till Pittsburgh so I can do it in the ladies' room. We get 45 minutes there, and I'm going to spend the whole time bawling. I'm not sure about what. I think it's just because I love *us* so much. I love John and me, and I love all our brothers and sisters, the ones we'll meet and the ones we won't, all riding around on Greyhound buses searching for America out the window and looking for cigarettes in their raincoat pockets while the moon rises over open fields, and wondering all the while if there'll be cops waiting at the next stop. When I look at John, with his bad skin and his hideous but gorgeous hair that doesn't look right being long, and his scared little chin and his big gray wide-open eyes, and his long pale boy's neck with the Adam's apple, and that awful Army coat, when I look at him, I see all of us, all the people who have to be true and real no matter what, and it just makes me very happy to know we're so fucking beautiful. But I will not cry in front of John. Tears freak him out.

Midnight

By the time we got to Pittsburgh, I was too sleepy to cry, so we decided to get out and look the place over. Nothing

25

much to report, it's more or less like Detroit. There must have been a thousand freaks pouring out of *Easy Rider* and a lot of them smiled at us. Then John got the worries again, he was afraid the driver would leave without us, so we got some coffee in cartons and came back to the bus and sat here drinking it. Now I'm wide awake again.

If I ever do write a book about my life, and I certainly intend to someday, these notebooks really will come in handy. *The Life and Loves of Gloria Random.* Maybe by then I'll have changed my name to Glyczwycz. Even if I don't find my father in New York, I'd like to be called that. Then when I become fabulously famous, he'll hear about me and the name will make his ears perk up. Maybe it should be Gloria Glyczwycz Random, so everybody in Belle Woods will know it's me, too. Mother of course will break out in purple polka-dot hives, but I can't help that.

In chapter one, I'll explain to the reader that even though my legal surname has a lovely bona fide wasp ring to it, I am a Jewess by blood, sired out of wedlock by a Polish Communist, and that I choose to mention this fact at the outset in spite of the embarrassment it may cause in certain quarters, so that my real father, wherever he is, will see what pride I take in my heritage.

But of course that doesn't ring true. Too bad I'm not more skilled in kidding myself. All I'm really interested in doing is rattling Mother's rafters by exposing her. What a delicious temptation! All her friends would devour every word of it. How the telephones would buzz with that first chapter! My dear, have you heard? Irene Random's daughter is not only a Jew, but a Jew bastard to boot! . . . On publication day, Mother would have a collapse and be forced to call in her

26

special emergency pal, Maude Dangerfield, to take over arrangements for the funeral of her reputation.

But I could never do it.

Could I?

This is a perfect example of my sun in Pisces in direct conflict with my moon in Scorpio. Gloria Pisces Me has compassion for her mother, knowing how sad the poor bitch really is, still secretly in love with her gorgeous Polack lover. Gloria Pisces Me even suspects that whatever happened between them must have had some really powerhouse depth to it, and that Hank Glyczwycz is really a great and wonderful man. Because whenever Mother talks about him, which is *never* by choice, there's no hatred in her voice or in her face. Only nervousness. And a kind of fake disdain. She tries to make him seem inconsequential, as if he were nothing more than a minor blunder of her girlhood. "You know, darling, he wasn't much, just a pushy little refugee with all sorts of pretensions, a typical Communist." "But was he awful?" I asked. "I mean did he beat you or bore you or sit around picking his toes, or what?" But Mother won't be pressed. She just gets up and walks away.

So. Gloria Pisces Me would bet her eyes Mother still thinks longingly of their nights together. And at the same time Gloria moon-in-Scorpio Me is just as certain the only reason she wouldn't marry him was because he was poor and had every prospect in the world of staying that way. She could have got used to the idea of becoming Mrs. Glyczwycz, and somehow she'd have swallowed the Jewish part, but never ever *ever* would she have borne doing her own housework and giving herself home permanents. For some weird mixed-

27

up Karmic reason my mother's fate was to be born a poor Irish Catholic from Corktown, birth a Jew bastard, and then become a rich WASP who spends her afternoons under dryers and chasing down bargains in antique stores.

I dislike my moon-in-Scorpio self for holding all this against her. I try to remember how she must suffer for not having had the balls to marry the man she adored. But it doesn't work. Because no matter what I tell myself, there are all these *other* evidences of mother's balls all over the place. And they're not tiny. They're the size of avocados and you can practically hear them klunk against each other when she walks.

So maybe she *didn't* love him. Maybe she slept with him for some other reason. Curiosity, say. Because I'm not really sure she has any deeper feelings. Maybe her ego does, but not her heart. Heart feelings are just things she mimics because she's heard about them and knows how useful they are. Like money and credit cards and membership in clubs. Feelings can be flashed around on the power market. I could sit here and document this conviction, but the subject of my mother is bringing me down. I think I'll have some more career fantasies instead.

What if I leave off the Random altogether and just call myself Gloria Glyczwycz? No one would ever be able to pronounce it, but I could always induce my publishers to print a pronunciation guide right on the dust jacket.

THE AUTOBIOGRAPHY OF GLORIA GLYCZWYCZ
(pronounced Gliz-Witch)

Wow! I have just stumbled upon the fantastic nom de plume of all time. Gliz Witch. What a great name! Better yet, I'll turn it around, Witch Gliz. People are always telling me I'm a witch, so why shouldn't I be called that? John and I have decided to take new names for our new lives anyway.

28

He *has* to, but that's not our real reason. We want names that suit our souls.

The Gliz part isn't too great, but it'll do.

Miss Gliz, what are your views on the revolution?

I can always ask Dick Cavett or Johnny Carson or whomever to call me by my first name.

Just call me Witch, Johnny.

What a tender, lovely name!

Hi, Witch!

Witch, could you come here, please?

I love you, Witch.

———————

I just tried it out on John.

"John," I said, "I've got my new name."

"Really? You've got your new name al*ready?*"

"Mm. Are you ready to hear it?"

"But I haven't got *mine* yet!" He looked like he was going to panic, so I gently reminded him we had all the time in the world. Then I told him.

"It's Witch. Witch Gliz." I watched while it moved into his head. Then, when I saw his eyes open in a certain way, I knew I had a big hit on my hands.

He repeated it. "Witch Gliz?"

"Mm-hm. Glyczwycz, spelled phonetically, syllables reversed. What do you think?"

"After your real father, right?"

"Right. Can you dig it?"

"Far out! But what if you meet him and don't dig *him?* Then you'll have to change your name again."

"Not a chance. I *know* I'll dig him."

"Witch Gliz. Hm. Are you going to have it that way on your books and all?"

"I'm not sure yet, but I thought you'd help me decide."

"Okay. Say it again and then keep still and I'll see what it does to my head."

I repeated it very clearly, and now John is thinking about it.

But I'm not. I'm thinking about John.

For his sake, I can't help wishing he weren't gay. I've heard that it can be a real hassle when you're not good-looking. And John isn't. His beauty is inner and most gay people seem to go for shoulders and good complexions. Not just gay people of course. Everyone does. Still, it doesn't seem fair. I'm hoping in New York he'll find a whole different scene, some really tuned-in types who have their heads together enough to appreciate Who He Is. John's truly fabulous assets are also the reasons I worry about him. It's very difficult to be 19 by the calendar, 45 in mental powers, 10,000 years old in the soul, and yet have a 9-year-old's overall ability to cope with this really psychotic mess the Piscean age has made of the world. Actually though, he's grown up tremendously in the last two years, ever since I turned him on to pot.

Which was June 4, 1967. I remember the date because I got turned on myself about two hours earlier, and there are certain dates a girl just never forgets.

(I wonder where I got all this *speed?* I'm writing like there's no tomorrow and digging it totally. I think I'll write all the way to New York! Why not? I'm free! I can do as I please!)

After a school dance, Arthur Hunnicut, this fairly groovy senior took me out to Belle Isle and we parked. Nothing memorable about the circumstances. He just turned me on and that was it. We didn't make out or anything. (I forget why. I guess his MG was too small or something.) But the main thing that stands out in my memory is the grass and this wild grin it gave me. I was smiling all the way down to my navel. (And that's not poetry either. The navel is exactly where a marijuana smile originates.) Anyway, I couldn't wait to turn John on, so I talked Arthur out of three joints and when he took me home, I went right next door to John's.

He was down in his lair watching the 11 o'clock news on TV. John's lair is the Ultimate Pad (or *was*—all that's behind us now, alas!), full of super sound equipment—plus a real lion's skin with a real head and tail. It would take me an hour to list all the groovy things John had in that basement. Dr. McFadden has money oozing out of him like sweat. He doesn't really dig John, so he used to buy him all sorts of things to make up for it. Actually, I don't mean to knock Dr. McF. He wasn't really square, just a nothing. A boxy little psychoanalyst who Knew Everything and Did Everything Right. John's turning out such a mess, by straight standards, was an awful puzzlement for Dr. McF. Here was John with a high IQ, flunking everything in sight—a perfect diet and pimples out to here, etc. Everything fucked up. Usually he blamed John's mother, who was tall and skinny and beautiful and alcoholic. (Aquarius, I think. Aquarians sometimes tend to get bored and go to pieces when things don't go right.) When John was eight, she was hauled off to *a place* and died a few months later. John and I think she set fire to her room, but we haven't got the full story. Anyway, she cooled.

Then Dr. McF hired a housekeeper to pretend she was John's mother so the Environment would continue to have all the Essential Elements for Child Rearing and blah blah blah. I don't know where he found her. She was the sort of person Ford would turn out if it was turning out mother substitutes instead of cars—all the latest gadgets but none of them really worked. She was a *down* masquerading as an *up*. Which is about ten times worse than being a good old-fashioned straightforward down. Her name was Mrs. Putz. That can't be the right spelling, but it sounded like that, *put* with a *z* on it. Anyway, Mrs. Putz did everything right, Cooked Hot Meals, Was Cheerful, Took an Interest, Showed Affection, right down the old list, all for $600 a month and a room with her own TV. And so naturally between her and Dr. McF the whole situation got so plastic John nearly freaked out. He could take everything but the freeze-dried cheerfulness and the Saran-wrapped affection. The first few weeks were unbelievable. Then John and I got together and worked the whole thing out. We as much as told her that if she liked the job—and she did—she'd better play ball. So John got his Nice Hot Meals delivered to his lair, unbeknownst to Dr. McF, who was practically never there at mealtime anyway. (I think he lived on sandwiches choked down between patients. After all, when you can cop 50 to 100 bucks an hour, you don't go squandering your time on meals. Not if you're Really Responsible.) So John got left alone from then on and managed to cultivate his genius without too much bullshit. Mostly he stuffed his head with books.

However. Back to the night of the first grass.

I slip into John's fabulous lair, my mind all fluffed up with this highly memorable Virgin High, and three joints stuck in my belt. John's watching Huntley-Brinkley. Only if it was 11 P.M., it probably wasn't Huntley-Brinkley, but anyway it was the news. News is sacred to John. He really studies it and knows what it's about. Everything that passes before his eyes seems to grab the full attention and interest of this stunning mind of his. I've always had a deep natural respect for John's concentration, so I sat perfectly still and tried to watch the screen. News is always a problem for me, but on grass I find it impossible. Suddenly it seems to me the news is over and they're showing this bad-bad movie, some sort of comedy takeoff about a little Oriental dictator. I said, "John, did you switch channels?" He said, "No, why?" I said, "What happened to the news?" He said, "This *is* the news." I said, "John, you're kidding, you mean those are real people?" And then he shushed me, and during the commercial he started to clue me in about what was happening in Vietnam. Fantastic. Uncle Sam pretending to the world that this little shit is the People's Choice and not allowing free elections because the Communists would *win!* I told John it was too horrible and I didn't want to think about it.

Right there and then I whipped out the grass and turned him on.

Some people don't get a thing the first time. But John's a born head. He got the Great Grin from Within on his third toke, and by the time we finished the second joint, we both contracted a powerhouse case of the Psychedelic Giggles. For a while, maybe half an hour, everything was wildly funny. We went outside and ran around the yard looking at things like a couple of brand new angels set loose in paradise. It was still the same old yard, of course, but our eyes had changed. They'd gotten clear, like the eyes of small children, and we were able to see the magic of everything again, the way we used to, the real natural magic of the world that's usually lost on you when you're straight. For instance, trees don't just stand there neutral. They're friendly and want you to touch and admire them, and flowers quiver with pleasure when you look at them. Then we climbed the fence into my yard and sat on the teeter-totter for a couple of minutes. It was the first time we'd used it in years and years and a squirrel came out to watch. While we were teetering, John said, "Gloria, we're criminals, do you realize that? It's against the law to feel like this!" So we lay on the grass for a while thinking how peculiar that was, and while we were lying there, John said, "How do we know the sky isn't down instead of up? Maybe we're just hanging by our backs!" And so suddenly the sky was beneath us and earth became the heart of heaven instead of just the outskirts. Then we held each other and vowed eternal love, and went back to John's basement to play "Sergeant Pepper" on the stereo.

It was fairly new then and neither of us had really gotten into it before that night. Grass makes your ears enormous, you hear with your Whole Self. John has these Koss headphones that are always breaking, but that night they didn't. You could actually hear an entire Lonely Hearts Club Band sitting inside your soul broadcasting through your bloodstream to every nerve you had. We lay on John's lion skin with our eyes closed, holding hands. After "Mr. Kite," John got up to turn the record over, and suddenly he had a whole new feeling about the lion. It was real. *Really* real. Lying on its skin became too savage for words. He petted its face and apologized to it, and from then on he kept it in his closet.

Anyway, when he finally got the record turned over, he brought the album cover back with him and we sat there studying the photographs of these four fantastic men. On the inside cover, they're all looking right at you, 100 per cent decent and lovable and sweet and manly. And you get the feeling that if they knew you, they'd dig you exactly the same way you dig them.

"A Day in the Life Of" blew our minds totally, so we played the entire album all over again. For me it was a joy trip. I felt joy about everything, even the sad parts. That's why the Beatles are geniuses. They give you the feeling that the world really *is* a ghastly mess, but it'll be okay in the end because we're all so beautiful. Stay high, they tell us, and the world will gradually come around. And you believe it, because it's obviously true.

When the record stopped, John just went on lying there with his headphones on, staring at the ceiling.

I sat up and put my hand on his brow. He took my wrist and clung to it for dear life. I didn't say a word. I just waited for him to show me what he was feeling. Pot gives you these flawless emotional instincts. Then, after the longest time, he said, "Gloria, I'm in love."

And I thought, Wow, with whom? *Me?*

At this point I wasn't sure John was gay. Once when we were 12, I tried to seduce him—not out of any real interest, it just seemed like a good idea at the moment. But John was more or less embarrassed, so I dropped it.

I said, "Oh, John, that's thrilling."

And I waited some more.

He sat up and lit a cigarette, a regular one, and we passed it back and forth. Then he said, "It's sort of a bummer, because it's like I'm in love with George Harrison for godsake."

Then he folded his arms tight against himself and sat with his shoulders all hunched up as if he were in pain.

I said, "John, I am, too. I'm in love with *all* the Beatles. How come you're uptight about it?"

"Because it means I'm a fag, doesn't it?"

"That's ridiculous. Men can love men without being fags."

"Yeah, but I'd like to *ball* him."

"Me, too. All four of them. *At once!* But it doesn't have to be a hangup, does it?"

"I don't think you're hearing me, Gloria."

35

I was hearing him. I knew just what he was bugged about. But I was stalling. Because I didn't have the faintest idea what to say.

"Do you know what I'm telling you now?"

I looked at him. "I guess I do."

We sat still for a while. Then John said, "Are you disgusted or what?"

That really annoyed me. "Am I *what?*"

He didn't answer.

"John. What do you take me for, some dumb shit? You are the most beautiful person in the entire known world, so how could I be disgusted?"

"Well, you weren't saying anything, so I just wondered."

"If I don't say anything, it's because I'm trying to think it over. I'm trying to think how you must feel and all."

"Oh."

"I guess I can sort of sense why it's a bummer, but in a way I'm not really sure. I mean, what's the difference whether you're balling guys or chicks, as long as you're digging it?"

"I don't know. I guess the main thing is I'd like to have kids."

"There are millions of kids around. Do they have to be your very own?"

"I'd like for them to be. But I guess that's just an ego thing. Do you suppose?"

"Probably. I never really thought about it. John, listen, you're not even sixteen yet. How do you know this fag bit isn't just a phase?"

"It might be, but I don't think so."

"Because, you know, all last year I was in love with Cecilia. I wrote her notes and everything."

"Did you want to ball her though?"

"No. But I *would* have. I'd have done anything for her. And now I hardly ever even think about her."

36

"Yes, but then you had that big thing with Delano. That's because you're normal. You dig guys, don't you see?"

"Mm. And you just don't dig girls at all?"

"A little. But not like I should."

Then he said, "Another thing. My father. He'll shit."

"He doesn't have to know."

"He'll figure it out. He's already sniffing around asking questions."

"Listen," I said. "I'll tell you what. If your father doesn't like it, fuck him! Okay?" John smiled. It was nice to see his sense of humor coming back. "And you and I'll run away from home," I said, "and go live in Pepperland, forever. Are you with me?"

He was.

So we smoked the last joint, got stoned all over again, and played the Bee Gees.

There's something about this bus that makes me write like a demon. It's actually sort of compulsive, I don't think I could stop if I wanted to. I keep getting ideas for novels, but the very thought of writing one makes me want to go to bed and die. How could anybody go through all that labor just to invent a bunch of bullshit, when writing the truth is so much easier and groovier. The only exception I can think of is *Siddhartha*, but that's not really hard-core bullshit like most fiction, because it's based on a man's life.

John just did something so cool and so John. He tapped my hand and leaned in, without even looking at me, and said, "Hey, Witch, are there any Mallomars left?"

I reached into my bag and pulled one out for him. He started eating it, and I said, "Oh, John, that was nice. I really got a thrill out of it. How did it feel to *you?*"

"Fantastic. I mean if you really feel like that's who you are, I'll be able to dig it just great. Shall we start calling you that full time?"

"Why not? Sure."

"Okay. No more Gloria Random."

"What a scary, terrific thought!"

After about a mile or two of no talk, John said, "Hey, Witch."

I said, "Yes, Roy?" And blew his mind completely.

"Roy?" he said. "Is that me?"

"I don't know, it just came out."

He said it over a couple of times. "This is very spooky," he said, "but I'm going to tell you the truth. I feel like I'm Roy!"

"It just came to me."

"Where do you suppose *from?*"

"Maybe from *royal*, I don't know. I always think of you as a royal prince."

"Remember just now when I said, 'Hey, Witch'?"

"Yeah?"

"Know what I was going to say? I was going to say 'Hey, Witch, remember that chick named Gloria Random?' "

"And I would have said, 'Vaguely, what about her?' "

"Then I'd have said, 'Oh, I was just thinking, if it weren't for *you* being so groovy, I'll bet I'd miss her a lot.' "

I said, "I love you, Roy."

But I lied. I don't love him. I worship him.

_____

Breezewood, Pennsylvania, in the ladies' room

Either I am delirious from lack of sleep or I have just invented something fabulous. It's called the Secret Zap, and I know it could catch on like wild except for one terribly fundamental snag. If I tell everybody about it, it won't be secret any more.

Anyway, here's how it works.

You see somebody that looks plain or sad or boring or mean, in other words somebody you don't really adore on sight, and what you do is you keep on thinking about him until you can imagine what his soul must look like, and when you think you've got it, you say, under your breath, "Thou art God." That's all there is to it. What happens next is sensational, but I don't know how to describe it.

Back on the bus

The Secret Zap is even more sensational than I realized. It also works on people you *do* like. I just tried it on Roy, and he opened his eyes *instantly* and smiled like an angel.

I feel like I'm tripping. I wonder if this is what people mean about getting repeat flashes from psychedelic drugs?

Still on the bus, 3:30 a.m.

Roy looks like he's asleep now. But I'm sure he's not. His mind has probably fainted though. I better turn out the light.

---

5 a.m.

We're almost in Philadelphia. I don't think I've slept a wink. And yet, I must have, because I had a dream. It was ghastly. It was all about the death of Lake Erie, where Aunt June has her cottage. The lake's been polluted for ages, so why am I just now getting around to dreaming about it? What's *really* weird is that in the dream, *I'm* Lake Erie. At the beginning, I'm all alive and blue and shimmering with beauty, and then all kinds of people start shitting poison in me. But lakes have no voices, so they can't protest. I just become more and more miserable, and then I die. But the minute I die, I'm not the lake any more. I'm me, and Roy and I are running away on his Vespa, and the lake is like a big black *thing* trying to catch us. I wonder what it means? Maybe if I go back and read over some of the stuff I wrote at Aunt June's, I'll get some big flash about it. Besides, I've been holding this pen so long my fingers are getting mad at me.

At the Lake, Sunday, July 13, 1969

Aunt June and Uncle Arthur are stuck in Detroit for the weekend. So the only ones at the lake are my cousins Junior and Sheila and Sheila's boy friend, Martin. Plus John and me.

It's really a stoned morning. Sky, sun, air, utter perfection. Consciousness kisses my head like a dream lover. I wake up feeling angelic, a person who is 100 per cent herself and digging it all. Still lying in bed, I swear a sacred vow not to do a thing all day long that isn't pure Gloria.

I hear sounds from the big main room. Voices, coffee-cup klinks, "The Millennium Begins" on the stereo. I'm excited because my friends are awake and they've already got the day going for me. So I jump out of bed, intending to run in and wish everyone good morning, and *bang!* I run smack into my first hangup. I *should* get dressed first.

But I don't *want* to. Therefore, knowing that if I think about it too much I'll start being real second rate and come up with all sorts of reasons for copping out, I start moving.

Blithely through the door, naked as Eve.

Junior and Sheila are at the table in bathing suits, having

coffee and rolls. John's lying on the floor, fully dressed, reading *Siddhartha*. I don't know where Martin is, probably still in bed. (Officially, the boys are all sleeping in one room, and Sheila and I each have our own. But Martin spent most of the night with Sheila, creeping back into the boys' room at dawn. I have no idea what this sneaking around is about. Probably Sheila's idea.)

I pass right by Junior and Sheila and go to the stove for coffee, saying something like "Hi, kids, fantastic day." They say good morning, and while I'm pouring I see that Sheila has caught my act and is busy nudging Junior under the table with her foot. She says, "Junior, if you want to see some skin, better get with it."

Junior glances at me, and then he looks. And then he smiles and nods approval. And then he goes back to his coffee.

Sheila says, "Looks like you could use some help with your zipper, Gloria."

This gets John's nose out of Hermann Hesse's head long enough to dig what's happening.

"I decided I wouldn't wear any clothes today. Unless I I want to later. Anybody mind?"

John, unable to care less, goes back to *Siddhartha*. Sheila looks like she's trying to come up with an objection that won't sound square. Actually her deepest secret is that she *is* square. Therefore, most of her behavior is super-hip to hide how uptight she really is. Finally she comes up with something—but it's hardly a winner: she's worried about her boy friend.

"What about Martin?"

I say, "Don't you think he'll dig it?"

"Oh, he'll *dig* it all right. But *still!*"

"Still what?"

"Well, I just wonder what he'll *think*. All the rest of us

dressed to the nines, and my cousin running around in her skin!"

"*You*'re dressed to the nines? Sheila, I can see everything but your nipples and your pubic hair."

"*Gloria!*"

"It's true! You know what that bikini looks like to me? It looks like something some tacky go-go dancer would wear to tease old men. I don't know why you don't take it right off. What do you think, Junior?"

Junior says, "I don't care what she wears." Junior's got a beautiful grin, which comes from not having an uptight bone in his body.

Sheila's really off balance now. "You mean," she says to Junior, "you don't care if your sister runs around naked in broad daylight in front of her boy friend?"

Junior gave her an are-you-kidding look, thereby deftly reminding her that she and Martin have been making it every chance they could get for the last three months. Then he says, "I could dig going naked myself. Okay, Shee?" Junior's his own man in practically every department, but at sixteen he's still having these little-brother reactions around Sheila.

"Listen, I honestly don't care what you kids do," she lies. "But what if somebody drives up or something?"

Junior is already slipping out of his trunks. "If somebody drives up, we put our clothes on."

"Precisely," I chime in. "John? What about you? The rest of us are going naked today."

"*Not* the rest of us!" Sheila says. "I'm checking with Martin first."

John, wearing T-shirt and jeans, is having a tough moment. I'm not sure he likes his own body. But wow, if he could get used to having it seen, what a boost it would be for him.

43

He says, "You really want me to, Gloria?"

"Only if *you* want to." I have to be careful of a certain moon-in-Scorpio tendency to push other people into going along on my trips.

John stands up and starts to undo his belt. He tries to appear casual as he walks out of the room taking off his T-shirt, but his face is somber. As usual, I'm tempted to worry about him, but I remind myself I'm not really his mother. And even if I am, it's time he was weaned.

Then Martin comes in, holding a towel in front of himself. "Morning everybody. John says we're going naked." He looks at me, and then at Junior, and then he takes his towel off, tosses it back into the bedroom, and comes across the room to kiss Sheila. He comes over to the stove and I pour him some coffee.

Sheila says, "Martin, what about me? Shall I?"

"Shall you what?" The gorgeous thing about Martin is that he really didn't know what she was talking about. Martin's totally natural. He's 21, has this wonderful chestnut-colored page-boy-length hair. I always think of him as the perfect child of the universe, truly free and un-hung up. (Not entirely. Money bugs him, mainly because he doesn't have any, and he's always making messy little deals with his father.) (But I don't hold money against anyone. It's a perversion anyway. John, my beautiful friend-guru who understands practically everything, says that during the Piscean Age, the entire world operated on money—sort of like oil—and that now, in the Aquarian Age, money doesn't really work any more and it's lousing everything up. He says the new oil will be love, and when people get used to the plenty that technology is producing for us, they'll stop hoarding and grabbing. Money will disappear altogether, love will take over, and everything will be fine.)

44

Anyway, Martin the Almost Pure says to Sheila, "Shall you what?"

Sheila says, "Never mind," and takes off her bikini.

Then poor John comes slinking back into the room, working very hard at *not* hiding his darling little genitals with his hands, and I find myself loving him more deeply than ever. That's the thing with John and me. Everything he does, every breath I catch him taking, makes me love him more.

He lies on the floor again, reading, his cute white butt all perky and shiny. Actually his body looks quite nice. The sun is doing wonders for the pimples on his back, and even the old acne scars are sort of blending in. His shoulders are not fantastic, but they're okay, and with a few more pounds on his ribs, he'll be fine.

A while later, sitting on the porch swing, I look up from my writing and watch all my beloved friends and cousins in the midst of their high, happy Sunday, enjoying the freedom from threads I had the good sense to nudge them into.

Junior. Fly-casting off the dock, but not using bait because all the fish are dead. He does it for practice.

Martin and Sheila. Stretched out on sun chairs. Their fingertips touch and they get up, as if each of them heard the same signal, and wander down to the water together, hand in hand, a perfect Adam and Eve. But they can't go swimming because Paradise is fucked up.

That's the awful thing about lakes when they die. There's no burying them. They just go right on tempting you with their beauty, shimmering and splashing away same as ever. We hardly ever talk about its deadness any more, because of a sort of unspoken pact not to bum each other. But I know the others are always thinking about it, too.

John, for instance.

He's sitting cross-legged under the weeping willow, facing out across the water. This Hesse book has him really turned on to meditation. I'm hoping he'll learn how and show me, because I'm a lousy meditator. You're supposed to empty your mind, but mine won't empty. The more I try, the fuller it gets.

And so, hoping John has discovered something he can teach me, but not wanting to disturb him, I walk softly down the grass and sit in the lotus position about twenty paces behind him.

I study John's naked back. Owing to his extreme skinniness, the long line of marbles running down his spine is very distinct, each marble glistening in the sun. The earth mother in me wants to cover him up. Not to hide him, but to protect him. From what? The sun? I don't know from what.

I close my eyes and try to empty my mind, but it seems impossible. Every thought I get rid of is replaced by ten others. Finally I decide to sit still with my eyes open and just groove on everything.

Way out in the middle of the lake a boat passes by. Some butterflies are doing a number in the willow tree. An ant crawls on my foot and tickles my instep. I send the ant a thought telegram: Dear ant, you are welcome to walk around on me if you like, but please walk where it doesn't tickle. Because if I brush you off you could easily get hurt. The ant gets my message, he parks on my toenail and sits perfectly still, probably trying to meditate with John and me. I'm so pleased about getting through to the ant that I close my eyes.

And, wonder of wonders, my mind is actually empty for a few seconds. I see this beautiful light inside. It's not blinding or anything, and I know I haven't reached any fabulous stage of illumination, but for a moment at least, I'm not thinking about being me. I'm *being* me. And I'm quiet and happy. And then I hear something, but not quite with my ears. I look up, and I see John. He has moved over and is sitting down near me. My soul smiles. So does John's. We look at one another.

He says, "Gloria, I got something to tell you."

I know it's something wonderful. My eyes say, Go ahead, John, what is it?

And John says, out loud but softly, "Lake Erie is Jesus."

I don't know what he's talking about, but with John, I've learned to shut up and listen.

"What happened was this," he says. "I'm looking at the lake and I'm thinking, Wow, how can you be dead if you're so fucking beautiful?" (I'm tempted to interrupt him, to tell him I was having the same thought, probably at the same moment, but I restrain myself.) "So I decide to meditate," John continues. "I close my eyes and sit still, and in just a couple of seconds, I'm way off in the most *outer* outer space there is, looking back at the world. And suddenly I get this super-multi-megaton blast of clear vision, and I see Lake Erie. It's like a powerful white light, and out of the light comes this image of Jesus in the tomb, right after He was wasted. And that's it."

He stops talking and looks at me as if he expects me to understand, but I don't. So he continues.

"Jesus died for what? Our sins, right?"

"Did he really? I thought you told me it was a political thing?"

"Oh, it was! Definitely it was political. Christ was a fan-*tas*tic radical. Only . . . Only now I'm getting mixed up."

"I should have kept quiet."

"No, that's okay. I'm getting it again. Oh, now I've got it! Christ comes along and he says, 'Listen, you bunch of nin-nies, don't you know you're divine? Well, you are! You're

47

just like me. And I'm God, for Christ sake. And so are you. That means you got to love each other because that's what being God is all about.' *So!* What happens is the fucking state lays a wiretap on him. Caesar overhears this love rap Jesus is putting out, and he gets very uptight about it. Because naturally if you got people loving each other all over the place—you know, trusting and sharing and all the other love goodies—well then, what's the state going to do? It's fucked, don't you see? It's not needed any more, it goes out of business. Are you with me so far?"

I nodded.

"Okay. So they kill Jesus to shut him up. But does he really die?"

"No."

"Right."

John falls silent. After a moment, I say, "Go on, John. I'm getting it, but I haven't really *got* it yet."

"Um. What was I saying?"

"Christ didn't really die."

"Right. Jesus cooled. But not Christ. Christ is the *idea*. And the idea of love grew. It grew very very very slowly for a couple of thousand years, but it *did* keep growing, until, um."

"Until what?"

His eyes suddenly went blank. "I don't know. My mind's sort of wilting. I can't keep it together."

"Have you been smoking?"

"Junior and I had a couple of tokes."

"Well, don't hassle your head. I'll write down what you said and we'll look at it later. Okay?"

"Okay. But I think I'm really saying something, aren't I?"

"*Definitely!*"

Dear Gloria,

I hope you don't mind me writing in your notebook like this, but I didn't want to wreck your nap just to ask your permission. Anyway, about this Christ and Lake Erie business.

Christ's love rap kept growing really slow for about 2000 years and then all of a sudden just quite recently, probably while you and I were kids, something like exploded. Love started to really take hold and that's why the shit's hitting the fan. The state is bigger than ever and there's not just one Jesus any more. Thousands and thousands of cats, maybe millions, are going around now laying on his rap and all the Caesars are trying to shut them up. You know what I mean by Caesar. The state. And not just the USA either, but all the governments in the world. And the Jesuses aren't just longhairs, they're all the people who dig this love rap. I hope you can follow me now. I was a little stoned before. Excuse me for scribbling in your notebook, but you don't care, do you? Oh, I almost forgot about Lake Erie. What I meant was Jesus died to teach us love of man, and Lake Erie died to teach us love of the earth. So long. See you when you wake up.

Love,

John.

P.S. You look pretty sleeping, in case you want to know.

On the bus, 5:45 a.m.

Each moment of my life is some new kind of magic. For instance, at this very moment I am inside of an enormous machine, roaring across the Western Hemisphere of the planet Earth. For the last several miles, until I sat up to write this, I've had my head resting on the shoulder of a

49

skinny young creature named Roy, half angel, half animal. It wasn't very comfortable, but it was fabulously cozy. Traveling at night on a bus with a good friend next to you is a whole special thing.

WESTERN UNION OFFICE, NEW YORK CITY, FRIDAY, SEPTEMBER 5, 1969

I'm miserable. I'm ashamed. I'm frightened. I'm numb. I'm nervous. And I'm grinding my teeth from that Dexedrine of Roy's. I could kill him for giving it to me.

Oh, God, I don't mean that, truly I don't. It's not poor beautiful Roy's fault. Each of us is the captain of his own head. Nobody has to drop any pill he doesn't want to drop. It's myself I'm angry with. I know I can't handle speed in any form and yet I took it the second he offered it. I exonerate Roy entirely. I and nobody else am the dumb shit who swallowed the wicked thing.

Take ten deep breaths. Think of the Buddha within.

There. I feel better now. Not a whole lot, but a little. At least I've stopped thinking about my fucking self long enough to pray that Roy is not lying dead in a gutter somewhere. And I've stopped grinding my teeth.

Dear Roy, wherever you are, please be alive, please be brave, please survive whatever awful thing is being done to you. Please come back in one piece. Please heal me with your love.

I can hardly bear to record what's happened to us, but I've got to because if I don't my mind will run away with me in a total, uncontrolled freak-out.

I am sitting at the Western Union office on Third Avenue waiting for a money order from Belle Woods, Michigan. Two hours ago, I telegraphed the following lies to Mother:

IN DIRE STRAITS   COMING HOME   SEND EIGHTY DOLLARS BUS-FARE AT ONCE   I WAS WRONG ABOUT CERTAIN THINGS   LOVE GLORIA

All lies, the whole thing! Lie #1. We were not in dire straits. We weren't even hungry. We were only broke, and not even completely. We had $19 left.

Lie #2. We have no intention of going home.

Lie #3. I don't believe I was wrong about *anything*. I only said so because I know being right gives Mother a temporary high, which I'm counting on to induce some generosity so she'll send more than I asked for.

Lie #4. Love. That's not what I was feeling at all. I was feeling cute and smart and darling. Whereas the simple fact is that I'm cheap and stupid and calculating. Two days here and we've flopped already. The worst aspect of our failure is not just the unearthly speed of it. We haven't even been behaving well. Not we. *I!* Roy is a saint. I'm the one who's mean. I don't smile. I don't feel any love. Not much anyway. Just a little for Roy. No. It's more than a little. It's quite a bit actually, but it's being crowded out by panic because my bad-news bells are ringing away inside of me right now and I'm terrified for him.

How can I keep on sitting here? It could take hours for the money to come and my composure is coming apart. Composure? Ha. I haven't had a scrap of it since yesterday morning.

We got off the bus feeling like a couple of zombies. We'd only slept about an hour the whole trip, but we didn't feel tired until the bus got into New York. Then I started hallucinating beds everywhere I looked. I wanted to lie down on a bench right there in the terminal but it was hot and grim and noisy and against the law, and Roy talked me out of it.

We went to a telephone booth and tried to find Glyczwycz in the Manhattan directory. No luck. Roy said I should try the Bronx and Queens. No luck there either. I was furious. I hadn't expected it to be easy to locate my father, but I'm a badly spoiled chick. I want miracles. All the time. And when they don't happen, I get pissed off, especially when I'm tired.

We leave the bus station and find ourselves in the streets of this godawful city, dragging our bags and our little butts behind us.

I can't go on. This is putting me on a bummer and I refuse to do it. I'm simply not willing to wallow all over again in the misery of the past two days just for the sake of my goddam autobiography. I'll do it in shorthand:

New York hell. Insanity commonplace. Dog turds everywhere. Constant noise. Air filthy, causes nose and skin to itch. Traffic thick. More horns than cars.

Roy says, Look, Witch, here's Broadway! Witch not impressed. Obsessed with thought of bathtub. We head for East Village. Roy leads way to subway. Ha-ha. End up in Brooklyn. I refuse to cry. Waiting on platform for Astor Place train, Roy whips out two Dexedrine caps. Witch grabs one. No water fountain. Ladies' room requires nickel. No nickels. I pop Dexy. Can't swallow. No spit. Much choking. Full panic. Roy grabs soft drink from Puerto Rican lady.

Puerto Rican lady too helpful. Each time I try swallow, she slaps my back. Train comes.

Get off Astor Place. Walk to Third. Check in at awful hotel. Feel like fugitive in hiding. No hot water. Mattress damp. Wonder from what? Dexedrines take effect. We lie down. Try to rest. Giggle instead. Hug each other. Get excited about seeing East Village. Start out. Pass prostitute and customer in hall. Roy and I flash peace sign. Prostitute flashes it back. Our first sister in New York.

Hideous streets suddenly seem fabulous. Roy consults Delano's map. We start flying. Down Third toward St. Mark's Place. Brothers and sisters everywhere. Groovy shops. Underground books. Posters. Bead shops. Head shops. Electric Circus. New York like downtown Detroit. 100 per cent business. No houses!

Roy spots Fillmore East. We race down there. Theater closed. We stand in lobby, soak up leftover vibes from Timothy Leary, Mothers, Jefferson Airplane, Doors, etc. I get goose pimples. Roy's mouth falls open.

Suddenly black cat crosses our path. Name is Winston.

No more shorthand. I've got to slow down to do Winston justice.

Winston is black, handsome, well built. He speaks softly, has an accent that sounds sort of calypso and turns out to be Virgin Islands. He's elegant and cool, has penetrating, gentle eyes. Wears a suit. Never smiles. Never blinks his eyes.

"Hello, my friends." He nods at me, then turns to Roy. "How you doing, mon?" The word is man, but he makes it sound like a title. We fall into conversation, exchange names.

"Witch?" he says, and his eyebrows go up. I think, Wow,

on those islands, they may not dig witches. So I smile and tell him I'm a white witch and my magic is love.

"Love." He nods agreement. "I'm with you, mom." Was he calling me ma'am or mother? I'll never know. "Love," he says, "very good thing. Peace, too."

Much agreeing, nodding, flashing of peace signs. Brotherhood is established. Now we get to what's on Winston's mind.

"You like to score some hosh, mon?" he says to Roy.

Roy says, "Hosh?"

And I say, "Hash, Roy. Hashish."

Winston looks to the right and to the left without moving his cool head much at all. Then in an even quieter voice than usual, "I can get you top grade hosh-eesh, mon."

Roy's so thrilled, he doesn't know what to do. It's not the hash that excites him. It's the *scoring*. This would be his first dope purchase in New York. I dig it, too, but mostly I dig Roy's digging it.

"How much?" Roy asks.

"It all depends. You want quantity?"

"Yeah, quantity. But just a small quantity. Because we don't have much bread."

"How much?"

Roy looks at me, says, "Small conference?"

By this time we're out in the sunshine, leaning against the fender of a parked car. Winston bows elegantly. "You like for me to step aside, good people?"

"No, no," Roy says. "It's okay."

Roy and I talk, using the ultra-quiet secret language, no melody, no facial expressions. It sounds like mumble-jumble to everybody but us. Winston discreetly scans the sky and steps back a pace.

ROY: What do you think we can afford?

WITCH: I don't know. What do you think?

ROY: How much we got?

WITCH: About twenty-nine dollars.

ROY: Is he really a brother?

WITCH: I can't tell.

ROY: Me either. I thought maybe you could.

WITCH: He's too good-looking. My judgment is wrecked.

ROY: I know what you mean.

WITCH: You dig him, too?

ROY: Sort of. But how come he never smiles?

WITCH: Doesn't blink his eyes either.

ROY: Maybe we better forget it.

WITCH: Right. We haven't even got jobs yet.

ROY: Okay.

WITCH: Besides, who needs hash? We're high anyway.

ROY: True.

Roy tells Winston our decision. We apologize for using up his time and offer to buy him a cup of coffee.

He bows. "No, thank you very much, my friends. I bid you good day, long life." Still no smile, no blink. But he nods nicely.

Roy and I proceed to Tompkins Square Park. It's late afternoon now. New York is looking great. Everything is either gorgeous, or gorgeous-awful. The only thing that's *just* awful, period, is the junk all over the streets and side-walks. Every kind of garbage imaginable. I mention it to Roy. Roy, fantastic guru that he is, suggests that if our heads are in the right place, we can groove on it, get to where we really dig the litter everywhere.

I tell him I agree entirely, but I wonder if we can ever learn to dig the dog turds. Roy is convinced we can. So we sit on a bench and look at some dog turds, trying to groove on them. About three benches away, an enormous German shepherd is dropping a nice steaming specimen for us. Roy and I both spot it at once, and exchange a glance.

56

"How you doing?" he says.

I shake my head. "I'm not making it. How about you?"

"A little headway, maybe."

"Fabulous. Tune me in."

"Well," he says, "what I'm doing is I'm thinking about the soul of that dog."

"I'll give it a try."

So I try it. I think of the dog's soul, and I give it a Secret Zap. Then I say, "Roy, that's not his soul crapping up the sidewalk."

Roy nods, ponders a while longer. Then he says, "Everything that comes from the human body is sacred. Shit, piss, cum, spit, hair, the whole thing."

"That's *humans* though. Right?"

"You think human turds are better?"

"I guess not."

"Besides, dogs are sacred, too. Aren't they? All living things?"

"Absolutely. Every little cockroach."

Roy looks at the fresh pile again, regards it with great seriousness. Then he says, "I don't know if I can make it a hundred per cent in one afternoon though. Can you?"

"No," I say. "Let's not force ourselves."

"Right."

We walk over to Avenue B, where everything gets really thick. Every kind of person imaginable, all colors and sizes and styles and genders, milling madly around, each on his own trip. I fall in and out of love three or four times, very quietly, nothing wild. Each affair lasts a half a block or so. Suddenly it's twilight. Roy and I both find ourselves hung up on an old Slavic lady with great cheekbones and an enormous junk collection. Lots of people like junk, but this lady carries hers with her in these miraculous shopping bags that somehow hold things even when they're terribly torn. She stops at a wire trash barrel to collect more goodies, then empties out her entire stash to rearrange it on the sidewalk: jelly glasses, rusty coat hangers, broken clocks, magazines without covers.

I say, "Roy, she's got it made, she's learned to groove on litter."

Roy says, "Yeah, but I think she's hung up."

We move along.

We go into this weird cave-type coffee place where all the longhairs are mad at us. I wonder what for? We flash peace signs. Nobody flashes back. I *sotto-voce* to Roy, "They *look* like brothers. What's wrong?"

Roy shrugs. "Maybe they're on reds. Let's split." And I think, If that's what Seconals produce, they could really hurt the revolution!

Suddenly I got this awful fit of depression and had to stop writing. Then this kind Western Union man started a conversation. I guess I look scared and he wants to comfort me. But it made me even more anxious than ever trying to keep up a conversation when I know something awful is happening to Roy. That's all I can think about. Sitting still doesn't help, and kindness doesn't comfort me. I'll have to keep writing.

After we got out of that down-head coffee place, something must have clicked over in our heads, because we kept attracting bummers, one after another. Sick-looking kids— our age, more or less—kept stopping us on St. Mark's Place, asking for money. The first bunch were so scroungy-looking, we gave them a dollar. And then, I don't know exactly how it happened, but suddenly these sad-looking types kept appearing out of nowhere, telling us their stories, and we kept handing out our money like there's no tomorrow. Roy kept saying, "They're worse off than we are, Witch." And I kept agreeing. We'd given away seven dollars before I saved us from total ruin by giving vent to a neat little wave of fury. This filthy chick with electric hair was sitting on some steps, and she actually hollered at us when we walked by. "Hey! Give me some bread!" It was like a demand. I stopped dead in my tracks and looked straight at her. A total mess, pimples, pale, wild eyes, crud all over her clothes, God knows what under her fingernails. Her hair looked like it had died and gone to hell. Suddenly—why so late?—it dawns on me what's happening. I'd been vaguely wondering why our generosity had been bringing us down. Isn't love supposed to help your high? How come then both Roy and I kept feeling worse instead of better. The more we gave the more desperate and scared we felt.

I look at this chick's eyes, and they're like the barrels of a couple of mean little guns pointed at us. That's what gave me my big flash. All these people we've been slopping over with our darling icky kindness were just a tacky tribe of bloodsuckers spaced out on drugs. They acted as if all they knew about brotherhood had come from a quick course at the Pentagon.

Witch moon-in-Scorpio Me—I think I'm learning to respect my awful side—sprang like a snake. God knows what I told her. I was brilliant. Roy must have thought I'd freaked out. In a way, I had. I started with How dare she shout at me and make demands. Then she made her fatal mistake, she looked at me half amused, half disdainful, like I'm some up-tight little fluff from suburbia that doesn't know her ass from a hypodermic needle. So I let her have it. I told her she and everybody like her were undermining the entire revolution. It was a fabulous speech, I wish to hell I had it on tape.

But here's the really awful part.

She heard me.

She really heard me. I'd made her feel like a totally unsacred little dog turd. And she started crying. So I joined her. Pretty soon we're all sitting on this stoop, Roy on one side, me on the other, and this poor smelly little wreck in the middle, and we're all hugging each other and saying how all right everything's going to be. Pretty soon I noticed her eyes were scanning the street again. I suppose all three of us had begun to feel our thing together was over. Roy and I got up and walked away. The good-byes were more or less scattered. She hardly noticed we were leaving. I guess she had crystals on her mind, poor dear.

I don't know what time it was. Seems like it had been dark for ages. Roy and I walked back to Third Avenue and without even talking it over we headed for the hotel, holding hands all the way. The Dexedrine was still doing its number in our heads, but our bodies were tired. I simply ached all over, and I know Roy was dying on his feet because his beautiful big eyes were just a couple of pink slits and his pimples stood out more than ever.

At the hotel, we talked. No, we didn't talk. We rapped. We rapped forever. We went over every little thing that had happened. Our doped minds were like hot little tongues and they licked in and out of every little corner of the entire day. Then we tried to shut up and couldn't. Finally we got undressed and rubbed each other's backs. I noticed Roy's cock was shriveled up to nothing. Delano said men get that way when they're speeding. I don't know what happens to women, but if I'm any sample, they begin to feel like witches. Not white ones either. Old and purple and ugly.

60

We stayed in the room for quite a while. There was almost constant emergency-type noise. Banging in the halls. Arguments. Screaming. Sirens. Roy said we'd get used to it. I sat on the window sill trying to breathe but all the air was secondhand. Roy did his Yoga.

Then, sitting there looking into the street and hating everything in sight, I flashed on the ending of an old dream I used to have. There's not much to it. I try to scream and can't because my voice doesn't work. Then the dream itself came back, the whole thing.

In the dream, Mother's chaise longue is covered with the skin of a big black furry bear. I sneak into her room naked and lie there feeling the fur on my body. I turn over and lie on my tummy. The fur feels wonderful on my breasts, but just when I'm really getting into it, Mother comes and catches me. This memory is so strong I wonder if it was only a dream? But I know it couldn't actually have happened because there's no bearskin on her chaise. It's just chintz. Anyway, she starts calling me terrible names and comes after me, so I run downstairs and out of the house. The back yard becomes a great forest, but it's Mother's forest and therefore not a real one. (Nothing of Mother's is real!) And she's still chasing me. So I try to scream, but I can't. Because the rule of the dream is that your voice can't work unless the forest you're in is real.

"Roy," I said. "I know I shouldn't be rapping at you when you're trying to do your Yoga, but listen to me, will you, for a minute? Someday, before I die—as soon as possible in fact —I want to go into a forest naked and make a terrible noise. Can you understand that?"

I could actually *feel* him thinking it over. This is one of the reasons he's so perfect to talk to. He hears you. He takes what you say inside of himself and really gets the feel of it before he answers. Especially when it's important like this.

61

"What kind of a noise will it be?" he said. "A scream or a song or a prayer or what?"

"It doesn't matter," I said. "It'll just be the sound I make."

"A really *terrible* sound?"

"Absolutely terrible."

"Yeah," he said. "I could dig that."

"Roy. We've made a mistake, haven't we?"

He leaned back on his hands, legs still in the lotus position. "What we did wrong was we picked the wrong scene. We shouldn't have picked New York."

"It's my fault."

"No," Roy said. "We both decided."

"Yes, but I had this big thing about I've got to find my father. If it hadn't been for that, maybe we'd have gone to Boulder or Laguna Beach or Big Sur or someplace beautiful."

"We can still do that."

"With no money?"

"Not right away, but later maybe."

So we had fantasy talk about what it must be like in California, and about all the communities we'd heard about in Colorado. And when we ran down again, I said, "Roy, if you decide to split for Canada, I'll be with you completely. I just want you to know that."

"You think we should?"

"I don't know. But we ought to consider it while there's still some money left, don't you think?"

Neither of us felt we were thinking clearly enough to make a good decision, so we went for a walk, hoping the change of scene would help.

By the time we got dressed and into the streets it was 6 A.M. The sun was coming up and we got high just on dawn alone. You can't get a complete view of the sunrise in New York, but on certain streets you can see all the way over to the river where the light is strongest.

We walked over to West Village and had scrambled eggs and toast at an all-nightery on Sheridan Square, then walked all the way back to Third Avenue. People were climbing in and out of the subway holes, populating the day. It was sort of nerve-racking seeing all these people running around doing their thing, and us not even having jobs.

On the way upstairs, that same black prostitute smiled at us. I thought she must be headed for the streets again, and wondered if she wasn't getting awfully tired.

We lay down and tried to sleep and I think we succeeded for a while. But what I remember most clearly is lying there with my eyes wide open wondering what the fuck we were going to do next. For a while at least I must have blacked out, because when I opened my eyes I saw Roy sitting in the middle of the floor, fully dressed, in the lotus position. He said he was trying to get at his inner resources to help him through the day. I got down on the floor with him, but neither of us were able to meditate. There was too much clutter in our heads, so we decided instead to get into some old-fashioned praying. Roy said he thought if we were really serious about it we ought to do it on our knees.

"But if *we're* God," I said, "who are we getting on our knees to?"

Roy thought about the question for a minute. Then he said, "I don't really know. Praying isn't really my thing."

"Then what are we doing it for? Just in case?"

"God takes all these different forms," Roy said, "you and I are just two of them. I guess what you pray to is all the forms you can't see."

"Spirits?"

"Yeah. Like that, I guess."

"Okay. Let's go."

Then Roy said, "Listen, if we're going to pray to the spirits, I think I'll address a few of them by name. Why not?"

"Go ahead," I told him.

"Okay. I'll say the names, and you say them after me."

We got to our knees and Roy started right in.

"Dear Buddha."

"Dear Buddha."

"Dear Jesus."

"Dear Jesus."

"Dear Carl Jung."

"Dear Carl Jung."

"Dear Mohammed."

"Dear Mohammed."

"Dear Hermann Hesse."

"Dear Hermann Hesse."

"Dear Malcolm X."

"Dear Malcolm X."

"Can you think of anybody else?"

"What about Martin Luther King?"

"Sure. Dear Martin Luther King."

"Dear Martin Luther King."

"I guess the prayer is just Please help us get our trip together. Right?" He looked at me.

"Right."

"Shall we say it together?"

I nodded. And then, together, we said, "Please help us get our trip together. Amen."

While we were getting ready to go out, I said, "Do you think any of them really heard us?"

And Roy said, "In a way, I do. Don't you?"

"In a way, definitely. *Definitely.*"

————————

We spent the day looking for jobs. We split up for little intervals, each of us going his own way and meeting back at the hotel to exchange news. But there wasn't much to exchange. I went into about a hundred shops and asked if they needed any clerks. Nobody did. Roy went to Everything for Everybody. Delano said they could help longhairs get jobs, but the girl there told Roy you had to "join," which cost $15. Besides, she said, he looked too young to fill any of the openings they had today.

This age thing is a problem we hadn't considered. Roy's 19, but he looks 16, and he can't show his papers, because when you go underground, you can't use your real name. If you do, the Army can trace you.

He got this notion that if he wore glasses he'd look older. So we went to the dime store on 8th Street and bought a pair. I didn't think they helped at all, but Roy did. By then it was after five and the business day was ended, but Roy wanted to test his glasses on some late-hour bookshops, hoping one of them might need a clerk or a stockboy.

Meanwhile, I went back to the hotel and experienced a certain misadventure that I'd rather not write about. But I have to. Because if I don't I'll start thinking about the fact that I've been waiting here at Western Union forever and ROY IS NOT BACK YET!!!

That black prostitute was on the corner of 9th and Third Avenue when I passed by. We smiled at each other and I went upstairs. About two minutes later there was a knock on my door. "Just passing by," she said. "Thought I'd pay a visit." She came in and we sat on my bed and swapped names. Hers was Loretta. We rapped for a few minutes. I acted terribly surprised when she told me what she did for a living. I have to face the fact that when somebody throws me for a loop, my first reaction is to say something phony.

For instance, I said, "You'd never know it to look at you," when that's exactly how I *did* know it. It embarrasses me even to remember it. I did say one thing I believed though. I told her I thought prostitution was a perfectly splendid profession. At first she looked puzzled, but pretty soon I sold her on what a fine public service she was performing. Then I started rapping about all the great courtesans of history, their genius in divining the needs of men and changing the course of human destiny. I have no idea why I carried on so. The poor thing seemed so flattened by her life, I guess I wanted to fluff her up a little. Then she said, "Baby, if you think it be such a picnic, how come you looking for a job selling shit in some store? If a gal digs working on her back, what the fuck she want to be on her feet all day for?"

So I actually considered it for a while. Finally I said I didn't think I could do it and stay in a good head, because it might make me anxious and depressed. I tried to explain what I meant, and then suddenly I realized if I convinced Loretta that whoring was depressing, maybe it would start depressing *her.* I hate lying, but I hate even worse to bum somebody else's trip. So I tried to end the discussion by telling her she was right, it was all talk, and I'd just been trying to hide from her the fact that I was too chicken even to attempt it.

And then this totally wild thing happened. She put her arm around me and said, "How 'bout starting with me? Lie down with me a while, I give you fi' dollars."

So I just threw back my head and laughed and laughed. Said I thought she had the best sense of humor of anybody I'd ever met in my entire life. I managed to get off the bed by pretending the joke was so tremendous I had to stand up to finish laughing. By the time I'd worked my way over to the other side of the room, sides splitting all the way, I thought it was safe to look at her and check her reaction.

Loretta was not smiling. Not a flicker. Her face was as dark as a well, and at the bottom of it her eyes were peering up at me, steady as a cat's.

She said, "You think I'm funny?"

I said, "No! Oh, no! You and I are sisters, I don't think you're funny at all. But I thought you were joking. Honestly I did."

Next thing I knew I was launched into this big routine about how fabulous lesbianism is. There was a lot of truth in what I said, too. I just know the right woman (Cecilia, for instance) could turn me on to making love. But that room and that woman and that moment— Oh, God, I wanted out of there with all my heart.

Loretta wasn't buying all my fancy talk either. When I ran out of wind, she was still sitting there with that same expression on her face, and I was scared to death.

She stood up and came over to me. "You been playing with me, honey. You nothing but a big phony."

I admitted to being a phony, but I swore I hadn't been playing with her. I told her I loved her like a sister or a friend, and that I'd been trying to be worldly and clever. I apologized, I took vows, I rapped on and on. But she didn't believe a word I said.

She slapped me. Hard. On the cheek. She said she ought to tear me apart. And she slapped me again. Even harder.

Then she said, "I find you in this hotel tonight, I turn y'pretty white face into a mess of spare ribs." She wasn't kidding either. Her eyes told me she was just the kind of chick who could come up with the necessary kitchen equipment to get the job done, too. My mind saw cleavers and paring knives and can openers, all being used in ghastly ingenious ways. For a while I think she was considering getting at it immediately instead of waiting till night came. But then all of a sudden she left the room.

It took me no more than 30 seconds to get Roy's and my things together. I hated my cowardice and I loathed my fear, but violence is just unbearable to me.

I stood on the street and waited for Roy. I thought he'd never come, but he did. He was discouraged, too, and trying to hide it. I didn't tell him what had happened in detail. I just said there'd been some trouble up there and I thought the spirits we'd prayed to at noon probably felt it was time for us to relocate.

He was tired, so we went to Tompkins Square Park and did the bench scene until the sun had set. No sleep, of course, but we held hands while we rested and told our days to each other.

———————

Roy has never failed to give me the feeling that he loves me, ever since the first moment we became friends in the seventh grade. No matter how scared or worried he is, I always get *some* kind of a Zap from being with him. Even now, sitting here wondering if he's dead or alive and knowing that *whatever* has happened to him it can't be good, not in the least, I still feel this Zap coming at me. If only I knew from where! If only it was a ray of light I could see and follow and go to the end of and find him. But it's not. I'll just have to sit here until he comes, even if I wither up and die or get hauled off to a hospital or an asylum.

It is now Friday, September 5, 1969. Three hours ago (was that all?) Roy and I were sitting on a bench in Tompkins Square Park having the following conversation:

WITCH: I've been thinking.
ROY: Me, too.
WITCH: Money?

ROY: Yeah.

WITCH: How much is left?

ROY: Nineteen and some change.

WITCH: I've got an idea.

ROY: What?

WITCH: A swindle.

ROY: Really?

WITCH: Really.

ROY: Go on.

WITCH: I send a wire to Mother.

ROY: And tell her what?

WITCH: I'm coming home and have to have bus fare.

ROY: Wow.

WITCH: They can afford it. Do you know how much they were willing to spend on sending me to Radcliffe?

ROY: How much?

WITCH: I don't know. But plenty. And do you know where they get it? Stocks. General Dynamics, General Motors, every general you can think of.

ROY: Bombers, jeeps, rockets, flame throwers, napalm.

WITCH: That's the picture! So why shouldn't I promote a measly hundred dollars to help the revolution? Can you name me one good reason?

ROY: Well, it's . . .

WITCH: Dishonest?

ROY: Yeah.

WITCH: Shit.

ROY: I know. But still . . .

WITCH: Come on. Let's go.

The Western Union man told us it would probably take a number of hours, at least four or five, even if Mother wired the money immediately

69

Roy was hungry, so we went to the Paradox, this macrobiotic restaurant Delano had marked on the map. My stomach was having post-Dexedrine anxiety fits, but I had a couple of bites of Roy's fish and drank some tea.

Then Roy got this perfectly awful idea, which at the time sounded like sheer genius.

He said, "Look, if we're getting all this money, why don't we score some grass?"

The very thought of it undid me.

So we went flying up 7th Street, hoping to find a dealer hanging around in front of the Gem Spa on St. Mark's Place.

Something happened on the way that might have saved us a lot of hell, if we'd used our heads. But we didn't. We were too interested in getting them stoked! An Indian boy was sitting on some steps talking to a fabulous cat who looked like Prince Valiant. They both smiled even before I did, so we stopped and talked. The Indian boy's name was Carl, he came from Quebec. His friend was Danny, from Key West. We told them where we were at—waiting for money, looking for grass, no place to stay, etc. Carl said he was in exactly the same situation. But it didn't seem to worry him. He was into a craft called "macrome," making things out of rope, and while we talked he was working on a belt. He said he was at peace because he followed the wisdom of the *I Ching* and went along with whatever the oracle said.

Roy's ears perked up. He'd been wanting to throw a change anyway, so Carl got out his copy and helped. Roy borrowed my journal to make notes in. I wasn't paying much attention because I was too busy falling in love with Danny. By the time I realized what was happening, I found myself in full seduction gear. Much witchcraft on 7th Street. I emanated. I Secret Zapped, my gaze lingered and darkened, I wove dreams of gossamer into a little net and just as it was

70

falling about his 14th-century head, along came this let's face it beautiful Hungarian chick named Sandie and plucked him out from under me. Turns out he'd been waiting for her all along. Ah, well. I watched them walk away, watched them all the way up to First Avenue and watched them turn the corner. I wasn't sad, but I was depleted. I've had dozens of these spiritual quickies and I'm usually fairly philosophical about them when they end. But after putting out all that magic and then watching it disappear up the street, I felt the barrel was getting pretty empty.

So when Roy told me about throwing these trigrams and hexagrams and coming up with something called "The Darkening of the Light," I just nodded and said it sounded pretty accurate. But I wasn't really listening. He said the gist of the I Ching's wisdom—and Carl seemed to agree—was that we were supposed to persevere. So we said good-bye to Carl and started right in persevering on the trail of some grass.

Neither of us were surprised to see Winston again.

He was leaning on a mailbox at the next corner, right across from Fillmore East.

The negotiations were endless. Winston didn't like doing small quantities, but he said ten of our nineteen dollars would get us a fat gram of some truly righteous hash, and because we were brothers, he didn't mind going to the trouble. Then he said we'd have to walk with him clear over to the West Village, where the stuff was, because of course he wasn't carrying. ("No, mon, never carry. Never.") So we started walking toward Third Avenue, and I remember wondering why Winston seemed to be thinking so hard. He walked with his eyes straight ahead and I don't think he blinked once the whole time. At the corner he said he'd had some second thoughts about taking two people with him at once. The reason he gave was "too much traffic." I was too tired to protest, so he and Roy left me at the Western Union office and went off together toward the West Village.

And here I sit. He's been gone an hour and a half. And there's nothing left to think about.

Except Roy's I Ching notes. I just looked at them, and I'm terrified. It says, "A man of dark nature is in a position of authority and brings harm to the wise and able man."

CANAL STREET, SUNDAY, SEPTEMBER 7, 1969

Hare Krishna!

Roy and I have our highs back. Obviously we lead en-
chanted lives. The most hideous adventures imaginable
turn into miracles before our very eyes. Life is too rich to
bear. Everywhere we go, angels precede us and light our
way with love.

Must never *ever* lose faith again, even for a second. I
hereby vow not to.

At this moment I am sitting at a real kitchen table, watching over an enormous pot of vegetable soup, and my beloved
Roy is downstairs cleaning out the fireplace. We have become part of a beautiful family. There are about ten of us
altogether, and we live in a terrific haunted ramshackle house
just a block from the Hudson River. It looks like I'm becoming co-housemother, because out of four chicks, only two of
us can really get our heads into a cooking trip. I'm a little
edgy about it. They're on a macrobiotic diet and the kitch-
en's full of stuff I've never seen before. For instance, what
do you do with dried lotus root? Smoke it?

Who would have thought on Friday, when we were in
hell, that by Sunday we'd be comfortably established in the

Kingdom of Heaven? Comfortably isn't quite the word. I suppose compactly would be more accurate. Roy and I sleep on the floor in the hall. But we have a mattress all to ourselves, and it's right under the stairwell, which makes it super-cozy. At first we thought the cockroaches would be a problem, but we've already dealt with them superbly. Roy drew a magic circle around our part of the hall and so far not one of them has trespassed. Also, I have lots of ideas for turning our alcove into a darling little gypsy cave. Roy has already tacked up our Desiderata poster. He put it upside down on the slant above us, so we can read it lying down just before we go to sleep. It's our good-night prayer. When I get done with this entry, I'll copy it down in my notebook as a spiritual discipline. Ever since we got off the bus I've been speeding, and I've simply got to slow myself down to normal. I'm almost afraid to get weighed. I must have lost five pounds at least. But I look marvelous, very cheek-bony and low-key luscious. I suppose it's tacky of me to be so pleased about that, but looking pretty helps my high, and anything that helps a high can't be all bad.

This morning I read over everything I'd written since Roy and I got off the bus and I can hardly believe how much has happened. It seems to me absolutely urgent that I keep the record up to date.

Therefore, between stirrings of the soup, I will lure my mind back to the Western Union office:

While I was sitting there trying to think of things to write, I heard a sudden frantic knock on the window right behind me. It was John. I mean Roy (still haven't gotten used to his new name), and he was motioning for me to come outside. As a rule I'm not a screamer, but I must have let out some audible sound because the telegraph clerk came running up to see what was the matter. I told him everything was fine and ran out to the sidewalk.

Roy was all sweaty and out of breath, but I was so busy hugging him I hardly noticed the condition he was in. Also, his pants were missing. He had some old jacket thing tied to his waist by the arms, covering him like a skirt. It only came to his knees, so there was this long stretch of skinny legs coming out of his combat boots. He looked so funny and pathetic, I was afraid I was going to do something awful, like laugh or cry. But I didn't.

"Get me some pants out of my suitcase," he said. "I just got ripped off."

I suddenly felt wonderful. I'd been sitting there getting such a strong steady blast of horrible vibes, I hardly expected to see him alive again. And now, hearing he'd only been robbed, it was like getting good news.

At first Roy didn't want to come inside, but I assured him the Western Union clerk was a brother, and it'd be much better than putting on his pants in the street.

By this time, all we had left was 90 cents. But that was enough for coffee, so we went to a delicatessen on Second Avenue and sat in a back booth while Roy told me what had happened to him. I'd like to record the conversation exactly, but it was terribly disjointed and I had to ask a hundred questions. Still I think I'll try to put it down the way Roy would have told it if he could have gotten it all together without me interrupting every three seconds.

ROY'S ROBBERY
as told to
Witch Gliz

Winston and I left you there at Western Union and started walking across 8th Street toward Greenwich Village, rapping

75

all the way. I thought he was really a great guy. He told me all about life on the Islands and how he and his buddies stayed stoned all day and did nothing but swim and dive and pick bananas and mangoes off the trees. I asked him how come he was in New York, and he said it was just to make money. He's got a connection in the Islands that ships him this fabulous grass and hash. Of course I don't know how much of this is true, because if a guy lies, he lies, and you just never know. Anyway, Winston was talking all this great-sounding shit, and I bought it all. In fact, I was taking a big interest in his whole trip. I was wondering how long he'd have to be selling dope in New York to make enough bread to get back to his paradise. He said a few more deals and he'd have it made. He said he usually dealt grass in kilos only and hash in ounces or more, so the profits came in good-sized chunks. I told him I felt bad about wasting his time on our little dime of hash, but he said it was okay, Wednesday was an off night anyway. Then we stopped at a magazine store because Winston had to make this phone call. He said he had to make sure it was cool to take me where we were going. I didn't know how these things were done, so I didn't see anything suspicious about it. Besides, by now I loved the guy. When he came out of the phone booth I asked him if everything was okay. I remember now he didn't look at me. He just gave me a sign with his hand. So I followed him out to the street and we kept walking. Then he told me about the wild life he's got going here in New York. He said he had this roommate and each of them had a chick and sometimes all four of them went to bed together. It all sounded pretty groovy to me. When we got to Macdougal Street he stopped in a cigar store to make another phone call. All of a sudden, I started getting this scared feeling. So when he came out of the cigar store I thought what the hell, I'll level with him. I said, "Winston, I don't know why, but

I'm feeling kind of uptight. Is everything okay?" He put his arm on my shoulder and said, "My friend, it's natural to be uptight in this city. Never trust anybody until you know them as well as you and I know each other. Then you're safe." He went into this big rap about how careful you've got to be. And Witch, I've got to admit I really thought he was being straight with me. I kept on feeling scared, but I figured it was just my paranoia. So I followed him up this side street, I think it was 3rd or 4th, but I'd never be able to find it again because my mind was kind of scrambled from being scared. He stopped in front of this cruddy-looking building, then he picked up a couple of stones and threw them at a dark window on the third floor. I figured this was some kind of a signal. After all, what do I know about dealing in Manhattan, right? Then we went across the street and I followed him into this *other* tenement building that was just like the first one. I thought we'd be going upstairs, but he passed the steps and led the way down this long hall to another door that opened on some shitty little back yard. It wasn't like any back yard I'd ever seen either. It stunk like hell and there was nothing growing in it. It was full of junk, old furniture, torn-up mattresses, broken glass, every kind of crap you can think of. And it was dark. The only light was whatever came out of these high windows all around. I told Winston I thought this yard was a pretty lousy place to wait, but he said he'd picked it especially so I could try the hash and nobody would smell the smoke. In a way that sounded reasonable, but in another way it didn't make any sense at all. My mouth got dry and I started shaking. Remember how it used to be when we'd get caught for something at school and have to wait outside Miss Alley's office? Well, that's how I felt. My heart was going so hard you could see my entire shirt moving. Finally I couldn't stand it. I said, "Winston, I don't want to be here. I'm gonna split." But by the

77

time I got to the door it was too late. Because there were two spade cats coming down the hall. I tried to get past them but they were in the way. One of them asked me where I was going. I said I had a friend waiting for me, and he said, "Oh, no, man, you don't need a friend," and the two of them hustled me into the yard again and shoved me against the wall. They had their knives out. One of them was at my throat. I could feel the blade pushing really hard against my skin, but it didn't cut me. Winston had his knife out too and it was pushing against my stomach. Then this third cat stood to one side and started giving orders. He told me to take off my shoes and all my clothes and throw them to him, one article at a time. He searched everything, even my T-shirt, like he thought I might have something sewed in it, I guess, and he even ripped the linings out of my boots. Then the fucker took all my clothes except for my pants and threw them over this goddam high fence. All he found was the nineteen dollars because that's all I had. So he flashed his knife in my face and asked me where the rest of it was. I was standing there stark naked and they'd been through all my clothes, so it must have been pretty obvious I wasn't holding out on them. But I guess Winston had given these guys the impression they were going to get a lot more than nineteen dollars, because they started having this argument. Then the other guy, the one that was holding the knife at my throat, said it was time to get out. So they started to leave. I said, "Hey, what about my pants?" This one guy had them rolled up and tucked under his arm. But he didn't even answer me. The three of them just walked out and left me there bare ass. Obviously I couldn't chase them with my butt hanging out. So I thought, Well, I guess I'm fucked. And I tried to figure out how to get over the wall where the rest of my stuff was. Witch, it was really hell. I kept slipping and once I even fell. I don't know on what, but I scraped my balls

78

practically off. They still hurt in fact. Also, I cut my goddam knee. Anyway, I finally propped up this rickety old table with only three legs and made it over the fence, and there was this big-ass rat sniffing my boots. I swear, Witch, he was the size of a fucking Easter rabbit. Anyway, I must have scared him because he ran like hell. So I grabbed my jockeys and put them on and then I put on my T-shirt. But I knew I couldn't make it over the fence in these combat boots, so I threw them over the fence ahead of me. This turned out to be a really dumb stunt, because just as they hit, I realized this other building, the one I was in the yard of, had an unlocked door too, and I could have got out to the street again without climbing the fence. However, it's a good thing I was stupid, because just as I got over the fence again and was tying my boots, Winston came back and gave me a joint. I could hardly believe it, Witch, but it's true. I've got the joint right here in this jacket. What happened was he just came walking back into the yard with this joint in his hand, holding it out to me. He said, "Here, mon." At first I didn't want to take it, because I thought I ought to be too pissed off at him. But I wasn't. I really wasn't pissed off at all. In fact, I liked him. I still do. I figured he was just doing his thing. I mean, after all, he's a thief, right? And a thief doesn't have to come back and give you a joint or anything, unless he happens to be a pretty decent cat in some ways. I don't know, I'm not saying I'm right about this. I'm just telling you all that went through my head. And for all I know, maybe I *am* right. After all, there is a goddam revolution going on, and these things can be very complicated to think about. So I took the joint. Not only that, I said thanks. Winston stood there for a second, just looking at me, and I felt this kind of a sad little Zap coming out of his eyes. It was the first and only time he ever really looked at me straight on. Then he waved his hand around this crummy yard and he said, "This thing here, it's nothing personal." And then he left. If I'd had a match, I'd have smoked that joint right away. Not all of it though. Naturally, I'd have saved half for you. But my mind was really messed up. I didn't know how I was going to get back here in my jockeys, and there was nothing in that yard to cover up with. And I mean not a goddam thing. I got so panicky, I even tore apart this old window screen and tried to make a half-ass skirt out of it, but it looked like I'd freaked out. Anyway, I held it in front of me and went through the hall and out to the street and looked around. I thought, What the hell am I going to do? I was even tempted to find some cop, for godsake, so you can imagine how confused I was getting. I saw a garbage can at the curb, but there was nothing in it, so I tried to figure out how to hide behind the lid. All of a sudden, a woman's voice came from out of nowhere. "Whatsa matter, kid?" I looked up and there's this fat lady sticking out of a window, leaning there with her titties on a bed pillow. I tried to think up some lie. Force of habit, I guess. But I ended up telling her the truth. I said, "I been robbed, they took my pants." She said, "How much did they get?" I told her and she said, "The sonsabitches." Then she said, "You look pretty cute. How you going to get home?" I asked her if she could give me something to cover up with, so she told me to come inside. It was a typical poor person's pad, like the slums you see on TV. She had her clothes hanging on a pole right there in the kitchen. I stood there and watched her go through it all. She pushed each hanger aside, one by one, and each time she said, "I can't give you this," and "I can't give you this," until finally she came up with this jacket. I said, "I can't wear that for pants." She said, "Sure you can. Just put your legs through the arms and wear it upside down." I said, "It'd look pretty weird," and she said, "Aw, c'mon, you beatniks don't mind lookin' weird. It's a new style. Try

80

it." Naturally it didn't work. I couldn't even get my goddam feet through. Then it finally dawned on me, this old
broad was just having a good time for herself. She didn't
give a shit *what* I did. So I said thanks for the jacket. Then
I tied it around my waist and split. On the street, I figured
there was nothing to do but make a run for it. I looked
pretty freaky, but at least I was covered up. I ran through
Washington Square Park, and you know what? Hardly anybody even noticed me. And the ones that did just kind of
looked. They didn't even laugh, for godsake!

When Roy finished his story, we decided to look for a
place to smoke Winston's joint. It's hard to find a hiding
place in Manhattan. We ended up smoking it right on the
street, trying to handle it like tobacco. Our heads were so
hungry the first toke went right to work on us. By the time
we'd had three apiece we were flying, so we put it out and
saved the other half for later. Then Roy did this angel-shit
number on my head.

We were on 10th Street, headed for Third Avenue, when
all of a sudden he stopped walking, stood stock still, banged
his forehead with the heel of his hand and let out this 20-
megaton WOW!

I thought, Wow, that was quite a wow. This must be
something major—and waited for him to subside enough to
make an utterance.

"Witch," he said, "give me your hands."

I did. He took them in both of his.

"Listen, something fabulous is about to happen to us."

"What?" I gasped.

"I don't know, but it will. Do you realize what we just
smoked?"

"No. What was it?"

"Are you ready?"

"Yes. But give it to me fast. I'm dying."

"*Angel shit!*"

"*Angel shit?*"

"We have just smoked angel shit."

"I never *heard* of it, what is it?"

"Any grass that's given to you by a brother when you really need it is angel shit."

"Really?"

"And when you're high on it, something fantastic always happens to you."

I said, "How can *this* be angel shit if we got it from Winston?"

"Winston's a brother, isn't he?"

"He's not *my* brother," I said.

"Why not?"

"He just ripped you off, didn't he?"

"Yeah," Roy said. "But that was *before.*"

This is 100 per cent typical of Roy. I remember one time we were down in his lair listening to music. The basement window was open and this strange alley cat came by and looked in. After a few minutes she jumped in and sniffed out the place while Roy and I laid there and watched. She got into everything he had and Roy just let her do as she pleased. Then she jumped up on a table and knocked over a glass. The glass rolled onto the floor and broke. The sound of the crash scared her, so she jumped out the window and ran away. I'll never forget what Roy did. He sat up and said, "Hey, man, don't *split!*" And that's the way he is. You can break right into his pad, go over his whole place, take anything you want, and on your way out he says, "Hey, man, don't split!"

I'm digressing.

Back to angel shit.

Roy convinced me that Winston qualified as a brother, and it wasn't hard. He just said, "Either we're *all* brothers or we're not. Which is it?"

And while I was thinking about that one, he threw in the clincher: "Besides, if love only came from perfect people, there wouldn't *be* any. Would there?"

I said, "Roy, how come you never told me about angel shit before?"

And he said, "Because I just made it up."

Then he laughed so hard he fell down. Literally fell down. Right on the sidewalk. Then I started laughing, and nearly fell on top of him. At this point, a police car came rolling by all lit up like a psychedelic rat.

"Fuzz fuzz fuzz!" I fuzzed.

All mirth subsided abruptly.

We pulled ourselves together and proceeded up 10th Street, tightass as a couple of archbishops, and when the squad car turned the corner I said, "Roy, if we'd have got busted, would it still be angel shit?"

"Listen," he said, "you think you're pretty funny. Right? Well I'm going to tell you something. That shit was angel shit. The fact that I invented it doesn't disqualify it, does it?"

"Of course not!"

"I mean, I can create magic, can't I? I'm a god. Am I a god or not?"

"You are, you are!" I said. And I meant it.

"Okay then, watch! Something fantastic is going to happen to us tonight. Something fantastic and fabulous. In fact, it'll be something absolutely superpluperfectfantabulous*Mc-Thwirp!*"

"Rip that off again, will you?"

"I can't."

"Try."

"SuperpluperfectfantabulousMcThwirp!"
"Superpluperfectfantabulous*McThwirp*?"
"Right."
"*Love* the McThwirp."
"Thanks. Thought you would."
"This ought to be quite a night."
"It will be."

It was.

We met Sally Sunflower.

She was sitting at the Western Union office when we walked in, and greeted us with the biggest and beamingest smile I've ever seen. *Ever.* And since this smile has changed our entire lives, I must describe in detail the celestial being who produced it.

Sally Sunflower looks exactly like her name. Sometime when I feel like it, I'll write the story of how she came to be called that.

Sally's hair is blond and naturally frizzy. If my mother got her hands on it, she'd have it straightened in five minutes. But it's perfect as it is. It picks up every light within miles and makes this enormous shimmering 3D halo around her entire face And what a face! It's big and round and pink and gives the impression of smiling even when it isn't. She also laughs a lot, and her laughter is completely musical. In fact, her whole person is some sort of an instrument, a harpsichord maybe. Whoever happens to be with her is the sheet music she's reading and out comes this tinkling babbling little song, just for them.

What an awful paragraph! I make Sally sound like a real gorp, all sticky-drippy with banana syrup oozing out of every opening she's got. This is frustrating. You write the exact truth about someone you love, and out comes a complete falsehood. What can I say that would really capture her?

I suppose the Salliest thing to be said about her is that she's so pleased about other people. For instance: she's more pleased about *me* than *I* am even. That's the way she seems to feel about everybody. She is genuinely, totally, deeply enthralled and delighted and flipped-out over every last one of us.

Although Roy and I had no way of knowing it at the time —and she's much too modest to mention it herself—we've since learned that Sally Sunflower is practically a historical figure. No one knows how many soldiers she's talked into putting down their guns. At least two San Francisco cops quit the force after turning on with her *one evening!* She's been busted seven times, and is generally fabulous in every conceivable way. Sally's 22 (a Virgo with the moon in Aquarius), so of course she was one of the first flower children, saw the summer of love at the Haight, marched at Century City, helped exorcise the Pentagon. But she was in the Movement even before 1967. A close friend of Kerouac's turned her on to grass when she was 14. She had her first LSD in an electric cocktail on the Merry Pranksters' bus. She helped the Hog Farm pass out food at Woodstock. When Abbie Hoffman sees her on the street, it's Hi, Sally, Hi, Abbie, kiss-kiss. Ditto with Joe Frazier, Allen Ginsberg, Frank Zappa, Paul Krasner, and God knows who else. In fact, she's known just about everywhere as one of the highest heads in all the tribes.

Certainly she's the highest chick *I've* ever met. And living proof that a really high head can keep her trip straight even in New York.

And without money, too!

Sally's been here seven months and one of her major sources of income is Western Union. Whenever she's caught *really* short, she thinks of someone to send a telegram to and the money always comes. This time it was coming from her ex-grandmother in Las Vegas who makes barrels from gambling. I asked her if it bothered her to beg, and she said no, because it wasn't begging. Then she explained:

"Begging is a whole special trip and I'm not into that. I work for a living. I do embroidery. Right now I'm making a blanket. Would you like to see it?" She reached into her bag and showed us her work in progress, an old Army blanket she was transforming into a peace blanket by embroidering MAKE LOVE NOT WAR all over it with big psychedelic lettering. She started it a year ago, on the day a friend of hers went to prison for draft refusal. She figured it'd be finished by the time he got out and then she'd present it to him. I thought it was beautiful, but I didn't see how she could make her living by giving things away.

"It's easy," she said. "I live on a post-revolutionary economy."

Roy was fascinated. "What kind is that?"

"You do what you can for others, and when you need something for yourself, you ask for it. That's all there is to it."

"And that's post-revolutionary economy?" I could see Roy filing it away in his head.

"Right. My guru says that's what the revolution is for, and the only way to bring it about is to live as if we'd already *won.*"

Roy said, "He sounds like a very heavy dude. Is he a Marxist or a Christian or what?"

"Neither. All he believes in is consciousness. He says when people really *know* that all men are brothers, politics will disappear. We won't have to be religious any more either. We'll be *holy* instead."

"*My* guru says we're holy *right now!*" I couldn't resist sticking that in.

"Oh, *absolutely!*"

Then I said, "Roy's my guru."

"No, I'm not," he said. "We're each other's gurus."

"*Far out!*" Sally sang. "That's just what *my* guru says! He says all the people that really know are gurus for each other."

I said, "Yes, but aren't some people more gurus than others? For instance, I *know*. But Roy *really* knows, and that's how he can be my teacher."

Roy said, "Come on, Witch. You really know, too. What are you talking about?"

"What about before? Didn't you have to teach me to love Winston?"

Sally wanted to hear all about Winston, so Roy told her the story. Hearing it the second time through, I had the mad feeling he was telling about a love affair instead of a robbery. Sally was enraptured. She's a good talker, but she's even better at listening. And she doesn't keep interrupting the way I do either. Her face is completely alive to what you're saying, so you end up with the feeling that what you're telling is wonderful and important and true.

At the end of the story, the three of us went outside and did up the other half of Winston's joint. Sally thought it was terrific. It was her first toke in three weeks, so her head was practically virgin. Roy asked her if she'd been going without grass because of the famine, and that's when Sally first mentioned this family she'd joined up with. They were all dedicated to the *natural high*, trying to achieve it by the way they lived, in love and peace. She said none of them put down grass or acid, but they had this little non-rule they tried to follow: Use as little as possible, but stay high no matter what.

When we went back inside, the clerk said Sally's money had arrived. She put the cash in her bag and sat down with us again, because Roy wanted to hear more about living on a post-revolutionary economy. That phrase really had hold of his mind.

"What about the people you send wires to?" he said. "Do they live on a post-revolutionary economy, too?"

"Maybe not all of them," she said. "But I always assume they do. After all, you have to give people the benefit of the doubt. Especially if they've got lots of money. Haven't you noticed how uncomfortable rich people are? All the ones I've known are always going around embarrassed or ashamed. They try to cover it up, but I think they must feel like real freaks. Do you suppose that's why they keep to themselves so much? So they won't have normal people staring at them?"

I said I hadn't thought about it. Roy said he had, but he didn't know.

"If you let people have a chance to help you," Sally said, "it helps them get high. Have you noticed that?"

We said we had.

"But of course," she said, "you have to make it easy for them to refuse. For instance, you have to make it clear that you'll go on liking them even if they say no. And one thing I never do, no matter what, is make up emergency stories. Some kids do that, you know, but I just—well, for *me* it's wrong. Even if I was hungry I'd rather go without food and call it a fast. Fasting can get you high, too."

I noticed Roy looking at me, and I got sort of defensive for a minute. "I'll bet you're thinking about that wire I sent Mother."

Roy's lip pulled to one side and his eyebrow went up.

I said, "Sally, I'm afraid I do lie once in a while."

"So do I," Roy said. "We both do."

"Does that make you hate us?" I asked Sally.

She looked stricken. "Oh, Witch! Don't say such things! Nothing could ever make me hate either of you! You're both angels, don't you know that?"

Roy smiled. "I wouldn't say we lie a *lot*. And when we do, it's only to the Establishment." He looked at me. "Wouldn't you say that was true?"

"Definitely."

Roy wondered what Sally thought about that. She said, "It must be okay for you, because otherwise how could you be so beautiful?"

"No, but really," he said, "don't you think a person *has* to?"

"Look," she said, "if you live as if the revolution's already over, then there *isn't* any Establishment, is there? In post-revolutionary society, everybody's just a person."

Roy said, "Yes, but what about banks and insurance companies and parents and armies and things like that?"

Roy loves hypothetical discussions. One of his favorite subjects is morality.

"That's very tough," Sally said. "I suppose if you were in the Army and had to lie to get out of killing someone, then you'd just have to go ahead and lie. But of course that's an exceptional situation, because there it's like you're dealing with real maniacs."

"The Army?"

"Sure! Oh, I don't mean every soldier is a maniac, far from it. But the ones that go around ordering the men to kill against their will—what's *that*? Isn't that what maniacs are supposed to do?"

"Right," Roy said. "So there's a situation where it's justifiable to lie."

"That's silly, though, isn't it?" Sally said. "Because what would we be doing in the Army? We know better."

"Yeah." Roy glanced at me. "We do know better." Then he said to Sally, "What would you do if you were a man? Would you lie to stay out?"

"If I were a man," Sally said, "I'd tell the truth to stay out."

"And go to prison?"

"Hm-mm, not me. I'd go to Canada and marry the Prime Minister. Isn't he heaven? No, seriously, I think it'd be easier to get used to the cold than go to prison. So I'd go to Canada."

"And give up your citizenship?"

Sally shrugged and smiled. "Sure. What about you?"

"Well," he said, "I guess I'd go underground."

I said, "*Tell* her, Roy."

Roy looked around the Western Union office. There was no one there but the clerk, but he wanted to be sure. Then he said, "Sally, listen, we're underground."

Sally breathed a long, deeply impressed ooooooh! Then she said, "Now everything is beginning to fall into place. I'd planned to come down here in the morning, but I came to-night instead. Now I know why. Oh, this is so *spooky!* Did you notice me looking at you when you came in here tonight?"

We said we had.

"Well," she said, "that's because I picked up on both of you before you even walked in the door. Truly. I got distinct angel vibes just seeing you through the window."

"*Fantastic*," I said.

"Far out!" Roy said.

Sally's very persuasive. We both ended up agreeing with her. Without much struggle either. Let's face it, it's true. Roy and I *are* angels. If we happen to fuck up once in a while, what does that prove?

Sally was shimmering and glittering and twinkling from head to toe. "Give me your hands," she said.

Roy and I each took one of her hands in ours, and we formed a little circle.

When Sally noticed the Western Union man leaning on the counter watching us, she said, "Do you want to join the circle, too?"

90

He hesitated. You could tell he dug the idea. But he said no, thanks, he guessed he better not, and he went back to work.

Then Sally said, "Okay, let's close our eyes together."

We closed our eyes and sat in silence for a minute.

"I see this fabulous light, don't you?" she said.

I hadn't, but I began to, and it seemed to grow stronger. Roy said he saw it, too.

Sally said, "You know what that light is?"

Roy said, "I'm not sure. What is it?"

"That's *us*. And it's especially strong because there's three of us. And we're *together*."

We said wow.

Sally said, "Think how it will be when *the whole world's* together!"

Then the light in our heads went Zap! and multiplied about a hundred times, exploding in all sorts of forms and colors.

And while our eyes were still closed and our inner eyes were still getting this real acid-style light show, Sally Sunflower said, "I hope you'll come home with me and join our family."

That did it.

I fell apart. Tears. The works. It wasn't just me either. They had wet eyes, too.

The clerk came over to the counter at about this point to tell us my money order had come—$150 and a message.

DEAR GLORIA BUSES ARE NASTY TAKE A PLANE ALL IS FOR-
GIVEN WE LOVE YOU MOTHER AND DAD

I started to have a big guilt flash, but I decided to put it off till later. So I composed a message for her.

DEAR MOTHER THANKS FOR MONEY PLANS CHANGED LETTER
FOLLOWS

It sounded pretty naked but I couldn't think of any way to dress it up, so I just added LOVE AND PEACE GLORIA and sent it.

The Canal Street neighborhood is spooky at night. You have to walk through a couple of miles of dark warehousey streets to get to it.

We talked all the way. Sally filled us in on the family. The head of it, even though she said there wasn't one, was obviously Peter Friedman, this guru she'd mentioned. He used to be a psychoanalyst (Sagittarius) but he dropped out (Super-Sagittarius) in 1967. One of his lady patients, a fancy Hollywood talent agent named Doris, dropped out at the same time and came east to live with him. They took the top three floors of this four-story building about a block from the river. He wasn't rich but he still had some money left. So did Doris. Besides, the place was old and run down and not very expensive.

For a while it was just Peter and Doris. Then one day their Yoga teacher got evicted from his loft and moved in with them. And while the three of them were marching on Washington that fall, they met a cab driver. The four of them more or less fell in love, so he moved in, too. And that's the way it happened, and *kept* happening until pretty soon there were nine.

All the way over to Canal Street, Roy and I were stopping to pinch ourselves. I'd say, Do you believe what is happening to us? And he'd say, No, do you? I'd say, No, and we'd both say, Wow. The prospect of having a place to live, Sally

Sunflower for a friend, and a super-high guru like Peter Friedman thrown in on top of it all was almost more than either of us could handle.

As we climbed the stairs we heard "Hare Krishna" playing on the stereo, the same Swami Bhaktivedanta recording Roy and I used to groove on in Belle Woods. Even though everything else was strange to us, this chanting gave us a feeling of coming home. And the minute we walked in the door, we knew we *were* home. We were greeted by four people we'd never seen before, three guys and a chick, but each one of them was as familiar to us as our own faces. Sally introduced us as new members of the family and the next thing we knew we were sitting in a circle holding hands with our new brothers and sisters, being accepted without a word of questioning.

Then they told Sally what had happened that evening. Peter had received a call from California telling him his father was dying. So he and Doris were on their way to California.

I was too lost in wonder and amazement to listen very carefully to all that was said. I remember looking around the room a lot. The place itself was ordinary, but the overall effect was magical. There was an altar on one wall—just a little table, really, with a wooden Buddha on it, a candle and some incense. Around Buddha's neck someone had hung a big gold cross. The only other detail that hooked my mind was a long narrow table at one end of the room. It reminded me of the last supper.

I guess for Roy and me it was the highest night of our lives to date. Even after the angel shit wore off, the night got higher and higher and *higher!*

Roy was in a state of utter flabbergastation. Mouth open, eyes blinking. He looked as if he'd just wandered into paradise and found it even finer than its reputation. All the while the others were talking, the two of us kept looking at their beautiful faces, and then we'd look at each other and say wow over and over again.

Midnight

The previous entry was written in about a dozen different sittings. I haven't yet found a quiet place to work around here. Tomorrow I want to write brief sketches of every member of the family, but I think I'm in real danger of becoming a writing freak. It's so hard to decide what to include and what to eliminate. Everything that happens around here seems interesting and important.

For instance, mealtime is a real gas. (Not because of my cooking either. Everyone said it was good, but I'm not so sure. I think the rice was too soggy and Sally's the one who actually baked the fish. But that doesn't matter. I'll learn.) When we sit down to eat, we hold hands around the table, close our eyes, and send Zaps to faraway brothers. We start with Will, the one in Pennsylvania who's serving out his sentence for draft refusal. Then, if you want to Zap someone else, all you have to do is say his name and everyone in the family chips in his voltage to help you do it.

But that's enough, goddam it. I'm tired!

1:10 a.m.

I can't sleep. I'm wondering where my father is.

2:30 a.m.

Still can't sleep. Neither can Roy. We're in our cave under the attic stairs. He's lying next to me with his eyes closed, and I've got one leg thrown across his stomach to keep us feeling connected. We've just had a very realistic talk and decided we've both been flying a little too high in certain ways, and had better be careful of crashing.

I don't know how either of us could be so naïve as to think we could move into a perfect stranger's house while he's away and actually expect him to come back and be delighted about our being here. Obviously he's in the habit of taking people in, because there are all these others here. But did they move in while he was away? Didn't he have some say in the matter?

Earlier, I asked Sally Sunflower if she didn't think there was some chance Peter would be annoyed about our moving in on him like this. Her answer, even though I love her to pieces, made me feel she might be just a tiny bit manic. She said, "Peter trusts me. He knows I have good judgment." Smiling like mad, of course, the darling.

I said, "Okay, but what about Doris?"

"Doris trusts me, too."

"But Sally, they've never even *seen* us. And we've moved into their house, bag and baggage."

"I know," she said. "Isn't it groovy?" Then she hugged me and went off to some meeting. (Theosophy, I think.)

Roy said he never had believed our good luck was necessarily permanent.

I asked him what gave him his first inkling of doubt. He said it was that first night on the street when Sally mentioned Peter had been an analyst. Because of his father, all these alarms started ringing in his head. Then for a while he got carried away meeting all these new people. But before we went to bed, when I suggested he put up the Desiderata poster, he only went along with the idea because he didn't want to bring me down. But he didn't push the tacks all the way in.

He asked me what gave me *my* first clue. I said I guessed it was Sally. She sounded a little bit fanatical on the subject of Peter, and that made me feel he must have some really fabulous flaws that she'd failed to pick up on.

Anyway, I feel better now, because Roy and I are back to earth. We both realize our fates are far from sealed. We've got ourselves set up now so we can pack our things and be out of here in 60 seconds flat. The $150 from mother is a nice cushion, but we've decided to put part of it in the Grocery Pig.

The Grocery Pig is part of the post-revolutionary economy. The family has this ceramic gravy boat in the shape of a pig, and everybody chips in for household expenses.

Tomorrow we're going to do something about getting jobs.

Canal Street, Monday, September 8, 1969

I'm sitting on an upside-down bucket in the most wonderful office in the world. It's a greenhouse on the roof. Will built it before he went to prison. He's not only a carpenter but a plant freak. According to family legend, his thumb is so green all he has to do is lean on an old man's cane and it takes root right before your eyes. He even grows things you're not supposed to be able to grow at all, except in the tropics. For instance, at this very second I am looking at a hibiscus plant, a live one. Nobody else can get it to bloom, but Will can—even in winter! All the plants have tags on them. *Dracaenea. Dieffenbachia. Schefalerea. Adonidea.* Banana. (Banana!)

I'm learning to call each of them by name. Will told Cary Colorado (he's our Yoga teacher) this can be an enormous help when you're trying to get blooms from them. Talking to them by name lets them know your interest in them is more than just casual and they turn themselves inside out trying to please you.

Everything I've heard about Will makes me like him. There's a photograph of him on Peter's bulletin board. The face is all in shadow, but you can see he's fantastically tall and his shoulders are just enormous. One of these days I'll write to him and thank him for the use of this groovy office. Also, I just discovered that the alcove where Roy and I sleep used to be Will's, too. I wonder what his birth sign is? I hope he's an Aries.

Today I found out classes begin at City College on the 15th. When I hung up the phone I started trembling. Why?

I've been dreaming about my father for the last two nights. In one dream we were married and living in a foreign country. But it didn't *seem* foreign, it just was. Everything pure white and mysterious, and then the whole thing turned inside out and became murky. I think I changed into my mother or something.

Sally says she'll show me how to get to City College on the subway.

Mrs. Gretzinger in Senior English told me I'd probably write a book someday, but I shouldn't do it until I could do it with *authority*. I have a fantastic idea for a novel and I could really do it, too. There's this young girl in Elmhurst, Illinois, or Wild Earth, Kansas, or wherever I decide to put her. She knows Where It's At because she reads constantly. *Time, Look, Playboy, Newsweek, Rolling Stone, EVO, Screw,* everything she can get her hands on. But she hasn't had a chance yet to try her hip little wings in a real center of action. So the book starts with her arrival in New York. I'll use some of my own actual experiences. Roy's too. I'll have her get robbed and beaten up, put in *beaucoups* sex, plus I'll have her fall in with a gang of smackheads who try to turn her on to heroin, etc. A thing like this could really sell like acid at a festival and I could make a fortune. The girl ought to be a virgin, though. Or at least a virgin head, so if she doesn't have her first big sex thing in the book at least she'll have her first acid trip. Then in the movie version there can be all these psychedelic effects. Better yet, why don't I give her a virgin body *and* head and she can lose both cherries at once in a fantastic climactic scene?

I hate it. I really do. I really hate it. I'm so sick of all this virginity bullshit. I've *never* been a virgin and I don't know anyone who ever was. I think virginity must have been invented by dirty old men so they'd have something to defile. What *else* is it good for? Anyway, women have been hassled enough about it, and I'm certainly not going to write an entire book that'll do nothing but foster a lot of phoniness. Only why is it every time I come up with a really sensational idea for a novel, it's always got to be so disgusting I can't write it?

Okay. Back to the journal.

When we got here Friday night there were four members of the Canal Street family missing. Peter and Doris—and Will, of course. The fourth was away somewhere for the weekend, but I met him this morning. Archie Fiesta. My stupid hand lingers over the letters as I write his name. I loathe being in love. (Loving is great. Being *in* love sucks.) Archie's a Virgo with a moon in Leo and Aquarius rising, which means I've had it. Poor Roy, being Pisces like me, is having the same problem. Except that he seems to be digging it and I'm not. I suppose that's because he's got Virgo rising and Virgo men seem to love trouble. For instance,

Archie took him out this afternoon to show him the town, and Roy floated off like a bubble.

Archie Fiesta is the first . . .

I don't want to think about Archie now. If I do, I won't feel like writing, and I want to do little sketches of the others.

Neyeurme is a cab driver. He's probably about 30, but he looks like a big schoolboy. His skin is very dark and he has Afro hair. He's always reading and I get the impression he's a heavy thinker. His answers to even the most casual questions are pondered so carefully that after a while you begin to wonder if it was cool to place such a burden on his head. He has a big troubled forehead with a few hickeys on it, and I keep imagining there's some connection between the hickeys and all this heavy thinking. He's a double Gemini, which can't be too much fun. His name is a bitch to pronounce. The ghost of some archbishop appeared to him while he was tripping one night and laid it on him. This ghost is the only other person besides Neyeurme who can say it correctly because it has all these diphthongy tongue-strangling nuances to it. But it's his soul's name, so all his friends try terribly hard for a while and then give up and call him Nyoom.

Cary Colorado comes from Boulder. He used to be part of a very high commune there, before it got squeezed out by the local Establishment. His mother named him Cary because she was hung up on Cary Grant. But he doesn't look like a movie star. He looks like an ape. In fact, he's any girl's dream of what an ape would be if apes were really groovy and not *too* covered up with body hair. He has this compact little jungle-style body, too, probably from doing Yoga. He's known in the family as the Meditator, because his thing is putting out these blockbuster vibes. He's an Aquarius with Aries rising, and when you sit in a circle with him, it's sort of like being electrocuted with love. He's 22 and he's spent the last three years learning secrets for getting high without dope. He teaches Yoga for a living and he's happy *all the time!* But what delights me most of all about Cary Colorado is that he's a perfect ape. Everything about him, from his pie-face smile right down to his longer than normal arms, strikes me as simian-groovy.

Jeanette has perfect brown skin and her hair is the greatest Afro I've ever seen, an enormous mat-black living turban. The chick herself is as real as her hair. She's a Cancer, but a truly evolved Cancer with a moon in Capricorn. She's been to college, graduated *cum laude* in language, and makes her living translating letters and reviews for a literary agent. She works at home and she's so good at it, it only takes her a couple of mornings a week. Her best language is French, but the language of her life is pure black. Not Pearl Bailey either. Even better. Simpler. More peaceful. Not so ego-trippy. This morning she and I were talking about this fabulous educa-tion of hers and she said, "That's all a bunch of shit, Witch. What I dig most is keeping things straight." I asked her what she meant and she said, "You know, drawers, cupboards, closets. My head, too. I just like to keep it all straight." She's got Peter's books all catalogued and the entire family record collection is in perfect order. She also likes sewing and beading, and Sally's teaching her embroidery.

If I'm going to do this thing right, I'd better describe Percy the Cat. Even though technically he doesn't belong to our family, he's always here. His owner is an Italian lady named Mrs. Goldoni, who lives next door, but she only sees Percy at mealtime. He comes and goes through the window next to the fire escape. Percy is black, actually a kind of sable color, and he moves like a tamed panther who's gotten fat and lazy from living in captivity. Also, the jewels have been removed from his poor little scrotum and this must have something to do with his total lack of feline initiative. He's an ankle cat. He's always rubbing his ears against ankles, hoping for a massage. I suppose any definitive portrait of Percy has to include some reference to his flatulence. It's absolutely radical. He farts every time you pick him up and hold him. And his brand is special. They don't just rise up and blow away, they have staying power. Even when the room is full of patchouli and frankincense, Percy's farts hang in the air like lead clouds.

The only other living being in this house is a ghost. Nobody's actually seen it but everybody's convinced it's here and it seems to be located in the hall outside the Big Room. Sally described it as a column of cool air, and often when she passes by it she has the feeling it's alive. Nyoom has had the same experience and so has his girl friend, Mary. No one seems to mind. They've just gotten used to the idea of sharing the place with this invisible tenant. Ever since I heard about it, I pause in the hall when I pass, hoping to pick up some ghost vibes. Last night on my way to bed I actually *felt* something. My head's too programmed now to be objective, but I had the feeling there was this gentle little pocket of lonesomeness there, and it made me vaguely sad. When I got to bed, I told Roy about it. He said, "Did you say good night to it?" I hadn't. So I got up and stood at the head of the stairs and smiled down into the dark. Nothing seemed to be smiling back up at me, but I flashed a peace sign and said good night, just in case, and went back to bed.

Nyoom brought his woman to dinner. Her name is Mary something. She's a super-blond ex-WASP and he's jet black, so they look great together, very Yin and Yang. Also they're opposites in other ways. Nyoom loves to hold forth and Mary loves to listen. They seem to be a perfect couple in every conceivable way. (I'll bet they're fantastic together in bed!)

Mary doesn't call him Nyoom either. She gets it right, pronouncing every little nuance of his soul's name exactly the way he does, *Neyeurme.* She teaches bookkeeping at a high school in Brooklyn. You can tell she's intelligent by the questions she asks—but she never pushes herself forward in a discussion. You always have the impression she's sitting at Nyoom's feet, encouraging him to be brilliant. Furthermore, it works.

He was so brilliant tonight explaining the Black Panthers, the entire table was spellbound. He says they're actually engaged in Street Theater and their most powerful weapon is the TV camera. The plot of the play is to force the white power structure out into the open so the whole world can see the tactics it uses to hold the black man down.

Nyoom feels he knows exactly what's going to happen in the world during the rest of the century. He's got an entire timetable in his head. At first it sounded too fantastic, but I noticed Roy listening so intently I decided to pay closer attention. It goes like this:

Between now and 1972, we catch the government in more and more lies, most of them just as shitty as Vietnam. For instance, all the secret wars like Laos and Cambodia get exposed. Demonstrations. Counterdemonstrations. People beat each other up right in the streets. Much bombing. Crime rate zooms, everybody ripping off everybody else. Schools close down. Rich ladies hire armed guards to take them to the delicatessen. The whole country becomes as dangerous as the ghettos have been for years. Chaos up to *here*. Nixon and Agnew lay the whole thing on the students, the blacks, the peace movement, etc. The cops get caught on TV gunning down the leaders of radical movements. Word leaks out that shoot-to-kill orders have come from Very High Up. This causes mass public freak-out. (Nyoom called it "cultural shock," but Roy translated.) Scads of government employees all over the country split their posts in disgust. Nobody buys a single word uttered by any public official. This creates a "power vacuum." (Roy's translation: "Nobody left to do the dirty work.") So the police and the Army move in. Nyoom says they already run the whole thing secretly, but by 1972 they quit pretending. They just move right into the old White House, guns and all, and declare a national emergency for themselves. Half of the public thinks this is just divine, but the other half doesn't dig it at all. Civil war starts. Naturally, the generals cream. They've been revving up for this for years, and they know perfectly well the poor revolutionaries haven't got it together at all. Instant slaughter, quick roundup of dangerous types (like us!), and the whole thing's over. Very short war. Then the New Dark

Age begins. Martial law. Armored tanks in the streets. Curfews everywhere from Sutton Place to Gung Ho, Texas. Old ladies out looking for their cats after dark found shot to death in the A.M. Students caught listening to Beatles records suddenly disappear, never to be heard from again. Super uglies for breakfast, lunch, and dinner. Informing. Sabotage. Reprisals. Meanwhile, the rest of the world's getting it together for a change. Because the Pentagon's too busy making fascism work at home to do much exporting. America is finally isolated by its own bullshit, and Third World forces have to move in to liberate us. Do they get to us before the looneys push the button? Nyoom says it's touch and go, because the whole system's rigged for self-destruct.

Later, in bed

Roy earned $3 today. There's a sign painter on the street floor of this house, and Roy made a delivery for him. It's the first money he's ever earned and he's practically hysterical with pride.

I didn't do much about getting work myself. Spent most of the afternoon with Sally at the launderette. She taught me how to run the machines. They're easy. All we had to do was fold things. And talk. Is Sally *always* high? I'm beginning to think so. And she hardly ever smokes!

Peter called from California while we were having dinner tonight. His father hasn't died yet. Nyoom happened to be the one to answer the phone. When I found out it was Peter, I told him to say something about Roy and me, and to ask if it was all right if we stayed till he got back. But Nyoom can't do anything simply.

105

He said, "The population of this Canal Street Experimental Station en route to Utopia has increased by two examples of the genus *homo sapiens*, and, er, uh, the, uh, foundlings in question are indulging in a certain shall we say anxiety as to their status here. However, Sally Sunflower, that stunning example of celestial flora, has done what she could to assure them that the matter . . ." And blah blah blah.

Peter must be a saint to let him run on like that long distance. Anyway, I guess it's cool for us to stay till he gets back.

CANAL STREET, SEPTEMBER 11, 1969

Haven't been into a writing thing for three solid days, so
it feels good to have this notebook in my lap again. It's been
raining all day. Cary Colorado's out looking for wood. He
wants to build a fire and do his Yoga in front of it. It's not
at all cold, but it'll be lovely to see the fireplace working.
Percy the Cat is curled up at my feet and the whole scene
is so old-timey and cozy I'm having Emily Brontë flashes.
Sally Sunflower is Charlotting in the kitchen. It's her day to
cook. On my days she's always out there showing me macrobiotic secrets, but on her days she doesn't seem to mind
doing it all alone.

Peter and Doris are still in California. They phoned last
night to get in on the mealtime Zap. Peter's father is lingering on and on without showing any signs of getting better
or worse. I caught myself hoping he'd die, so Peter and Doris
could come back, and it didn't bother me at all to catch
myself being so selfish because I knew it was only a flash
and entirely human.

Roy's upstairs helping Jeanette clean out Peter's attic.
They want to have it all painted and spruced up as a surprise

for when he gets back. I've never seen Roy work so hard. The sign man downstairs hasn't had any more deliveries for him to make, but since that first $3, he's been obsessed with the idea of paying his own way. He volunteered to help Jeanette do over the attic, and the notion of repainting it was entirely his. It's strange. On the one hand, he won't even push the thumb tacks all the way in on our Desiderata poster, and yet he's painting the attic of a man he hasn't even met. I suppose he's trying to build up a little insurance against getting thrown out when Peter comes back. Also, I notice he digs being with Jeanette. It seems like whenever he's not with Archie Fiesta, he's with her, and I've sort of been missing him. The only time I see him is at dinner and in bed.

———————

The attic is my favorite part of the house. The stairs right above the alcove where Roy and I sleep open into this sort of loft that Peter uses for talking with people in private. I suppose it's actually his consultation room. The only furniture in it is an Oriental rug, two easy chairs and a mattress. Off to the side there's a little blue Buddha, some votive candles, and an incense burner, all on the floor. Also little stacks of books here and there and scads of newspapers and magazines, both underground and overground. On one wall is a bulletin board with a little of everything on it. You could stand there for hours (and I have) finding new bits and pieces that various members of the family and other visiting brothers and sisters have tacked up. Some are original and some are copied from other sources. I'll copy the whole bulletin board in here someday when I haven't anything else to write, but at the moment I want to get the titles of these books.

Peter's Books

The Autobiography of Malcolm X
The Politics of Ecstasy. Timothy Leary
The Strange Death of Marilyn Monroe
Reality Therapy. William Glasser
The Wretched of the Earth. Franz Fanon
My Wicked, Wicked Ways. Errol Flynn
Principles of Accounting
The Other Side. James Pike
Woodstock Nation. Abbie Hoffman
The Teachings of Don Juan; A Yaqui Way of Life. Castaneda
The Prophet. Kahlil Gibran
The Whole Earth Catalog
I Ching
Education and Ecstasy. George Leonard
Centering. Mary Caroline Richards
Post-Prison Writings and Speeches. Eldridge Cleaver
A Stranger in a Strange Land. Robert Heinlein
The Phenomenon of Man. Pierre Teilhard de Chardin
Thus Spake Zarathustra. Friedrich Nietzsche
Mandate for Change. Dwight D. Eisenhower
Vietnam: The Logic of Withdrawal. Howard Zinn
Points of Rebellion. William O. Douglas
Growing Up Absurd. Paul Goodman
Childhood's End. Arthur C. Clarke
The Ultimate Revolution. Walter Starcke

Periodicals

I. F. Stone's Weekly
Buy-Lines
The Minuteman News
Scanlon's
Playboy

Dr. Strange
Consumer Reports
National Observer
The Realist
Win

———————————

Now that I'm sort of into it. I might as well describe the
rest of the house. The street floor doesn't count, because it's
commercial. The sign man has his shop down there, and we
have the top three floors. Our first (which is actually the
second floor of the building) has three rooms. The one I'm
in now is called the Big Room. Practically everything happens here—living, eating, listening to music, etc. Then there's
the kitchen at the back, and off to the side a tiny bedroom
where Sally Sunflower sleeps. The second floor is nothing
but two enormous bedrooms and a big bathroom in between
plus the little cave under the attic stairs where Roy and I
sleep. And that's it. Except that in the attic there's also a
bedroom where Doris and Peter sleep.

The style of the house is groovy ramshackle. Everything's
either falling apart from age or on the verge. The toilet, for
instance, has to be flushed by drawing a bucket of water
from the tub and dumping it into the bowl. Nobody minds
any of this because the rent is super-cheap, $150 a month,
and the deal is that we agree not to ask the landlord for
anything, no matter what, even if the roof falls in. But we
can do anything we please, even build greenhouses on the
roof, as long as we don't bug him.

———————————

Why am I writing all this stuff? I seem to be in a Jeanette
mood today, sorting out little drawers in my head, telling

where everybody is, describing the house, etc. I'm avoiding something of course.

And I know exactly what it is, too. I've been noticing lately that the minute I ask myself a question like this, the answer's sitting right there staring at me.

Hi, Archie, you prick.

I might as well go whole hog and start from the beginning.

The first time I saw him, the morning after Roy and I moved in, he was sitting here on this very couch listening to a Steve Miller record, the one that starts with "Quicksilver Girl," a song I always think of as my very own. I was hardly awake yet, but when Sally introduced us, I nearly fell over in a dead faint, he's that beautiful. Puerto Rican and Italian with a little German thrown in, and the combination is utter pornography. His handshake alone is an aphrodisiac. And no woman should look at him head-on without sunglasses unless she wants to run the risk of making a fool of herself on the spot. Witch Pisces Me wanted to jump right into his lap, but somehow Witch moon-in-Scorpio Me has been able to maintain a certain cool—until this afternoon. Now I'm wondering how badly I blew it.

I have some secret thoughts about Archie Fiesta that I wouldn't divulge to a living soul, not even Roy. The thought of causing even a hint of dissension in this perfect, sacred family destroys me completely. Besides, Roy has taught me to dig the Eighth Commandment. Rather than break it, I'd undergo an abortion without sedation by a doctor using ice tongs.

But I'm not called Witch for nothing. I get definite flashes about people, and I trust them. They are whispered into my ears by angels or something probably. Who knows? But everything I am tells me Archie Fiesta is on a death trip. *Furthermore, he wants company!*

God, what a horrible thing to write down.

111

The really awful thing is that he's so excruciatingly attractive. And not just to me. He's got this entire family in a bag slung over his shoulder and just walks away with us in any direction he chooses. So great for instance are the prerogatives of beauty that he takes money *out* of the Grocery Pig while everybody else is putting it *in*—and no one seems to mind in the least. I can't help thinking if he really wanted us to live in peace, he'd mess himself up a little so we could all stop quivering about him. His hair is the reddish black Grandmother O'Malley used to try for with her henna packs, only on Archie it's real. His skin is even more translucent than mine, and his lips! I'd just as soon forget his lips. But it wouldn't help—it's his whole head and bod. He looks as if somebody had hired the top 25 greatest sculptors and painters of all time and said, Go to it, the sky's the limit—and what they came up with is Archie Fiesta. But I still can't forget his lips. They're curly and a little too big, and the skin on them is so thin you can see right through to the red, which is the red of ripe strawberry with the faintest hint of beige at the edges. And now, having lingered on them for a full minute, I'm ready to faint again. I hereby instruct myself to stop thinking about Archie Fiesta's lips. I must steel myself and proceed to his eyes. One of them moves straight into yours when he looks at you, but has a slight cast and seems somehow to be off on a trip of its own. The total effect is that Archie Fiesta is half here and half somewhere else, hung up on some glorious mystery. You get the impression he's remembering life on some other planet, or this chick he left back on Mars.

Along with all these radical physical assets, what really undoes people is his cool and his rap. He claims his cool comes from harmony, inner harmony. And that, in a nutshell, just about sums up his rap.

The first time you hear it, it sounds pretty good, but the second time it rings hollow. It's like he got hold of this magic code word, Harmony, and because he's so cool (stoned out of his mind is my guess—I'll bet my ass he munches mescaline for breakfast!) and so wildly good-looking, everybody seems to want to believe it. I wonder if Peter does?

Could I be wrong? Could it be just this mad physical impact of his that makes me feel he's simply got to be a con man? Scorpios are often suspicious of the people they want to go to bed with. But I'm hip enough to myself to take that into account.

So why does that left eye of his keep bugging me? It's like the rest of his face and his body were with you completely, but this one part of him is keeping an eye on the boss. And the boss is Satan.

I've just read this over. I disgust myself. I don't believe a word I've written. Now shut up, Witch, and copy the Desiderata. I order you to do it beautifully, in your best handwriting:

DESIDERATA
Go placidly amid the noise and the haste. And remember what peace there may be in silence. As far as possible without surrender, be on good terms with all persons. Speak your truth . . .

This is ridiculous. I just realized I'm still on my mother's old Catholic guilt trip, doing penance for having ugly thoughts. I refuse to defile the Desiderata by copying it down as a punishment. I'll wait and do it when the perfect moment arrives for it and not a second before.

I suppose I'm just trying to avoid writing what happened between Archie and me a few minutes ago. But now that I think about it, it's not so horrible.

There've been all these glances passing between us ever

113

since that first night. As a rule, when one of us gets caught at it, the other smiles, and nothing ever gets said. But today it was different.

I came down and found him here stringing his guitar, and like a fool I said, Oh excuse me, and started out of the room. But then he called me back and asked me why I excused myself.

"I don't know. Maybe because you're working. I don't really know."

"Have you got something else to do?"

"Nothing urgent. I was just bringing my notebook up to date."

"Why not do it here?"

I said I didn't know why not. And then I looked at him, really looked at him to see if I could find out what was in his head. He was sort of smiling in a knowing way, and I got the feeling he knew I was attracted to him and was teasing me about it.

I said, "Archie, you look like you're amused about something. Am I right?"

"I don't know. Do I look amused? Maybe I am."

"Yes, maybe you are. I always feel you're teasing me."

"*Teasing?*" His right eye and his entire face found the idea incredible—but his left eye went right on doing its little number on my head. I got annoyed. But I didn't let it creep into my voice. I spoke reasonably.

"Yes, Archie. Teasing. And I don't dig that, because I'm not into games."

"Games? You think I'm into games? Listen, my rap is harmony."

"I know," I said. "I've heard your rap. It's very beautiful." I said it as if I meant it.

"But you don't buy it?"

114

I just looked at him. His whole face was working together at putting out this big sincerity blast. Then Cary Colorado came into the room with his arms full of kindling and started to build the fire. He must have picked up on the voltage we were putting out, because without even looking at either of us, he asked us to make a circle with him. Archie had my left hand, and he squeezed it in a way that made me feel he was begging me to believe him. My right hand was in Cary's, so naturally I was getting these really powerhouse vibes. Between the two of them, my mind turned to mush and everything got simple again. I loved them both and they loved me. Pretty soon we were all smiling at each other and feeling this invisible white sweetness passing through us.

I said, "Archie, was I hassling you before, when Cary came in?"

Archie said, "No, I didn't feel like I was being hassled."

Then Cary grinned like an adorable little ape and said, "Look, Ma, no hassles," which made us laugh again. So we broke the circle, and Cary started his Yoga.

Archie said he had to go out and would I walk him down to the street. I said sure. And when we got down there, he said, "Listen, Witch, if you should happen to feel like getting in bed with me some night, just crawl in."

Thank heaven he wasn't looking at me, because I was wrecked. Of course, being a large phony, I was careful not to betray myself. I said something breezy like "Fantastic idea, Archie," and ran upstairs.

But why did I get so angry? It seems to me now that under the circumstances this was a very cool thing for him to say. He looks like a god; can he help it? He sees this chick obviously freaked out over him and he invites her into his bed—at her convenience. What more can a girl ask for? Wedding rings, annuities, promises? It's absurd. I'm the one that's off base in this entire matter. Thank heaven I have a notebook for this drivel so I can keep my head free of it.

(*But I still don't trust A.F.!*)

CANAL STREET, SEPTEMBER 12, 1969

ROY SPENDS THE DAY IN THE BRONX
as told to
Witch Gliz

I get this job through an ad. It's selling children's books door to door. I despise the idea of selling, but I decide to try it because I figure they probably won't ask for identification. On the first day, we drive up to the Bronx in the boss's car. There's myself, a black dude named Bristol, who was also a beginner, and this really tough black chick named Harriet, who's supposed to show us what to do. I'm the only one with a license, so I do the driving.

The day goes along okay. Nobody wants to hear about these books though. All they want you to do for them is go away and leave them alone. I get hollered at a few times but it's not terrible. Anyway, at the end of the day, Bristol and myself are sitting in the car in front of some apartment building, waiting for Harriet to come out. Across the street there's an elementary school. Otherwise it's just a regular neighborhood.

117

All of a sudden the car door opens and I'm being told to get out. Then I see the door on Bristol's side is being opened and somebody's telling him to get out, too. It's a pair of plainclothesmen. They show us a badge, shove us up against the car and search us. One of them, a fat-faced guy with little pink eyes, starts questioning us. What are we doing up here? I tell him, but he says I'm a fucking liar. That's his favorite word, he uses it about a hundred times.

I show h'm all the stuff in the back seat, the children's books, the flyers, all the order forms. And that's when it starts getting creepy. Because at this point they believe us. I can tell they do, and yet they keep on pretending not to.

They ask if we have police records. I say no. Bristol says, yes, for possession and assault. So what do they do? They leave Bristol alone in the car—*unguarded*—and they take me, the cat that doesn't have a record, into this apartment building. The pink-eyed one says, "Come in here and talk. It's cold outside." And they get me in there by the mailboxes and tell me to take off my sweater. I ask them what they're after, and the guy says, "We want to see if you've got tits and a pussy along with all that pretty hair."

Up to this point I'm being cooperative, because I'm afraid if they take me in they'll find out about my thing with the draft. But now it's getting too weird, because they start throwing me around and pushing me against walls and slapping me in the face. So I tell them I've got a right to know what's happening. Then the one that's been silent up to now says, "You're selling heroin to school kids and we know it. Look at you, tracks all over your arm." All the while I'm trying to figure out what they're talking about because my arms haven't got a mark on them and they know it. Then he shows me his fist and he says, "If I shove that in your face will you tell the truth?" Then the fat-faced one pulls out a razor, an actual goddam razor, and he says, "I'll

118

bet he jerks off fifth-grade kids. Is that what you do, you filthy little motherfucker?" He grabs hold of my hair and asks me if I'd like a haircut. But the other guy says, "No, don't cut his hair. We'll need it to hang on to when he goes down on us." Just then the inside door opens, and it's Harriet, on her way out of the building. She sizes up the situation pretty fast, and she's not scared of these guys either. She says, "What's the matter, Roy?" Suddenly the silent one gets very dignified. "You know this person?" he says. Harriet looks him right in the eye "Yes, I do," she says. Then he shows her his badge. "Narcotics squad. Routine check." And he turns to me. "Okay, you can go." Then they give me my sweater back, and we split.

On the way back downtown, Harriet says to me, "How do you like bein' a nigger?" I tell her I don't care for it. And when we get back to the office, I get fired for not coming up with any prospective buyers for the books.

MONDAY, SEPTEMBER 15, 1969, 11 P.M., 23RD STREET AUTOMAT

I'm wrecked. My mind won't stop. It's been leading me around by the nose all day long and I'm not going to let it get away with any more shit.

The Desiderata says, "Beyond a wholesome discipline, be gentle with yourself."

I haven't been gentle, I've been indulgent. I've been compulsive and foolish and reckless, and I've followed every single whim as if it were a command, and what's worse, my darling little mind has been justifying each disastrous step, one after another. The Mothers of Invention say the mind is the ugliest part of the body. Well, mine is in for a face lift. Or at least a good purge. I'm going to sit here at this table until I've written everything that's happened today, and when I get done, if my mind hasn't had enough, I'll just keep writing until it faints from sheer exhaustion. Yesterday I was so full of clarity and purpose and good sense, I felt like some kind of a saint. Maybe from now on when I'm feeling so absolutely certain I've found the Handle, I should take it as a clue that I'm about ready to fuck up on a grand scale.

120

For the sake of fairness, I should consider one mitigating factor. It's just faintly possible I was thrown into this spiral of stupidity by the shock of finding my father this afternoon. His being such a crushing disappointment might not have helped matters either.

Careful, Witch Gloria, don't let yourself off the hook too quickly. There's work to be done. Right now.

(Witch Gloria. I like the sound of that. A little of the old, a little of the new. I guess I've been missing my old name and didn't even realize it till now. Gloria. Hello, Gloria, dear old friend of my babyhood, dear bewildered, frightened, brave, lonely companion of my girlhood. . . .)

I paused just now for a cry. It was nice. The Automat gives you these paper napkins to blow your nose on.

And now, back to work:

This afternoon Sally Sunflower took me up to City College on the subway. Everyone was extremely helpful. But they have no Henry Glyczwyczes teaching in the History Department. I studied all the names in the catalog, hoping to find one that sounded like something you'd change your name to if your name was Glyczwycz. But there weren't even any Henrys. We walked around the halls for a while because I had a hunch I'd be able to pick up my father's vibes if he was on the premises. But there were no vibes either.

Coming back downtown on the subway, I got an awful

fit of anxiety. I told Sally I was afraid I'd never find him, that I'd spend my entire life expecting to run into him everywhere I went. In twenty years there'd be this skinny, haggard, frenetic little madwoman running around from city to city, staying in tacky rented rooms, passing her days hanging around History Departments looking for her father. Sally chose not to be comforting, and I don't blame her. Not now. But at the time I could have chewed her up and spit her out. Because she said, "Each of us can have any life he envisions for himself."

The brilliant thing about Sally is that in her sweet, wonderful way, she's absolutely uncompromising. She took my hand and said, "Oh, Witch, don't you know if you're supposed to find him, you will? And if you're not, you won't?"

I said, "Sally, I know you're right. Of course you are. But don't you see, I've got a moon in Scorpio, and Scorpios are *driven!*"

"Only if they want to be," she said. "If a person's not determined to grow beyond her chart, rise above all the negative things in it, she'd be better off tearing it up. Honestly, Witch. Astrology mustn't be a map you follow until you're in *hell*. It's got to be a guide for expansion of consciousness." The subway train was making a ghastly noise that made me feel even more desperate and anxious. I was in no mood for the truth, and having it shouted into my ear didn't help much. Even while I was hearing it, I knew she was right, but something in me wouldn't let me up for a second.

When we got to Columbus Circle, Sally said, "Come on!" She got up and walked off the train. Subway maps have me completely flummoxed, so I had no choice but to follow her out onto the platform.

She said, "I'll tell you what! We'll go to all the colleges, one after another. We'll do everything we can to find him. But if we fail, will you promise to give up?"

I promised.

Then she said there were two schools at this stop, Central Park J.C., and Hunter, right across the park. We decided to try them both, and if my father wasn't teaching at either of them, we'd give up for the day and try N.Y.U. and the New School tomorrow.

The first one we went to was Central Park J.C., and we found him *immediately*. It couldn't have been easier. We walked right into the Administration Building, went up to the desk and asked. No Glyczwyczes. Sally asked for a list of history courses. They gave it to her. The third one on the list was "Contemporary Events, Room 304. Mondays, Wednesdays, Fridays, 3 to 4 P.M. H. Gliss."

I'd already imagined his name might be something like Gliss, so of course it was perfectly clear we'd found him.

Sally said, "This is Monday, Witch, he's probably up there right now. What do you want to do?"

I said, "I want to faint."

"Oh, my God, really?"

"Really."

She guided me to the drinking fountain. Which turned out to be one of those wonders of modern technology where you open your poor dry little mouth, lean in, and get your entire face squirted off. My hair was drenched. Anyway, it cooled me off.

We sat on a bench in the hall and talked it over. What was I to do? I could see only two alternatives. Walk right into the class, introduce myself, and *then* faint. Or wait till it was over, catch him coming out, and keel over in his arms. Sally said there must be something else. And I said, "You're dead right, there is. I'll pose as a student, call myself Rita LaFlubb or something, and look him over. If I don't dig him, we can split."

"You mean," Sally said, "you could actually see you father

for the first time in your entire life, and walk away without telling him who you are?"

"Could I *ever!* Come on, let's go!"

Now that I had this sneaky little plan giving me fuel, I was operating like a dynamo. I flew up the stairs and down the hall, Sally right behind me, and waltzed into Room 304 without so much as a second thought. Furthermore, I sat in a front seat and looked right into his eyes.

It's a good thing I was sitting down. Because all my guts abandoned me the minute our eyes met.

He hated me. He absolutely hated me. And I hated him right back. His eyes were awful: I felt like they were calling me dreadful names. They were saying, You're stupid, you're superficial, you're late, you're a female, you're wasting my time, you're worthless, why don't you get the hell off this planet altogether!

And I was thinking, Watch your step, Professor Gliss, your daughter is a witch. She knows how to deal with hateful old bastards. She's been trained by experts all her life. So cool it and cool it fast, or she'll spit in your eye. And I could have too. My spit would have been pure carbolic acid and blinded him for life.

By that time, he was looking at Sally. She must have been smiling, because he said good afternoon. Then he glanced at me again and went on talking to the class.

My mind was chattering at me like some loony little bird. This is your father, it said, this is Daddy, this is Papa. One day a long time ago, this man got on top of your mother and planted *you* in her. The seeds of you came out of his balls. Those very balls are hanging there right now, inside of those awful baggy pants, and the stupid thing doesn't even know you're a part of him. He doesn't know anything, not really. How can he? He's full of hate and meanness, and there isn't any room left in him for knowing

124

anything. He doesn't like you and he doesn't like himself and he doesn't like the world and he doesn't like anything at all. How sad he is. What a sad man is my father. Gloria. Gloria dear, you are looking at Henry Glyczwycz. Isn't this what you've been wanting to do since you were born, or at least since you were twelve, when you first heard of his existence? This is Hank, this is your mother's lover, the very man your Uncle Mickey told you about when you were twelve. He'd just enjoyed one of Mother's superduper special putdowns for being drunk and he blurted out the whole works! "Hey, Gloria," he said on his way out to the car, "ask your mother how Hank is. Ask her if she's heard anything from her kike lover lately." You knew he was going to tell you something awful, but you knew you had to hear it because somehow you'd always known anyway. Besides, you're the kind of a chick who has to hear *everything*. And so you went to the car, drawn to it, magnetized, *hypnotized*, while your mother was screaming at you from the front walk. "Gloria, get in this house. Gloria Random, don't you go near that car." But you went near it all right. You got in fast and sped away and in thirty seconds you had the whole story, digging it totally right from the start. It was immediately and wildly thrilling to be the love child of a Polish Jew who'd been thrown out of three universities for preaching Communism, to be so nearly a bastard you had every right to call yourself one, because if your mother hadn't managed to drag that bloodless little broker to the altar in the nick of time, you'd *be* one for real. (But of course he wasn't dragged, he was delighted. His self-satisfied little tail must have wagged all the way up the aisle. And it wasn't in the nick of time either. The lump that was you was only three months along and probably hadn't even begun to show yet. How could it, under about six miles of virginal white tulle?) You carried around this new knowledge of Gloria like a shining secret

125

possession, whispering over and over again, I am not a WASP, I am not a WASP, I am not a WASP, until it all ran together and became IYAMNOTAWASP and lost some of its shine and nearly all of its sense. So you carried it over to John's basement and renewed it all by telling it out loud for the first time, and in the telling it got even better. "John, I just found out from my Uncle Mickey that I am a Polack Jew Bastard!" But careful! Careful this time not to squander the spell by repeating it too often. And then the phrase began to sink in, until it sank in deep, really deep, and became *knowing.* Knowing at last what you'd only felt before, that you were truly and truly and truly an alien in Waspland, an exotic foreigner even *by blood!* a stranger, caught—but only for a while!—in the land of the carpeted, insulated smile and the glossy stainless steel frown, where words were for hiding behind and not for showing who you were.

And now here you are 17 years later, sitting three yards from the man who made the lump. Why does he have to be so ordinary and mean and sad? Is he? Maybe he's none of those things. You're quite capable of making emotional judgments that turn out to be madly unsound. Pretend he's not your father and look at him again. Carefully. Look at him with your witch eyes. See who he is.

So that's what I did. And everything turned upside down. He wasn't ordinary any more. and I wasn't at all certain he was mean either. Sad? Yes, maybe. But then, most people in their forties, underneath all their attitudes and faces, seem awfully sad to me.

Maybe I'd been wrong about everything. For instance, why would any man *bother* to hate a strange chick—just for walking into his classroom a few minutes late. On the first day of school, practically everybody's late. Try to listen to him, I instructed myself. Try hard.

"So if you people come here for fairytales, stay home.

Skip class. Play hookey. Don't come at all. I'll give you C for honesty." He hit his tees too hard and said his final gees too carefully. He sounded like an overeducated dumbhead. His grammar was technically correct, but just barely, as if keeping it correct was a constant strain. He paced back and forth a lot, and his hairy hands were a burden to him. They kept going in and out of his pockets and making abortive little gestures. He fooled with the knot in his necktie, and I got the impression he was none too sure it was tied correctly and wondered how many of us were sitting there writing him off as square.

Finally I got around to seeing him through my mother's eyes. Supposing, I asked myself, I had to pick out the one quality in him that had seduced her. And the minute I asked, I knew: it was his fire. Mother's old Hank Glyczwycz might be a lot of things, tiresome, irritable, who knows what else, but he was alive. Packed with life. And lean, too. You couldn't really tell, in all these baggy brown tweeds, whether his leanness was jungle leanness or ulcer leanness. Maybe a little of both, because he was quick as a cat and uptight as a gangster. But either way, I could imagine my mother absolutely craving that energy, wanting to soothe it and control it and hold it close and contain it.

Then a weird mood struck me. Suddenly I'd begun to *sympathize* with my mother. I felt myself to be her as she was 18 years ago, a pretty, uptight, carefully groomed virgin (?) of 23, terrified of becoming an old maid, office-working at Random Hogan Random and Hodge in the daytime, and trying to stir up a little safe trouble for herself after hours by taking evening courses at Detroit U. And Bam! Alacazam! she meets this glamorous young refugee from Hitler's Europe, an angry, husky, sexy dynamo from Hamtramck, and gets *hooked!* I wondered if he was wearing the same necktie then. Probably not. But I bet he tied it with the same knot!

127

And I bet the backs of his hands were every bit as hairy as they are now.

Mother. My mother.

Dear mother, my babbling mind wrote her a letter, *I am in the presence of your old lover and I know how it must have felt to be with him. Forgive me for not knowing before. This afternoon I think I love you a tiny bit more than usual. Do you suppose we'll ever get to know one another? Peace. Gloria.*

After class a few people went up to talk with him. His answers were curt and tough and official. There was no real *hearing* in them, no softness, no warmth, just rat-a-tat-tats with built-in fuck-yous. I stayed in my seat. Sally Sunflower looked over and tried to come up with a smile for me, but all she could manage was one small anemic grin.

"Would you like to go up and talk with him?" she whispered.

I shook my head no. When everybody but Sally and I had cleared out of the room, Professor Gliss, my father, stopped at the door and looked back at us. He looked at Sally actually, but I had a feeling what he was really doing was *not* looking at me.

He said, "You girls want something?"

And I said, shocking myself terribly and knowing at once how wicked and hard it sounded, "Like what?"

He looked at me for a few seconds with a faint unpleasant smile on his mouth and said, "Careful, you might get it!" Then he kept *on* looking at me, nodding his head several times, and left the room.

I felt like I'd been slapped. Not by him, but by myself. Why would I act that way—*instinctively?* Was I really such a hateful little slut?

Sally said, "Are you all right, darling Witch?"

128

I started babbling about how marvelous I felt, how I'd wanted to see him and now I had and that was that, and what did she think we ought to do with the *rest* of the afternoon. She said it was such a pretty day why didn't we walk in the park. So we went down to the street and looked at the day.

It wasn't pretty. It was spectacular. I loathed it. It hurt. It was one of those perfect young back-to-school days, windy and sunny and yet cool enough to carry a sweater just in case, and I felt such a nostalgia for other days that had been like it, days when I'd been *really* young, with nothing grim working in my stomach. Had there been such days? Of course, thousands of them! So I began to *impersonate* one of them. I said, "Sally, I feel like a beautiful young girl!" She said, "You *are* a beautiful young girl!" And I said, "Yes, but what I mean is I feel *marvelous!*" And she said, "You *are* marvelous!" And I said, "I *know!* But Sally, please, listen. Do you suppose we can forget him entirely? Forget we ever saw my father? Just put him out of our minds and never think of him again?"

At that moment a boy and a girl came up to us with a petition. He was a shorthair cleancut number, and she was braided-and-sensible. The boy did the talking.

"We saw you girls coming out of Gliss's class, and we thought you might like to sign this. It's a petition. Are you new here?"

I said, "What's the petition?"

"We're trying to get him out."

"Trying to get *who* out?"

"Gliss. Last semester we got a hundred and forty signatures, including a majority of all History Majors. But they *still* haven't fired him. This is a protest petition."

"What's wrong with him?"

129

"Everything. Also we think he's a Communist. That's his business. But the point is he hates this country, all his courses are nothing but hate-America courses. We know our country's not perfect but we refuse to pay out good money to be taught contempt for the flag."

Dear Mother, I saw Daddy today and he's still up to the same old tricks. Peace. Gloria.

Braided-sensible said to Sally, "Will you sign?"

"I can't," Sally said. "I'm not really interested in flags and nations."

"Not interested," said B-and-S, "in what happens to your own country?"

Sally smiled one of her brightest sunflower smiles and said, "No, not really. I care what happens to our *world!*"

Shorthair cleancut gave B-and-S a knowing look and they walked away. I wonder what people with knowing looks *know?*

I said, "Well, if Professor Gliss has enemies like that, he can't be *all* bad."

"Do you still want to forget you ever met him?"

"Yes. Absolutely. Forever. We have a pact. Will you forget him, too?"

Sally agreed. So we went across Central Park West, climbed over the wall, and ran into the park. If anything, the day had improved. Blue was blue and green was green and air was air and people were people and I was me and Sally was Sally—and happiness was misery. Someone should invent spirit glasses that would do for your soul what sunglasses do for your eyes. Couldn't the glare of just *being,* on a day like this, blind something in you even more precious than eyes?

I knew I was in a dangerous mood. And I knew if I had half a chance I'd do something really foolish.

Which is exactly what I did.

After the park, we kept walking, and pretty soon we were at Bloomingdale's. While we were passing through Men's Wear on the way to the basement, somebody said hi to Sally. It turned out to be this friend of hers who was selling pajamas. I've forgotten his name already. But while we were standing there talking, the three of us, along came this dude named Edward— a friend of the one whose name I've forgotten.

Edward is an extremely sexy and magnificent-looking Leo, with a virile-plus body, and an Adam's apple. He's wearing an emerald-green shirt with a bright blue flowered scarf tied at the neck and tight-tight black bell-bottoms. The shirt's open to the waist, so all the while we're talking, I have to cope with this hairy hairy hairy chest. Obviously Edward sees his chest as quite an asset. He wears this shiny brass medallion hanging from a chain that hits him midway between navel and nipple. And just in case your attention happens to wander, there's this medallion flashing away like crazy to bring your eye back home.

From the start, Edward presents this big riddle. He comes on super gay, with a rich and witty tongue that goes like forever. But all the while he's talking, I feel he's looking at me the way a man looks at a woman. I'm confused, but not the least bit turned on by him, because whether he's gay or not, he's a peacock, and he talks too much. Edward's a make-up artist. "Probably the world's finest. I create faces," he says. "I make everyone a star. It's the answer, don't you see, to all the world's problems. If everyone is a star, and knows that everyone *else* is a star, then the entire world becomes this perfectly glorious TV studio, with everyone treating everyone else with the most s*upreme* deference. The theory's as old as Aristotle. Beauty is harmony. And if everyone is beautiful, there's harmony everywhere. Would America be committing genocide in Vietnam if it *realized* how fabulously gorgeous the Vietnamese are? Would we allow *stars* to starve to death in Biafra? As for police brutality, it would disappear overnight. When was the last time a star got beat up in a parking lot by the fuzz; or hassled for walking down a street? Remember what I'm telling you and think it over *carefully!* I have stumbled upon the greatest secret for turning people on since LSD. How do I know it? I've *proven* it! Everyone who comes to me for a face, I treat just like a star, and when they leave, I swear to you I have them so convinced, you can actually *see* stardom shooting out of them like *rays*. Instant Charisma. Naturally I charge for it. Money bores me, but I have to eat. Besides, I'm a star *too*, aren't I? So of course I have to live like one! Now tell me the truth, did you know I was wearing false eyelashes? Of course you didn't. Not until I *said* so. Men aren't ready to come out in the open yet, so for them you have to do imper*cept*ible things. But they're doing it, my dear, men have really *begun!* Would you believe me if I told you there is a policeman in this city, walking the Broadway beat at this exact second, wearing false eyelashes? I never lie. I swear this to you on my mother's eyes. I sold them to him myself and taught him how to use them. Within five years false eyelashes for men will be sold openly in every gas station from here to California—right in slot machines next to the rubbers. People don't seem to realize it, but we're having a goddam revolution, and it's *really taking place!*"

He pointed at me. "*You*, by the way, have a face already. I couldn't do a thing for you. You're already a star. And you" —he pointed at Sally—"are also a star. But your face could use some help. Too much sunniness, too much light. It wants a hint of darkness somewhere. Yes, yes, yes indeed! I know precisely what I'd do with you—a few shadows, mostly at the eyes. And then that fabulous frizzy hair would really pay off big. It'd go absolutely *zingo!* You'd step out into the street, traffic would come to a standstill, the National Guard would be called in, Congress would meet in emergency session, you'd be declared a public hazard and forced to wear *veils* for all public appearances! Incidentally, I'm in love with you both. I never sleep with women, because I'm much too much in awe of them. But I do worship them. I'm putty in their hands. Therefore I'm inviting both of you to my studio. It's exactly a block and a half from here on Madison, and I want you to come with me this minute. I have no more appointments for the day, we can just smoke a little grass, and, if you like, I'll let you play in my lovely puddles of paint. Now tell me, what do you think of this idea? Does it touch your little buttons? Does it arouse *anything?* Will you come?"

I don't think I'd said a single word the whole time. When somebody's as sparkling and overpowering in their rap as Edward is, I have a hard time getting my mouth together for a response.

Sally said she thought it would be fun, but it was her day to cook, so she took a raincheck. I might have gone home with her, but Edward was really insistent. Besides I wanted to go with him. When somebody seems to like me, I find him irresistible. Also, it occured to me that through Edward I might meet some groovy homosexuals and one of them could become a lover for Roy. So I told Sally I might not be home for dinner. Edward and I walked her to the subway and then the two of us went flying along 59th Street.

He said, "Witch, you're fan*tas*tic company, you know that don't you?"

I still hadn't done any talking or contributed anything, but I took the compliment as well as I could.

He said, "Let's skip! Shall we?"

Edward took my hand—and we *skipped!* All the way to Park Avenue. Suddenly I realized I was a young girl in New York, spending an afternoon with a glamorous, bizarre, slightly obnoxious but very sweet nut, and I really threw myself into it. I felt like I was acting in an old-timey Hollywood musical with Gene Kelly.

On Park Avenue they have this skinny little island running down the middle with grass and flowers. Edward said, "Watch!" Then he jumped the fence and did about a dozen cartwheels. Other pedestrians and even people in cars waiting for the light to change watched with their eyes popping. When he was finished, Edward took a number of bows and blew kisses at the traffic. A black boy about 12 wearing a baseball hat and an enormous grin was standing next to me when Edward jumped back over the railing. The boy said, "Hey, are you on TV?" Edward said, "Yes I am, I'm a great star, and so are you." Then he made a camera with his hands and pointed it at the kid's face and said, "Are you ready?" The kid said, "Ready for what?" Edward dropped the camera and took the boy's hand in both of his and pumped it full of congratulations. "That was perfect! Absolutely perfect! You did that scene in one take!" He took a roll of bills from his pocket and gave the boy a five, saying, "Do you realize your network is paying you at the rate of one dollar a second? That makes you the highest paid star in America."

Then the light changed. Edward took my hand and we ran across Park Avenue. Halfway across, I looked back at the kid. He was holding the five-dollar bill, and hollering "Do I get to keep it?" I nodded and said I guess so.

Edward said, "Witch, my one ambition is to elevate the entire world to stardom! Do you think I'll succeed?"

His studio, which he calls an *atelier*, is above an antique shop. Right at the top of the stairs there's a door with a sign painted on it in gold:

You enter the place through a small room with nothing in it but three bright-colored poufs like fluffy little mushrooms arranged on a white carpet, and three or four fashion magazines lying on the floor.

"Does a waiting room have to be a waiting room?" he said.

I just smiled. I realized by now Edward prefers to answer his own questions.

"Of course not," he said. "Besides, stars never wait. They may, however, choose to have their famous little butts pampered for a few minutes while I'm preparing to go to work on their faces. But that's not waiting, is it? Now look in here."

We passed through a white door, and inside everything was black. Edward flipped a switch and suddenly there were all these streams of light coming from everywhere. You couldn't see any walls or ceilings, just these columns of light. Edward drew me along behind him and everywhere I stepped I saw myself in some mirror, each one with lighting that was entirely different from the one before.

Edward said, "I'm vastly gifted in interior design, but I never design rooms. I dislike rooms, they're too limiting. I do interrupted infinities. Infinities interrupted by light. Besides, stars are accustomed to performing under great banks of light, *n'est-ce pas?* And this"—suddenly we were behind a screen—"is the corner where the magic takes place." There was an elegant little upholstered bench, which he said a friend had stolen for him from the *Cleopatra* set. Edward was holding up a big beige smock. "Step into this," he said, "and lie down."

When he was absolutely certain I was comfortably arranged on this couch thing, he turned to a little white table that was crowded with pots of paint, brushes, sponges, pencils. He looked back and forth from the table to me, rubbing his hands with delight. "Witch, this is terribly exciting. I feel

I'm about to surpass myself, and it's more than I can bear. Here, we'll start with hashish." He got out a Turkish water pipe and prepared it: a little chunk of hash on a bed of grass. We had two good tokes each, and then Edward went to work on my face. It seems to me he used every color and every piece of equipment on the table, and of course he chattered on as he worked. I wasn't allowed to see what was happening, but three minutes later he told me to get up, I was completed. Off went the smock, on went a silver lamé cape with fur hanging all over it. He said Angela Lansbury had worn it in *Mame* and I'm sure she had. Then he led me past the screen again, where all the infinities were interrupted by light.

"*Voilà!*" he said. "*Presenting! Witch Gliz!* Ta-taaaaaa!" Suddenly I saw this glorious movie star and I knew she was me.

"Now *preen* yourself, Miss Gliz," he said. "Glide about under the lights. Drink in the glory that is you! Suffocate, my dear, under the sheer impact of your own incomparable beauty!"

And that's exactly what I did. I saw myself from a dozen different angles, under every kind of lighting, and I was simply breathtaking. I don't know what he'd done to my face. But it worked. It may not have been *me* in these mirrors, but whoever the chick was, she was a *star!*

At the last mirror Edward said, "And the winner is Witch Gliz! For her performance in the Edward Atelier production of *A Star Is Born!*" He handed me a little gold statuette. It was an Oscar. I clutched it to my bosom, and for the first time all afternoon, I knew what to say. "Ladies and gentlemen of the Academy," I said, addressing faceless thousands in the dark. "My entire career would be nothing—if it hadn't been for a humble little man named Edward who happens to be the world's greatest cosmetician. Thank you." Then I sobbed and ran through the lights to the other side of the screen.

I must have really gotten into the part, because I was all flushed with excitement and had to lie down on the couch and catch my breath. Edward came in and stood looking at me with adoration. He was perspiring and there was almost a kind of pleading in his voice when he said, "Witch, is it fun? Are you having fun?"

If it hadn't been fun, I would have lied to him. Because he looked so dear and anxious to please. All I said was yes. He could see the rest in my face.

"Now let's go outside and show off," he said. We had one more toke apiece from the pipe and then went floating down the stairs and into the streets.

We ran, we skipped, we pranced, we took bows, we caused perfect strangers to smile, we made a personal appearance before God and all the angels at St. Patrick's Cathedral. We picked flowers at Rockefeller Center. Edward hired a winged chariot, and we flew down Fifth Avenue, soared high above adoring crowds, in and out of busy little skyways, between skyscrapers. We tossed flowers to children and nuns and peace signs to everyone we passed.

Edward held my hand in the taxi and put his arm around me. "You're more fun to be with than any girl I've known. Have you had fun being with me?" And then instead of talking on and on as usual, he waited for me to answer, and I realized he actually wanted to know whether or not I was enjoying myself. I could hardly believe it wasn't obvious to him, but it wasn't. So I told him that even though I'd had miraculous things happen to me since I'd arrived in New York, nothing had been more *fun* than this afternoon with him.

"Really and truly?" he said.

"Really and truly."

He seemed terribly happy, as if I'd given *him* an Oscar. So I thought I'd lay on a little more for him. I said, "You're a wonderful man, Edward."

"Am I?" he said, and then he looked out the window in a way that looked as if he were very seriously thinking about what I'd said.

I spoke to his profile and his wild Adam's apple.

"You really are. I've never met anyone before who tried so hard to make somebody happy. The only thing I wonder about is how you can squander your genius on something like cosmetics." He thought for a minute before he answered. Then, "Two reasons," he said. "One, I really do think it's a good way to turn on people who might not otherwise get the opportunity. And two, I'm a silly fucked-up shit who doesn't know whether he's coming or going." The more I heard Edward talk the more I respected him.

The last part of the taxi ride was quiet, and for the first time I had a chance to think about Edward without having to watch him perform and respond to his talk. I had a chance to realize he didn't honestly think much of himself. In his own eyes he was just a fag who was putting something over on the world. At times like this I wish I didn't have such insight into people, because it made me a little sad. I decided to spend the rest of the evening finding ways to make *him* happy. Since he was homosexual, I didn't even consider seducing him, but I was determined to do everything a woman can to make a man pleased about himself.

The taxi took us to Kip's Bay, where Edward has an apartment. A boy Edward knew got on the elevator with us. Edward introduced me as his sister from Detroit. The boy got out before we did, and Edward turned to me and said, "Was that okay? You don't mind being my sister?"

I said, "No, I love it."

"Can I tell everyone you really are my real blood sister?"

138

"Well, you *could,*" I said. "But the truth is even more exciting, isn't it? That we just suddenly met and loved one another?"

"Oh, you're right! You're absolutely right! It's *infinitely* more exciting! I *used* to want a blood sister, but now I don't. All I want is you." The elevator stopped at the 14th floor and we got out. As we walked down the hall, he said, "Did you really mean that though? That we suddenly met and loved one another? I know I love you, but do you love me, too? Really really really love me?"

We'd arrived at his door. He had the key in the lock. "Do you?"

I looked at him and smiled and nodded real hard.

"And you don't want me to go to bed with you or anything?"

I shook my head and kept smiling. "No. I just love you, that's all. No hangups."

Edward's pad has hot pink walls, Oriental carpets, and a cushion on the floor the size of a double bed. One wall is entirely glass and it looks out on the East River. The only furniture in the entire room is this enormous paisley cushion and a big round brass cocktail table near the window. The minute we got inside the door, Edward started taking his clothes off. "I always run around naked, do you mind?"

I said, "No, of course not. Can I?"

"*Paradise!*"

So we got out of our clothes and admired each other's bodies for a minute. Edward piled some records on the stereo and then he said, "Watch!" and took off like a bird, leaping across the room and landing on his belly on this giant cushion near the brass table. I oh'd and ah'd and applauded and sat next to him, and he said, "Now it's time to stoke our heads, don't you think?" And he went to work loading a pipe with grass.

The table had all sorts of interesting things on it: incense burners and exotic little boxes and pipes for smoking every kind of dope imaginable. Real flowers, too, red roses. And candles of all sizes and shapes. We lit them all, and a dozen sticks of amber incense, too. Then Edward got some goodies from the refrigerator—cheese and chicken and Sara Lee banana cake and Coca-cola. We had everything we could possibly want, and I began to feel my crazy anxiety again. Everything was too perfect. The view from his window was just too staggering. There were thousands of tiny lights from skyscrapers all over town, but it was still twilight and you could see the sky, a clear starry blue. Obviously it was all real. It wasn't a stage set or anything, but still it seemed *un*real. And that was how Edward suddenly seemed to me, with his craggy, tense face and his splendid physique. He was just *too high*. And so was his apartment. It was too thrillingly comfortable, too breathtakingly beautiful. Everything about him was too much. Too much in wonderful ways, but still *too much*.

I thought about the rickety old tumbledown home Roy and I had found on Canal Street and about everyone sitting at the table, probably at that exact moment, eating Sally's meal. Or maybe holding hands in thanksgiving, Zapping each other and the whole world with love.

Edward picked up on my mood and it made him anxious.

"Are you all right?" he said. "Is anything wrong?"

"Yes," I said. "We forgot to Zap the meal. I told him about the custom on Canal Street and he was all for it. So we sat there cross-legged facing each other, holding each other's hands.

"What should I do?" he said. "Should I pray or something? Because I'm not sure I believe in God actually. It's not that I *don't*. But I haven't really gotten into religion yet."

"I don't know if I believe in God or not either," I said.

"But I believe in *some*thing. Because otherwise, how could we be so beautiful?"

"That's true, Witch. There must be something even more fabulous than *we* are—to think the whole thing *up!*"

"That's just what my guru says."

"You have a *guru?*"

"Yes. He's also my best friend. His name is Roy. He's nineteen, he's gay, and he knows all about God."

"Fantastic!"

"He really is."

"Will I get to meet him?"

"Of course."

"Is he sexy?"

"Terribly. But it depends what turns you on."

"Am *I* sexy?"

"Definitely."

"To you?"

"Yes, very."

"Witch, may I touch your breast?"

"Of course."

He did, and it sent a shock all through me.

"I guess you better stop."

"Why? Did I excite you?"

"Yes."

"Oh, my God! I'm excited, too. This has never happened to me before, Witch."

"Really?"

"Never with a woman. I don't even know what to do!"

"You don't have to do anything."

"But shouldn't we make love or something?"

"Only if we want to."

"I do, Witch. I want to. Do you?"

"I think it'd be beautiful to make love with you."

"But I don't know how and I'm afraid you'll laugh at me."

141

"How could I laugh? I don't know how either."

"You mean you've *never?*" he said.

"Oh, I've made love lots of times. But it's always different. I mean there isn't any special way. You just enjoy the person, in whatever ways you can both dig."

"But what if I don't satisfy you?"

"Well, that's the breaks! Maybe I won't satisfy you either, but I'm not going to worry about it."

"Isn't that the whole *point?* To satisfy each other?"

"No," I said, "the whole point is to *love* each other. Isn't that how it happens with another boy?"

"I guess. But then, I don't know really. Because I'm always so interested in being *terrific* that—"

"Edward, nobody's terrific *all* the time with *every*body! Are they?"

"But I feel like I've just *got* to be. Don't you see?"

"Wow, isn't that an awful drag?"

"Look! I'm not excited now."

"Neither am I!"

"You're not?"

"No! Should I be?"

"I guess not."

"Can I finish your drumstick?"

He didn't answer, so I started eating it anyway.

"Goddamnit," he said, "I shouldn't have *talked* so much!"

"Why?"

"Because now we're not making love."

"That's cool. I mean, after all, we had things to talk about, didn't we? Aren't you hungry?"

"No. I'm depressed."

"Have another toke."

"Fantastic idea."

While he was holding the smoke in his lungs, he said, "Are you disappointed, Witch?"

"You mean because we're not making love?"

He nodded.

"Edward, I didn't come up here for that. I came here to be with you."

He let out the smoke and said, "You know, Witch, you're saying all the right things."

Suddenly I felt caught. Because he was right. I had been trying to say all the right things. I wanted to please him. I wanted to be the first woman he'd ever made love with and leave him feeling manly and terrific about himself. Then I thought, My God, he's *impossible!* What does he want me to do, say all the *wrong* things? So I put down the chicken bone, all set to tell him how difficult I thought he was being, when he took my hand, the one that had held the chicken, and started licking my fingers. He was really enjoying himself, too. So was I. Just then a new record plopped down on the turntable, and the Stones started singing: " 'She's like a rainbow, she comes in colors everywhere.' " And he made love to me. *Terrifically.*

I just know I could write some rich pornography right now. I could describe everything that happened between us, and sell it and make pots of money. The plot would be about these two people who both have overwhelming urges to be terrific in bed, and what happens when they get together. They both try so hard to please that they *succeed!*

And they're left feeling empty. At least the woman is. She doesn't feel empty because of what happened between them but because of what happens right after.

The man falls asleep on this enormous cushion. The woman lights a cigarette and sits cross-legged behind him with one hand resting on his hip. She sits there thinking the whole

143

thing over a hundred times, what splendid angelic animals they both are, and how great they'd been for each other. She's always been eager to prove to herself how sexy she is. Up to now, she suspected herself of being a bit of a phony. But here's this man who had never made love with a woman before, and he's lying next to her now, asleep, happy, and exhausted. She's not only shared a miraculous and special experience with him, she's also presented him with proof that he can please a woman.

She goes to the mirror in the bedroom so she can have a look at this remarkable chick, and while she's standing there savoring the full impact of her wondrous self, someone else appears in the mirror. It's not the man. It's someone else. *Another* man. He waves at her, says, "Hi, there." The woman hides her breasts and screams like some stupid little virgin.

The man says, "It's all right, I won't peek. I just want to change clothes." He goes to the closet and starts taking off his shirt. The woman sees her clothes on the bed. She grabs them and runs into the bathroom. Apparently without realizing it, she's been apologizing all over the place. Because the man comes to the door and talks through it while she dresses.

"No reason to be uptight," he says. "We're always going around naked. Please don't be upset. Are you all right?"

"Yes, I'm fine," she says. "I'll be out in a minute."

When she comes out of the bathroom dressed, she feels better. The man's wearing dungarees now and a Levi jacket painted all over with Day-Glow designs. He starts hanging strings of beads around his neck. He turns to her, says, "I'm a plastic hippie," and grins. Then he reaches into a drawer and comes out with a longhair wig and puts it on.

The woman says, "I guess you two are roommates."

"Yeah," he says, "but there's no problem. We both make it with chicks, too."

144

The woman doesn't get the full import of this all at once. But slowly it dawns on her. She can't believe she's heard correctly. She draws him carefully into telling her more about their arrangement. They've been lovers, but it's a completely open situation. Actually, they prefer women.

"Does *he* prefer women, too," she asks.

"He *adores* them. Let's see what he's done to your eyes." He studies her painted face. "Beautiful! He never repeats himself."

"You mean," she says carefully, "he paints each of his chicks differently?"

"Mm. Isn't he fantastic?"

"Yes. He really is, really fantastic."

"Have you seen a couple of Fillmore East tickets anywhere? Oh! I know where they are!"

He finds the tickets in an old coat pocket and leaves the apartment.

The woman is left with her sleeping lover, but she feels entirely alone. She looks out the big window. The sky is black now but there are millions of lighted windows.

A sleepy voice behind her says, "How come you're all dressed?"

She doesn't look at him. "I thought I'd better go now," she says.

"Will I ever see you again?"

She thinks for a minute. "Probably not," she says.

After a long silence the man says, "Okay, I understand. I'm the same way you are. Once usually does it."

The woman thinks she'd better get out of this place pretty fast. But she takes a few seconds to kiss him on the cheek and tell him he's a magnificent lover.

When she gets to the door, he jumps up to open it for her. They smile at one another. She walks down the hall and while she's waiting for the elevator, he steps out into the hall, still naked and splendid, and calls to her. "Don't forget you're a star," he says.

"Oh, I won't!" she says. "Not ever."

In the movie version, the elevator should arrive at that exact second. But in real life she has to wait quite a while for it. However, this dame is her mother's daughter, i.e., a colossal phony. She's able to fill in with small talk and cigarette lighting.

SHE: Hey, mister, your fly's open.

HE: (*Laughs and laughs. Funniest joke ever.*) Oh, that undid me utterly! Please, marry me tonight! I'd give my soul to have such wit in my life.

SHE: Sucker! It wasn't even original.

HE: Screw originality. It's *timing* that matters.

SHE: Go inside, you'll get busted for lewd vag.

HE: Listen, I can use the publicity already!

SHE: Blah blah blah.

HE: Blah blah blah blah blah blah blah blah blah.

SHE: Blah blah blah blah.

HE: Blah blah blah.

SHE: *Blah!!!*

———————

Coming down on the elevator, I saw a little electronic eye that seemed to be and probably wasn't a television camera. Anyway, I tripped out briefly, imagining myself on TV being watched on a home screen by some elderly man. He's in his bed watching the Witch Gloria Show with great fascination. It's in black and white and he's been watching all day long. Now he sees me on the elevator leaving my lover's apartment. He's a nice man, straight, oldish, like forty maybe, no hair left on top, a hurt, disappointed-looking cat, not bitter but a little sad. And he turns to his wife, who isn't even listening—she fell asleep, but he hasn't noticed yet—he turns to his sleeping wife and says, "This girl doesn't seem to be having much fun after all, does she?" And he switches channels. They're doing "The Star Spangled Banner" on this one, so he knows they're about to sign off. This makes him feel a little desperate, because he's not even sleepy yet.

———————

Neither am I.

CANAL STREET, TUESDAY,
SEPTEMBER 16, 1969

This morning when I woke up, I reviewed my disaster of yesterday and decided it was definitely minor. I'm not pregnant, because I'm on the pill, so nobody was hurt. My ego got knocked around a little, but that's okay. Roy says ego bruises can bring about an increase of wisdom, so the whole thing could hardly be called a disaster. Just a blunder—or maybe a blunderette. No, not even that. I had a very good time with a very dear, superficial, attractive ass, not to mention gaining lots of new experience for my autobiography. At first, when he poured Drambuie all over my breasts, I thought he'd freaked out, but when he started licking it off, the whole thing began to make sense. Edward may be part fink, but he's tremendously imaginative and free. I tried to top him by putting his penis in my mouth (another first!) but I don't suppose he dug it as much as he pretended to. Anyway, I'm glad I tried it, because now I'll be able to write with authority on the subject. I'll explain to my readers the ritual value of penis-sucking, how every real woman should take joy in paying homage to the fabulous male organ from

148

which emerges the sacred seeds of human life. Besides it's sort of groovy.

Roy wasn't in bed last night. When I came in, post-blunderette, I needed him. But he wasn't here. And then I began to realize I've seen very little of him since we moved in here. I've been running around with Sally and Cary, and he's been spending practically every waking minute with Archie and Jeanette. I hope we're not drifting apart. I miss him. I guess what I miss most is his needing me. What good's an earth mother without any children? But that's not all of it. Roy is my beautiful lifelong friend and brother, my soul's tender lover, and I would like him always to be in my life. I also missed his skinny little body in the bed. It's a bummer to run all the way home from a foolish, lonesome experience and not have somebody to hug. I suppose I could have hugged Sally or just about anybody, but it's not the same.

Tonight while we were doing the dishes, I told Roy about seeing Hank Glyczwycz teach his class. Something about that entire thing is still bugging me, and I was hoping Roy'd be able to help. I asked him if he had any idea why a person would continue to think so hard about someone they weren't really interested in any more. Roy said, "After all, he's your father. It's only natural you'd keep thinking about him for a while—even if you don't dig him."

I suppose he's right. But I'm still not satisfied. One thing that really freaks me out is that I can't remember Glyczwycz's face any more and it's only been two days. Everything else about Monday afternoon is still perfectly clear, but when I try to pull his face into focus, all I get is a blank. It's so frustrating I don't know what to do.

CANAL STREET, FRIDAY, SEPTEMBER 19, 1969

Having a completely blah day. Might as well copy down the rest of the bulletin board.

There is neither Jew nor Greek
There is neither bond nor free
There is neither male nor female
For ye are all One in Christ Jesus

—John 17:22

God respects me when I work
but he loves me when I sing

—An Uphead's Song

Where your head is is your wealth.

—Gene Robeson

I don't mind dying as long as I have a big grin on my face.
—Archie Fiesta

151

Learn wisdom from the pupil of the eye that looks upon all things and yet, to self, is blind.

> —A Persian poet,
> according to Malcolm X

Aug. Phone bill—$38.50. Message units up 112 from last month.

> Love,
> Jeanette

P.S. Whoever made the call to Colorado, it was $12.20. Oh, hi, Cary!

Each soul is like a drop of water without which the whole world would thirst.

> —Ugo Betti

Merely being alive is such a fantastic
privilege. The only maintainable thing to
do is to get into life and dig every second.

> —Danny

There will come a day when you won't even
be ashamed if you are fat.

> —The Mothers of Invention

To live outside the law you must be honest.

> —Bob Dylan

We are everything you say we are, and more,
and we are proud of it.

> —Jefferson Airplane

Any well regulated life has its share of sex and dope—and irregularity.

—Peter

If you can love one person, yourself, you can love the world.

—Ty

When one eats, he fills his stomach.
When one loves, he fills his soul.
Once he found this, he'll never give it up.

—2 Friends

There is no insight without Love.

—Choo Choo

The ultimate product of materialism is shit.

—Cary Colorado

We Are Love—
You and I and
We are all Love
And if God is Love,
Then we are God—

—Aman

The kernel of all jealousy is lack of love.

—Carl Jung

The earth is a flower—opening.

—Swami Choochitananda

I used to think joy had to be paid for in blood
and pain. It doesn't. It's free. Joy doesn't
increase our debts. It increases our capacity
for more joy.

> —One who learned this

We're living in the world's most beautiful day.
If we're more aware of the darkness than ever
before, it's because there's more light penetrating
it in more places.

> —Peter

Just being is holiness itself.

> —Socorro's Life Said
> This to Us

Fighting for peace is like fucking for
virginity— But it's great!

> —Subway men's room,
> Astor Place stop

The only way you can win a war is by seeing
to it the enemy has everything he needs.

> —Will

You only meet yourself on an acid trip. If
there are aspects of your life, your self,
your past, your future, that you're afraid
to look at—don't take the acid.

> —Peter

I'd love to blow your soul.

> —Archie Fiesta

154

Television is education. That's why all
the schools are dying.

> —A TV student

A girl who's sleeping with your brother isn't
your sister-in-law. She's your sister outlaw.

> —A deep thinker

May the longtime sun shine upon you, all
love surround you, and the pure light within
you guide your way on!

> —The Incredible String Band

Butterflies are flying flowers.

> —Swami Choochitananda

Be yourself: No one can ever tell you you're
doing it wrong.

> —Good John

If community is to come it will come from
one-to-one, perfected.

> —Neyeurme

Let us overcome the angry man with gentleness,
The evil man with goodness,
The miser with generosity, and
The liar with TRUTH.

> —Old Indian Wisdom

NOTE TO ALL LAUNDERETTE TRIPPERS
Don't forget we've got an enormous
box of low phosphate soap now, so take some
with you. Their detergents fuck up the
rivers!

                              —Cary

No more paranoia! It attracts persecution.
                              —Jeanette

You must find God in whatever you are doing.
                              —Mike Pollack

Everything is wrong that forbids the freedom
of the individual.
                              —Dylan Thomas

He drew a circle that shut me out—
Heretic, rebel, a thing to flout,
But love and I had the wit to win:
We drew a circle that took him in!
                              —Edwin Markham

If we live what we know, our life will be our rap.
                              —Cary Colorado

We are the people our parents warned us about.
                              —Some hippie

All beauty is head food.
                              —Jim Coan

It is not how we love, or who we love,
but that we love.

—Unsigned

UNDESIRABLE DISCHARGE
FROM THE ARMED FORCES OF THE UNITED STATES
OF AMERICA   '
This is to certify that

Harry Wilson Jones, Jr.

Was discharged from the United States Navy
On the 29th Day of April, 1968
As Undesirable

—Modern American Wisdom

When the pupil is ready, the teacher comes.

—Buddha? Meher Baba?

Anyone who takes the sure road is as good
as dead.

—Carl Jung

Fuck is no longer a four-letter word.

—Neyeurme

Resist biologically—be erotic.

—T. Leary

Anything that can enslave you can also free
you.

—Starcke

Life must be guileless, roleless.

—Mark Stern

Nirvana is pure gamelessness.

—James

Lies tend to isolate you.

—Jeanette

Life is learning what you can grow.

—James

Love is a humble dragon
Hate stands alone . . .

—Chinese Wisdom
Translation, Brad Brasfield

Bank Balance for July $1,907.06
Bank Balance for Aug. $1,540.22

I hear and behold God in every object, yet I understand God
not in the least,
Nor do I understand who there can be more wonderful
than myself.

—Walt Whitman

CANAL STREET, SATURDAY, SEPTEMBER 20, 1969

Stoned out of my mind on LSD. Fabulous visions, impressions. Feel great urge to write it all down. Can't. Words get in the way. Reality is reality and words are words. Besides, my pen is turning into a rose.

CANAL STREET, SUNDAY,
SEPTEMBER 21, 1969

Last night we all dropped acid. The stuff had some speed in it and I ended up rapping too much and grinding my teeth a lot, but I don't regret it, because so many groovy things happened.

A. I heard the Electric Prunes' *Mass in F Minor.*

B. I stopped being hung up on Archie.

C. Doris came back from California and caught us all stark naked and tripping. (Why do I say *caught?* Is my life forever to be plagued with guilt? I think I'll do C all over again.)

C. I made a new friend. Her name is Doris and she's heaven.

D. I made a second new friend. Her name is Sara and she's a ghost.

Archie had come in about an hour before dinner with a dozen tabs of orange sunshine. He said it was the same very high stuff Timothy Leary recommended in an *East Village Other* interview in the spring. Anyway he passed it around.

Nyoom frowned at it for a moment. Then he said, "If this is the sacred substance recommended by the High Priest himself, one can hardly decline." He took a tab and popped it into his mouth. Sally said she preferred to abstain, but assured us she'd be tripping right along with the rest of us on a contact high.

Cary Colorado said he hadn't tripped since Boulder, and he was interested in seeing what it would do for him. (Later I asked him how it compared with the high he got on meditation and he said he found the acid pretty sloppy.)

Jeanette took a tab without comment.

Roy looked at me and said, "What do you think, Witch?"

I told him it was his head.

"Yeah, but are *you* going to?"

I said yes. So Roy and I dropped, too.

Gary put the new Donovan record on the stereo, the one about Atlantis. By dinnertime we are all having rushes and nobody was interested in eating. We all took our clothes off. Cary's idea. At first I was nervous about being naked with Archie. I was afraid I'd start hallucinating the two of us making love all over the place, or that we'd get into a pure lust thing that could put me on a bummer. (What's wrong with pure lust? I don't really know, but if just thinking about it can put you in a down head, what would the experience itself do?)

Anyway, I needn't have worried. Because seeing Archie under acid, clothes or no clothes, had the opposite effect on me. Aphrodite went out the window. Earth Mother moved in. I stopped wanting him, and don't think I ever will again. His body is as lovely as his face, but the acid made him seem so helpless and alone. Maybe acid makes what your soul is more important than what your body is. I don't know. But I was seeing auras all night, like on my very first trip. Archie's was a color I'd never seen before, indescribable, sort

161

of a dark puce with very little light in it. It's almost *not there*. Also, I saw not just auras but souls, too. At least I *think* I was seeing souls. It was as if all of our bodies existed inside of a quivery watery sheath. I tried to write about this last night but I couldn't. I guess there are things that refuse to allow themselves to be written down. Or maybe I don't know enough words. Anyway, with acid, hiding doesn't work. You show who you are. Archie's whole being comes through as a selfish, pouting lost child. He was beautiful, too. I suppose all souls are, if you really *see* them. I had no interest in Archie sexually, and yet my breasts actually ached. I felt as if my soul wanted to suckle him and nourish him, but it didn't know how to go about it.

Seeing Archie so clearly gave me a real insight into the dangers of acid. My own trips have been pretty glorious experiences, but I've always had high friends around who could help me *use* my paranoia and turn it into a growth trip. For some reason I've never really had major problems about keeping my head straight, but Archie is a mess. A half a dozen times through the night someone had to be with him holding him and comforting him and telling him everything was all right. At one point he thought the house was on fire and couldn't be talked out of it. Finally we all had to put our clothes on and take him outside and show him everything was okay. Then we brought him back inside and he cried with relief. But a few minutes later he was whispering to Nyoom, "The house isn't on fire. Right?" And Nyoom said, "No, Archie. The house is beautiful. So are you, and so am I. And everything's cool."

———————

The first really interesting event of the evening was meeting Sara the Ghost. Sally and I had been up on the roof in

162

Will's greenhouse trying to see gnomes in the flowerpots. Sally's convinced each plant has a little invisible creature tending its roots and she was hoping with acid we'd be relaxed enough to see them. We weren't. But on the way back downstairs, just as we were coming to the first landing, Sally stopped and said, *"Far out!"* I said, "What's happening?" And she said, "I'm getting extra strong ghost vibes. Just stand still right here and see if you can pick them up."

I stood still for a few seconds, looking into the dark, and I didn't pick up any vibes, not a one. But I saw the ghost. There was this big watery-looking oval of space, like a full-length mirror with blurry edges, and she was sitting inside of it in a rocking chair, watching me with an enormous grin on her face. The most far-out part of it all is that I wasn't even surprised.

I said, "I can see her, Sally. She's right here."

"Oh, Witch! Can you truly?"

By this time the ghost was waving at me, so I waved back and said, *"Hello* there!" She had on an 1890s-ish costume and her hair was all braided tight across the crown of her head. Her face was homely but nice to look at, and the expression on it was terribly dear. She looked so pleased, you'd have thought we were old friends.

Sally said, "Oh, Witch, I'm so excited! Please! Tell me what she's like."

I described her as well as I could, but it was hard to talk to Sally because the ghost seemed to be talking at the same time.

I said, "Are you talking to me?"

She nodded brightly and said, "I certainly am. You're the only one in this entire house that can see and hear me!"

I said, "Good lord, am I? *Why,* do you suppose?"

The ghost shrugged. "I just knew you'd be able to, if you

163

ever really looked. And tonight you're really looking. I'm *so* pleased."

"Would you like to tell me your name?" I asked

"I'm Sara. And I know yours already. You're Witch."

Sally said, "Witch! You're having a *conversation* with her! Please tell me everything she says. I'm just *dying!*"

I tried to describe Sara's voice to her. I couldn't actually hear it with my ears but I could see her mouth going and I knew what she was saying. I don't think there was any sound involved at all. It was just pure communication. Except that *I* spoke out loud. Maybe Sara would have heard me even if I hadn't, but it didn't occur to me to try. I had a voice, so I used it.

So the ghost and I chatted for a while. Sometimes I asked questions for Sally and relayed Sara's answers. It all seemed very natural at the time. And now as I think about it, it *still* does. The lady was dead, but so what? Body or no body, she still had things to say. I can't record her words accurately, of course, because I wasn't actually hearing, not in the usual sense. My head just sort of supplied words to go with her meanings. And this is the story that came out of it:

Sara had been living in this house for more than 100 years. Before that she and her father had lived in Puerto Rico, where he was an exporter. Then they moved to New York and she'd lived here ever since. By the time he died, in 1890-something, Sara was a full-fledged old maid, and afraid to leave the house. She said the streets were dangerous then. I wanted to say she ought to have a look at them now, but I didn't want to interrupt. Anyway, after Sara died, she was *still* afraid to leave the place, and simply stayed in. She told how awful it was to stand by and watch while all the family furniture was moved out and their effects disposed of, but there was nothing she could do about it. (Somehow I guess she was able to salvage that rocker—or maybe it was just a

164

ghost rocker. We didn't get into that.) Over the years a series of different families moved in and out, none of them very interesting to her, so she sort of checked out most of the time. I didn't ask how ghosts did that, but I suppose to protect themselves when they're bored, they have their little checking-out mechanisms just like other people do. . . . In the 1920s a couple of honeymooners moved in and she fell in love with both of them. Soon they had three sons, and everything went along beautifully for about ten years. Then the depression came along and the couple started quarreling about money all the time, so Sara began checking out again. She still loved them as much as ever, but when they were unhappy their conversation was repetitious and tedious to listen to. The boys grew up and went into the Army, and one of them, Sara's favorite, got killed. World War II, I guess. Sara kept hoping he'd come back as a ghost and live in the house with her, but he never did. So Sara took the gold star that had been hanging in the window to commemorate his death and began wearing it around her neck. I'm very confused about how ghosts pull off these little stunts, but I suppose the gold star is a ghost like the rocker, and like Sara herself. After the war the house was full of grief and sadness until finally quite suddenly the people moved away. I asked Sara if she'd ever spoken with any of the members of that family and she said, "Yes, I talked to them a great deal at first, all of them. But the only one who ever heard me was the one little boy, my favorite. I used to tell him bedtime stories and in the mornings he'd tell his mother about the lady in the rocking chair that visited him at night, and at first his mother said, Oh, that's nice, dear, but after a while she started getting angry with him. So one night I told him I thought I'd better not talk to him any more for a while. I was afraid as he grew older our conversations might confuse him, so I forced myself to be still. Later, years perhaps, or perhaps just days later, I'm not sure, I tried to talk to him again but he couldn't hear me any more." Sara smiled rather sadly at this point. "That's life," she said. "People come and go." Afterwards there was a long series of people in the place, none of them the least bit interesting to her. Then suddenly a couple of years ago Peter moved in and began to accumulate his family of freaks, and she'd been fascinated with life ever since. She said if she was forced to carry on a conversation with a straight person right that minute, she didn't think she'd remember how. She threw her head back and laughed, then she rocked back and forth a couple of times till she'd calmed down. I asked her how she felt about the life style of Peter's family. She thought it was wonderful and beautiful and brave. "Just wait," she said, "until you meet Will. You're going to fall in love with him." I said I thought I already had, in a way. And she said, "But you *really* will, when you meet him. Do you know what he's going to do? He's going to bring an end to war!" I tried to question her further about Will, but she started going on about the others. She said she'd learned to meditate with Cary and whenever we formed a circle she always joined in. Her favorite event of the day was the mealtime Zap. "Tonight," she said, "I'm stoned on acid." That blew my mind. I told Sally. Sally said it made perfect sense, you didn't need a body to get high. "In fact," she said, "you can probably get higher without them!"

Then Sally said, "Listen, Witch, I think you should ask Sara if there's anything we can do for her."

I said, "Like what?"

"I don't know," she said, "but ask."

So I did.

And Sara said, "Yes, as a matter of fact, I'd like your advice. Do you think I should leave here? It's been a hundred years now. Often I feel I should move on, but I'm still so frightened I just end up staying. And of course I'm more torn than ever now, because I'd miss you all so. I can't tell you how much you've helped my head."

Sally loved that. "Oh, we've helped Sara's head," she cried, clapping her hands together. "Isn't that *super?* Tell her she's helped mine, too. Tell her every time I pass her in the hall I dig her cool. From now on, of course, I'll *speak!* I think I'll speak now." She looked into the corner where I'd been looking and gave a tentative little wave of her fingers. "Hi there, Sara dear," she said. And then, to me, "What'd she say, Witch, did she hear me?"

I reported that Sara thought she was an especially beautiful person, and Sally clapped her hands with joy.

But I was interested in getting back to Sara's problem about whether or not she should leave Canal Street. I wanted to know why she was asking *my* advice. I told her whatever experience I may have had as a ghost in the past had completely slipped my mind, so I didn't know what to tell her.

Sara said, "Yes, Witch, but you know as much about it as I do. And you're much more level-headed than I am. Please, take a moment, imagine yourself in my shoes. What would you do?"

Suddenly I knew exactly what to tell her. "If it was me," I said, "I'd stick around here and groove until it wasn't interesting any more. Then? Who knows, if I felt like it, I'd probably take off."

"Even if you were frightened?" she said.

I told her if it seemed the right thing to do, I thought I'd try to leave even if I was frightened, but I couldn't be sure.

By this time we'd been talking for a long time, probably an hour or more. The conversation must have been taking tremendous energy from me, because suddenly I felt totally depleted. I told Sara I thought I'd like to rest for a while. She understood, but she was disappointed. "I'm not usually

167

so selfish," she said. "It's just that you're the first person in more than forty years who's heard me when I spoke." I said I thought that must be really awful, and she said, "You get used to it. Now go rest, Witch Gloria, there'll be other days." When she called me Witch Gloria an odd little look went with it. I was just on the verge of asking her if she realized I sometimes called myself that secretly, when she said, "I watch you write in your journal. I hope you don't mind. If you do, I'll stop. I promise."

"No, it's okay," I said. "I don't think I mind. Is it interesting to you?"

"Oh, *yes!*" she said.

Wow, I thought. I've got a reader!

It must have been around mid-trip when we got into the Electric Prunes. Before that each of us had been pretty busy doing his own thing, Archie alternating between playing his guitar and freaking out, Nyoom and Cary spending most of their trip squatting Buddhalike in a corner trying to get into samadhi, Roy and Jeanette appearing and disappearing all over the house. At one point they took a shower together, giggling like children and playing games with foam from the shampoo. I was invited to join them and might have except that at the moment they asked me Sally and I were on the way up to Will's greenhouse to visit the gnomes. Anyway, the Electric Prunes' *Mass in F Minor* brought us all together. When the Kyrie started, everyone more or less fainted with rapture on the Big Room floor. Roy lay next to me and held my hand and whispered how glad he was we were tripping together, because I was his favorite person in the entire solar system. It's a good thing I was lying down, because his words gave me this enormous love blast, which

I can still feel even now. A lot of the things you experience on acid seem (whether they *do* or not) to disappear into thin air the next day, but the loving never does. You remember it and keep on feeling it. At least *I* do. Also, Roy and I had shared a whole big Electric Prunes trip back in Belle Woods, so the music made us aware again of all the terrific highs we'd had together.

After the Gloria, I said to him, "Isn't this music absolutely superultramysticalMcZapp?"

He said, "Superultramystical*McZapp?*"

I said, "Right!"

He said, "*Loved* the McZapp."

And I said, "I thought you would."

When it was time to turn the record over, Cary came up with the notion that we should all lie on our backs, each of us making the petal of a flower, with our heads touching in the center and our legs pointed in seven directions, like this:

He said we'd be a living mandala and all the power of the trip and the music would be centered in us and give us an experience of spiritual union.

It did. And there's nothing I can say about it. I don't know how to describe spiritual union in words. You're not you. You're everybody. And not just those who happen to be present. You're everybody who ever lived or died. I don't mean you're brothers either. I mean you *are* them and vice versa. ·

Even Percy the Cat seemed to feel the power of it. He climbed onto Nyoom's stomach and laid there with his motor running and didn't even fart. The little tiny part of my mind that was still *me* felt safe and beautiful and holy and perfect. It was as if I'd slipped out of my body and joined the music at its source, and the source was—well, I suppose the word is God, but maybe I'm jumping to conclusions. Anyway, I was getting a tremendous light show behind my eyes, too, an endless river of color and form flowing through the middle of my head and then spreading out, filling my entire body and extending even beyond it until there was nothing but this infinite river containing every form I could possibly remember or imagine, ivory columns, marble statues, perfect colors, fourth of July fireworks, faces, celestial landscapes, fishes, maps, abstract forms all in 3D and full color, masks, exquisitely carved images, mosques, fruit, animals, cathedrals, fantastic butterflies, serpents, birds, flowers—I could fill pages and pages. It went on and on and I can't remember all I saw, because the flow was so constant there was hardly time to dig each thing separately. All you could do was groove on the flow itself and hope it would never stop. Every once in a while one of us said wow and I remember feeling absolutely certain each of us was tuned in on the same flow of images. But there's no way of knowing for sure. It went so fast you couldn't compare notes. Somewhere along the

170

way I had this thought that what I was seeing was the river of life. It was flowing through me and I was its banks. But now that I write it, it doesn't look right.

When the record ended, Cary Colorado said, "Does everyone have his eyes closed?"

We all said yes.

"Is everyone getting a light show?"

We all said we were.

Then he said, "Don't change the record yet. I want to recite something from *Demian.* Is that cool? Because it's a very heavy thing. Would everyone like to hear it?"

Most heads tend to be Hermann Hesse freaks, so of course we were all delighted and urged him to go ahead.

It was beautiful. Cary was so stirred up by what he was saying that the words sort of quivered out of him like cum, and yet the sound he made was strong and clear because he was seeing the truth of it all so thoroughly. I couldn't concentrate on the full import of each thought, but later I got him to find it for me and now I'll copy it here word for word as it appears in the book:

> If the outside world were to be destroyed, a single one of us would be capable of rebuilding it: mountain and stream, tree and leaf, root and flower, yes, every natural form is latent within us, originates in the soul, whose essence is eternity, whose essence we cannot know but which most often intimates itself to us as the power to love and create.

When Cary finished reciting, there was a long super-high silence.

Then Archie Fiesta said, "Would it be cool to play the Doors? I could dig Morrison right now."

Nobody answered. I guess the others felt as I did, that nothing could be cooler at that moment than silence. But Archie got up and put the Doors on, and we all lay there and listened. I felt myself gradually being brought down. We'd been on a space flight and this was re-entry. The process was gentle and the rock beat was good but the over-all effect was sad and bitter and down-headed. Listening to Morrison, I felt I was hearing the song of Archie Fiesta's soul.

> *Can you give me sanctuary*
> *I must find a place to hide*
> *A place for me to hide*
> *Can you find me soft asylum*
> *I can't make it any more*
> *The man is at the door*

I felt someone stirring, so I opened my eyes to see who it was, and there was this strange woman standing there. Not a ghost either, but a real flesh-and-blood lady with great bosoms and enormous eyes, smiling at us. I was so surprised, my first reaction verged on freak-out. Then Carry said, "Doris!"

I was relieved to know it wasn't a stranger, but then I had a guilt flash. Why is it when I'm tripping I always imagine a straight person sees this big strobe-lighted sign on my face flashing, *This Chick Is Doped to the Eyeballs,* in psychedelic colors?

Ever since I got to New York, I've been seeing practically everything with Mother's eyes. I never used to do that at all, not even when I was living in the same house with her. But now I always finds myself wondering what she'd think if she could see me. I'd like to get over this because it tends to turn everything sour. I don't want to look at the world through the eyes of anyone but Witch Gliz—unless of course

I chose to enter into somebody else's trip, and I certainly wouldn't choose to enter Mother's.

Archie turned down the stereo and there was much hugging and kissing and everyone talked at once. Peter's father had finally died. Then Peter and Doris had decided she should come back to New York alone while he stayed on for a few days in L.A. to take care of his father's affairs.

After my first big Oh-Christ-Mother's-Caught-Me-Tripping-Again paranoia flash, I took a look at Roy. He was in a state of alarm, too. I guess we must have looked like Hansel and Gretel lost in the woods, because pretty soon Doris noticed us standing there together and she smiled at us. Then Jeanette introduced us.

By this time Doris had begun to look familiar to me. On acid you often seem to feel you knew everybody in some other incarnation. I said I wondered if we could have met before somewhere.

She said, "I don't know. But maybe it's like they say, we're all members of some ancient tribe, and we're just beginning to know one another all over again. Anyway, you're Witch, and you're Roy, and I'm Doris." Her voice is wonderfully low with just a hint of gravel in it. She has enormous eyes with a lot of lid showing, and when she looks at you, you feel as if you're really being *seen*. The three of us eyeballed one another for a while in a kind of sweet, profound silence. You'd have thought she was on acid right along with the rest of us.

I knew we liked each other. But Roy still looked scared, as if he thought there was still a good chance of being thrown out. Doris seemed to pick up on his fear, because after a few seconds, her mouth started to scrunch up like she was trying to keep it from melting. She loved him. She loved us both. But how could she? How could she love us so? How could we mean anything to her? Then Roy's face

173

cracked open in the biggest smile I've ever seen from him. The next thing I knew he was getting hugged against these great bosoms of hers, and I was having jealousy rushes. I guess she knew it—she seems to pick up on everything you're feeling—because one arm reached out and grabbed me and then the three of us huddled for a long sweet moment. Roy was getting something he needed and hadn't had any of for about a million years, and I felt like I was getting earth-mother lessons from the number one expert of all time.

A few minutes later, when Doris went up to unpack, Roy and Jeanette and I followed her to the foot of the attic stairs, waiting for her reaction to all the work they'd done up there. For a full minute there wasn't a sound, and then all of a sudden Doris let out a great *ooh*, followed by a whole series of them. And in a minute she started flying down the stairs until she saw us there looking up at her. Then she said, "Angels have been here! Angels have been here!" and her face was all wet with tears. So we all three went up while she raved about every little detail. I hadn't lifted a finger up there, so I said, "It wasn't me, it was Roy and Jeanette."

She must have carried on for five full minutes, blowing her nose and wiping her eyes and frowning with the heavy import of it all. She said it was like a miracle. Spirits had come with magic wands of love and transformed her hovel into a palace.

Roy was in Seventh Heaven. When Doris began to run down a little, he started pointing out exquisite details she'd missed. For instance, he'd painted the *inside* of Peter's closet! Doris thought that was sensational. She carried on about it as if no one in history had ever come up with such an inno-vation. Then Roy became modest. He said it wasn't really that hard to do, but it was the sort of thing that often gets missed—unless a person is thorough. Everything he said for the rest of the trip seemed to be geared to pleasing Mama. He was making plenty of headway, too. Once, for instance, Doris stopped in the middle of a sentence and looked at him. "God, you're adorable," she said, and then went right on with what she was talking about.

After a while Jeanette went downstairs, but Roy and I stayed on. The three of us must have rapped for a good two hours at least, so I'll have to leave out a lot.

Roy wanted to know what Doris thought about his being in her house while he was hiding from the Army. She said the place wasn't hers any more than it was his, since Peter paid the rent, but she didn't think Roy had anything to worry about on that score. Peter was rabidly anti-Pentagon and liked having opportunities to undermine it.

All the talk was delicious. I wanted to go downstairs and get Nyoom's tape recorder but Doris said she thought it might "put a crimp in our style." Doris has a good rap, fast and wisecracky and warm. She uses all sorts of phrases I've never heard before, but acid has a weird effect on my memory, so I'm afraid I'll miss a lot of them. She reminds me of some super-bright ex-stripper you'd see on a late night TV talk show, an older chick that's lived plenty and really knows where it's at. Her face does great contortions when she's making a point. She doesn't wear make-up, but she's sort of got make-up scars, as if she'd just plucked her eyebrows and cold-creamed all the paint away about five minutes ago and you can still see where it was. Also her hair is still half dyed (reddish brown like Mother's) and half not. The real color is brown streaked with white. When it grows out, it'll be like some real sneaky super-authentic $100 job from Elizabeth Arden's. She's tall, too, which I envy, and her body is full with these big cozy-looking boobs that'd be terrific for crying on. (With any luck, mine will be like that in a few years.)

Doris was into a big plastic scene in Los Angeles when she first started going to Peter. That's how they met—he was her analyst. She was a talent agent in Beverly Hills, very appearance-conscious and ambitious (Aries, moon in Capricorn, Pisces rising) and spent a lot of her time in beauty parlors and fussing with clothes. Lots of things about her remind me of Mother, except that Doris broke out of it. No, that's not true. She doesn't really remind me of Mother. They're not alike at all. It's just that Doris is Mother's age and came out of the same bullshit. Seeing how groovy she is makes me wish Mother could have been that way, too.

One of the things she went to Peter for was to get help with this losing battle she was waging with the calendar. She said by the time she got adjusted to being 20 she was 30, and before she could dig being 30 she was 45. (Sally says Aries are often behind or ahead of themselves in time.)

Doris's first marriage had given her ego a real beating. She said Peter had done wonders for her head, wiped out her sex guilt almost entirely, and helped her like herself a lot better. I noticed there was still a little residue though. She doesn't dig her own feet. They're sort of big and shapeless if you're into a high fashion bag, and even though she's out of all that now, she still has this tendency to hide her feet and make slighting references to them, as if they were ugly stepchildren.

The one part of the conversation I'd like to be able to capture here has to do with acid. Doris wasn't too surprised to learn we were all tripping when she arrived.

"I thought that ceiling was pretty high when I came in," she said. "Well, how's it all going? Any bummers?"

She was sitting in one of the easy chairs with her feet tucked under her. Roy and Jeanette and I sat on the floor.

176

We told her Archie had had a few problems but everybody else was having a peaceful trip.

Roy asked her how she felt about acid in general.

"In a nutshell," she said, "it scares me to death. I've had three trips myself and they were glorious. But awful things really do happen with it. Now look, sweetheart, are you sure you want to go into this now? You're tripping, and I don't want to make you anxious." She stopped to pull a piece of tobacco from her lip. Doris is nearly always smoking. I get the impression she's addicted to Winstons. "I don't know what I'm worried about though," she said. "You seem to be handling it great. How many trips have you had?"

Roy said he'd lost count on about the 30th trip.

"Well, I guess you know what you're doing by now, don't you?"

"I *think* I do. But I'd like to hear your feelings about it."

"Why, darling? My expertise extends only to gin and tonic. Why should you listen to me?"

"Because I like your head."

"Well! I'm very pleased! Now let's see. Acid is two years old in my life, four years old in Peter's. He's tripped eleven times and once on peyote. Neither of us feels his experience is so impressive as to make him an authority on the subject. But we've stumbled upon a few guidelines we follow. The guidelines, by the way, are for ourselves. We're not out to convert, or to get anybody off the stuff. First—when to drop." She looked at Roy and me. "How do *you* decide that question?"

I didn't know what to say.

Roy told her he dropped acid whenever he thought it might be groovy.

"I think that's the way most younger people do it, but you're braver than we are. Peter and I keep wondering about things like long-term effects, so we only take it when we

177

feel we need it to stay high and keep growing. For me, one toke of good hash or grass usually does the job. Peter, too. He says if we took acid just for that, it'd be sort of like using a power crane to do the job of a shoe horn."

I asked her when she thought the power crane was called for.

"If we feel really stuck in one spot and don't seem to be moving at all; it's as simple as that. But first we exhaust every other resource we have, inside and out. Then, if we can't get things moving, it's time for soul medicine, LSD, the great spiritual power crane. May I tell you how my first trip came about?"

We all squeaked and nodded and said please tell.

"One afternoon I came to see Peter in a really awful state. This was before we got together. He was just my analyst at this point. Anyway, there I was, suicidal, weeping, hating my life—I forget what the crisis of the moment was, but after I'd blurted it out, Peter stood up and came around the desk and stood next to me. He said, 'Mrs. O'Neill, do you suppose there's any purpose to human life?' I was really knocked off balance. His whole mode and manner was different than I'd ever seen it. Suddenly he wasn't my doctor, he was just this person, this big terribly impressive man, and he was standing right next to me. He repeated the question, and I said yes, I supposed it had a purpose, but I hadn't the vaguest notion of what it was. And he said, 'Oh, yes, you do, you have some notion. That's how you've gotten through it so far. You've been riding some notion. Tell me what it is.' I thought for a while, but I kept coming up with blanks. Then I asked him if he could put the question in another way. 'I could,' he said, 'but it wouldn't help. Why don't you just answer it?' Frankly, I was getting annoyed but I was afraid to say so because I didn't want him to throw me out. Then he repeated the question. He said, 'What do you conceive to be the purpose of your life?' So just to shut him up, I said the first thing that came into my head, 'To save my goddam soul, I suppose!' I guess I expected him to be irritated, but he wasn't at all. In fact it was perfectly obvious I'd rung some kind of a bell. I couldn't have been more surprised. He was nodding his head and knitting his brow. And then he said, 'Do you suppose you might have it upside down? Do you suppose the purpose of your soul might be to save you?' I knew he wasn't just playing with words either. He was dead serious. Bells went off in *my* head. I was learning something and I knew it was important, and by God I was determined to get it through my skull. You see, all this time, since I was a little parochial school brat with chubby knees and a guilt complex, I thought that I, Doris, was supposed to take this messy little wreck, myself, and make something of her, make her into a Worthwhile Person. Save her soul, in other words. And now here was this great man, who happened also to be a hundred-dollar-an-hour psychoanalyst with qualifications up the iddy-wah, and he was asking me, in all seriousness, if I thought I might have the thing upside down. Maybe my soul was supposed to save *me!* I worked the thought over in my head for a few minutes and then I asked the Big Question—*How?* And at that precise moment Peter ceased being my analyst. He sat down and looked out the window and he said, 'I'm not really sure how.' I nearly flipped. My analyst was *leveling* with me. They don't do that as a rule, you know. They have this *code!* Anyway, Peter decided to screw the code and he took me out to dinner. We talked till midnight. Mostly he talked, and I listened. *Really* listened. He said he'd begun to discover there was a faculty in man that had fallen into disuse, and he had a sneaking suspicion it was the most important faculty of all. The soul. He said it was a constant in each person, the *only* constant, whether the person was aware of it or not—and it was there to run things, to be relied upon and consulted and to be made friends with. The following Sunday we took LSD together. We've been together ever since, by the way, but that's not my point. The point I'm trying to make is that LSD is soul medicine. It's like peyote, which is infinitely better and much harder to get hold of. It helps you get in touch with your own soul. That's the only thing Peter and I use acid for. We don't happen to think, as so many youngsters do, that it's just head candy, to be popped into your mouth like a maraschino cherry every time you yawn. Peter researched the stuff, he read everything he could lay his hands on, Huxley, Leary, the works. And he's convinced it's a tool for releasing light into man's consciousness, and that it's just plain stupid to let in *more* light if you haven't already made good use of the light that's there already. Now I don't think either of us will be taking another trip until we're convinced, really convinced, that our daily lives—the way we're actually *living* —is already reflecting all the night we've gained in the past. I realize full well of course and so does Peter that there are any number of adorable little hedonists with hair down to their butts who think we're both too rigid on this point. They tell us pleasure is motive enough. Well, perhaps so, but then we're right back to the shoe horn and the steam shovel. Who needs anything that strong just for pleasure? If you need a little help relaxing so you can enjoy pretty things like bed and food and music, puff on some grass! Nobody worships the senses more than Peter, and I'm in a position to know about that, my dears. He's marvelous! But I don't want to spoil his pleasure rap for you. It's one of his best and he loves giving it. He feels the senses are teachers. They make us more aware of who we are. Look, here's something he wrote down under peyote." Doris went over to the bulletin board and came back with a note that had been pinned to it. She read it over to herself first and then read it aloud. "'Learning the senses is learning to be an animal who is conscious.' And blah blah, there's some stuff here I don't understand, and then it says, 'When a man becomes truly aware of all the subtle powers of the senses, a terrific magic enters his consciousness. This is the consciousness of God, which is beyond all senses.' Now that is hardly the manifesto of an old puritan who's uptight about dope, is it? It's just that Peter has such a tremendous respect for it he doesn't like to abuse it. His real hope is that a day will come when a great deal more is known about these things. By then, who knows, the whole world might be having mescaline every Sunday morning for breakfast instead of just going to church. Can you imagine an international sacrament that really packed a wallop? Why, we might even stop blowing one another up!"

———————

All these new thoughts were so exciting I asked Doris if she'd mind if I ran downstairs and got my notebook. She smiled, and then she laughed. And then suddenly she got terribly serious. She looked at me and held my face in her hands. "Good lord, how you frighten me, sweetheart. You listen so beautifully, and you make me feel like such an old fool. Please, I'm not an oracle, truly I'm not. I'm just an old relic from the big-band days. I was weaned on Pepsi Cola and the dollar bill and 'God Bless America,' and I've made an awful mess of my life. For two years now I've been happy, it's true, happier than I've ever been before—but I'm no authority. Neither is Peter. We don't know what the hell we're doing, any more than you kids do. This is a whole new age we're heading into, and nobody but *nobody* knows what it's going to be. All we can do is dream and try and hope and flounder. And *talk!* We can talk, can't we? *God,* how we can talk! Forever it seems. I love you both. I loved you both on sight. And now I'm going to bed."

Canal Street, Monday Noon, September 22, 1969

Conversation with Roy:

ROY: I'm an escaped convict. No, I'm not. I'm a fugitive from justice. No, I'm not. I'm a—what the hell *am* I anyway?

WITCH: What are you talking about?

ROY: Today's the day I didn't report for induction.

WITCH: Is it? Is this really it?

ROY: Monday the twenty-second. The letter said seven o'clock this morning. And I didn't go. Wow, it feels weird. I'm a—what the hell am I—I'm an underground character. I—I'm a draft refuser. No, I didn't refuse, I just didn't go. So I'm a—I don't know what. What am I? I'm in *hiding!* Witch, do you realize I'm in hiding?

WITCH: Do you think you can dig it?

ROY: No. Not yet. Maybe I'll get used to it though. But right now I feel awful and it's some whole new kind of awful.

WITCH: Can you describe it?

ROY: Well, it's like I'm used to breaking laws, right? Because who isn't? If you don't break the law, you can't, you know, do anything. I mean you can hardly breathe or smoke pot or you-name-it without breaking some law. So I'm *used*

183

to that. Only now, for godsake, my whole entire *life* is illegal.

WITCH: That's really heavy.

ROY: It's heavy all right. It's as heavy as boiled shit, and I don't dig it at all.

WITCH: I don't think I would either.

ROY: I wonder what it would be like to live in a free—you know—country.

WITCH: In Sweden I hear they go around depressed a lot.

ROY: Yeah, but not because they're free. It's the weather.

WITCH: They are free though, I hear.

ROY: Yeah, that's what I hear.

WITCH: Where else are they?

ROY: I suppose on some islands somewhere there are free places. You know, the South Pacific and places like that.

WITCH: Really?

ROY: I don't really know. Maybe not. Maybe there aren't any yet.

WITCH: Actually the entire world is struggling to be free. Isn't that fantastic? Wouldn't you think it could just *be* free without all this bullshit? (*Long pause.*)

ROY: You know what today is for me? Today is the first day of the revolution for me. I mean from now on there's no kidding around about it. I am a fucking revolutionary.

WITCH: Committed.

ROY: Right. Committed. Whether I can dig it or not. That's the part that really frosts my balls. I don't have any goddam choice!

WITCH: Except to go be a hired killer for the imperialists.

ROY: That's a choice?

WITCH: No, you're right. There isn't any.

ROY: You know what I'm doing today?

WITCH: What?

ROY: I'm getting so stoned my eyes'll float right out of my head.

184

WITCH: Me, too.

ROY: In fact I got to split right now. I'm meeting Archie in the park.

WITCH: Oh. Right.

ROY: I'd ask you to come but . . .

WITCH: Oh, no, listen, go ahead. I've got stuff to do. Are you and Archie having a thing?

ROY: I don't know what we're having. It's weird.

THE STATEN ISLAND FERRY,
10 P.M. OF THE SAME DAY

I sometimes wonder what's running my life. This afternoon I went tearing uptown on the subway, got off at Columbus Circle, ran all the way to Central Park J.C., up to the third floor, and by two o'clock, there I was, out of breath, waiting for Contemporary History to begin, and wondering what other plans I had for myself that I hadn't let myself in on yet.

However, once there, I decided to make the most of it, observe H. Gliss in action, and try to keep from making a fool of myself. The hour went by quickly. He gave a really interesting lecture on the Constitution, and there was not one word of hate-America in it. In fact, he praised the Constitution so extravagantly you'd have thought he was being paid by the State Department. Then he did something truly sly. He asked if anyone knew or could guess which of our old World War II allies had admired the American Constitution so much he'd copied it for his own country's use. No one knew. No one could guess. Then he announced quietly it was Ho Chi Minh. I got so caught up in what he was saying that once or twice I forgot who he was and why I was there. By the time class was over, I sort of liked him, and I began to realize I intended to go up and talk to him, which sent me into full panic. Especially since I didn't know what I'd be saying to him.

So! While I was waiting to catch him alone, I cooked up a plan. And when everyone else had left, I went up to him and asked permission to audit his class. Without actually lying, I made it sound like I was enrolled at the University. He asked me why I wanted to audit; and I said I was interested in knowing why, if the Constitution was such a fabulous document, America was in such rotten shape, and I had a feeling I could probably learn that in his class. I thought it was a fairly mealy-mouthed little speech, but he actually got so excited by it he invited me for a cup of coffee in the cafeteria. Mostly I think he believed me, that I was really interested in government. But it was probably unusual for him to be sought out by students, so he was a little suspicious of me. Still, he kept on talking, answering all my questions, and every once in a while slipping in one of his own, like where do you live, and what's your major. He even asked me if I was a hippie. I said I believed in peace and love, but I didn't belong to anything—except the human race. Then he asked me if I believed in free love. I said I didn't know about any other kind, so he dropped the subject. Now I remember feeling a certain relief. I guess I knew even then he was having some ideas about what might happen between us. I suppose I kept them out of my mind because I wanted so much to keep them out of his.

We talked for over an hour and then he said he had to catch the ferry.

I said, "What ferry?"

"Staten Island."

"You're kidding!" I said.

"No, why?"

"Because that's where I'm going."

Amazing, the things that come out of my mouth!

"You live there?" he said.

"No. Just visiting."

So I went with him. The ride was lovely. I saw the Statue of Liberty. He bought me an orange soda. We talked, but not the whole trip. Sometimes we just looked at the water and at the other boats. I began to wonder what I'd do when we got to Staten Island, but I decided to leave it to inspiration. For one brief moment I played the game of pretending we were a father and daughter who were really on their way home. Then I thought, I've come this far. I'm determined to see where he lives.

"Does your wife meet the boat?" I asked.

"No, she's in Pittsburgh," he said. "The kids, too. We're separated." He didn't mention her again. I got the impression the subject was painful, but I couldn't resist asking about "the kids." After all, they are my siblings and I felt I had some sort of a right. He pulled out his wallet and showed me a photograph. There are two, which means I have a half-sister 11 and half-brother 9. I studied the photographs so carefully and for such a long time he asked me if I had some special interest in children. I said I did.

My sister, whose name is Marie, looks like our father, and she looks like him in a way that makes me realize I do, too. It's in the bones; we both have broad faces with sturdy cheeks and jaws. I'm blond and my father has dark hair, and perhaps that's why I hadn't noticed before how similar we were. Marie is blond, too. And my brother, whose name is Andrew, is dark like our father, but I can't tell much else about him. In the photograph, he's wearing a cowboy hat and most of his face is in shadow.

Then I asked a dangerous question. I said, "Do you have any other children, or just these two?" And while he was thinking about the question, frowning and looking out across the water, I had to hang on to the railing because my legs had turned to spaghetti.

"Why you ask so many questions?" he said. I tried to shrug it off lightly, but he kept looking at me with a certain smile he has—if you can call it a smile. Actually it's just a way of holding his face; he squares his jaw and lets his mouth wrinkle up on one side. "You do," he said. "You ask many questions."

I told him I'd always been inquisitive by nature. I said people often found my questions offensive, and I apologized.

We were quiet for a while, and I thought, Why in the hell don't I tell him he's my father and get it over with? At the time, I couldn't come up with an answer. I just felt some awful danger in the situation. But now I don't know what the danger was. Partly of course I wanted to see what kind of man he was, see how he behaved with a girl he didn't know. Maybe even get some clue about how he'd treated my mother. If he knew I was his daughter, he'd start acting like a parent, i.e., phony, and I'd *never* find out who he was.

Apparently something in me really wanted to let him have the truth, because I kept saying dangerous things. Once, for instance, when he was looking at me like a woman (I was coming back from the ladies' room and he was watching me walk toward him), I felt a certain alarm about leading him on, and decided to look for some way of turning his thoughts about me in a safer direction. So I said, "You know something? From far away, you look just like my father!"

"Your father!"

"Truly, you do!" I said. "*Exactly*, in fact!"

He didn't seem to care much for the comparison, so I tried to make it more palatable. "My father was a very handsome man, so you should be highly complimented."

"Okay. I'm complimented."

"Really! He was a wonderful man, too. Strong principles, and a terrific sense of—decency. You'd have liked each other. You have *every*thing in common. Except of course, he's dead. And you're very much alive. Listen, do you know what I'd like to do? I'd like to cook for you some night. In fact, I'd *love* to! Would you let me?"

"You want to cook for me?"

"Yes!"

"Tonight?"

"Wonderful!"

"I thought you got a date?"

"That's easy," I said. "One little phone call. Okay? Will you let me?"

"Okay. I let you cook. You know how, huh?"

"Mm, I used to cook for my father."

"Am I gonna hear about him some more?"

"No. I won't mention him again, I promise. But you do remind me of him."

"I don't know, maybe I don't like that."

"Why? I told you he was handsome."

"Maybe I like to look like me."

"You do!" I said. "You look exactly like yourself."

Staten Island looks like small towns must have looked 40 years ago. Everything looks out of date. A stranger plunked down in the middle of it would never believe he was in New York City, especially not in 1969.

We drove for about ten minutes in his ancient Ford station wagon and then turned down an old road lined with trees and into a driveway next to an enormous old wooden house. We got out of the car. Behind the house was a barn and the autumn remains of a vegetable garden, and all around the

190

edges of the place were trees. In a place like this, I thought, I could finish my old dream. I could take off all my clothes and go naked into the trees and make awful noises and perform nature rites and . . .

"It's a farm!" I said. "You live on a farm!"

"I *know* I live on a farm." He was smiling. "You like farms?"

"I love them! But I've never been on one before!"

"Come look." He led the way to the barn. There was a hayloft without any hay in it, and several storage bins with potatoes and carrots and onions and apples in them. He handed me a basket.

"You come to cook," he said, "get vegetables."

While the stew was cooking, my father showed me every little corner of the farm. He has three and a half acres with lots of trees, a house with seven bedrooms, a big barn and two small ones, a chicken coop, twelve chickens, three ducks, two cats. As I inspected it all, I kept whispering to myself, "Witch, you are the farmer's daughter!" Somehow his not knowing it made it more true.

I could tell this farmer wasn't used to having company. He was feeling the same things I feel when I let a special person read something I've written. I read it with them—using their eyes. And that's what Hank was doing. He was looking at his place through my eyes. Naturally, I let him know how wonderful I thought it was, and this fresh view of his kingdom brought him a great deal of excitement. Before dinner he had a second drink, which he said was unusual. He asked me why I didn't drink, and I said because it didn't make me high.

"Me either," he said, "but I like the fire." He pointed at his chest and belly.

Dinner was all right. There was no wine for the stew, but I used lots of garlic and lemon. I noticed something was depressing him, but I don't think it could have been the food, because, even though he didn't offer any praise, he ate a lot of it. For dessert the only thing I could find was some home-canned peaches in a little pantry off the kitchen. There must have been a dozen jars there. I asked him if it was all right to use them and he said, "No," very decisively. Then he said, "You eat some if you want. Not for me." Obviously, the peach discussion had made him even sadder. I suppose his wife had canned them in happier times, so I left them on the shelf and had bread and jam for dessert.

It was dark outside now and very quiet. I felt as if we were way off in the country somewhere. My father's mood became heavier and heavier until pretty soon the entire house was forelorn. I was tempted to try to bring the place to life by chattering, but something told me not to. I made coffee. He used bourbon in it instead of cream and kept sipping it in silence. Every once in a while he'd say something so declarative it didn't seem to invite an answer. "I'm not a drinker." "There's no woman here any more." "Sunset comes too soon." "This place is big." And he'd look around the huge old dining room and out the window into the dark. The only time he looked at me was when he thought I wasn't noticing. He liked my being there, but still I knew my presence made him feel awkward about himself. After one especially long silence, I said, "I like it here." He looked around, using my eyes again.

"It used to be better," he said.

I know he was talking about the days when his wife and Andrew and Marie were still with him. My father is an extremely articulate person—not in his speech but in his face and body. I knew what had happened between him and his family without being told. I can't be really sure, of course, but still I would bet my eyes I'm right in many of my guesses about him and his life. Some of my guesses might have been set off by certain scraps of information that came out, but most of them are based on the feelings I could see passing through him, especially in his eyes. When the liquor had relaxed something behind them, they became completely open and naked. And all the troubles that usually live in his forehead moved into these big brown show windows.

Fifteen years ago, he'd married one of his students. They'd lived together in some awful Manhattan slum where they began to dream of a good life somewhere in the country. One day when the children, my brother and sister (I love writing "my brother and sister"), were still small, they took a ride on the Staten Island Ferry and spent the afternoon driving around the island. The station wagon was probably new in those days. Anyway, they bought the farm and moved in, and somehow, after only two or three years, the dream began to go sour. Maybe it was too hard teaching in the city and working the farm at the same time. I feel certain, too, that he began to expect too much from his woman and from the two children, that he'd been really hard on them and had finally driven them away. And now he was full of loneliness and regrets and confusion and pride. It would be hard to guess which of those things was the most painful for him to bear. Probably the regrets and the pride.

There must be something in me that's terribly attracted to sadness. I suppose that's sick and I wonder about it but I don't really care. Yes, I do. I *care*. But I care more about the sadness. I have this tremendous desire to make it go away. I've always known this about myself, but I'd never experienced it so sharply as I did just an hour ago at my father's table. And it caused me to do something foolish.

Really foolish. But I don't really regret it. (Furthermore, I'm getting pretty sick of being told by myself that I'm foolish! *So cool it!* I am who I am.)

I got up from the table and walked around to my father and stood behind him. I put my hands on his head, rested them on his forehead, and prayed that something in them would cause everything in his whole heart and mind and soul to be soothed. But in my eagerness to heal, I'd forgotten that this poor lonely beautiful man has a body, too, and that he could easily misunderstand my affection for him. And of course he did. Completely. After a few seconds, he took my hand and lowered it to his mouth and kissed it. And he kissed it in a way that caused me to realize I'd made a really ghastly blunder. Then he stood up and pulled me toward him and pressed himself close to me and kissed me. Suddenly I found myself trembling and crying. I felt the most tremendous love for him, and at the same time an overwhelming horror at the situation I'd created. It seemed hopeless. And while I stood there crying and trembling, I said—to myself, I think, or was it out loud? I hope not—I said, God help me, what have I done? And whether it was out loud or not, something in him heard me. He put one of his thumbs on my face and took some of my tears and licked them off. "Crying tastes good," he said. But he wasn't smiling, he was dead serious. "What you think I am?" he said. "Some old man with the fire gone out? I'm forty-four years old, far from dead yet. I like to lick tears from a girl's face. And that's not all. I like to lie with them, too. Oh, boy, look at you, big surprise, huh? Ach! Come on. I take you to the ferry, crazy dumb chick."

He took out his keys. I got my bag and followed him out to the car. We drove in silence for a while. Then I said, "I wasn't teasing you. Honestly I wasn't. I like you an awful lot. I think you're a wonderful man. I just didn't realize— how I was acting."

After a moment he looked at me. "How old are you?"

"Seventeen."

"Why you call yourself Witch?"

"It'd take a long time to explain."

"Crazy name. I don't like it. What's your real name?"

"On my birth certificate it's—well it's complicated. I don't use my real name."

He shrugged. Then he said, "You never have any experience—with a man?"

I tried to think what I might say, and how it might sound to him, and nothing seemed right. The reason is obvious to me now. Nothing *would have* been right—except the truth. And the truth was something I was no longer even tempted to tell. So I kept quiet.

At the ferry building, he stopped the car and as he reached past me to open the door, he said, "Good meal."

I said, "Thank you, and I'm awfully sorry I—"

"Why don't you shut up?" he said.

I admitted that was a good idea, and then I kissed him on the cheek and got out. He drove away without looking at me.

The father drove away without looking at his daughter.

Why can't my mind stop playing with these simple facts? Why can't I get it through my head that except for some meaningless accident of blood, this man and I are nothing to each other?

Canal Street, Wednesday, September 24, 1969

Roy wasn't here all day yesterday. I started out the day merely worried and ended up obsessed. I tried to work on some pornography for a while in the afternoon, partly to get my mind off Roy, but I couldn't really get behind it. That worries me, too, because I've got to come up with some way of making money.

This afternoon Doris asked me where I thought Roy and Archie were. I tried to play it lighthearted and unconcerned. I said I supposed they were out on some mad adventure. Ha ha ha. (When will I stop being such a phony?) Saying it out loud was the first time I'd actually formed the thought —*some mad adventure*—and the words scared me. Not the words, but the possibilities that lurked behind them. When I'm worried like this, my witch sense is none too reliable. It's got too much imagination mixed up in it and all it does is present me with clammy little still photos from horror movies that couldn't possibly be true.

But why not? This is the city where those movies *take place!* Roy's already had a knife aimed at his gizzard and one cooling off his throat *simultaneously,* and I personally have come within inches of being beaten to death by a black lesbian prostitute. For all I know, he's been mashed by Godzilla and turned into hambu

Someone's coming up the stairs. Let it be him.

Half an hour later

It was. It was Roy. We've had a talk and a hug and now he's taking a nap. I'm supposed to think everything's okay. But I don't. He doesn't look right and he doesn't act right. He's all splotchy-looking and pale, and his eyes have disappeared. He's not *behind* them.

He said Archie had the use of a pad on Spring Street that belonged to some friend who'd gone to California, and they'd gotten hung up over there with "these people."

I said, "What people?"

"Just people Archie knows."

"Roy, where are you? You're not behind your eyes."

"Oh, that's only because I'm asleep. The rest of me is sitting up talking to you, but *I'm* really asleep."

"Well, then, you'd better go join yourself on the bed."

I went upstairs with him, mother-style, plumped the pillow, fussed with the sheets. I said, "Roy, I hope we'll do something together tomorrow. Because I've been missing you something awful."

He said, "Okay, sure."

He got in bed and I tucked him in and kissed him. Then I thought what an icky female trick I'd just pulled, beating him over the head with how much I'd missed him, making him promise to spend tomorrow with me.

I said, "Roy we don't *have* to. I was just . . ."

But his eyes were closed, and I thought, Oh, Witch, shut up and let the poor kid sleep!

197

Canal Street, 7:10 p.m., Thursday, September 25, 1969

Peter is back and all hell has broken loose. I've borrowed Jeanette's typewriter so I can work fast. We're having dinner at eight-thirty and I'm giving myself until then to get this up to date. I have a feeling this is going to be the most interesting evening since we arrived in New York.

He got here at about five while Roy and I were out shopping, and the place has been in an uproar ever since. I'm in an absolute panic to get it all written down. If events continue to pile up at the present rate, my autobiography is going to be the longest book ever written.

———————————

Our first view of Peter Friedman could hardly have been more terrifying. He was in a rage, like a wild man. His eyes were shooting flames and his face was pure white, he was making violent noises with his hands by socking them together, and he was shouting at the top of his voice. He's quite tall and his shoulders are massive. He has a high forehead with black wavy longish-but-not-long hair, and sideburns that are so full they're semi-muttonchops. I don't know whether or not to describe him as handsome. The word impressive seems more accurate.

His behavior scared me, but in a way it was a magnificent surprise. I'd heard such fabulous things about him that I'd been expecting some kind of a saint, and of course I didn't expect to like him at all. I was afraid on the surface he'd be a real goody-two-shoes, peaceful and wise and sensible, but underneath there'd be this terrible flaw that only I could see, and I'd have to go around pretending I didn't.

But it's not like that at all. If he's a perfect person—and I have a hunch he is—it's not because he's flawless but because he doesn't hide his flaws. He digs himself. Cary Colorado turned to me the minute the explosion was over and said, "Isn't he great? He lets it all hang out!"

Roy and I weren't here for the worst of it. We'd gone to Bleecker Street to get some fresh dill and watercress for dinner. This is Sally's night in the kitchen, but since Peter was expected back, the whole house has been pitching in to make a sort of welcome feast. I wasn't sure he'd be able to appreciate it, with his father just freshly buried this morning, but it was Doris's idea and she probably knows what he'd like better than anyone else. Anyway, he was supposed to come flying in to JFK at four P.M., so with the traffic and all we expected him about five-thirty. Somehow he got in earlier though, and Roy and I missed his arrival. I had to piece the story together from bits and scraps people told me later, mostly Jeanette and Doris. They were here for the entire movie.

Apparently the actual arrival scene was very high. Peter wasn't at all depressed. He even felt good about his father being dead.

The old man had been a rabbi. His voice must have been stupendous. He had a big reputation as a cantor and was always being asked to do his thing in other people's synagogues for special occasions. He was also super-orthodox, so Peter's childhood was full of hassles because he didn't dig the synagogue all that much. There had been a long strain between the two of them that ended in an uneasy truce a couple of years ago, but the deathbed scene was completely harmonious. The old man held out against taking morphine until the very last. Peter sat by the bed for days and days. He didn't even go to bed in all that time, just nodded off once in a while in the chair, and then he'd wake up with the old man clutching his hand. Finally they had to give him injections because his mind started to go and nobody could stand to watch the suffering.

Anyway, Peter came home in high spirits and full of love, and right in the middle of all the excitement the doorbell rang.

It was three young men asking for Archie Fiesta. Nobody'd ever seen them before. Archie was out, so they asked if they could wait for him. They looked like sharpies from Newark or somewhere, but they weren't unfriendly or anything, so they were allowed to wait.

Peter and Doris went up to the attic. Peter wanted to unpack and lie down before dinner. While they were up there, Doris started to show him all the things Roy and Jeanette had done to improve the place, but Peter didn't seem to be listening. Doris asked if anything was bothering him. He said yes, those young men downstairs. So he got up and went right down to the big room in his stocking feet.

Doris had a feeling something was going to happen, so she followed him down. The three strangers didn't stand up when Peter came in the door. He stood there and looked them over for a minute, and then he said, "I get the impression you guys are interested in scoring." The three guys looked at each other, then one of them said he guessed it was cool, and another one spoke up and said yes, they'd been told they could score some crystals from Archie. Peter said, "Well, that's not the case. In fact, Archie's moving out of here this afternoon, so you might as well leave." At this point he was still very calm, and when they left, he turned to Nyoom and Cary, who had come in to see what was happening, and asked very quietly if they'd help him get Archie's things together.

Just as they were starting up the stairs, they heard some footsteps. And there was Archie, on the lower landing, looking up.

Peter said, "Did you see your friends on the street?"

Archie said, "Yeah, I did."

"Did you tell them to wait while you came up and got the stuff?"

"What stuff? I haven't got anything." Everyone knew Archie was lying. Peter included. He said, "Oh, I see. It was just a misunderstanding, huh? Come on up here, Archie. Let's talk it over."

Archie said, "How was your trip?"

"How was my trip? You want to know how my trip was?"

Now they were both standing on the landing outside the Big Room. Peter gave Archie a push and said, "Get the fuck up those stairs."

Archie said, "What's the matter, Peter? What's happening?"

"*You*, shitheel, *you're* what's happening. You're leading the way to your stash. It's in your room, isn't it?"

"I haven't got anything in my room. I don't know what you're talking about."

They were on the second landing now, and Peter slapped Archie hard across the face. He said, "Go get it. Fast."

Archie went to his bedroom and lifted up the mattress. There was a little brown bag hidden under it. Peter reached in and pulled out a handful of small tinfoil squares. Then he dropped them all back into the bag, except one. He unfolded it and found about a quarter of a teaspoon of white powder.

Peter said, "What is this? Methadrine? Heroin? What is it?"

"Meth," Archie said.

"How long have you been dealing out of my house, motherfucker?"

"Never. I never dealt out of here, I swear. I was just going to deal this one batch. That's all I was going to do. Honest, Peter, I'm telling the truth."

"Get out."

Then Peter started pushing Archie down the stairs.

At this point Roy and I came in the street door downstairs. I was opening the door for Roy, because his arms were full of groceries, and when I opened it I saw Archie sort of falling toward us and this wild man shoving him from behind and raving like a lunatic. He kept saying, "Faster, faster! You're not moving fast enough. Move faster, you little prick, move faster."

When Peter saw us, he held Archie by the shoulders from behind. I suppose he thought Roy and I were two more speed customers. "Who are you two?" he said. "Who are you?"

Roy couldn't get his mouth together at all.

I said, "I'm Gloria. I mean *Witch!*" And felt foolish for correcting myself.

Doris called down from the top of the stairs, "They're ours, Peter. Those two belong to us."

"All right, but stand aside!" he said. "I'm taking out the trash!"

Then he pushed Archie out the door and out onto the sidewalk and followed him out, hollering all the way. Archie ran over to a lamppost and sort of hid behind it. And when Peter stopped hollering at him for a second, he said, "Can I have my stuff?"

Peter still had the brown bag in his hand. I hadn't yet been told what was in it, and couldn't even imagine. Peter acted like it was poison. He dropped it on the sidewalk and started to grind it with his foot. But he was only wearing socks, so after a few seconds he gave up and came back toward the house. Roy and I got out of his way. He walked right past us and up the stairs.

Roy looked at me and said, "Hey, that was Peter, wasn't it?"

"I guess so."

Archie was down on his hands and knees, gathering up the contents of his brown bag.

Roy said, "Archie, what's happening?"

Archie was crying. "I just blew my scene, man. He threw me out."

"He found your crystals, huh?"

Things were happening so fast I couldn't get it all together immediately. But later I realized what was in the bag. And not only that—*Roy knew*. This fact kept hitting me all through dinner.

(But I'm getting ahead of the story.)

Roy went over to Archie and said, "Please don't cry, man, please."

Archie said, "I'm not crying!" But he was. And then he started to run. He was running so fast nobody could have caught him. Especially not Roy, with grocery bags in both arms.

Now I'm going to record what was happening in the house while Roy and I were downstairs on the sidewalk with Archie. Doris told me this part:

Peter came up the stairs. Doris was waiting for him on the first landing. She said she didn't have any plan, she didn't know what to do. She was just *being there* for him. So Peter came up to the landing and looked at her. Then he looked down the stairs, and back at Doris again. She said his expression was so strange and distant she was actually frightened for him.

He went into the Big Room walking like a stick man and everybody was standing around looking at him. A couple of them tried to smile, but his mood was so queer, no one knew what to say or do. Then he looked at Doris again and said, "What did I do just now? What happened?" His voice was quiet, but he still wasn't himself. "Tell me," he said. "What happened here just now?"

Doris said, "Well, Peter, you put Archie out of the house."

"I threw him out, didn't I?"

"Yes, you did. We have a family agreement against hard drugs in this house. And against dealing of any kind. Archie broke them both. He broke our family agreements. And you put him out of the house."

I'm not absolutely certain, but I think this is the moment Roy and I walked in on. Because when we did, Peter looked past us both without even seeing us. He went to the landing and looked up and down and up and down, and he kept saying, "Oh, Christ. Oh, Jesus. Oh, Christ. What did I do to the boy? What did I do to him?"

He ran down the stairs and out onto the sidewalk, calling after Archie. But Archie had been running, and so of course he was gone by then.

Peter came back up the stairs and looked at us for a minute. He was like a person waking up from a nightmare. He

said, "I'm sorry, I guess I just don't know what I'm doing."
And then he went up to the attic. Doris followed him up,
but she came down a minute later and told us he wanted to
be alone for a while, and we were to call him when dinner
was ready.

I asked her if he was all right.

She said, "I think so. He's watching the seven o'clock
news and that's a good sign. Peter's a news freak, you know."
She told me that even in California when his father was
dying, he left the sickroom every evening to watch the
Huntley-Brinkley report in the hospital lounge. "He says
this is the only world he's got, so he has to keep an eye on
it, no matter what."

I just went down to see about dinner. It's almost ready.
The table looks beautiful. The whole place does. Nyoom
brought some of Will's plants from the greenhouse on the
roof and arranged them in corners and on window sills. Cary
built a fire. We still don't need one, but it makes the whole
room glow.

I'm awfully excited about the evening coming up. Peter's
presence in the house has changed everything. Even with
all this disturbing Archie-drama fresh in everyone's mind,
we're all feeling about twice as high as usual. Roy's in the
bathroom putting Clearasil on his pimples, and I noticed
he's wearing his special-occasion shirt, the blue madras
Delano gave him.

I suppose I'd better stop now. My hair could stand a
brushing.

Hours later, about 1:30 a.m.

I'm alone in the Big Room, wide awake, full of new thoughts and feelings. The ashes are still warm in the fireplace, and there are a few live coals left. I'm writing by candlelight, sitting at this great long wooden table. Typewriters make too much racket at night, so I'm doing this by hand. I love the silence of New York nights. It's a kind of roaring silence that you feel everyone in town is contributing to even in their sleep. When you're awake at these hours (as I often am, writing or thinking or just lying in bed next to Roy) you can actually feel all the foghorn tooters on the river and all the ambulance drivers and truckers and cops and burglars and whores keeping you company. It's nice. It's also a little creepy. But I like it.

All evening I've been getting flashes of some other time, some earlier century. I don't know which one though. All pre-20th centuries seem pretty much alike to me—I suppose because none of them had electricity. Tonight the only light we used was firelight and people light, and I'm still feeling the tremendous glow of all that's taken place here in the past few hours.

At dinnertime we were all seated at this table when Peter came in.

He stood at his place at the head of the table for a minute, and then he said, "What about somebody else sitting here tonight?" Nobody responded. Nyoom was sitting at about the middle place on the left side of the table. Peter said, "Hey, Nyoom, what about you? Will you swap with me?"

Nyoom seemed delighted to have been singled out. He rose with a self-important frown and gave up his seat to

Peter, then went to the head of the table and sat down. Now I was sitting across from Peter, and Roy was right next to him. Doris, who was at the opposite end, said, "Well! That's nice, to shuffle things up once in a while. Sally, why don't you switch with me tonight."

Sally made a happy little game of it. She switched places with Doris, and that put Doris right across from Peter, and next to me.

Food was passed, and when everybody's plates were filled, Sally Sunflower extended her hands and said, "Zap time!" We made a chain of hands around the table, and everyone closed his eyes. Then the current started flowing through us. It was the strongest hand-chain Zap I'd ever experienced. At one point I took a peek at Roy to see how he was digging it. He had his fingers wrapped tight around Peter's right hand and Jeanette's left and I could see he was really impressed with the voltage coming through. His face was completely slack and his eyelids were fluttering.

The first Zap is always for Will.

Then Doris said, "Let's send a Zap to Peter's father."

After a few seconds Sally said, "My ex-grandmother in Las Vegas broke her foot."

The whole thing was getting so heavy I didn't want to waste it. I started thinking of all the people I knew who could use a Zap—my father in Staten Island, Edward the world's greatest cosmetician, Sara the Ghost—and just as I was about to open my mouth, I heard Roy's voice. When I think of it now, I'm amazed at how strong and clear it was, because what he said must have taken guts, and it caused a good-sized shock wave to travel around the table.

He said, "Shouldn't we send a Zap to Archie Fiesta?"

Peter said, "Yes!"

A few seconds later, as if on some inaudible signal, Zap time was over and everyone was busy eating and talking. I don't know what I expected Peter's mood to be now, but he seemed gentle and open and full of life. Doris told him Roy and I were sleeping in Will's place under the stairs. He wanted to know if it was comfortable enough, and both Roy and I started raving at once about how perfect it was. Then he asked us where we were from, and whether or not our parents knew where we were. Roy looked at me, so I just told the truth: that they knew we were in New York, but we hadn't given them an address.

Then he looked at Roy and Roy looked back, terrified. He seemed to be steeling himself for a terrible blow. Maybe he thought he was going to get thrown down the stairs for looking young.

But Peter wasn't even thinking about that. He said, "That white paint between the rafters up there fills the whole place with light. I can't get over the difference. Was that your idea?"

"It was Jeanette's," Roy said. "She picked the color."

Jeanette was pleased. "Roy swings a mean brush," she said.

Peter said, "I could tell it was a professional job. No big globs of drippage, no spilling over. What'd you do, use masking tape?"

"No, I was just careful."

"You must have a steady hand."

"I guess I do have a pretty steady hand. Because I'd never painted anything before or anything."

Peter said, "Did you enjoy it?"

"I did, I really did. I just got behind it and dug it. That's the way I am. I get right behind a thing, whatever I'm doing, and I make myself dig it. Did you notice the skylight in the hall?"

"Did I *notice* it? I noticed it first thing. Did you do that?"

"I thought it'd be better to let the light in. So I just took

208

out the wood and put in some glass. It doesn't leak either. I tested it. I went up on the roof and threw water at it really hard, like a bad rain would do, and not a drop went inside. So it won't leak or anything either."

"I lack the patience for a job like that," Peter said. "A craftsman has to have patience. What does your father do?"

"He's a psychoanalyst."

"That's what I used to do, you know."

"Yeah, I know, but you quit, right?"

"Right. Is your father any good?"

Roy shrugged. "He gets a hundred dollars an hour. Sometimes a hundred and fifty."

"That's not what I meant."

"You mean is he *really* good?"

"Yeah."

"I don't know how to tell."

"What would be your guess?"

"*I* wouldn't go to him if *I* was freakin' out."

"Why not?"

"If you want the truth, I think he's sort of an asshole. I mean that respectfully." Everybody laughed—except Peter. Then Roy continued, "I mean, I'm not sure he listens. No. He *listens* all right. But he listens too fast. He thinks he knows what you're telling him before you get it all out. And so what happens is you *never* get it all out. And so he's telling you what to do and all, but he still doesn't really know what's happening. Only I guess he's different with his patients. I don't know how he is with them. I just know how he is with me."

"Have you spent a lot of time with him?"

"Yeah. Every other Sunday he'd stay home in the afternoon and we'd talk. He'd ask questions and all, and I'd answer him, sort of."

"Didn't you see him every day?"

"Not as a rule. He had all these patients from early in the morning till late at night. Saturdays, too, and once in a while on Sunday. But most Sundays he spent at the yacht club, except when we had our appointments."

"Appointments?"

"Yeah, they were like appointments. I guess he thought he ought to *counsel* me. Because that's what our talks were all about, they were all about my getting *counseled*. It was a drag, it really was. Naturally I didn't want him to know what was *really* happening, so I used to make up problems. Like, I'd say, Gee, Dad, my mind wanders during geometry. Why do you suppose that is? Then we'd spend the hour getting *that* all patched up, and I'd have him off my back for another couple of weeks."

"Was he on your back a lot?"

"No, it wasn't like that. What I meant was his *conscience* would be clear because he'd been giving me all this *counsel*, you know what I mean?"

Peter nodded. "Yeah, I know what you mean. How do you *feel* about him? Apart from thinking he's an asshole. Do you like him at all?"

"Once in a while I feel sorry for him. I tried to turn him on to grass once but it didn't work."

"What happened?"

"I told him about this friend I had that turned on with *his* father. There wasn't anybody like that, I made it up. Anyway my old man said this *other* father must be a very disturbed man. He tends to think everybody needs professional attention."

"He knows you smoke grass?"

"He knows I *have*. But I told him I quit."

"Why?"

"I didn't want to be hassled about it. I know that's no good. I should've told him the truth, right?"

"I don't know."

"You think it's all right to lie to them? Parents?"

"I don't know, I really don't. Seems to me there are times when a person doesn't have any choice. It takes support to tell the truth. You got to have something behind you, something underneath you, something to hold you together when the shit hits the fan. And if you don't feel you've got that, then you lie."

"I should've had all that, though, right?"

"I don't know where in the hell you'd have *gotten* it—living at home. I was still lying to *my* father when I was thirty. Not that I'm carrying any big regrets either. I did what I had to do and to hell with it. *Now*, of course, I feel differently about all that. I won't lie to people any more. Just to institutions. You know, the government, the telephone company, the Army. Institutions don't have ears, so I just try to figure out what information *works* best—and feed them that. But people, I, uh, I just can't do that any more. I can't lie to people. I find it hurts me immediately! I get immediately depressed by it. So I've cut that out pretty much."

He'd been addressing a lot of these remarks to all of us, but at the end he swung his face toward Roy and said, "What about you? Do you still lie to people? I don't mean your father. I guess he's an institution, isn't he?" His face cracked a little, so Roy snickered. And Peter said, "But what about now? Do you lie to your friends?"

Roy said, "I don't think I do. What about it, Witch, do I lie?"

I said I thought he just lied to institutions and to people who acted like institutions. But never to me.

Nyoom, who was having a ball playing Papa at the head of the table, picked up the subject of Archie. He said, "The episode earlier this evening, involving our *pater familias* and the, uh, erstwhile Mr. Tambourine Man, seems to present a fascinating ethical problem vis-à-vis the question of the state versus the individual."

Peter said, "Tell us about it, Nyoom."

It took Nyoom several minutes to find phrases pompous enough to cover the matter. But finally, after a few other people thinned it out for me, I got his point, and I found it just fantastically impertinent. He was saying that Peter had chosen to protect the household against Archie by throwing him out. Therefore, in his behavior he had actually sided with the state against the individual.

But Peter wasn't at all annoyed. He listened with perfect interest to the whole thing, even helped Nyoom find the right wording to make his point. Then Cary Colorado started defending Peter's behavior. He said there was a revolution going on, and Archie's behavior had placed us all in jeopardy. In an ideal society—pure anarchy, with everyone governing himself—people wouldn't be going around shooting up hard drugs in the first place. Besides, he said, nothing would be illegal, so there wouldn't be any police breathing down everyone's neck.

Peter interrupted. "Now hold it, whoah," he said, "now just wait a minute! We're going to *have* to have police, man! Oh, yes indeed! In these early stages of Utopia, a police force *must* be maintained! Absolutely. It'll be needed, don't you see, for maintaining public health when people are found running around spreading contagious diseases!"

"Yes," Cary said, "but that's what *you* were doing—in a way. You were stopping the spread of a—"

"Now please, man! My behavior can't be justified! Forgive it, please do, but don't justify it! You just *cannot* have police behaving the way I behaved with Archie! Throwing a boy down the stairs? That's sick!"

Doris said, "What do you suppose we'd better do, arrest you?"

"No. Let me off. My record's good. Besides, you've all rehabilitated me. I'm peaceable now. But *listen!* Think about this! What's to be done when *men in high places* act like I did? Say they suggest warlike solutions to problems? Won't those dangerous individuals have to be arrested? Won't they have to be placed in isolation? For their own sakes as well as society's?"

Cary said, "What would we do with them, keep them in prison?"

"No, no, no! Rehabilitate! Rehabilitate! And who knows, we may have to dedicate all the powers of science to the job —but that's okay. Everybody's worth the trouble. Everybody's worth all the trouble in the world. Is there a kinder way—no, let me put it like this: *Is there any other way at all* to help carriers of the most virulent disease known to man? I don't know. I can't think of one. But you'd better, you kids had better get at it, figure out how to handle this thing. It's all well and good to toss peace signs around in the streets, but how you going to handle it when you're running the world? What are you going to do when some dear beloved brother goes berserk—like I did an hour ago, running around here like some Old Testament Jewish papa who'd as soon knock a—"

Everybody interrupted at once, including Doris. But Peter kept raving on, like a man in the grips of some wild, marvelous obsession, and he was utter heaven the whole time. I adored him.

"No, no, goddamnit, I'm serious," he said. "I realize I pay most of the bills around here, but please, for Christ sake, all of us have got to remember that what we've got to form on this planet is a society where money doesn't get any special privileges. Ideally, we do away with money entirely. But that's not going to happen tomorrow, and it's not going to happen next year. So we've got to learn to live *with* money.

And the first rule is Don't let the moneyman get away with any shit. In the past, money was influence. But not here. All of us at this table are compatriots in the future. We've got to do it right. And that means we've got to realize Peter Friedman is no fucking angel.

"Let me tell you what happened in California last week. I'm sitting at my father's bedside, holding his hand. I think he's asleep, so I'm just sitting there looking at him, thinking what a tough old fucker he was, and how maybe he wouldn't have *had* cancer if he'd been just a little less hard-ass. If he hadn't been *right* all the time, and so goddam sure of himself—well, I don't want to get into that. I don't know what cancer's all about. Forget I said that. All I want to tell is what *happened*. I'm sitting there thinking all this shit about him, when suddenly his eyes pop open and he's looking straight at me, and he says—now get this—he says, 'You are my immortality.' And then, quick as a wink he shuts his eyes again. And that's the last thing I heard out of him. Oh, he talked some more after that, but nothing very clear. From then on, he was on the way out. But that was the last thing he shot at me. He said, 'You are my immortality.'

"And let me tell you all something right this goddam minute. He was right! *He lives in me*. . . . Who did you think that was this afternoon hollering his lungs out and throwing Archie Fiesta down those stairs? It wasn't Moses and it wasn't Eddie Fisher and it wasn't Dick Nixon. It was me. I am my father's immortality. And I proved it here about an hour ago. So *watch* me! This is exactly how the shit gets rolling in this world. The president of the United States drops a turd that burns millions of people, Asians and Americans alike, *people*—sacred human persons, dead and mutilated! And what happens? All his high-paid helpers, the Cabinet, the Chiefs of Staff, all the advisers, they sit around forever after, telling him what a great man he is, and how dare these fucking gooks, these slanty-eyed Communist farmers try to run their own country and cause all this trouble for our president. *He means well! He's trying to protect us!* So the fuck what? He's still out of his goddam mind, isn't he? Bullshit. I'm not getting into that act. I'd rather have Archie and every little speed freak in Manhattan descend upon this place and burn it to the ground.

"By the way," he said, "is Archie a speed freak?"

Everyone looked at everyone else. Roy said, "You mean is he shooting speed? Or is he strung out on it? Because a speed freak is somebody that's strung out on it, isn't it?"

"Well, either way," Peter said. "What I'm wondering is what shape Archie's in. That's what I should have been thinking about when I found that shit in his room. Was he just selling it? Or is he shooting up, too? Do you know?" He put the question to Roy.

Roy got flustered. It looked pretty obvious to me, probably to Peter, too, that Roy knew *something*.

Nyoom said, "I get the impression Roy would like to invoke the dictum of, I think it might have been John Lennon or one of the Beatles, who, when asked by the press if some other famous personage was a marijuana smoker, simply said, I think everyone has a right to blow his own cool. And perhaps he has a point. Because you see—"

"Nyoom," Peter said, "let me interrupt, may I?"

"I relinquish the floor."

"You just said something that strikes me as very serious, if I understood you right. You think Roy doesn't want to rat on Archie. Right?"

"Very succinct!"

"Mm-hm. And you know what that means? That means I'm the fuzz in this situation."

Nyoom spoke up quickly. "I didn't mean that!"

Peter said, "Yes you did, Nyoom." Then he put his arm on

Roy's shoulder and spoke softly. "Listen, son, how could I blame you? The first time you lay eyes on me an hour ago, what am I doing? I'm performing a raid, making a bust. Naturally you see me as someone to protect your friends from. In your shoes, I'd be doing the same thing, and for the same reasons. Furthermore, I admire you for it."

"Perhaps," said Nyoom, "there is still another reason for which Roy is disinclined to share information about Archie's, um, shall we say, habits."

"Shit!" said Jeanette. Her eyes were all a-snap with black anger. She looked marvelous. "Nyoom baby, I'm gonna tell you something. Your mouth thinks too much!"

Then Doris spoke. "Let's have a quiet moment now. Shall we?"

Sally Sunflower, who had begun to look like she'd been rained on, suddenly bloomed again. "Oh, yes," she cried. "Let's!"

We all held hands quietly for a while, and you could actually see and hear the return of peace to the room. Faces relaxed and smiled. We started tasting the food again. The fire crackled in the fireplace. Percy the Cat jumped into Peter's lap. A foghorn belched and I felt we were all safe from darkness and from the sea and from everything outside the door.

Peter was the first to speak. "Does anyone know where to find Archie?"

Roy said, "I do. *I think* I do anyway."

"What do you all think of this idea?" Peter said. "I've got a truly righteous ounce in my pocket, superduper Santa Barbara hothouse shit. Maybe Roy wouldn't mind going to fetch Archie, and we could all go up to the attic and have a powwow later on. I could use a little head-straightening. What do you think?"

Everyone liked the idea, but Roy was thrilled by it. He

left the table even before dessert and ran lickety-split down
the stairs and into the street.

When Roy returned with Archie about an hour later,
Sally and Cary and Doris and I were still in the kitchen putting away dishes and cleaning up. A few minutes later, when
we were finished, we went to the attic and found the others
there silently passing joints.

Peter and Archie had their arms around each other's
shoulders, and Roy was sitting across from them looking
at them with open adoration.

(Later, I said to Roy, "I guess they've talked it all out."
And Roy said, "No! No, they didn't! They didn't say a word!
Archie came in. They looked at each other, and *wham*. That's
all there was to it!")

I had the feeling Roy had never in his life seen an older
man and a younger one love each other in such a simple,
open way. Like an ideal father and son. No, not even like
that. Like friends! His mind was blown through the entire
evening, and I know now that's what blew it. There was a
whole lot said by all of us last night, but not by Roy. He
hardly opened his mouth, except when it fell open involun-
tarily from sheer amazement.

Actually I didn't say much either. I was getting Holy
Family blasts one after another. We were really brothers and
sisters, every last one of us, deeply and truly connected. I'd
felt brotherhood before, but I think this was the first time
I'd ever experienced family-hood.

For the first half hour nothing was said that was worth
writing down. The talk was beautiful but not very interesting. What I dug most was the way we ended up arranging
ourselves on the floor in this kind of loose, happy circle,

enjoying the closeness. Roy somehow angled his way over toward Doris, who was sitting next to Peter. Then he stretched out on the floor and made it quite clear his head wasn't at all comfortable. Obviously he wanted a lap, and naturally Doris picked up on it. She's not only an earth mother, she's an *old* earth mother and she knows just how to do it without even thinking about it. She took hold of Roy's face with one hand, patted her knee with the other and said, "Come here, Roy." So he was lying on Mama's lap, Mama was sitting next to Papa, and Papa had his arm around Roy's beloved brother, Archie. And I was holding Roy's foot. What more can a man ask for? He was in heaven and he knew it.

After a while Peter began to talk about his father again. Mostly, I think, for Archie's benefit, he repeated some of what he'd told the rest of us at the dinner table, and then he went into a fabulous rap about parents and children. He said one of the great differences between the new age and the past would be that, from now on, children would learn to inherit more and more light from their parents, and less and less darkness. We'll learn to be *aware*, we'll learn to watch ourselves in such a way that when the ghosts of our parents show themselves in our behavior, we'll be free to pick and choose. We'll take what's wise and beautiful, and be happy that it's a part of us, and we'll simply reject what's ugly and dark.

"I don't want to give the impression," he said, "that my father was nothing but a bastard. He wasn't. And none of your fathers was either. I hope you all realize that. I don't suppose there's a one of us who didn't have some serious differences between himself and his old man—or his mother, or both of them. But when you really look, you can always see valuable stuff in them. And those are the things you *want* to inherit from them. The thing that scared *me* today was finding myself acting like the sonofabitch my father so often seemed to be. But who could have guessed he was an angel, too? He was though. My father was really a fucking angel. He was honest. By which I mean he honored himself, honored the things he believed in. That's no small matter. I need that in myself. I pray for it. I do. I hereby pray that my father's honor will move into me and live on forever. Who knows, maybe it will. Another thing, the fucker could sing. He was a real cantor. When a cantor sings, he's calling God into the place. He's calling up all the powers of God to come and visit the tribe with strength and good health. And my father knew how to do that in spades. Maybe it wasn't your God he called, and maybe it wasn't mine, maybe it was some old power-mad prick of a God who had a temper like a bulldog and would tear apart anybody who crossed him up. No matter! The point is that when God was sung forth by my father, *He came!* He was there! You could feel Him in the whole synagogue! Now, to tell the truth, I found Him to be one highly spooky old fuck, and for my money he could've stayed where he came from before my father opened his mouth. But again, you see, what I'm trying to make clear is this: My father had this *power!* Now why shouldn't *that* be my inheritance?

"I want you all to help me. Will you? Will you help me right now? Everyone? Hold hands and make a prayer with me."

We all held hands. Percy the Cat moved closer to Peter, sat next to his leg. Roy gave up Doris's lap long enough to sit up and get with what was happening.

"I know a God," Peter said. "He lives within me. He lives within each one of us. My prayer is that He'll live our lives for us. My prayer is that whenever I'm unaware of his presence in me, I'll remember to call Him out." Peter closed his eyes.

"My dear father, Sam, Samuel, Rabbi Friedman, I've felt you here ever since this morning when we covered up your grave. You've been inside of me ever since. I pray that you stay with me forever. I pray that your honor increases my own. I pray that your strength will add itself to mine. My dear father, splendid cantor, I pray that whenever my voice rises to sing forth the God that lives within me, all your beauty and light and power will come forward to help me."

Peter's father was here. I know he was. I'm a witch, and I know these things.

We stayed in the circle for a long time, maybe three or four minutes, it's hard to judge. Just when I was beginning to feel we'd *had* the experience, because my hand was sweating and I was aware of a lot of stray thoughts trying to get into my head, Peter suddenly broke the circle. He jumped to his feet and said, "Did he shit, did he shit? Have I got any on me?"

Percy the Cat had broken loose with one of his midnight specials. His farts are always terrible but at night they seem to get worse. Peter's reaction to this one was so wildly ser:ous the rest of us started to laugh.

Cary said, "I don't think he shit, Peter. It was just a fart."

"Just a fart? Oh, thank *God!* Because if that was a fart, what's to become of us all when he starts *shitting?*" Jeanette was howling by now. She actually fell over and doubled up, hugging her belly.

Percy just lay there showing no interest whatever in the scene taking place "Look at him, look at this cat," said Peter. "He emits this fatal gas, the worst fart I've ever smelled in my life, and acts as if nothing had happened, nothing at all! We've simply got to get Mrs. Goldoni to stop feeding him six times a day. He's fat! Look at the size of him! He looks like the cat of some German! I'm ashamed, ashamed of him. Percy, for Christ sake"—he leaned over, looking straight down at the cat—"you've got to cut down on your eating! Be a cat! Be lean! Be a real panther! Go chase pigeons! Cease and desist this constant nightly farting!" Peter gasped and clutched his throat. "Oh, sweet Jesus help us, he did it *again!*"

By now we were all falling all over the floor, and the more we laughed, the more Peter carried on. He's a fantastic ham, and you could see he was digging it even more than we were. He swooped down and picked up Percy and deposited him at the top of the stairs. "Please, Percy!" he said. "Fart else-where!"

"Now I ask you," he said, rejoining the circle, "how in God's name are we to create a golden age if people like me keep shoving their own trips off on to others? That's exactly what I'm doing, you realize! It's true, it's true! It's my hang-up! I've just spent five minutes teaching a cat when to fart."

Jeanette was absolutely wrecked. She let out a whoop at this point that caused Peter to break up altogether. Pretty soon he was laughing and hollering, with the rest of us, and Jeanette was begging him to stop. "Help!" she cried. "My face hurts! I can't laugh any more!"

When we'd pulled ourselves together, somebody said they could dig some ice cream, and then everybody got a radical and virulent case of the Munchies. We all headed for the kitchen. Sally whipped out some really far-out date-and-nut cookies from Nature's Cupboard on 7th Street. And in a few minutes we were all sitting around the big table having ice cream and cookies.

Then I heard Peter saying something to Archie that made my ears pick up. "Archie, may I ask you a personal ques-tion?"

Archie said, "Sure."

And Peter said, "Are you on meth?"

"Am I *on* it?" Archie said.

"Mm. Do you shoot speed?"

"I *have*. Yeah, I've shot up once or twice."

"Now come on with that once-or-twice shit. How often? Have you shot up a lot?"

"No. Not a lot."

"More than once or twice, though. Right?"

"Well, *altogether*, yeah. But just once or twice lately."

"Tell me what you get out of it?"

"I don't know. I guess the main thing is the first rush."

"The first hour? The first big blast?"

"Yeah."

"And you feel how? Like you can do *anything?*"

"Right."

"That's what I figured. But *can* you do anything? Or does it just feel like it?"

"Well, I guess mostly it's like you *think* you can do anything. But you tend to spend the whole trip getting ready to. And you don't really do much. Except talk a lot. And everything's clear. You know what I mean, Peter? You can see everything really clear. All kinds of things make sense."

"What kind of things?"

"Oh, people, I guess. And things. You feel like you know just how everything *works*. And you do!"

"And then what?"

"Well, then you keep *on* knowing. For a couple days sometimes. Like if somebody asks you something, you can tell them the answer."

"Can you remember the answers later? For instance, now, can you remember some of the answers?"

"I, I, I, um, I wonder if we could talk about it some other time."

"Sure. But why not now?"

"I'm getting, um, *nervous*."

"Okay, we'll stop talking about it. But just that one question I'd like to get straight right now. The answers you get, on meth, they don't really stick to your ribs, huh?"

"I don't know. I guess not."

"And when somebody asks you about it later, does it always make you nervous?"

"I'm not sure. I, um. Nobody's asked me before, so I can't remember. But I really would like to stop talking about it though."

"Would you like to shoot up right now, Archie?"

"Would I like to shoot up right now?"

"Mm."

"Sure. I'd like to. I don't mean I'm going to or anything. But I'd like to. Because it's—it's really . . . Well, I'd *like* to, that's all!"

"Are you hung up on meth, Archie?"

"Hung up? No! I don't *ever* have to take it again—if I don't want to. Listen, just because a person takes it once or twice, that doesn't mean they're *addicted.*"

"What did you do with that little brown bag?"

"That little brown bag?"

"Yeah. What'd you do with it?"

"I got rid of it."

"Where?"

"I stashed it."

"Where'd you stash it?"

"This place I know."

"Your pocket?"

"No!"

"I love you, Archie."

"I love you, too, but why is everybody looking at me like—"

Sally Sunflower said, "We love you, Archie. You're our beautiful brother."

"Amen!" said Jeanette.

Doris said, "Archie knows he's very much loved in this family."

Nyoom said, "Perhaps at this juncture we might proffer a small Zap to Señor Fiesta."

"Oh, great!" said Cary Colorado. "But let me go pee first. I don't want to have kidneys on my mind."

While Cary was in the bathroom, Archie said, "Listen, I feel really good right this minute. I really love you all. I know I broke our thing, and I feel like a real turd about it, but I swear on my life I'll never do it again."

"Do what?" Jeanette asked. "Shoot up?"

"That, too. But what I meant was, I'll never bring hard dope in this house again. I swear."

"Better take it slow, Archie," Peter said. "Don't swear you'll never shoot up again. Unless you mean it. Because broken promises are, well, they're bad news. They can do real damage."

I had a hunch Peter was right. I've always had a very spooky feeling about promises, that they have to be kept. But I wondered exactly what kind of damage breaking them could cause. So I asked him.

"Well, lots!" he said. "But the main thing is, they can cause a person to not like himself. And that's the worst."

Cary Colorado came back with an empty bladder and all revved up for the Zap. He said, "You waited for me, didn't you?"

"Of course," Doris said. "What kind of a second-rate Zap would it be without you?"

We all sat at the table and joined hands. It felt good. It always does. But it wasn't one of your really major Zaps. My mind kept going and I couldn't even get it to slow down. I kept thinking, Why hasn't Archie promised never to shoot up again? I hoped he'd speak up right in the middle of the Zap and make that promise. But he didn't. Then I thought, Maybe I'm hoping *too hard*. You're not supposed to have specific desires for specific results. You're just supposed to be open and empty-minded and feel love going through you. So I relaxed every part of my body, consciously, and for one split second my mind was empty. And I thought, Ah, my mind is empty! And then of course it was *full!* Full of pride. And I knew I had to let go all over again.

I took a quick look at the others to see if their eyes were closed. Jeanette and I caught each other peeking, then we smiled and closed our eyes again. At that moment I saw, sitting right smack in the middle of my head, Hank Glyczwycz. His eyes were black with sadness and he was looking right at me. Without even thinking about it, I opened my eyes again and spoke up. "I'm sorry, everyone, but I'm not doing very well. My mind's all cluttered up."

Peter looked at me. "What kind of clutter?"

Everyone opened his eyes except Cary, but we all kept on holding hands.

"Mostly worries. For instance, I just saw the face of this man I know, a new friend who lives in Staten Island. And he's terribly sad."

"Anybody else got a cluttered head?" Peter looked around the table.

"Well," Doris said, "I might as well confess. My mind just baked a blueberry pie. That only took a few seconds. And before that—I'm sorry, Archie, this is all just in my head, remember, but I might as well say it—I was going through your *pockets!* Doesn't that take a nerve? Anyway, I'm afraid I wasn't doing much zapping."

"I get the feeling," said Cary Colorado, "that somebody here is afraid of the rest of us. It's almost as if someone is sitting here thinking the rest of us are all full of shit." Then he opened his eyes and looked at Peter. "Do you suppose there could be anything to it?"

Peter said, "I don't know, maybe. Does anybody here think we're all full of shit?"

Jeanette said, "*I* don't. I think we're all just wonderful!"

Then Archie said, "I don't think anybody here's full of shit either. I think you're all very *groovy* in fact. But I think the rest of the world is shit. Maybe that's what Cary picked up on just now. We're all sitting here holding hands and that's great. But all I'm thinking is, These people don't really know *what's happening!* Well, I *do*. This whole fucking world is doomed. And it should be, because it's a lousy place. And *I* say *that's* what's happening—*fast!*"

"I must say," said Nyoom, "there is massive evidence to be summoned in support of such a view. But I'm not certain it hasn't already been summoned and found wanting. That is to say, I find the view myopic."

"C'mon, man," Archie said. "What the hell's 'myopic' mean?"

"Short-sighted. I speak with affection, and respect, Archibald, dear brother. I realize (A) that your father has retired to the drunk tank at Bellevue, (B) that you have recently received a rather urgent communication from the draft board, (C) the musical group you had such hopes for has dissolved, and (D) that you have developed what is perhaps a somewhat worrisome fondness for Methadrine. I can see how in such circumstances one might imagine that the sky of *communitas* under which we labor here might seem just faintly overcast with futility. However, it is possible to view these—"

"Nyoom," Archie said, "I'm going to have to level with you. You're my brother and all, but I don't know what the fuck you're talking about, man. I really don't."

Nyoom raised his hands gently, palms up, and nodded. "Lucidity has never been my long suit. I yield the floor."

I think everyone expected Peter to take over at this point, but Cary was bursting with things to say. His eyes were glittering and his face shone. He licked his lips and said,

"Can I say what I think Nyoom might have meant? I think he was trying to say we can't judge *real* reality by the material scene. Because, man, *God* is reality, and anything you can look at with your eyes is just one of the faces He's wearing. It's all Maya, illusion, appearance. What's real is the thing *behind* what you see. Call it God. Or the Creative Force. Or call it *Schmidlapp!* It doesn't matter. Because all it is is *life*. The life principle. Livingness. Man's task is to fit himself into life. No, he doesn't even *have* to. He doesn't have to fit himself in. He *already* fits. His job is to see *how,* and then *cooperate like mad!* Please let me get this point over, because I'm dying to say it out loud." At exactly this point poor Cary's eyes went blank, and his face took on a desperate expression. "Oh, *shit!*" he said, "I lost it! God-fucking-damnit, I lost my thought!"

I told him I could fill him in if he wanted me to. He grabbed my hand across the table and said, "Oh, please do! Only I guess I shouldn't be getting so excited about it, should I?" He smiled. "What if I *do* lose my point? There's still God! Oh!" He pounded the table with the palms of both hands. "Now it's all come back! This is *tremendous!* Do you see what's happened? I gave up! I remembered the only thing that's important is God, and the second I did that, I got my thought back. Wow!"

Peter and Doris were right with him, smiling and beaming and nodding their heads. But Archie wasn't.

"I'm getting really nervous!" he said. "I don't know what the fuck *any*body's talking about!"

"Okay, okay, okay!" Cary cried. "I'm going to get really specific, *right now!* Okay? Let's say a person has to go downtown and hassle with the draft board, right? Is that specific enough? Okay, what does he do? He thinks, Ah, God is taking the form of the draft board today, only the draft board doesn't *know* that. I do, though. And I know I'm one of God's faces, too! Therefore, I'll just go right downtown and tell them who I am!"

"Right, right," Archie said. "You just trot down to the draft board and tell them you're God, huh?" Archie scrunched his face all out of shape to show what he thought of the idea. But he's one of these people who always look beautiful even when they're thinking ugly and taking the grimmest possible view of things.

"No!" Cary shouted. "Of course not! What do you think I am, a complete asshole? Naturally you don't go down and tell them you're God. You go down there and *act like a person who knows it!* That's what I did in Denver. I called them Sir, because I respected them! I said, 'Sir, I know you people are mistaken about this entire war thing. The Vietnamese are my brothers just like you are. If you insist upon taking me against my will, I promise you I'll fuck up, because I can't cooperate with the murder of my brothers. *That's final,'* I said. And I didn't get drafted."

"Will did it that way, too, baby," Jeanette said. "And he's in prison."

"That doesn't matter!" Cary pounded the table. "He's still God in prison! And he's not killing innocent people! What's prison? I could get through it. 'I can fast, I can meditate, I can think.' Isn't that what it says in *Siddhartha?* Prison is fabulous for fasting and meditating and thinking. Look at Malcolm X! Look at Eldridge Cleaver! Those guys were *created* in prisons. They got together with God and created *themselves.*"

"You're doing beautifully, Cary," Nyoom said. "Now why don't you proceed to the question of Methadrine? I've been given to understand that behind bars it's in rather short supply."

"Methadrine is shit!" Cary said. "I know because I've had it. All you get is this one stupid rush, and then you spend three days wishing to Christ you were unconscious! There's

228

no real high in it, man, it's just *hysteria!* I can get a better high from meditating—and no crash landing either."

"Well that's just great for you," Archie said. "I'm just tickled to death to hear about how high you are all the time. But *I'm* not. And neither is 99 per cent of everybody else in the world."

"I'm *not* high all the time, and I didn't claim to be. But I'm learning. And so are a lot of other people. Millions. Millions of people are learning to get high and stay high. And that's because we're waking up. The whole world is waking up. The whole world is God and God is waking up and learning how to stay high. Amen, goddamnit!"

Jeanette said amen. Then I said it. And pretty soon we were all saying it at once. Except Archie and Peter. Archie said, "Amen my ass." And Peter said, "I'm going to bed."

Then he got up from the table and picked up his ice cream dish and his water glass. "You all realize the day I've had? I buried my papa this morning and flew across a continent. I feel like I'm about to collapse."

Roy said, "Let me take care of your dishes?"

"No, no. Thank you, lad. Everybody wipes his own butt around here. Including me."

We all paraded into the kitchen with our dirty dishes, but Archie stayed at the table, alone and forlorn. Through the doorway I watched him blinking and squinting his eyes nervously while he finger-traced the ring left by someone's water glass. Peter went back in there and stood behind Archie. He put his hands on his shoulders and said, "I feel too poor to go to sleep without a toke of grass. You want one with me?"

I couldn't hear Archie's answer, but it was super-affirmative. Doris watched the two of them go upstairs together and when she saw me watching, too, she said, "He never gives up on anyone. He doesn't know how."

WILL'S GREENHOUSE, SUNSET, FRIDAY, SEPTEMBER 26, 1969

I can't see the sun itself from up here. There are too many buildings in the way. But I can see what it's doing to the sky and I find the whole thing much too beautiful.

Cary just left. He brought some of the plants back up. While he was here, we watched together for a while. I asked him if he could stand it. He said, "Yeah, I can stand it. It *wrecks* me—but I like to be wrecked."

I'm not sure I do. When a thing is too beautiful, something in me aches, and I don't entirely dig it. I suppose it's lonesomeness I feel. Cary isn't much help either. He's got this thing going with God and it's obviously so heavy and so satisfying to him, he doesn't seem to need other people as much as I do.

When he left just now, I looked at the sky again and shivered all the way down inside, even though it's not at all cold. Then I found this old denim jacket of Will's and put it on. It feels really good to be inside of a man's sleeves.

Will must have shoulders like that gold Prometheus at Rockefeller Center.

I wonder if my father missed me today?

I didn't get to class because I was too busy writing. It took me all afternoon to get last night's entry completed. I left out the interruption for sleep because it didn't seem important, but now I feel I have to confess the omission so my journal won't catch me lying to it. Anyway, the break came when I was describing Peter's reaction to Percy's farting.

At that point, when I went to bed—it must have been at least four, maybe five o'clock—there were still sounds of activity coming from the attic. Archie and Peter were still up there talking. Archie was probably operating on leftover speed, but I don't know where Peter gets his energy. Anyway, with the attic right at the top of the stairs over our alcove, I couldn't help but hear a few choice bits, especially when Peter raised his voice. I suppose you could call it shouting, but I think of it as passionate oratory. These are some of the scraps I picked up:

"Of course God's a fuck-up. Why shouldn't He be? Aren't you? How can He straighten out if you won't?"

"I'm going to say one last thing, and then we're both going to sleep: Your generation is the luckiest generation in all human history. Your fathers have handed you a technology capable of transforming the planet earth into the kingdom of heaven—in your lifetime. Unless you blow it. And I mean you, Archie Fiesta. Who the hell did you think was running this show? You are, boy! You are!"

"*Mr. Fiesta. I'm sorry to inform you, you're not turned on yet. You're a head, but you're not turned on. Learn the difference fast, or the whole world will go down the drain!* . . . *No, it won't! No, it won't, goddamnit! Because I won't let it! Do you hear me?*"

———————

"*If you keep seeing shit everywhere you look, don't you know that's dangerous? Don't you know you're going to build your life in the form your vision takes?*"

———————

"*You want to know why I take such pains with you? It's because I need you! That's why, shithead!*"

———————

"*Consciousness, goddamnit!* Consciousness! CONSCIOUS-NESS! *CONSCIOUSNESS!*"

———————

I think it must have been at just about this point, when Peter was shouting for consciousness, that I finally lost mine. Or a part of it anyway. It didn't feel like real sleep, because there was too much going on in it. Anyway, when I woke up just before dawn I felt sure Sara the Ghost had been here visiting me. My mind was so tired I might have been hallucinating. But I'm inclined to think it was really Sara and that she was trying to tell me something.

She had some other people with her, real darlings, too, but I can't remember anything specific about them. I just remember feeling pleased that Sara had found some other ghosts to keep her company, and wondering why they were all hovering around our alcove. But in the state I was in I couldn't ask. My mouth wasn't working. Or maybe it was just my will that was out cold.

Sara was saying, "Bodies are awfully important, honey, bodies are awfully important." I knew she meant something specific and terribly simple, and yet my mind couldn't get hold of it. So I began to feel a kind of panic, and it was the panic that made me open my eyes and sit up. I heard myself saying, "So what? What about it?" right out loud—and I'm afraid my tone was awfully irritable.

Suddenly, I knew.

All sorts of things I'd been puzzled and alarmed over clicked instantly into focus, and *I knew*. But still I had to go through all the motions of finding out, just as if I didn't know.

Roy was next to me. He seemed to be fast asleep, but it was too dark to tell. Ever since he repaired the skylight upstairs, we get a little light in our alcove each morning, but it was too dim for seeing what I had to see. So I lit the candle and held it near his arm. It looked so frail and skinny sticking out of his T-shirt. Even before I saw the needle mark, I had to clench my jaws to keep from crying. And there it was, a tiny pink hole right over the vein in the crook of his arm.

I asked myself, What are you going to do now, earth mother? Sit here and cry? Lay your head on his shoulder, bathe his arm in kisses and tears? As much as I wanted to do those things, I couldn't. It would be like some truly unforgivable act of disloyalty, or faithlessness. After all, this wasn't just some skinny little jackass with tracks on his arm. It was Roy. No, not Roy, *John*. It was John, ally of my childhood, John, my wise guru, my strong friend, my tall son, my loyal brother, my soul's lover. Knowing these things about him, making them new and real all over again, there was nothing left to cry over. And the minute I felt truly okay again, Roy opened his eyes and looked at me with a truly okay smile.

I said, "How long have you been awake?"

"Long enough," he said, "to know you've been checking out my needle mark."

"Well," I said, flashing defense, "if *I* showed up with a needle mark, wouldn't you check it out?"

"Sure, I would. Listen, I'm not bummed. I'm glad we're talking about it."

"You shot up with Archie, right?"

"Yeah."

"What was it like?"

"Groovy. And super-horrible. I'm sort of glad I did it. Now I know I could never be a speed freak."

"Did you do it a lot?"

"Twice. Once one afternoon, and then about four or five hours later. Remember the other day when I came in all fucked up?"

I nodded.

"Well, it was a couple of days before that. But it took a lot of time to come down, it was really shitty. I had to stay stoned out on grass to keep from falling apart. I thought I loved him, Witch. And I *do!* But I mean I thought I was *in* love with him, and now I know I'm not. Witch, I want to tell you my new theory. Being *in* love isn't ever *really* loving, it's just wanting. And it isn't any good. It's all aching and misery. I say fuck it! Do you think I'm right about this?"

"I don't know, but I'm going to think about it a lot. Because it sounds just like what I had with Delano that summer. Remember how I just cried and ate for two whole

234

months? I hated it, and I gained seven pounds. Did you know I was starting to get that way about Archie, too?"

"Yeah, I figured you were. But you broke it during that acid trip, right?"

"Right. I saw his soul, Roy. It's very beautiful, too, but it's dark and sort of heavy-looking. Did you see it that night?"

"No, I was just digging his bod, and it almost freaked me out. You know something, Witch? I could become a sex fiend, a real maniac."

"Couldn't anybody?"

"I only know about me. I would have done anything, just to touch him. That's why I shot up with him. Because I figured then we'd go to bed and all. It's really spooky to think about."

"Did anything ever happen?"

"Bedwise?"

"Mm."

"Yes and no. We went to bed. But then I realized Archie wasn't digging it, so nothing really happened. I don't think he digs sex, not with anybody, not even chicks. All he wants to do is keep his head fucked up with dope."

"Why would he go to bed with you at all if he didn't really want to?"

"I hate to say this, Witch, but I think he was hustling me. I had forty dollars left of that bread from your mother, and I let him buy a quarter of an ounce of meth with it. It was stupid, I know, but I was sort of hypnotized. So was he. He was hypnotized by the idea of getting some speed and I was hypnotized by the idea of going to bed with him. Only we didn't really talk about it, we just sort of got into it. It was a mess. Then after we shot up, Archie decided to sell off half of the stuff in dime bags to raise bread for some more."

235

"What are dime bags?"

"Little ten-dollar packages. You get about two blasts each out of them. Anyway, the next thing I knew, we were into dealing. Or *he* was. Because that's when I cut out on him. I said, 'Archie, I love you, man, but I'm not dealing out of Canal Street.' "

"Well, why did *he*? I mean if he had to deal the stuff, why not do it out of that other place, the one on Spring Street?"

"That's another story. Spring Street is hot. That whole building is crawling with dealers. You never saw such types in your life, Witch, real hoods, and they deal heavy. I mean *quantity!* And there was a bust there three days ago. I saw the whole thing from the window. About eight cops' cars, a real fucking *raid!* I thought we were next, and so did Archie. But you know what he did? You won't believe this. I said, 'Archie, let's flush this shit down the toilet, *quick!'* And he said, 'Never panic, man,' and he put the stuff in his pocket, walked out in the hall and down the stairs, right past the cops. He even shot a peace sign at them! I swear! I was right behind him! But I wasn't carrying anything, so I figured I was reasonably safe. Then he brought the stuff over here and stashed it in his room.

"Let me tell you what scares me about Archie. He likes that stuff so much, he'd take any kind of a chance for it. No kidding, you should just get a look at some of the goons coming in and out of that Spring Street pad. Remember Winston? Well, I never see him—but those two buddies of his are in and out of there all the time. I recognized the one that took my pants."

"Did he see you see him?"

"Yeah, he saw me see him all right. It was on the corner, about a half a block from the building, and there were two cops right across the street. I thought, Wow, I could get this cat arrested! But y'know I felt like I'm more on *his* side than I am on the cops', does that make sense?"

I said I thought it did.

Roy said, "Witch, you know what I really hate about this revolution? It makes you think about *sides*. You always have to think about which one you're on."

I've just been doing some figuring, and something has to be terribly wrong. It's only 16 days since Roy and I got on the bus in Detroit. I've written enough in that time to fill a whole book. If I keep going at this rate—say 5000 pages a year for 50 years, my life will be 250,000 pages long and fill 1000 volumes! This is really distressing. Because even if I cut down to a measly 10 per cent of my present output—which doesn't seem at all likely—it'd still be 100 volumes long, and my publishers would force me to cut even more! Using small print, maybe it could be crammed into 50 books.

CANAL STREET, SEPTEMBER 27, 1969, 4:30 A.M.

Ingmar Bergman calls this time of night the hour of the wolf. The darkest thoughts in your soul come to the surface and you can't *not* look at them.

What's scaring me is something Peter said about the United States government. It's the single most horrifying thing I've ever heard in my entire life.

He said the U.S. government is certifiably insane because it demonstrates the three classic symptoms of psychotic paranoia:

   a. Delusions of Grandeur (Thinks God intends it to run the world.)
   b. Persecution Complex (Convinced the other guy is out to get him.)
   c. Repressed Homosexuality (Gun fixation.)

What makes it psychotic is that it's gotten out of control. (Murders a couple of thousand people a week.)

CAPRICORN CAPERS, INC., MONDAY, OCTOBER 6, 1969

This is my first entry after a ten-day fast from writing. Now my literary body is all purged and lean, and I have a wealth of rich material for breaking my fast.

First: A *ménage à trois* has been going on at Canal Street right under my nose, and I didn't know a thing about it until yesterday morning.

Second: Archie has disappeared. His clothes are gone and everything.

Third: Sally and I have jobs. We mail catalogs and samples for this novelty manufacturer on East Broadway. It's probably temporary, because pretty soon they're installing an addressograph system. But meanwhile we get two dollars an hour, and it's sort of fun for a change to *have* to be someplace every morning. Besides, now I can contribute to the Grocery Pig again.

Fourth: Roy moved out of the alcove.

———————

Sunday morning, while Roy and I were still in bed, Jeanette came down from the attic in her robe. She said hi and trotted on down to the kitchen. I didn't see anything unusual or even interesting about it until a few minutes later when she traipsed by a second time—on her way back up with a tray of coffee cups—*three* of them!

A few minutes later when Roy woke up, I told him about Jeanette taking coffee up to the attic in her robe. I said, "Do you suppose the three of them sleep together?"

He said, "Sure. Didn't you know that?"

I was flabbergasted, mostly because he knew about it and I didn't.

"Why didn't you tell me?" I said.

"I didn't think it was important."

"Well, it's *interesting*, isn't it? I mean isn't it worth telling, for godsake?"

"Yeah, I guess. But I took it for granted you knew."

I was so pissed off, I started to pout. "You don't tell me hardly *any*thing any more."

"That's not true. I just told you about Archie and me, didn't I?"

"I guess. But still, I feel sort of—I don't know—*left out*. You mean Doris and Peter and Jeanette have been sleeping together up there all this time, and everybody knows it but me?"

"I don't know *who* knows it. But there's nothing secret about it, Witch."

"Who told *you*?"

He thought for a minute. "Archie."

"Where *is* Archie, by the way? He's never around any more."

"I don't know where he is. Peter told me they'd made an agreement, and then Archie just sort of disappeared."

"What agreement?"

"Archie promised he'd never shoot up again unless he came to Peter first. The deal was that Peter would hold his stash for him up in the attic, hidden in some secret place only Peter'd know about, and then if Archie ever thought he just *had* to have a fix, Peter promised he'd give it to him himself."

"Wow! Do you think he would?"

"He promised, so he'd *have* to! But first he'd try to talk Archie out of it. That was the whole idea behind the agreement. Peter wanted to get a crack at him sometime when he was on his way to the needle."

"What happened? Did he bring Peter his entire stash?"

"Nah. Just the one dime bag he had in his pocket."

"Then he *did* have something in his pocket that night! Remember how Doris's mind picked it up when we were all trying to Zap him?"

"Yeah. Then Peter picked it up from Doris. So did Archie, I guess. Anyway, he gave him what was in his pocket, and Peter's got it hidden up there."

"And now Archie's disappeared entirely?"

"Yeah."

"What about his things?"

"They're gone, too. He must've snuck in when nobody was here. Nyoom noticed it a couple of days ago."

"Do you suppose he's at that Spring Street place?"

"Could be. But he doesn't answer the door. I've been there four times looking for him."

"Roy, do you think Archie is doomed?"

Roy took a moment to think about it. Then he said, "I don't want to make guesses like that, Witch. It's like writing a person off, to say he's doomed. It doesn't seem fair."

Suddenly I had a dreadful idea. "Roy, why don't you move into Archie's bed. It's empty, isn't it?"

He said, "Don't you want me here with you?"

Obviously he liked the idea. My heart sank. "Well, it's awfully *nice* sleeping with you. But maybe we'll both dig being able to stretch out. This *is* awfully narrow you know. How do *you* feel about it?"

He thought for a minute. "Okay, I'll move in with them. And whenever we want to sleep together, we can. Right?"

I knew he wouldn't want to, and I'd be too proud to suggest it.

"Right," I said.

Last night I missed him terribly. But how can you snuggle with someone who wishes he were somewhere else? The answer is, you can't! Not only can't but *mustn't!*

WEDNESDAY, OCTOBER 8, 1969

I've been wondering lately if all the others get the same thing I do from our mealtime Zap, so last night at the table I asked everyone to say what they were feeling.

SALLY: We all know we live inside of God's head, right? But when we close our eyes together, we can see how really *pretty* it is in here.

CARY: It's communion. Jesus said do this in commemoration of me. And then they passed the potatoes. Only they should never have called it the Last Supper. They should've called it the First Zap.

ROY: Me, too. That's what I get out of it. I dig the super-Christiness of it, knowing we're all in the same place in our heads, loving each other all at once. Only I'm not *thinking* about it like that. Mostly I'm just *into* it. And then after, if I was nervous or anything, I start being calm instead.

JEANETTE: I can't say, because for me it's not a word thing. It just *feels* great. I feel like, *Man, I've got company!* You know?

DORIS: I welcome any opportunity to hold hands with a tableful of beautiful people. It makes me happy, that's all.

NYOOM: The Zap is a spiritual apéritif, if you will. Infinity visits the alimentary canal, sanctifies the digestive system, as it were. Hmmm?

PETER: I can't add a thing. I agree with everybody.

THE AUTOMAT, FRIDAY, OCTOBER 10, 1969

Horn and Hardart make delicious macaroni and cheese, but I can't even taste it today. I've been in a down head all week. No, it's worse than that. I've been teetering back and forth between vaguely miserable and desperately depressed, with only the briefest letups in between, and I don't know what's wrong. *Everything* seems to be—but I can't single out the thing that bugs me most.

I just got paid a few minutes ago. It didn't help at all. And I'd sort of been counting on it, too, because last week, getting the first pay envelope of my life really turned me on. It only had $28 in it, but to a girl who'd never earned a dime, $28 can do a real number on her head. The first thing I wanted to do was buy presents, so I spent the afternoon shopping (and staying away from Central Park J.C., where I'm headed the minute I finish this entry—my first class since the day of the Staten Island disasterette). I thought having earned the money for the presents would make me feel as if I'd made them by hand or something. Maybe so. But I couldn't find anything anybody'd want in any of the stores. So I contributed half the money to the Grocery Pig, and got this fantastic wage-earner's high out of it that lasted the whole weekend. I also chipped in with Nyoom on a lid of grass—another very heavy first—and that pushed me right over the top. I was flying.

Monday the dark moved in on me. All week long everything's been unreal. Today at noon when Mrs. Oggins gave me my second pay envelope with $31 and some change in it, I hardly even bothered to count it. How quickly one becomes jaded! All week long I've been feeling like a wage slave, and seeing these little scraps of money only made it worse.

But that's not what this big depression is really about. I know if my head was straight, I could get behind the job and dig it.

For a while I was *sure* keeping this journal was screwing me up. I was so tired when I left Will's greenhouse after my September 19th entry, I swore off these notebooks for good. I'd been overdoing it, so I decided all writing must be some kind of sickness. Anyway, I was so certain I was right, I went around for ten days in a great glow of virtue like some drunk who's just given up the sauce.

When this sadness began to move in, I wanted terribly to write about it and was afraid to. If writing about really interesting things is sick, then writing about sadness would have to be downright evil.

One night I asked Peter if he thought keeping a journal was a sick ego thing.

He said, "I don't play the sickness game any more. I've given it up."

"You mean there's no such thing as real sickness?"

"Nah. It's just a variation of the old Us-and-Them game. It used to be Us is good and Them is bad. Now it's Us is healthy, Them is sick."

"I'm confused. Aren't there people who really need help?"

Peter nodded about three times. "You betcha. Everybody needs help."

"But nobody's sick?"

"If you're playing that game, sure. *Everybody's* sick. But the game doesn't really help any more. It got too popular. All the nuthouses are jammed. It's a bust. None of the old games are worth a shit. We've got to give them all up and start seeing it like it is."

"Well, all right, but how *is* it?"

"That depends," he said. "What are we talking about? Are we talking about journal-writing?"

"I'd like to, because it's been bugging me a lot."

"Well then, *you're* the expert here. You better say how it is. Don't ask me. How *is* it, anyway?"

Continued a few minutes later, on the uptown subway

I thought for a minute or two, while Peter lit cigarettes for us. "I guess what bothers me is I don't know why I'm doing it. I used to think I was taking notes for my autobiography so I could get famous and reveal to the world what a big phony my mother is. But I don't *really* want to hurt her."

"Then why not find a way to show your *own* values without hurting *any*body?"

"Yes, but then I think, Who am *I?* Sometimes I have these big delusions of grandeur about writing some fabulous book that makes the whole world high. Which is really stupid, because I'm not all that high myself!"

"Maybe not, but that doesn't mean you're sick! Is that what you do in that journal of yours, call yourself ugly names?"

"Sometimes."

"Does it *feel* good to do that?"

"No. But I'm trying to be truthful."

"Then *be* truthful. But don't play games, and don't engage in name-calling. Let me ask you something. Isn't it just possible you might write a book someday that could shed one tiny ray of light on some little corner of the world? Of course it's possible. *Any*one might do that. So isn't it conceivable that someone with a little talent might even do somewhat better than that? *You*, for instance? Hey hey hey! Why are you trying not to smile?"

"I guess because I'm embarrassed."

"Dear little Witch," he said, "you have a capacity for spreading love in the world. That's an *angelic* capacity. There's nothing at all embarrassing about it. Do you understand what I'm telling you?"

"I have an angelic capacity?"

He looked at me and nodded. "Mm-hm. We all have. That's why people are so special." Then he said, "Tell me something. You're the head psychiatrist around here. Do you think I'm sick to believe that?

"No, I think it's *beautiful!*"

"Well, then, I think I'd better tell you that my case has been diagnosed by another crack professional, and according to him, you're wrong. There's nothing beautiful about it at all. No kidding, I mean it. An old colleague of mine from the Coast stopped here in the spring. He took a look at my life here on Canal Street, spent the afternoon, had dinner, the works—and in the evening he declared that I was not only sick but a positive menace to all the people in this house. He diagnosed them, too. He said they were without exception incapable of adjusting to the real world. He told me what I'd created here was a monument to neurosis held together by the demonic force of my own conceit. We were all riding for a fall, a big one! He could guarantee it! He said the minute these victims of mine were forced by reality to hit the streets again, they'd fall apart like dolls made out of matchsticks and library paste. Now what do you think of *that*, Doc?"

"Well, obviously I think he's *insane!*"

"Now now! Steady there! No name-calling!"

"Well, not insane, maybe. But he's badly mistaken." After a moment of quiet, I said, "Isn't he?"

"Not necessarily. Maybe in a certain sense, by the rules of his game, some of us *are* doomed. Maybe all of us, who knows? It's dangerous as hell to live by your own sense of reality. I can't promise any of you you won't end up in prisons or concentration camps or insane asylums. In fact those are all very real possibilities. You realize that, don't you? The old games still have a lot of power over us, Witch, and most of them have the law behind them."

"I was just thinking of Will, in prison."

"Me, too. I'm always thinking of Will. Shall we send him one?"

He held out his hands and I took them, and we sat there on the floor of the attic sending love to Will in prison. After a few minutes, with his eyes still closed, Peter said, "Will is in prison because he believes in the wisdom of the Self. The Self is the only master. Do you know what the Self is, Witch?"

I said, "No, not really."

He opened his eyes and smiled. "Well, neither do I, come to think of it. But I know where it's to be found. In our desires. We have to trust them and follow them and experience them. We have to live them out."

"No matter what?"

"No matter what. If we desire a thing, a hundred per cent, with everything we are, heart, soul and body—then we'd better get at it."

"What about the mind, Peter?"

"Oh, the mind's nothing, just an instrument. Don't give it too much importance. If you do, it'll drag you into game-playing. The mind is a servant to the Self. Keep it that way. Keep it peaceful and efficient. Don't let it take over the show. They sometimes do that, you know. Quite often in fact. The mind tends to be a usurper. It's always grabbing up authority that really belongs to the being itself—the soul, the heart, the body. And it doesn't work. You can't *think* your life. It's got to be lived—with everything you are."

———————

My hand is trembling as I write this. Just as I was trembling when Peter said it. He noticed it, too. He put his hand on my head and said, "You're frightened, aren't you?" I nodded because I could hardly speak. He said, "Is there anything else you want to talk about tonight, Witch?" And I said no.

Why? Why didn't I tell him the truth? Why didn't I tell him it wasn't just writing that frightened me, but my entire life? Why didn't I tell him I'd been wandering around in a daze for the past week? Why didn't I tell him I'm worried about my father to the point of obsession? Why haven't I told him or anyone else about my visit to Staten Island?

———————

Peter said, "Why are you trembling so, Witch?"

"What you said. It's very scary. A person's got to live his life with everything he is. Wow," I said, flashing on the old personality. "That could get a gal in real trouble, couldn't it!" Ha ha ha.

249

And Peter said, "Yes. It could. But then, what's wrong with trouble? Is there some other route to the Self?"

I just missed my goddam stop. Which means I've got to ride all the way back to 96th Street, change trains, and then go all the way downtown to Columbus Circle. By the time I get there, class will be half over.

I wonder if something in me made this happen on purpose?

Maybe I should go back to Canal Street and leave my poor father alone. Besides, what would he think of me in this fucked-up condition?

Subway platform, 96th Street

An old memory just popped into my head for no reason whatever, and for no reason whatever I think I'll write it down:

Mother is standing in the doorway of her gorgeous Belle Woods kitchen, a kitchen gorgeous enough for a magazine cover. Her face is all splotched with frustration that looks just like terror. She and I have just come back from Bowling Green, Ohio, dragging behind us in a U-Haul trailer some old wreck of a cabinet called a Hoosier kitchen, which she "practically stole!" from an old lady there who didn't know what it was worth. All the way back to Detroit she's been gloating over her triumph, marveling at the skill with which she wields her checkbook, only to discover, the very second she sees it installed at home, that the "absolute steal!" doesn't fit in with Formica and General Electric and Vinyl. It looks, in fact, like someone has taken a rather untidy but generously proportioned turd and mounted it exquisitely in the show window of Hudson's Department Store. Mother is an antique freak, and the shock is more than she can bear. She goes into a depression that lasts for days and days and days. My own sympathies of course are with the old lady who's been robbed! I wonder why Mother doesn't simply haul the hideous thing back to her and forget the whole matter? And now I wonder why I'm *still* wondering about it a thousand years after the fact?

On the downtown subway

I bought some Chiclets a minute ago and saw my own face in the mirror over the gum machine.

Witch, shall we lay it right on the line? The face you're wearing these days is your mother's, isn't it?

Sorry. But yes.

THE LADIES' ROOM AT CAPRICORN
CAPERS, MONDAY, OCTOBER 13, 1969

I'm sitting on the toilet, constipated, but it gives me a place to write.

My sadness continues, and the weather is torturing me. It's perfect. The sky is such a piercing blue it goes right through my heart like a dagger. Every time I glance *up*, I feel the blade twisting. Even the air today is clean. My unhappiness grows fat on it. But I don't have any tears to shed. I just feel dead. I drag my body around like a corpse. And act. I'm always acting these days. Scorpio has taken over my life. I feel this excruciating shame for the mood I'm in and so I disguise it when I'm with others. Which is seldom. I've been avoiding everyone, even the ones most likely to help me. Why don't I go to Peter? He was wonderful to me last time. Or to Doris? Or to my dear brother, Roy? Or to my beautiful, wise sister, Sally Sunflower? Or *anybody?*

I feel some ugly, stubborn secret inside myself. It's like a lump of tightness right under my belly button. Jesus, I'm probably giving myself cancer right this second! And what's worse, I don't even care. So what if I died? Big deal. There'd be one less phony in the world.

The most awful thing to bear is that everything I've been so certain of seems to be collapsing inside of me. Roy and I vowed to stay high no matter what. I've broken the vow. I've been doing a what-if-we're-wrong scene for days now. What if I and all my friends are wrong about everything? What if the Vietnamese really are dying to get their hands on San Francisco? What if marijuana is really the devil's weed? What if misery is the natural condition of man and it's really foolish to fight it? What if love is just a soft, decadent blight wiping out man's powers of survival? What if war and booze and $ are really the keys to the kingdom of heaven?

What would Timothy Leary say to me in this mood? He'd say, "My dear child, your thinking is psychedelically unsound." And he'd laugh at me. No. No, he wouldn't. He'd give me a joint and tell me to be happy.

But I don't want a joint. I want to know what's wrong with me. I want to know why I've been running all over New York for the past week wearing my mother's face. I want to know what happened to my own.

Don't I?

Later, Central Park J.C. Cafeteria, after class

The 15th will be Moratorium Day. This morning at work I started wondering if my father'd be holding class on Wednesday. So, having nothing better to do with the afternoon, I decided to come up here and see what's going on.

It was horrible, of course. Everything is these days. But I don't think I mind as much as I did last week. I'm getting used to being a miserable wretch, pretending to my loved ones—who never believe me—that everything's fine.

When I went in, Hank looked at me in a friendly way, but

253

he didn't actually smile. It was obvious he'd never expected to see me again. But there I was, and he didn't quite know what to do about it. Poor man, how could he when I don't know myself?

Anyway, he was conducting a Questions and Answers session on Vietnam. But he did it sort of mechanically, like a sleepwalker, or someone too tired and sad to care what was happening. I wonder if he was depressed before he saw me, or *because?*

The discussion was pretty tacky. I felt as if I'd heard it all a hundred times. All the arguments began to rhyme with one another.

Some painted-up chick with a bouffant hairdo said she didn't understand how the United States could be *completely* wrong. Hank said no country could ever be excused for going against its own constitution and the United Nations Charter.

"Not even to save people from Communism?" she said.

Ordinarily I think he would have lit into her, but not today. All he did was look at her and shake his head. "No, miss, not even for that."

A boy named Terry spoke up. "I'd like to ask *her* a question. I'd like to know where we get the right to save *any*body from *any*thing—if it's something they *want.*"

"How do *you* know what they want?" the girl shrieked.

"Because they been fighting for it for twenty-five years, and nobody's been able to beat them—not even *us!* That's why!"

"If we haven't beat them," she spat out, "it's only because we're too *humane* to use the H bomb!"

"*Neither* side is using the bomb," Terry said, "so that doesn't make any sense! We haven't beat them because we can't! And if we're so *humane,* what are we using napalm for?"

Somebody else got into it then, and pretty soon the whole room was in an uproar. Hank just watched. I don't think he was even listening, but he might have been. After a while he took a piece of chalk and printed with big letters on the blackboard: NO CLASS WEDNESDAY. It was only twenty minutes to four, but he picked up his notebook and walked out of the room. Some of the students left a few minutes later. One boy passed out black armbands. I took one and thanked him for it.

Then I came down here to look for Hank. But he wasn't here.

And neither am I, not really.

I died.

My ghost is riding home with my father on the ferry. The rest of the world is sunny today, but there are dark clouds over Staten Island, and all along the ferry route the bay is choppy. An angry wet wind tears through my father's dark hair and his face is wild with despair. He looks into the distance, but his eyes are missing, and the black sockets aren't really seeing. I know if I weren't with him, by his side at this railing, protecting him, he might

A few minutes later, on the subway platform, Columbus Circle

I'm obsessed! Obsessed with my parents! They're all I think about!

Suddenly I saw, *really saw*, what I've been doing! This whole hangup I'm developing of seeing my father as a tragic figure in need of his fair daughter's rescue is a bunch of shit. How can *I* save anybody? I can't even keep my *own* head straight!

And that's what I came to New York for. To get away from families and all the horror that goes with them. The

255

fact that I sprang from the loins of H. Gliss no longer has any novelty value for me. I stopped toying with that little number about two weeks ago, when I gave up writing in this notebook long enough to sit still and *think*.

As for my mother, I don't even know who she is! When I close my eyes and try to think of her, all I get are three pictures. None of the three is real of course.

But then, how could they be, my dearie, when *your mother* isn't real?

Picture A. She's a little girl, skipping rope, trying to impress hell out of somebody across the street, but she tripped and fell. The picture was obviously snapped one second after the pratfall, and one second before the full indignity of it hits her. It's the realest of the three, and although I don't dig the chick, she is kind of touching.

Picture B is a real specimen of my mind's evil. It seems to have been snapped at midnight in the kitchen of some whorehouse where she's bawling out the girls.

I'm the girls—all of them! All you can see of Mother in this one is a red housecoat, a lit cigarette, two deadly eyes, bitter as the shit of little beetles. These really tough, nutty, nasty eyes are letting you have it straight, they're not fiddling with the facts for one second, they're laying it right on the line: You're a louse and a bitch and you caused the *Whole Thing!* (What whole thing? The ruin of her life. What else?)

Ten seconds later, on the subway

Now in *Picture C* we have a change of mood. Mother's just as happy as a little piss ant in this one. She's been to Maine Chance, where they not only did her up brown (Roux #7) but flattered her butt off in the bargain. At the moment of posing, Mother begins to enact her own favorite self-portrait, and her performance is stunning. She's all teeth and dinner ring, a poisonous green emerald the size of her elbow, and it's glittering away like mad. Mr. Random, whom I refuse to call Daddy in my notes . . . (To his face, I used to do it, but not in here. Not in here, I can't! This notebook is my fucking castle, and the token I used to get on this train was bought by me. I'm no longer eating your food, Random, no longer driving your cars, no longer— Um, excuse me! Back to the photo of mother.) She's posing, that is to say she's got her teeth and her jewels and her hairdo all propped up in front of the cameras, on a Very Special Occasion. Mr. Random has just been elected president of the world and *somehow* (!) word has leaked out that Mother was secretly responsible for the entire thing. She's being sublimely modest about it, so charming and self-effacing in fact that the photographer will have to scrape her off his lens with a blowtorch.

And this is the dame I've been worrying about *hurting?* Christ! Maxwell's Silver Hammer couldn't faze her.

As for Hank Glyczwycz: All I see is a schoolteacher who's such a flop his students are trying to get him canned. And why shouldn't they? He's morbid. He's bitter. He's angry. And he's probably suicidal.

Tough Ka-shit-ski, says the Polish-Jewish-Irish bitch, Gloria Glyczwycz. It's time to save *yourself*, doll-baby. You've been doing okay so far. You've been keeping your head reasonably straight for an ex-WASP semi-bastard from Belle Woods, Plastic County, Michigan, in the heart of Amerika. Now is no time to get sucked back into the old blood-ties-are-strongest fairytale. Your fascist mother and your Communist father are nothing but two spooky profiles of the same old head, a pair of matching relics from another age, the Piscean age of super-materialism, when everybody was a producer and a consumer and if he wasn't goddam good at both, he got bumped off the merry-go-round because he wasn't good enough to play with.

Bye-bye, you hideous wretches. Gloria doesn't live here any more. The pair of you can fuck off!

Chock Full O' Nuts, five minutes later

I've just reread the last three pages as if they were the work of some other person altogether. The verdict isn't nice. *Whoever* she is, I loathe her guts. Furthermore, I don't think she makes much sense.

QUESTION: If her father is such a pain in the ass, why is she always trotting uptown wagging her tail in his face?

QUESTION: If she lived in the same house with her own mother for 17 years and then writes in her precious notebook that she doesn't know who her mother is—and means it— what makes her think she's so *bright?*

QUESTION: If both her parents are nothing but worthless poops from a diseased bygone age, what does that make her? Heaven with whipped cream on it?

And, is this the same darling little lovepuff who thinks she knows how to make over the world? How does she propose to do it? In her own image?

If my mother and father are only my mother and father— and blood doesn't really matter any more—aren't *they at least my brother and sister?* Aren't all men brothers? *They must be!* Because if they're not, then all the things Roy and I believe in really *are* false, and if that's the case

Leaning on the window at Barricini's

Well, I blew it at Chock Full O' Nuts. Had to leave because I was crying. Been walking all over the Village for 15 minutes, bawling like a baby. Lost, too. Haven't the faintest idea where I am.

In my alcove at canal street, BEDTIME, TUESDAY, OCTOBER 14, 1969

Yesterday morning I told Doris about my constipation and she stewed some prunes for me. I ate about a dozen of them and this morning I actually got a little high from the relief they gave me. After work I took my poor little head up to Will's greenhouse and spent the afternoon writing pornography, which I later tore up because it was so disgusting.

In Chapter One, I had this family of scientists trying to colonize the moon. For the first few days everything's cool, but gradually they begin to discover that outer space is all charged up with these funky rays that work like an aphrodisiac. It creeps up on you until pretty soon your feet are practically cloven hoofs. In Chapter Two, the head scientist and his wife, his virgin daughter, and his adolescent son are all smeared with honey. Then they release the laboratory animals, white mice, guinea pigs, etc., who haven't been fed for three days and—well, there's no reason to go into it all over again. The point is that it brought me down from my teensy-weensy high, and left me feeling worse than ever. So I mentioned it at dinner just in case anyone here had any thoughts about what I was doing wrong.

Cary asked me why I was trying to write pornography in the first place, and I said I'd hoped it might be a groovy way to make some money and couldn't understand why it wasn't.

Nyoom said hard-core stuff like mine wasn't groovy because it wasn't art. If it were art, it'd make you high. Art always does that, he claimed, and that's how you could tell good art from bad. Sally Sunflower said she didn't believe there was any such thing as bad art; there were just people doing art, and each one's work showed where his head was at. If your head was in the same place as the artist's, you'd call his work good. I said, Okay then, how come I don't like this stuff that's coming out of *my own head?*

Cary said, "We know, don't we, Peter?"

"*The Integrated Man?*" Peter said.

"Yeah. Tell it."

"You tell it."

"Okay." Cary gets a certain glow when he's about to divulge a spiritual secret. "Peter and I got stoned on grass one night—not stoned, just nice and high—and we came up with this fabulous book that we decided not to write. We were going to call it *The Integrated Man,* and later I'll tell you why we didn't write it. But here's how it was: In this rap, we decided that people were divided into three parts. There was a lover, a thinker, and a doer. If you had all these parts going full steam at the exact same moment, you'd be at your most beautiful. Because you'd be *together.* That's why, in head language, we're always talking about Getting It Together. We want to have the lover and the thinker and the doer operating simultaneously, because that's when a person feels the greatest. And the longer you can maintain that state of being together, the more beautiful you get."

"And the increase is permanently yours," Peter said.

"Right! Because every single second of being *together* that you have in your life increases the beauty and power of your soul! That's it. That's *The Integrated Man.*"

Peter said, "Great. Now show Witch how this applies to pornography."

"Oh! Okay! It's like this. Pornography tends to be *un-groovy* because it puts the whole burden of sex onto your thinker. It gets over-amped, and the doer just sits there panting and slavering. I mean nothing's happening to your *body!* You're not kissing or petting or fucking or sucking or *anything*. And of course the lover is completely idle, too. He just *has* to check out, because he's got nobody to love. I mean, it's not Rosemary Christ or George Christ or Frieda Christ you're digging in a dirty book, it's just these characters using their genitals, right? So! What's happening is this: Your mind's getting all these multimegaton blasts of sex, but your body and spirit aren't helping you assimilate the impact. Am I saying this okay, Peter?"

"Fantastic. Press on."

"Um. What else? Didn't we decide that masturbating might help a little?"

"Well, we thought it would at least help keep your thinker from blowing a fuse. But the lover would still be getting short shrift."

"Right, right! Have I left anything else out?"

"We talked about vice and virtue, didn't we?" Peter said. "About how vice, down the ages, has always been thought to bring about *dis*integration? So we thought maybe you could define virtue as anything that makes you feel *together*. And vice as anything that makes you feel *untogether*."

Roy piped up and said, "What about dope? Smack and speed make you feel like you're together."

"Yeah," Cary said, "but they both lead to bummers. And you *know* that when you take it. You know heroin and amphetamine and all hard stuff are going to hang you up."

"Okay," Roy said, "but then you can't really say virtue is anything that makes you feel *together*, can you?"

"Well, I suppose not strictly," Cary said. "I mean if a person digs jumping off cliffs, it's only a virtue till he hits bottom."

"And that," Peter said, "is why we didn't write the book. Books on topics like this tend to throw you into think gear. And our book in particular would do something even worse. It'd make you see yourself as all divided up into parts."

I could see Nyoom frowning with frustration. He thought he had a new theory for his hungry mind to munch on, and now Peter was snatching it away from him. "Isn't that your entire thesis, for Christ sake?" he said.

"That's the thesis," Peter said, "and it sounded pretty good to us. It still sounds okay. And maybe it is. But I smell some bullshit on it, don't you, Cary?"

"Yeah, kind of. It's too slick. Nobody knows what makes a person tick, not really."

"All we know about man," said Peter, "is that he won't fit into any system of thought. And if you know that, you don't go rushing to the typewriter to fit him into one. Unless of course you're trying to make a career out of snowing people."

There was more talk but I don't feel like writing it down. The point is that I've decided to retire from my career as a pornographer.

A few minutes later

Wide awake again.

Jeanette said something during the Integrated Man rap that I'm afraid of losing. She said there were three English words that shared the same Greek roots. (Or was it Latin?) Anyway, the words are heal, whole, and holy, and ever since I turned out the light, they've been banging around in my head like silver pinballs in a slot machine.

When I am whole I am holy.

Wholeness heals me.

Health is wholeness is holiness.

Wow.

THE SHEEP MEADOW, CENTRAL PARK, WEDNESDAY, OCTOBER 15, 1969— MORATORIUM DAY

Something superoverwhelminglyfantastic-plus has happened! The entire city of New York has turned on to love and peace. Businessmen, old ladies, longhairs and shorthairs, no-hairs, secretaries, bums, children, even soldiers and sailors. Everyone is wandering around in a spell, as if they can't believe what's taking place. I feel I'm participating in an occasion so momentous it would make dancing on the moon seem like a great big so-what. Peter's at home glued to the TV set. Nyoom talked with him by phone a few minutes ago, and he says the entire country has stepped down out of the skyscrapers to reclaim the earth and return it to the people.

I'm with Nyoom and his girl, Mary. We're resting on the grass in Central Park. It's cold, but the sun is shining. Nyoom is beautiful today in his African shirt, and Mary's blond head is like a sunburst on his shoulder. I've never seen him in such a sweet, open mood. His mind seems to have been blown out of orbit by all the things we've seen. He's not even making any pronouncements, but once in a while he exclaims. A minute ago, for instance, just after we sat down and got comfortable here, he looked around at this enormous crowd, a staggering mixture of types and sizes and colors, and he said, "America is blessed! *Why* is America so blessed?" And it's true, it must be. People are still dying, thousands every week, because of us—and yet we're given a day like today. Fifth Avenue is one long church. Ordinary people smiling at strangers and carrying lighted tapers. But they're *not* ordinary. Nobody is. And nobody's a stranger either. Sally Sunflower is absolutely right when she says everybody in the world is high and beautiful—when they're given a chance to be. We left her a couple of hours ago at Bryant Park. She and Roy and Cary Colorado are passing out black armbands. She's been concentrating on the police and so far she's got three of them wearing the bands right over their uniforms. She says we mustn't call them fuzz or pigs any more, and I promised I wouldn't. And I'm not spelling Amerika with a *k* any more either.

It's terrific to be thinking about the world again, instead of myself, and to realize I've got my high back without smoking pot. Now I can smoke it again if I want to, and it won't matter. Last night at dinner I told Peter what I'd been going through—no details, just that I'd been depressed and was seeing it through without dope, and wondered what he thought about it. I set off quite a discussion, and in the end everybody was in agreement. Each of us feels marijuana has helped him become a better person. More open and honest and gentle, freer and kinder and stronger, more forgiving, more peaceful, more optimistic. Deeper. *Happier.* But the whole point of smoking it is to use less and less, not more and more. Then Peter said something that amazed Doris. He said if pot was legalized, he might be tempted to go back to work again, and use it in therapy. But when he saw Doris's mouth hanging open, he said, "No, I wouldn't. I'm just talking. If you know what love is, you don't go making a profession of it."

The irony of it is fantastic. The thing that really qualifies Peter to help others is the very thing that made him stop. And yet, Roy's father, who hasn't the vaguest

WILL'S GREENHOUSE, TUESDAY, OCTOBER 21, 1969

It's been a week since I started that unfinished sentence, but it feels more like six months. These few days have been the most important days of my life, not only for me but for Roy. And maybe for my father, too—but that's only a guess. The notes I took are so messy they're almost incoherent, so I've decided to come here each afternoon, after work and lunch are out of the way, and work at least three hours a day until I've reconstructed all the things that have happened.

Thank you, dear brother Will, for providing such a beautiful place for me to work. Your banana tree is having a new leaf. It's unfolding like a scroll, and it's the tenderest green I've ever seen. The weather's cooler today, so I'm wearing your blue denim jacket again.

I hereby dedicate this task to my soul. Each word I write will be a prayer, a prayer that by the time this notebook is up to date, I'll know what to do next. Amen.

As I was sitting in the Park with Nyoom and Mary, writing that unfinished sentence, I became aware of a man's legs a few feet away. And in the next split second several things seemed to flash through my mind at once. I knew those legs were both familiar and terribly important, and that the person who owned them was looking at me, and had been looking at me for a long time.

It was my father, Hank Glyczwycz. He was standing there alone (is he *always* alone?), wearing the same old brown knit tie, slightly askew, the top two buttons of his tan shirt undone, his hands in the side pockets of the same old dark brown corduroy jacket, legs wide apart, looking at me. No, not looking. *Studying.*

I don't think just seeing someone has ever made me feel such a wave of truly ecstatic happiness. It was as if God and all the angels and saints got together to give me the Super Zap of my entire life.

And all I said was hello.

He wrinkled one cheek into a kind of token smile, nodded at me, and kept right on *studying* me. Even at the time, I was amazed that being studied by your father could give you such a beautiful feeling. Maybe it was because he liked me, and I could tell it, even though he didn't say a word and hardly moved a muscle.

I went over to him and offered my hand. He looked at it for a few seconds before he shook it, and when my hand was in his I had the feeling he wasn't exactly greeting me, but continuing his study of me. I don't mind being studied when I'm feeling good about myself, as I was Wednesday in the park. In fact, I enjoyed it. Hank Glyczwycz couldn't be more different in every way from Edward, the world's greatest cosmetician, but he did make me feel like a star, radiant and beautiful and unique. I told him I was surprised to see him there. He shrugged and said, "I'm just looking it over."

I said, "It's a great day, isn't it?"

But he wasn't committing himself to any such extravagance. "It's a day," he said.

"You don't have an armband. Would you like one?"

"That's going to stop the war?"

"If enough of us wear them, it might help."

"Okay, I wear an armband."

While I was getting one out of my bag for him, I introduced him to Nyoom and Mary. Hank doesn't have any small talk, and he doesn't seem to care whether or not he's being friendly. Chances are he'd like to be, but doesn't know how. Nyoom and Mary were pretty much wrapped up in one another anyway, so the moment was actually more empty than awkward. I suggested to Hank that we walk around and see what was happening.

So we left Nyoom and Mary sitting on the grass and wandered off together through the afternoon. I don't want to describe the whole thing. Going through it once was enough. For me, the whole trek was uphill and the climbing didn't seem to get us anywhere, certainly not *up*. Hank automatically takes the negative view of everything he sees. His eyes and his voice always seem to have in them the unspoken comment that all enthusiasm springs from a shortage of intelligence, and of course high spirits are just plain silly. If you think something is beautiful—*anything at all*—you're just being duped by appearances.

But I didn't give up. I had a tremendous urge to show him the day through my eyes. I guess I wanted to *convert* him. Down heads often make me feel like this—*challenged*. I want to make them high. And with Hank I tried harder than I ever had with anyone. I gave it everything I had. I pumped and pumped and pumped. I overlooked his rudeness. I radiated. I smiled. I worked like a stevedore. No, I can be more

267

accurate than that. I worked like my mother works at a cocktail party.

And the worst of it is that, at the time, I didn't know why I was doing it. I was just too busy to give it a thought. Too driven even to consider what it was that was driving me. And now I wonder whether or not, if I'd stopped long enough to ask myself, some little voice inside might have told me what was happening to me?

At Rockefeller Center we noticed a lot of people smoking marijuana right out in the open. Suddenly I was inspired with the idea of getting Hank turned on. Just as I was looking around to find someone I might score a couple of joints from, Hank said, "You want marijuana? I got a pocketful."

"You're putting me on!"

"Look here." He pulled open the side pocket of his jacket.

"Wow! Shall we smoke one?"

"Here?"

"Sure."

"And go to jail?"

"Everybody's smoking," I said. "They can't arrest us all."

He shrugged. There's no real point in my writing "He shrugged" over and over again. My father shrugs almost every time he speaks. I don't know if it means that nothing matters to him—or that *everything* does, terribly, and he wishes it didn't.

So he took out a joint and lit it. I could tell the way he was trying to be super-casual, handling it like a regular cigarette, that he didn't know what he was doing. Heads can always spot an amateur.

I said, "I didn't know you smoked pot."

(Shrug.) "I thought I give it a try."

"This is good. Where'd you get it?"

"Some kid in the park sold me a handful. Ten dollars. What the hell, why not?"

I knew he wouldn't get a high from it unless he held the smoke longer, but I didn't want to tell him what to do. I always have the feeling his ego's about ready to fall apart anyway, so I tried to give a clear demonstration without saying anything, and on the next toke, he copied the way I did it.

"Do you smoke a lot?" I asked him.

"Once before. But nothing happened. What about you? You take a lot of dope, huh?"

"I've had a lot of acid. Maybe thirty or forty trips, but I'm not taking any more for a while."

"Why not?"

"I haven't liked where my head is lately." I could see from his face that more explanation was needed, so I said, "If a person's not really together up here"—I tapped my head—"acid can backfire on you. Unless you're with somebody who really knows where it's at."

"You haven't got a good head?"

"Not as good as I used to think it was."

"Something happened?"

"Not really. But I've been sort of confused lately. I do things and I don't know why I'm doing them." The conversation was beginning to make me uncomfortable. So I said, "No big deals. I haven't killed anybody or freaked out or anything. I'm just playing it cool for a while."

"You ever try to jump off the roof?" He was dead serious.

"No."

"I read a little about it," he said. "People jump out of windows sometimes, huh?"

"Nobody *I* know ever has. But I guess it's happened. How's your head?"

"My head?" (Shrug.) "It's just a head."

"No, I mean right now. Does it feel high?"

"Nah. This stuff doesn't do anything to me."

"To me it does. I feel *great!* You want to smoke another one?"

(Shrug.) He took out another joint and lit it. Then he offered it to me, but I said I'd had enough.

A man in dark glasses and a big bushy beard came up and asked Hank for a toke. Hank looked at me for guidance, but this time *I* did the shrugging. I didn't much like the man's looks. He seemed to be a kind of freeloader type who asks for things too easily. I suppose if it'd been my joint, I'd have given it to him anyway. But Hank said, "Sorry, sir. I don't know you."

The stranger said, "Man, don't you know we're having a revolution?"

"I *still* don't know you." Hank took my arm and as we walked away, the man shouted *peace* after us. I turned around and shot him a peace sign, and it was okay. He was smiling. Hank hadn't bummed him.

"Revolution!" Hank started grumbling and he kept it up for several blocks. "What's a revolution? Is it getting diseases from strangers? Revolution. A lot of crap. This country doesn't know what revolution means. Smoke marijuana. Wear an armband. Grow a beard. Make peace signs. Some revolution!"

I kept quiet. Hank said, "That guy's a bum. I know bums. You think I'm wrong?"

"He *might* be a bum," I said. "I just don't know if he is or not."

"You let a stranger puff on your cigarette?"

"Sometimes I do."

"What about diseases?"

"It *is* taking a chance."

"And the *nerve!* What about the nerve he's got?"

"Oh well, it's all over now. It doesn't really matter."

"It doesn't matter! I'm disagreeable, huh? You think I should have . . ." His voice trailed off. "Where are we going?" he said.

"I guess we're just walking."

Then he stopped and looked back. "What's happening here?"

I said, "I think you're beginning to feel the marijuana."

"Oh yeah?" He stood still for a minute. "Maybe." Then he added begrudgingly, "*A little.* Maybe."

We walked for another half a block, and he said, "What were we talking about?"

"It wasn't anything important."

A few steps later: "Are you *sure?*"

"Mm. We were talking about smoking after strangers."

"Ah! I remember."

"But it wasn't important. Shall we go to Bryant Park?"

"Too many people. Too many bums."

"Would you like to go to Canal Street then? You could meet my friends and we could all have dinner."

"What were we talking about?"

"Hank, listen, would you? I want to explain something to you. Okay?"

"Explain. Go ahead."

"Well, it's just that, when you're smoking pot—you know, marijuana—you sometimes forget what you're saying. And it never really matters at all. You just let go of the thought, whatever it was. And if it was important, it'll come back again. I just thought I should explain that to you."

"It makes you forget what you're doing?"

"Sometimes."

"Well! *That's* a hell of a thing!"

"But it can be very nice!"

"Nice? To *forget?*"

"Yes. Very."

"I don't see how that's so nice!"

"Just think about it a minute, will you? For instance, we were just talking about that man, right? The guy who asked you for a toke from your cigarette?"

"Yeah, I remember that bum."

"Yes, but the thing is, he wasn't really *important.* So if we've forgotten him, that's *good.* Isn't it?"

"But suppose I don't *want* to forget something." He raised a finger, teacher-style. "You see? You forget. Some things are important to remember!"

"Well then, *those* things you can think about some *other* time! When you're not smoking marijuana. Marijuana isn't for remembering. It's for pleasure."

"Aah! Yeah! I see! Pleasure! Mm-hm! Yeah! *Sure!*" He shook his head. "You kids. You think a revolution is for *pleasure!* You got something to learn, I can tell you *that* much!"

"Hank." I stopped walking again. "We're not talking about revolution. We're talking about smoking marijuana!"

"It's the same thing! Listen to me, I know what I'm telling you."

"Really? Well then, would you tell me again?"

He looked at me with completely blank eyes, and I knew he didn't have a thought in his entire head. Obviously the pot was trying to quiet his mind down and let him have a little peace, but my poor father was struggling against it for all he was worth.

I did a terrible thing. I laughed. And I couldn't stop myself.

"I'm funny!" he said. "You think I'm funny!"

I said, "Hank, it's not *you.* It's the marijuana that's funny. Why don't you just laugh!"

272

"This is very serious!" he said. And he was so stern and convincing I tried to *be* serious.

"*What* is?"

Then he drew another blank, and at first he seemed so concerned about it I got really worried. I'd never seen anyone actually freak out from first-high paranoia, but it looked like it was happening to Hank. And then, thank God, he saw the humor of it, and we both laughed together. We stood in the entranceway at Brentano's and laughed for at least five minutes. I wasn't really that amused. I was forcing it a little, to keep him company. Because you could tell how badly he needed that laughing. I could imagine all kinds of busy little fingers working away in his guts trying to untie all the knots in there. And it made me happy. The sight of my father laughing for all he was worth doubled my high.

Later, maybe as much as ten minutes later, as we were waiting for the subway train to come, he was still thinking about it.

"Laughing doesn't hurt," he said.

In common with my mother, I have the makings of a third-rate manipulator of people. I should give up. My big unspoken motive in taking Hank Glyczwycz to Canal Street was to get him tuned in by Peter Friedman. It didn't really work in quite the way I'd hoped. Maybe it would have if Hank hadn't stopped at a liquor store on the way home to buy a gallon of wine. His contribution to the dinner, he said, but by the time we sat down at the table he'd drunk several glasses of it. And with each gulp his politeness toward Peter increased until it was almost insulting. Right from the start, he looked at Peter in a narrow-eyed half-smiling way that said, So you're the old nut who runs this asylum. And I

273

kept expecting Peter to grab the bait. His head, by his own admission, is half old warlike Piscean, and half young peaceful Aquarian, you can never be sure which half's going to show itself. So we had this mini-tension all through dinner.

Also there was a cop at the table. Sally and Roy found him in front of the Library. He was wandering around completely spaced out on acid—his first trip—when Sally and Roy came along and decided to take charge of him. Not that he was having any difficulty. In fact, he seemed as happy as could be, but Roy was afraid all that psychedelic smiling, in full uniform, might cause him to lose his job. Sally agreed, so they brought him home.

In all, there were fourteen at the table. Nyoom brought Mary home with him, and Cary Colorado came in with old friends from Boulder, three beautiful heads who looked like they'd just stepped down from a covered wagon. Joshua, with a long craggy frontiersman's face shining out of a bushel of cornsilk hair and beard. Lu, half redskin and half black, with a smile that started in his feet. And a tiny little blond called Motherlove Ford. Motherlove did the cooking. Watercress salad and a great casserole made of rice and beans and sesame seeds and peanuts.

Hank's paranoia let up slightly at the dinner table. He was a little self-conscious about the pre-meal Zap, and probably would have resisted if he hadn't felt outnumbered. Sally was the only one at the table who realized he was my father, but she didn't let on. When I had a chance, I whispered the fact to Roy. He was fascinated and kept studying Hank every chance he got.

In spite of Hank's presence, Peter had a pretty good high going for him. He likes it when the table's so full we have to bring in nail kegs and orange crates to seat the extra people. I think it makes him feel like the patriarch of some enormous tribe. And of course he *is*. There must be hundreds of people

274

who love and trust him, and he really digs the feeling it gives him. I heard him tell Jeanette he felt like a king. And she said, "You are a king, baby." He thought about it a minute, his face glowing like mad, then he said, "Okay. But that means everybody else at the table is at least a prince or a princess." Then she took a look around and said, "I believe you're right." Hank picked up on this little exchange, too. He didn't say anything, but he made sure Peter caught the comment his nasty smile was making.

For a while everyone was talking at once. We all had stories to tell about things that had happened through the day. Peter started giving Joshua and Motherlove his Golden Age rap. I'd never heard it firsthand before, so I started listening, too, and pretty soon everyone else at the table stopped talking to tune in on it.

"Someday, and you'll all live to see it," he said, "all the world will be at peace, and there'll be a great international coming together of man. Every man, woman, and child on the planet holding hands around the world. It'll happen, I swear it will. Each tribe, each town, each city neighborhood, every nation on earth will form its own chain of hands. Just as we do here at the table each night. This thing'll be coordinated by television and Telstar, you see, because that's what they're for. That's their real function. In fact, I'll go farther, I'll say this: The ultimate use of *all* technology is to bring men together. Anyway, when that day comes, listen to me now, I'm telling you, *there'll be such a Zap!* this entire planet will *shimmer!* Everyone alive will enter into a new day. And what will the new day be like? All you have to do is imagine. Think about it. What will happen on this earth when the people who inhabit it become *fully human?* When we all realize that *this* is the kingdom of heaven. In other words, when we all learn to love. Because love is man's destiny. We know that, don't we? It's not just a dream, or the invention of some hippie stoked out on acid. It's man's *thing*. Man's great potential is as a lover. In the past we didn't have much time or energy to concentrate on getting this thing together. We were too busy. We had to hustle for food and shelter and fuel. But now we've done all that. The hustling for survival is over. We've got our knowledge now, we've got our technology. We're learning at last, after eons of struggle, we're learning how to be free of purely animal concerns. What a fantastic stroke of luck to be alive now, at this moment, of all moments in history. You and I, every one of us alive, are taking part in an event we've been growing toward for thousands of centuries—the flowering of the human person. We're it. It's here. It's happening. The hour is upon us. Love's magic can go to work now. And it is! It is! It's working! All the hell and horror in the world at this second is nothing but a death rattle, the last terrible sigh of a poor fucked-up savage who was forced for a million years to subsist through greed and violence. It's true. Man has arrived at the great moment of his destiny. Man, the old monster, is in a profound state of change. Man, super-terror of the Milky Way, is in metamorphosis. Man, the animal who dreamed that one day he might become a lover, is about to get his wish. The only real problem we've got now is we're not digging our success enough, our fabulous success as a species. We're all in danger of getting sucked into this big transition-blues bullshit—and missing out on the miracle. No wonder of course. It's so *big!* It may take a few minutes to get it through our heads. Meanwhile, our poor leaders go on hustling for us day and night, just as they did in the day of the monster. They still lie and grab and defend and kill for us—not realizing the necessity for it has passed. We don't need our greed any more. We don't need our violence. We don't need to hoard any more. There's *enough* now. For the first time in all human history, think of it, there's enough!

No, I should put it this way, there's the means of producing enough. Buckminster Fuller tells us the entire present population of the world can be housed *comfortably* in the British Isles, or *compactly* in Haiti. Or have I got that turned around? Never mind, the point is that overpopulation is only a *threat* when people don't dig each other, when we don't dedicate our resources to taking care of one another. But when *caring* has been learned—and it's happening now, it's happening fast—when *caring* arrives, comes into its fullness, we'll think there aren't *enough* people! Woodstock taught us a little something, didn't it? Isn't it interesting, by the way, that Woodstock and the moon landing took place in the same summer? I'm in danger of losing my point here, but I think it's worth the risk. Let me make a point about Woodstock and the moon landing. This hashish and all your beautiful faces are giving me a red hot flash of insight into these two mind-blowing events. Now look! That rocket to the moon was man's greatest exploration of outer space. And Woodstock was his greatest demonstration of the possibilities of inner space. The moon landing, technology's greatest day. Woodstock, brotherhood's greatest day. And they happened simultaneously. Don't you all agree that this is the most astounding sort of *accident* imaginable? The timing, think of it, the timing is staggering! I can hardly believe it! And yet I *do*. I believe it because I witnessed them both on that extraordinary machine upstairs. And I believe it because we all knew 1969 would be the Big Year. We all felt it. And so many of the prophets and astrologers foresaw it too, didn't they? We *knew* 1969 had something earthshaking to deliver and we all wondered what it would be. And now it's happened! The past is the past. The future is the future. And these two birds don't look so much alike any more, have you noticed? It used to be they were so similar you could hardly tell them apart from year to year. But now the past is really and truly over with, in some radical new way. It's so over with, in fact, it's *irrelevant*. We've lived out our history. It's done. All of its lessons are still available to us of course, but fuck 'em, we don't really need them any more. All we need's the lesson of 1969. We need to know that we're not just poor put-upon little earthlings any more. We're not doomed forever to be creatures of violence and greed and misery, not any more. Because by our own efforts, our own genius, we've become *spacelings*. We've learned, because our young have demonstrated it to us, that we're lovers. Creatures of joy. Jesus Murphy! this is big, folks, this is *big!* We don't have to see ourselves as lowly earthbound killers ever again. Think of it. After this glorious summer we're all spacelings and lovers. Amen and hallelujah!"

Doris and I served the tea and dessert—a carrot cake she'd made in the afternoon. When I came in with the mugs, I heard Hank saying to Peter, "Excuse me, I missed perhaps something important. Would you help me? I don't understand. Exactly *for what* do we celebrate? The war is over? The dead walk? Widows and orphans are not widows and orphans any more? The races are united? Hungry people are eating?"

Peter took a good long look at Hank. I think he was trying to decide whether to throw him down the stairs or just gently let him know he was acting like a pain in the ass.

He said, "Hank, were you actually listening? Because somebody should've warned you about people who smoke dope. Y'see, what happens is they get high and they talk this really awful shit. You should never listen to it seriously."

Well, I thought, at least he hasn't thrown him down the stairs.

Hank took a moment, then nodded his head and said, "Oh. Oh, I see. Thank you. That explains it."

Peter's face broke into a smile. He wasn't faking it either. He was really amused. Then Hank, not wanting to be caught with *too* many square bones sticking out of his head, laughed too. Except he laughed quite a bit too loud. The moment was sad and awkward and touching and a little bit tense. I knew if Peter wanted to he could say something sweet that would help us through it. Joshua spoke up instead. His blue eyes were bright with feeling and that wild cornsilk hair framing his face made him look like a sunburst. Sally Sunflower was digging his act with wide-open admiration, and I flashed on what beautiful babies they could make if they got together.

"Excuse me for butting in here, good people," he said, "but with all due respect to *everyone* present, I just wanted to say I've been digging what Brother Peter had to tell us." Joshua's whole style is cornball-beautiful. "I been listenin' with every ear I got to m'name, and my nose was workin', too. And I can tell you for a certainty that I did not pick up the scent of shit. In fact, I'll go farther. What I picked up sounded to me just like the nitty-gritty itself. I say, Amen and hallelujah!"

His approval was taken up all around the table. Motherlove Ford burst into applause. Lu stood up and said, "Right on!" The acid-tripping cop said, "I am getting rid of this goddam uniform," and proceeded to take off all his clothes.

Hank was having a problem with his eyes: he couldn't believe what they were showing him.

Joshua turned to the acid-tripping *ex*-cop. "A fine idea, brother," he said, "a fine idea." And then, to Peter, "Brother, would you have any objections if some more of us here got down to our skin?"

Peter said, "I'm not wearing a blue uniform, am I?"

279

"No, no, brother, you're sure not."

Joshua's little family began to take off their clothes, then Nyoom and Sally and Cary—and pretty soon I lost track. There were petals falling everywhere.

Meanwhile I was having this little dialogue in my own head:

"Why aren't *you* stripping, Witch? As a rule you lead the parade. What's happening?"

"I can't take off my clothes in front of my *father!*"

"Oh, really? What's your hangup."

"I don't know *what* my hangup is, but I am not disrobing."

"I can remember when you used to *face* everything. Now all you do is get uptight and tell me to shut up."

"That's right, and I'm telling you now—*shut up!*"

So I changed stations and tuned back into Peter and Hank.

Peter was saying, "I think we're all high on this Moratorium thing. I think we feel encouraged. Don't you?"

"Encouraged?" Hank said, trying hard not to notice the sudden flowering of naked bodies all over the room. "No, I don't. I'm sorry. I don't feel encouraged. My subject is history. If a man knows history, he never feels encouraged."

"Wow, man!" said Cary Colorado, hanging his trousers over the back of his chair. "If you really mean that, you ought to give up that history trip. It sounds like a bummer."

"Wait a minute, though," Peter said. "It's not a bummer for Toynbee. Toynbee says the twenty-first century will be the century of the unity of man—if the United States doesn't louse it up."

"*If?*" Hank said. "It's not *if* any more! She's doing it. Right now."

"Yes, I know," Peter said, "but Americans aren't going to let it go on any longer. Today proved that!"

"*Proved?* Proved *what?*"

"The country's waking up!"

280

"A few thousand New Yorkers."

"*Not* a few thousand New Yorkers. Millions," Peter said, "all over the country. I'm telling you, I saw it on TV. The tuning-in rate is gaining fantastic velocity everywhere. Listen, do you know how many Americans are deserting from the armed forces this year alone?"

"A few thousand, that's nothing."

"But it's not a *few* thousand. Would you like to take a guess at the actual figure?"

The guessing traveled around the table. The only one I picked up was Joshua's. He pushed his great face forward and declared, "There must be a million at least?"

"Not quite," Peter said. "It's 79,000 and some. Nearly 80,000."

Everybody said wow except Hank. He challenged it. "Where do you get that figure?"

"From the Pentagon," Peter said. "That's the Pentagon estimate for 1969. It was in the *Times,* all the wire services carried it, it's official. And that's double the figure for 1967 by the way."

"If it continues at this rate," Nyoom informed us, "there won't be an Army in 1980."

"And what about the thousands," Roy said, "who've gone underground? How many of *us* are there? Nobody even knows."

Cary said, "And the refusers. Guys like Will who've gone to prison. There are thousands and thousands of them. And what about all the thousands that pretend to be gay?"

"And all the cases," Peter said, "that are on the federal dockets right this minute. Something like 28,000 of them."

Nyoom's quiet little Mary spoke up. "Does anyone know how many of our boys have gone to Canada?"

Peter turned to Hank again. "How many of the lads in your classes are there to keep out of the Army?"

"About half," Hank admitted.

"Okay then. Now you know why we feel like celebrating. Peace is getting almost as popular in America as . . ." He paused to look for a word. Someone threw in "fucking," and somebody else said "money." And then everyone talked at once for a while, and when a lull came, Hank filled it up.

"Not peace," Hank said. "Opposition to Vietnam—*maybe*. Peace? No. Peace is not popular."

"Then what was today all about?"

"It's a nice day. They walk around in the streets, burn a few candles."

"You don't think the word has gotten around finally that peace is *urgent?*"

"People are stupid, my friend."

"Not when they're threatened with extinction."

"Oh yes. Especially then. Man is threatened with extinction at this minute, and he chooses Mr. Nixon to lead him over the edge."

Cary Colorado said, "That wasn't fair though. The only opposition he had got assassinated."

Hank said, "Another example of the popularity of peace, huh?"

"Wow, I don't want to argue with you, man. I love you. Besides, we want to go upstairs and chant for peace."

Cary and the three Colorado people got up and began to clear the table. Then our bunch joined in and when it was done, Cary said to Hank, "Would you like to come chant with us, sir?"

Hank said no. Not no thank you. Just no.

Sally said, "What are you going to chant?"

"Oh, any old thing," Cary said. "What about *Nam Myoho Renge Kyo?*"

"*Far out!* Can we come, too?"

"Sure! Anybody that wants to."

Sally and the cop and Nyoom and Mary followed Cary and the Colorado tribe up the stairs. Which left the house divided neatly into two groups. Upstairs, the naked chanters. Downstairs, the dressed talkers. The latter group included Doris and Peter and Jeanette and Roy and Hank and me. Jeanette brought in what she called the *deuxième infusion*— the teapot with its second infusion of water.

While we were still pouring, Hank said, "That kid was right. Robert Kennedy might have been elected. But he wasn't. The good men get murdered. They don't fit in with the stinking mess, so they have to die."

Then he helped himself to what was left of the wine.

"Is that the way you see it?" Peter said.

"That's not the way it *is?*"

"Good men do sometimes get murdered, Hank. But can't you see other things going on, too?"

"Yes," Hank said. "I see more than that. I see good men performing wonderful deeds, smoking marijuana and feeding LSD to cops, telling fairytales about the future. Spectacular things, no doubt. But where? In the White House? On Wall Street? No. These wonderful things happen in tenement buildings, in the slums, in dying cities. Forgive me if I don't expect these, uh, these—great things—to change the course of history."

For some reason Hank was being openly hostile. Doris had one hand resting on Peter's knee. Peter himself was quiet. I think he was trying to listen to Hank in the deepest way he could. Roy glanced at me. Neither of us were breathing. We could hear the chanting upstairs, *Nam Myoho Renge Kyo, Nam Myoho Renge Kyo, Nam Myoho Renge Kyo.* Jeanette suddenly sprang from the table and on her way out of the room she said, "Man, that chanting is *heavy!* I got to get in on it."

There was silence for a moment. Then Peter said, "Please go on, Hank. I'd like the benefit of your insight."

Hank looked suspicious. He thought Peter was putting him on. Then Doris said, "So would I, Hank. We sometimes tend to get a little insular. Tell us what you see. Please."

Hank's expression, the way his face looked at that moment, made his entire trip clear to me. My father was a damaged person. His life had taught him to land the first blow, to strike before he was struck. He'd never been into peace. He'd lived in a world of attack and retaliation. I'll bet I'm right about all this. In fact, I just *know* I am.

Anyway, for at least a brief moment, I think he trusted us. He folded his hands on the table in front of him and stared at them for a minute. Then he began to talk.

"I see plenty. I see fear. I see a country paralyzed with fear. Everybody afraid the end is coming, and grabbing what they can. Strikes. Shit, I'm an old-line Socialist. I like strikes. But I'm telling you, the wrong ones is striking. It should be the poor. Only it's not. It's the middle class, the fat union workers. The poor don't strike. We shut them up with welfare money, just enough to keep them alive—but so weak they can't revolt. It's a crazy country. The world never saw anything like it before."

While he spoke, his hands were locked in a death grip, fighting to hold each other still. But his thumbs kept trying to escape. And the harder they tried, the tighter his hands kept gripping one another. As for me, I kept wanting to put my hands on his, but I couldn't talk myself into it. My mind is always getting in the way of my earth mother impulses. All I could do was listen and watch the struggle.

"It's not nice to tell you these things," he said. "I am a foreigner, a refugee. I want to be grateful. America let me in here, and if it didn't, I probably be dead like all the other Jews in Poland. I come to Detroit, a young man, and they give me a job. I go to night school, I learn the new language, I get an education. It's all a dream, too good to be true. For these things I want to be grateful. Right? But I am not, my friends. I hate this country. Why? Because it seduced me. It gave me my life back, it gave me job, education. But *why* is it so generous? *Why* does it give me all these things? I'll tell you why. So it can start crapping on my soul." He looked around the table. "You don't know what I'm talking about."

Peter said, "Not exactly. But keep talking. Maybe we will."

"Okay," Hank said. "I try again. A smart man with a big drive can get drawn into the system here. He can become a little king, have his own back yard and a fence around it. He can buy Coca-Cola, a television. His wife can go to the drugstore and come back smelling good. He can buy a car and drive fast on big highways. Superhighways. Everything super. He is a little king because he's got a little intelligence, a little ambition. But you know something about kings, even little ones? They can't see good. They can't see millions of other people still desperate, still hungry. The fat grows up around their eyes. They don't see *the millions of poor who don't fit in the system.* And the poor? What about them? They not even angry, my friends. They think it's their own *fault* to be broke and out of work. They're not angry. They feel guilty. They live in the greatest country of all, where every man can be king, but they look in the mirror and they see a piece of shit. They don't know what the hell they do-ing wrong. If they get drafted in the Army, that's good

285

luck. Maybe in the war they find a way to fit the system. Otherwise, stay home, get drunk, die.

"This is why I hate America."

Nobody spoke for a while. The tea wasn't hot but we all sipped what was in our cups.

Peter said, "What about *you*, though, Hank? I mean you personally. You said America seduced you and then started crapping on your soul."

Hank took a long time to think about the question, and then he said, "America made me a little king, no better than all the others. I get seventeen thousand a year. I talk history. Nobody listens. Except a few. And the few, what do they do? They hate my guts. They pass petitions, they try to get me fired. I don't care. I've lived enough. The world is all over. It's true, you know. America was the last hope. And it went crazy. So now everything is finished."

Roy said, "Tell me something, will you, Professor Gliss. If you're a Socialist and all, how come you say America was the last hope? What about Russia and China?"

"They didn't have a chance, boy. From the start, they are forced into militarism, totalitarianism. Germany and America did it to Russia. And now America and Russia both together doing it to China. It's crazy. China got two choices. Give up totalitarianism, get destroyed right away. Keep it, get destroyed a little later. Doesn't matter, of course. Too late now."

"Isn't there a chance though?" Roy said. "Couldn't people's heads change and make everything right? Couldn't the United States just quit scaring everybody shitless?"

"How? This country's too crazy already! Got a million soldiers in Asia, rockets pointed at everybody's head. Why?

The president says we got Chinese trying to get into the back yard. Where? You see any Chinese? Not me. I see Chinese in Chinatown. But the president's got everybody crazy with fear. If he decided to tell the truth, if he got on television tonight and said, Excuse me, people, we were mistaken. We have discovered the Chinese are not interested in conquering America and so we bringing our soldiers back home—you know what happens then? A hundred million fat American kings and queens start shitting their pants and impeach the sonofabitch. Because it's too late now. They're too crazy already. They been scared so long the truth sounds like a big Communist plot. Just like people in a nut house, they think everybody's after them with guns. The only ones not scared is the president and a few of his buddies, a handful of generals and billionaires. They're not scared because they think power and money will save them forever. There's blood in the streets already, but that's okay. These men live in palaces. They think they can shoot the failures or lock them up in prison. They doing it, too. You watch and see, boy. They getting away with it. Sure. More and more men going to get shot and thrown in prison. You think Bobby Seale and Abbie Hoffman, this bunch of clowns in Chicago, you think they're going to get off? That's not what they going to get. They going to get locked up. And the Black Panthers, you think they the only ones going get murdered? That's nothing, not even the beginning. America will be the worst police state yet in history. And it won't be saved by this schoolboy revolution. The schoolboys think they can win a revolution with dope. Typical reasoning for the sons of fat kings. And the blacks, they buy a handful of guns in the hardware shop and they show them on the television! But that's not how you win. That's how you lose. In fact, they already lost. It takes peasants to win a revolution. America hasn't got peasants. It's got kings and failures."

"How do you see us?" Doris said. "The people in this house, what are we? Are we kings or failures or what?"

"I don't want to be personal," Hank said. "I am your guest. You are friendly people."

No one said anything. I'm almost sure Hank expected to be pressed for an answer. But no one repeated the question. Hank's hands were still joined and resting on the table, but mentally I think he was rolling up his sleeves for a fight. He turned to Peter and said, "I've talked so much. Don't you want to go upstairs now and chant?"

Peter considered the idea. "No, Hank. Not right now."

"But it's for *peace!* Don't you want the guns to stop?"

Peter smiled. "It's very tempting. But at the moment, I think I'll just sit here and listen to you tell me what a shithead I am. Isn't that what you'd like to do?"

Hank laughed. It was a sneaky laugh. "What do you *mean,* my friend?"

"You think I'm a fool, don't you?"

"Oh, please," Hank said, "if I offended you, my English is clumsy. We're just two humble men exchanging our views."

"That's not true, Hank, is it? We're not humble men. We both think we're right. In fact, each of us is thoroughly convinced that if the world doesn't listen to us, it's going right down the drain. That's not humility. That's arrogance."

"All right. We're arrogant. So what?"

"So don't say we're humble. We're not. That's all. And if we're going to keep talking, we'd better not ridicule each other."

For a minute Hank almost let his hands get away from each other, but they didn't quite make it. "Okay, okay," he said. "But I listen to you talk at dinner, and I hear one thing only. This fine man, this Peter, with his beautiful ideas, he is Mr. Nixon's best ally. He works for the generals and the

288

billionaires and the corporations. He takes the young people and he keeps them soft in the head with all his hashish and his dreams. They should be out organizing and plotting the takeover of the government, but he puts them to sleep instead with his talk of love. Very fine talk. The whole world holding hands. Beautiful. There should be such a world. And perhaps it comes. Who knows. It could happen—*ten thousand years from now!* In the meantime, some other things going to happen first. America will be obliterated. There is no other fate for such a cancer of rubbish and greed. Europe and Russia will go, too. And for hundreds of years this land will be cemetery land, with Asiatics and Africans and South Americans picking over the bones. *Our* bones."

At that moment there was a really gruesome coincidence: Hank stopped talking and the chanting from upstairs came to an abrupt end. It was as if his hideous prophecies had brought about this sudden awful silence. Hank's face muscles were working, and his jaws were clamped tight shut. He seemed to be overwhelmed with emotion, but I couldn't tell what the emotion was.

Peter stood up. "You know what I'd like to do?" he said. "I'd like to see the sky. Does anyone want to come with me to the roof?"

Doris said, "Oh! *I* do!" And Roy said, "Me, too!"

I looked at Hank. "Will you come with us?"

He shrugged. It's hard for him to say yes to anything.

Peter led the way. We climbed the stairs in silence. The closer we got to the attic, the better I felt. On the top floor we stopped and looked into the attic. There in a circle, surrounding a votive candle and holding hands, sat ten beautiful people. All their eyes were closed, and each of them had a smile on his face. I could tell by the way Hank stared that he'd never seen anything like it, and so for a brief moment I looked at the scene through his eyes. Ten naked people experiencing peace together, real peace. I suddenly realized how unusual my life is, and how exceptionally lucky I am to be me, to have such brothers and sisters. We don't even know very much about each other—certainly not things like facts and histories—and yet we are intimate friends. I'd never even seen the Boulder people until three hours ago, and yet I knew I could show myself to them, inside and out, with perfect trust.

Another thing I flashed on was how different each of them *looked* sitting there in that circle. The range was celestial. Everything from the fragile super-white of Motherlove Ford to the great ebony elegance of Nyoom—and all the different shadings of sex and color and hair and size in between. I thought of all the different moon signs and sun signs and rising signs each of them lived under, all the different pressures and problems and hangups each of them had to cope with, and how many different backgrounds they'd come from—ghetto and suburb, east and west, rich and poor. And yet they were together, *really* together.

Seeing them like that—maybe because of Hank's presence —was an overwhelmingly strong experience. I'm trying to isolate the things I felt most keenly, so that I can name them. But it's hard. A lot of it was love, I'm sure. But I know security was part of it, too. They say there isn't any such thing as real security. Maybe not. But there is something that *feels* a lot like it. Also pride. I felt as if I'd invented them all, or written them, or given birth to them.

If Hank is right, and something awful has to happen to America, I hope whatever it is will come at such a moment, when I'm with my brothers and sisters sitting in a circle. If

290

it did, I feel it wouldn't matter so terribly much. Our souls would just go right on holding hands.

———————————

The time it took for all these thoughts to flash through me was actually quite short. We'd only been standing there a few seconds when Cary opened his eyes and smiled at us. Then all the others looked at us, too.

Cary said, "You want to join us?"

And Peter said, "No. We're on our way to the roof. We want to see the sky."

———————————

The stars have to be extra bright to counteract the lights of New York. Otherwise they don't have much impact on you. On this night everything was bright, the city, the stars, all of our faces looking up and out—and Hank's eyes.

Especially Hank's eyes.

Moonlight washed away so many of his years, I saw him 20 instead of 45. But it wasn't groovy to see him that way. It made me feel the most excruciating wave of anxiety. And I didn't even realize why—until later on, in the street, when he said something that forced me to know what was happening to me.

———————————

On the roof, in the midst of all these confusing feelings, Roy started talking to Peter, and he said some things that shook everyone up. Not Hank. But Doris and Peter. And seeing these two giant types knocked off balance made me feel the earth was trembling underneath me.

During most of it, I was studying Hank, and Hank was studying the uptown skyline. At least that's what he was doing with his eyes. But I had a feeling his ears were quivering with interest.

Peter put his foot on this low wall, then leaned on his knee with one elbow. His other arm was draped around Roy's shoulder.

PETER: Tell me, lad, if you could start from scratch, what kind of a world would you make?

ROY: Wow, you mean pretend I'm the absolute ruler or something? And I can just *say* how it's got to be?

PETER: Yeah. What would you do?

ROY: Well, I personally would make it so everybody was free to do his thing for real reasons instead of money. That'd be number one. And the only way you could have that, I guess, is if you gave everybody the basics to start with. I don't mean in exchange for work either. I mean just for being born. I'd get on TV and I'd tell everybody to stop being uptight about other people not working. I'd try to make 'em understand that there was enough for everybody, and all those thousands of years of people having to sweat their asses off was over with. We could find real cool ways of getting the necessary work done. Like say, if nobody wanted to empty the garbage, I'd think up ways to make it a *gas*. Maybe I'd put stereo in all the garbage trucks and pass out free joints. And I'd make the world so fantastically great, young guys would be glad to put in a couple of years as garbage men. It'd be a goddam *honor!* You know, like being a soldier used to be. So then it'd not only be groovy but patriotic. A guy would love the world *so much*, he'd really dig getting his hands dirty for it. And he'd be born knowing he'd always have enough food and shelter and wheels and medicine, too. And all around him he'd see these millions of other happy people doing their thing, and he'd get the idea working was kind of great. He'd never think of it as a hassle, because there'd be nothing around to *give* him that idea. And then when he got to where he knew what his own special thing was, he could start doing *that.*

DORIS: What if somebody's "special thing" was having a lot of money?

ROY: Well, then, I'd let him have it, I guess. Because nobody else'd want it. I really think money is something people want just so they won't be hassled for *not* having it. Isn't that true? I mean if nobody's hassling you about the rent or the phone bill, then money's not going to be such a big thing to you, is it?

DORIS: I don't know about that. People like power, and that's what money means to them, doesn't it?

ROY: *Now*, yeah. But what if you couldn't *buy* people with it? What if nobody had to put himself up for sale any more? Then money would stop being power. In fact, I'm not even sure you'd have to have money at all. I'll bet you could just paper the walls with it and forget about it.

DORIS: Oh, Roy, you've got such beautiful ideas in your head, it makes me worry for you.

ROY: No, but I really mean it. Think how much safer the world'd be, too. You wouldn't be getting mugged and ripped off all the time either. And you could practically close down all the courts and jails.

PETER: He's right. Money'll have to be done away with sooner or later, or there's just no hope.

ROY: And you know what else could close down? Banks and insurance companies and places where they do just middleman crap and bookkeeping. They could all close down. And you wouldn't need salesmen or tax collectors or stockbrokers, and hardly any lawyers and cops and judges. Cops could be just public helpers. Like if some poor asshole is hurting somebody else, then the cop could just gently stop him, and lead him away to some really nice place where he'd get turned on. So instead of jails you'd have these turn-on-orariums with experts teaching people to be groovier.

PETER: It's true, it's true! I know he's right! It could *work!* I know it could! And I'm a fucking authority.

DORIS: All right now, let's just back up a minute. I want someone to tell me what's to become of all these poor sales-men and bookkeepers, all these people you just threw out of work. What's to become of them?

PETER: Don't you see? The way Roy's got it figured, they'll be just fine. He'll get on TV and tell them all to relax and go fishing or make love or something.

DORIS: I know you're both half serious. Aren't you?

PETER: No, not half. *Completely.*

ROY: Me, too.

DORIS: Something's terribly wrong with all this. Isn't there?

ROY: I don't see what's so wrong about eliminating this whole big fantastic load of work that money causes. Why *not* leave people more and more free? Free to groove and just enjoy this absolutely super planet. And there could be this whole new science, the Science of Enjoyment. And all these people that don't know how to do anything but work, they could be *retrained.* You know, rehabilitated. They could be taught to be happy. And you could have all these experts teaching them how.

DORIS: Fine. And where do you get all these experts?

ROY: Me!

PETER: All of us! That's *something* we're all getting pretty good at, isn't it? And there could be lots of movies and TV shows showing people how.

ROY: And probably acid would help, too.

HANK: Jesus Christ!

ROY: Why not? It's good for that, isn't it? So why not use it?

294

HANK: Holy God. Such Communists this country produces.

ROY: Okay, so maybe we're not Communists. I never said *I* was, you know. I just think what I think, that's all. I haven't got any big fancy political name for it.

HANK: Boy, I'm telling you something. I'm twice your age. Wouldn't hurt to listen. LSD is a product of decadence.

ROY: But how do you know that, sir? I'll bet you've never even tripped.

HANK: I don't say any more. I talked enough tonight.

(*Long pause.*)

PETER: You know, Roy, I really like your utopia. It's a lot like mine. Tell me something, do you suppose we'll ever live to see it?

ROY: Sure we will. And it'll be really good, too. If I didn't believe that, I'd just check out.

PETER: What do you mean, check out?

ROY: Oh, I'd just find some way out. Drugs, or kill myself, I don't know. But I just wouldn't want to live in a world where it *could* be beautiful, and the only thing that kept it from being beautiful was bullshit.

PETER: Okay, now what about this: Do you think it'll come about through the media, and TV, and everybody getting turned on? Or do you think like Hank does, that America'll have to be smashed first?

ROY: You really want a straight answer?

PETER: You know I do.

ROY: Then I have to say I think you're both right. The world'll get really beautiful—but this country—well, it'll probably have to get smashed up pretty bad first. (*Pause.*) I don't like to say that, because I don't like to bum you. But it seems to me like, well, it's already *happening*. And it doesn't seem to be slowing down any. (*Pause.*) I think I'm bumming everybody. Am I bumming everybody?

PETER: That's not important. We have to know what you feel. And think.

ROY: Maybe I'm wrong, though. I really *hope* I am. What I'd like is to see America get liberated in some nice peaceable way.

PETER: Liberated, huh?

DORIS: Tell me, baby, what do you think's got hold of it?

ROY: Capitalism.

(*Peter and Doris glanced at each other in a way that made me see them in a new light. They were like some suburban couple who have just discovered their son has some radical thoughts in his head.*)

DORIS: Don't you think capitalism can be *reformed?*

ROY: No. Because who needs it any more? You know what I mean?

DORIS: No, I don't, Roy. I really don't.

ROY: Well, it's not making things better for people, not any more. All it does is go around defending itself. Isn't that true? I mean it's all courts and cops and soldiers now, isn't it?

DORIS: Yes, darling, but Communist countries have all that, too, don't they?

ROY: Yeah, but they wouldn't have to have it so *much,* would they, if it wasn't for us?

DORIS: Oh, but sweetheart, they're fighting among themselves, too. China and Russia are at each other's *throats.*

ROY: Well, *let* them be. Maybe Communism's lousy, too. I'm not talking about that, I'm just talking about capitalism.

DORIS: But, honey, if they're both awful, what else is there?

ROY: I'm getting sort of mixed up. See, I'm not really sure *either* of them are a hundred per cent awful.

DORIS: Whew, that's a real relief to hear you say that.

ROY: Why? You mean because—

296

DORIS: It's just that I'm glad you realize capitalism has some value. I was beginning to *worry*.

ROY: But I'm not sure it *has* value. I think it *used* to though.

DORIS: And now it's done its thing? Past tense? . . .

ROY: Yeah, because it's not doing it any more.

DORIS: Please tell me what it did that it isn't doing any more.

ROY: Um, actually, what it did was, it developed stuff, stuff that really needed developing. You take your real old-timey capitalists, they were fucking geniuses. Like Henry Ford, he put wheels under millions of people, and that was just a fantastic thing to do. He wasn't just sitting around, you know what I mean? He was really *doing* something, and those old cars he made were really put together. Okay. So that's what capitalism *used* to do. It used to develop this really good stuff. But then, instead of spreading the good stuff around to the whole world, it started developing *shit*. You know, cars that fall apart. Bombs. Flamethrowers, napalm. Toothpaste with stripes. *Real* shit. And so what it seems like to me is this—you get to a point where you've had *enough* capitalists, and then when you keep getting more and more and more, pretty soon you've got too many. And none of them are really *doing* anything any more, so naturally the whole thing has to go. For instance, my dad, he says he's an analyst, right? But what he *really* is is a capitalist. He wants to get hold of enough money and invest it so he can sit on his ass. And most of the people you meet that dig capitalism so much, that's where they're *at*. They don't care about developing something fabulous like old Henry Ford did. All they want to develop is more money. And when you get to where millions and millions of people are in this money bag, well, my personal opinion is, this is really sick.

(*Pause.*)

DORIS: Peter, why don't *you* answer him, darling? I know something's awfully wrong about all this, but I'm just not terribly political.

PETER: Neither am I. And I suppose that's one reason the country's in such trouble. None of our generation was terribly political. Roy's given this whole thing a lot more good clear thought than I have.

DORIS: Oh, God.

PETER: What's the matter?

DORIS: I'm sort of wrecked.

PETER: Me, too. Maybe we're learning something.

ROY: I'll bet I know why you feel sort of wrecked.

PETER: Why?

ROY: Because Americans tend to get democracy and capitalism all mixed up in their heads. They're not really all that connected though.

PETER: How do you mean?

ROY: Well, one's a political thing, and one's economic.

DORIS: Should that make us feel better?

ROY: I don't know, but I think a lot of Americans are depressed because they feel like *democracy's* what's fucking everything up. And they're scared to *think* it even. Because it'd be just really *sad* to think of all our founding fathers and the Gettysburg Address and Thomas Jefferson and the flag all going down the toilet, you know? And if *democracy* doesn't work, what the hell else is there? Right? So naturally this is very scary and depressing. But it's *not* democracy that's fucking everything up. It's capitalism. The kind of capitalists around now, Jesus, old Thomas Jefferson, he wouldn't *fart* in their direction. And why should he? They *exploit* democracy, they sell it right down the river. Like Vietnam, they want you to think when you go there you're defending democracy, they want you to be really confused about all this. And most guys are, too. You talk to Army guys, they don't say they're fighting for capitalism. They say it's freedom and democracy. And if you say, No, it's capitalism you're fighting for, then they say, What're you, a *Communist?* I mean, let's face it, these guys are programmed. Even after they get over there and *see* what it is, a big fascist cesspool with no free elections and no free press—they *still* fight for it. That's how fucked up they are. And meanwhile, the generals are all running around going crazy trying to figure out why seventy-five per cent of these cats are smoking grass. Man, if *I* was over there, I wouldn't be smoking grass, I'd be *shooting up.*

(*This confused Hank. He had to have it explained to him that shooting up didn't mean shooting up the Vietnamese, it meant dope. Then Roy went on.*)

ROY: Man, I think people have got to feel good about what they're doing. Otherwise it makes them really crazy. And I don't think Americans feel really good about what they're doing any more. Not only in the war either, I mean right fucking *here!* For instance, why does my dad want to be a capitalist? This is nuts. He works six days a week because he wants that half a million, and I think this is pretty disgusting. For instance, why isn't he interested in healing people? If he felt good doing that, he wouldn't want to *retire*, would he? He'd be digging his work too much.

DORIS: Aren't you being pretty hard on him?

ROY: Well, maybe. But I don't want to get into my father. He's only a symbol anyway.

DORIS: Tell me this, how do you feel about Communism? Do you really think that'd be a solution?

ROY: It's hard to know, because there aren't any countries that have it yet. Take Castro. Some people think he's fabulous, but *I* don't. He's getting rid of money, which is just great, but he's also putting all the gay guys in concentration camps.

DORIS: Don't you suppose there might be a pretty interesting clue there? Couldn't it be that Communism just isn't that groovy?

(*Doris looked at Hank.*)

HANK: I don't speak. The boy speaks.

ROY: I don't know if it could be groovy or not. But I'll tell you what drives me crazy. Nobody seems to be able to think up any alternatives to capitalism except Communism. It's true, capitalism is falling on its ass all over the place, but if you say so out loud, right away you're a Communist. It freaks me out.

DORIS: Well, aren't there other alternatives? Does it *have* to be either/or?

ROY: I just don't know. All I know is you can't go on forever having a country where everybody's robbing everybody else. And it's getting worse all the time. I don't mean just burglars and rip-off artists either. And it's not just the utility companies and big corporations. It's plumbers and doctors and lawyers and landlords and you name it. If you ask me, capitalism does that to people. It makes everybody freak out over property and money, like there wasn't anything else worth having in your life. For instance, work isn't groovy for hardly anybody, and not only that, it doesn't even pay the rent. You got to be in on some kind of a hustle or you don't make it. Guys know it, too. They look around and they see how it works, and if they can't hack it, they go on smack and then they become burglars or dealers or something like that. What else is there? If they want to be a carpenter or an electrician, say, or something *real*, they can't get in the goddam unions. I'll bet some of them wouldn't even mind running a fucking elevator, only they didn't graduate from some stupid college. I mean the whole thing has gotten too *weird*, you know? And what it amounts to, it seems to me, is if you've got a country where everybody's looking out for himself, then in the end *everybody* gets fucked. And that's where it's *at.*

(*At this point, I got into it myself. I hadn't expected to either. It just happened.*)

WITCH: Didn't you use to believe everybody'd end up getting turned on—and *that* would change the system?

ROY: That was before I came to New York. Now it just looks to me like everything's too rotten. Being underground really stinks, Witch. The only thing good about it is Canal Street. But every second away from here is a hassle. I can't get a job, I can't get a driver's license, I can't get a library card. I can't even tell people my real name. I don't like it. And I'm not gonna live my whole life like this either, hiding out just because I'm not a killer. I won't cooperate with this bullshit by running away from it forever. I'm nineteen now and I haven't got my shit together yet, but when I do—and it won't be long either—anyway, when I *do* get my head straight and the time is right, I'm putting in an appearance *above* ground. I am. I'm gonna say, Hey, this is John Mc-Fadden. Not *Roy* either, Witch. That's a name for hiding behind, and I dig it, but I won't *always* dig it, because I won't always dig hiding. What I'll really dig someday is standing up to all this shit.

WITCH: You know what you sound like?

ROY: What?

WITCH: You sound like a, well, a person that's in favor of —*violent revolution!* Are you?

ROY: Like I said, I haven't got it all together in my head. I'm reading Cleaver and Malcolm and Che and I'm talking to guys, and I don't know where I'm at yet. But Cleaver says if somebody's holding you down with their boot heels buried in your neck, there comes a time when you got to say, "Let

301

up, motherfucker!" And you got to *mean* it. And you got to let them *know* you mean it. Otherwise the crap goes on forever.

———————

There was silence for a while. Then all at once everyone seemed to realize it had turned cold. Roy put his hands into his pockets. Hank turned up the lapels on his corduroy jacket and pulled them close to his neck. Doris put her hands into her sleeves, using her sweater like a muff. Then she said, "I'm getting cold. Have you all noticed how cold it's getting?"

Roy said, "Yeah, you can see your breath even."

Peter opened his arms. "Let's make a huddle."

Doris moved into his right arm, and Roy moved into his left. Then Doris and Roy held out their arms for Hank and me. I moved in next to Doris, and that left Hank all alone and puzzled, looking at us as if we were Martians.

I said, "Come on, Hank?"

"What is this?" he said.

"It's cold. We're making a huddle."

"A huddle?"

He shrugged, and then he joined us, standing between Roy and me. For a while, in silence, we all stood in a circle there on the roof, with our arms around each other's shoulders.

Peter said, "I've got my eyes closed. Has everybody else?"

Doris said, "Mm-*hm!*" and Roy said, "Yeah," and I said, "Me, too."

Hank didn't say anything, so I took a look. His eyes were closed, too—tightly closed. When I saw that, I started feeling good about *everything*. I wanted to say so out loud, because I always want to put everything in words, but I knew it wasn't necessary. The current running through us was so strong you'd have to have been a corpse not to feel it. It was probably love. Whatever it was, it was *good*. And nothing else seemed to have any importance at all. Then gradually I felt the arms around me had begun gently to squeeze. Each of us took a little step forward and inclined our heads until they were touching. For a moment after we'd moved, I was aware of each of us again, Hank as Hank, Roy as Roy, Doris as Doris, Peter as Peter. I looked at our feet for a few seconds, the flower they made, each foot a petal, and I thought how extraordinary we all were to be together in such a perfect way, and when I closed my eyes again, I felt we were all one, just one eternal creature.

When the circle broke, everyone was smiling. Except Hank. I felt that he'd been moved, maybe even deeply, but his mind was still acting up. His face looked terribly puzzled and he didn't seem to know what to do with his eyes.

Doris and Roy and I started toward the stairwell, but Peter and Hank seemed to be doing some kind of a waltz with their minds. They hung back a little as if there were still more to be said. Peter pointed out the lights on the Jersey shore, said they always reminded him of a necklace. But I don't think that's where his head was. He was just chattering.

Then Hank said, "You have a high view of mankind. I don't share that. However, maybe if I take a little of your hashish . . ." He laughed and spread his hands as if to say, Then maybe I go crazy, too.

"Well, actually," said Peter, "a little hash *might* help. Would you like a toke?"

For a brief moment, Hank seemed to be tempted. Then he said, "I got to catch the ferry."

"There's always an extra bed here," Peter said.

"No, thank you. Another time. It was very enjoyable. I like to come back."

"I hope you will."

"Why?"

"Why what?"

"Why you hope I come back? For what?"

"I don't know. Talk some more. Who knows?"

Hank was in a peculiar mood. In a way he seemed to be elated. But he was confused and troubled, too.

Down below, on the sidewalk across the street, an old man appeared from around the corner. He was a scroungy-looking old thing, and he was having a hard time making progress. I couldn't tell if he was lame or drunk. Maybe both. Hank and Peter watched him for a few seconds. Then Hank said, "You see? That's man! That's mankind. There he is! Look!"

Peter nodded. "Doesn't look like much, does he?"

They kept studying the man's form as it moved haltingly down the street. Then he stopped, leaned against a wall, and slid slowly down to the sidewalk, all done in.

"Rest in peace, old man," Peter said. Then he said, "A man alone isn't much. In *twos*, he may improve somewhat."

"But not necessarily," Hank said.

"No, not necessarily. And in groups? Well, it's still touch and go, isn't it? And cities and towns aren't much either, are they?"

"One little earthquake," Hank said. "One little bomb— and good-bye."

"And nations, too. It's the same thing," Peter said. "They come and they go."

"Right!"

"But *mankind!*" Peter grabbed Hank's shoulder. "I swear to you, because I know this, I really do—you put all men together, Hank, and what you've got is God himself! And when we come to know that—really *know* it—we'll begin to *witness* something on this planet. When we get ourselves together, we'll bestow such blessings all around that every measly little motherfucker among us will become the great god, Man! *Overnight!*

"Talks a lot of foolishness," Hank said to me later, in the doorway downstairs, "but he's okay."

Then he looked at me. "Well! I go," he said. But he didn't move. He just kept looking at me. I said good night, but he didn't say anything. And he still didn't leave.

It was windy in the street. He pulled his coat collar up around his neck, and kept on looking at me. Then he said, "*You!*"

"What about me?"

He shook his head. "Smart girl, huh? Know everything about life. That Hank Gliss, you know all about him, too, huh? Angry old sonofabitch square, that's what you think." I started to protest, but he said, "Shut up," and took hold of my shoulders. "I know," he said. "I know. I know what I am. And I know something else, too." The tighter he held me the weaker I felt. I couldn't have spoken if I'd wanted to. I was in a daze, frightened, hypnotized. "You want to sleep with me," he said. "You want me to make love to you." He nodded. "Yes, I feel it from you. It's there. I know it is." He pulled me closer to him, but still not quite against his body. All I could feel was his closeness, his hands on my arms, his breath in my face, stale and manly and exciting. "I don't understand women," he said, "but some things I understand. I understand *some* things about women very well." Then for a moment, he seemed to be considering what might happen

305

next. I could see the act of love taking place in his eyes. Suddenly his jaw muscles tightened and through clenched teeth he said, "But I can wait."

And then he left.

I leaned back against the doorway, my heart pounding, feeling such a dizzy, weak looseness in the pit of my stomach my legs almost buckled under me. I wanted to step out onto the sidewalk and watch him moving up the street. But I couldn't stir myself. My will wasn't there. I wanted to run after him and say, Yes, yes, it's true, everything you said is true. Take me with you. Take me home. Take me. But my body was locked. So I just leaned against the doorway, still aware of the pressure of his hands on my arms. I hadn't gone with him, but I was his, and I knew it. The memory of him held me as firmly as his arms had. I'd never really wanted a man before, not really, not ever like this, not ever so completely. And it was such a relief to know at last, in my body and in my mind, what my soul had been trying to say to me for weeks. I stood there for a century or two, maybe five full minutes, smiling to myself, feeling warm and weak and sensationally happy. I kept saying to myself, Something's happening to you, Gloria. Something's happening to you. You have a lover, you have a lover, you have a lover . . .

Standing there in the doorway, dreaming myself into his arms over and over again, Hank began to seem like a dream to me. I couldn't even remember what he looked like. My mind had worn out the memory of him. So I stepped out into the street and looked around. Of course he was gone now, probably on the subway, or on the platform, waiting, thinking of me. I was sure of that.

The fact that the man was my father didn't seem too interesting to me. It was just a little side issue at that point, a minor inconvenience, no more of a problem, say, than if he'd been married or couldn't speak English or something. It would take some thinking about, some handling perhaps, but it wasn't going to stop anything beautiful from happening. Nothing would. I was sure of that.

So I went upstairs to my alcove and lay on my bed with my eyes closed. For the first night in weeks I wasn't thinking of Will or Delano or Archie or Edward. And I wasn't even thinking of Hank Gliss, not really. I was thinking of my lover, and I felt him there with me. He hovered over me, weightless, but with the most tremendous radiance. He said —but not with his voice, and I heard not with my ears— Gloria, I want you. And I said, I'm yours. And then he lowered himself over me until he was so close his radiance became electrical and shocking, and millions of tiny lights exploded all through me and through the entire house, and Gloria wasn't there any more. She'd stopped existing. The union with her lover had caused her to dissolve entirely.

Doris and Peter were at my side, holding me, and I didn't know why. It was the middle of the night and the house was quiet.

I didn't realize I'd been screaming and crying out until Doris asked me to remember what had caused it. I said I'd been having a bad dream, but that was some sort of a childish lie. It hadn't been a bad one at all. Had it? And so learning that I'd screamed confused me completely. Peter asked me if I'd like to talk about it and I said I would. So we went up to the attic and arranged ourselves on the Persian carpet.

At some point, Doris brought a pot of tea and some mugs and then left us alone again.

Peter took a little chip of hash and put it in his pipe. I didn't question whether or not I should have it, because he handed it to me like a doctor or a priest—the hash was clearly a part of his ministration.

"It's all about Hank Gliss," I said.

Peter nodded. "You're in love with him, huh?"

"Yes."

"It's got you pretty upset, hasn't it?"

"I guess."

"You're not sure?"

"No."

"Are there problems?"

"I suppose there are."

"You feel like getting into it?"

"I guess I'd better. But I don't know where to begin. I don't know what it is that's bugging me about it. I know he's the kind of person I could get really hung up with. He's such a perfect Virgo man, virile and yet super-vulnerable. But, Peter, I'm just—well, I'm *afraid!*"

"Why shouldn't you be? You say it's your first really power-house attraction. That can be pretty scary."

I couldn't think of anything to say. I felt we were getting off the track or something. Then Peter said, "Just what is it you're afraid of?"

"I think it's a certain kind of involvement that scares me. I just don't want to get that hung up over anyone. Even though part of me wants to terribly. I feel like such a fool. I'm babbling, aren't I?"

"No, you're not babbling. You're talking. Quit putting yourself down. You're a splendid chick."

"Am I really, Peter?"

308

"You sure are. If I could have my choice of any daughter in the world, there's none I'd rather have."

"Honest?"

"Honest."

"Doesn't it worry you that I fall in love with madmen? My God, Hank Gliss! Look at him! You saw him, Peter! Negative, bitter, uptight about everything. He'd probably make me miserable. And yet, I want him more than . . ." I couldn't think of anything or anyone I wanted even *almost* that much, so I had to leave the thought unfinished.

Peter said, "He wants you, too."

"I know."

"What makes you think it'd have to be a deep involvement?"

"Well, I guess it's because he's so—in need. I've got this mother thing going in me. I know I'd want to take care of him. He seems so sad and lonesome and helpless. I couldn't just sleep with him and leave him. I know he'd never let go of me."

Neither of us spoke for quite a while. Then I said, "Peter, why do I have to go falling for someone like Hank?"

"Oh, I can't guess about things like that, Witch. You'll have to help me."

"Okay, how do I help?"

"We'll just keep talking and see what we find out. We might as well start with the obvious. I suppose you've considered the fact that Hank's just about the age your father would be, haven't you?"

I nodded.

"Well then, it might be fairly simple. You've probably had some romantic feelings about your *own* father— and you've transferred them to Hank."

I shook my head. "No. No, it can't be that."

"Now don't go rejecting the idea *entirely*. Give it some time. It might seem unlikely, and possibly even a little *shocking* to you, but I promise you it's the most common thing in the world. Millions of women in fact end up *marrying* a carbon copy of the old man. They may kid themselves because the guy is young and they don't notice the similarity. But it's there. And they just live their lives, continuing the romance with Papa, and don't even know what's happening. But what they've married is a papa substitute."

"I'm absolutely certain that doesn't fit me, though."

"If you're *sure*, okay. But how *can* you be?"

"Because there's something I didn't tell you about Hank. And now I'm sort of ashamed of myself for not having mentioned it earlier. Actually, I guess it's sort of important."

My mouth was suddenly as dry as cotton. I took a sip of tea. Then I said, "Peter, he *is* my father."

"What do you mean, he *is?*"

"I mean Hank is my father! He really *is!*"

"Now, Witch, don't talk in metaphors. Give it to me straight. What are you saying?"

"Hank Gliss is my father. His real name is Glyczwycz. He was my mother's lover. She got pregnant, and I'm it. I'm his daughter."

Peter was flabbergasted. It took him at least a full minute to get the bare fact set in his head. He waved his hands, he paced the room, he hit the side of his head a number of times with the heel of his hand, all the while shooting questions at me.

I told him the whole story from the start. I told him about the day Uncle Mickey spilled the beans, and everything that had happened here in New York and that day on Staten Island. I brought him completely up to date. It was a tremendous relief to be telling someone. I hadn't realized how much I needed to do that.

At the end of the story, Peter said, "One more question, Witch. Why didn't you think to *mention* this little detail?"

"I guess I didn't realize, you know, *fully*, just how important it was. I know that sounds awfully strange, doesn't it?"

"Well, it might be worth thinking about a little. Don't you suppose?"

"Oh, I see! You think I was *repressing* it, or something like that?"

"It's just vaguely possible."

"But why would I do that? I'm not afraid of incest, am I?"

"You might be, mightn't you?"

"Wow, that just seems so tiresome and old-fashioned. After all, what *is* incest? It's just *a word!* I mean, the *important* thing is that he's a man and I'm a woman, and we want each other."

"Is it really that simple?"

"I guess you don't think so, do you?"

"No. And neither do you. Don't forget, you're the girl who was screaming in her sleep just now."

"Yes, that's true. But I can't *remember* screaming."

"Nevertheless you did. And when I asked you what it was all about, you *knew*. You said, 'It's about Hank.' Isn't that what you said?"

"Well, I knew the *dream* was about him. He was making love to me."

"Did you like it?"

"It was beautiful. Fantastically spiritual. I could feel his soul coming into me. The only bummer about it was *after*. It was like I didn't exist any more, and I knew that was why —because we'd made love."

"How did you feel about not existing any more?"

"I didn't like it at all. I knew I'd been terribly foolish, and it made me sort of panic."

"That must be where the scream came from."

"I guess."

The tea was wonderful. I drained the mug and felt the heat go through me like some soothing medicine. And while I was pouring more, I suddenly knew what he'd been driving at. "Oh! I know what you're telling me! You think my dream is warning me not to have an affair with Hank. Is that it?"

"It's your dream. Your soul produced it. What do *you* think it's telling you?"

"I can see it's some kind of warning. But does it have to be connected with the fact that he happens to be my father? Couldn't it be something else?"

"Maybe it's something else, and maybe it isn't. Let's leave the dream for a while."

Peter started fooling with the incense. He drew me into a discussion of the relative merits of sandalwood and frankincense, and when he had me really sucked in, he sprang a trap on me. Out of the clear, utter blue he said, "Why didn't you tell Hank you're his daughter?"

I felt *caught!* And it was an awful feeling. But at least I didn't start babbling and lying. I tried to be really truthful.

"I'm not sure," I said. "At first it was because I wanted to observe him like a stranger. I thought, If he *knows* he'll start acting some part instead of being himself. Then when I got to know him better, I just—didn't tell him. I don't know why. I've wondered about it though."

"I'll *bet* you've wondered about it. And what did you come up with?"

"I didn't come up with anything. I just went around depressed for about three weeks, and I couldn't think straight. At that point I still thought I was hung up on him *because* he was my father—but it wasn't romantic. I didn't know there was anything romantic about it until last night."

"And *he* told *you* last night. Right? And how did it make you feel?"

"I guess I was sort of shocked. For a second. But no more than that, because it was, well, it was really very groovy. I felt—like a woman in love. That's all. I was sorry I didn't dig his character more, but that seemed like a pretty minor consideration. And Peter, honestly, I didn't have any big reaction about the incest thing at all. I really didn't."

"Maybe you didn't. And maybe that's just fine, too. But I can tell you this, it's awfully goddamned unusual to be that liberated from a taboo as strong as the one against incest. I don't think there's a deeper one in the whole human lexicon. You kids! You never cease to make my eyeballs pop."

"Do you think we *should* feel all those taboos?"

"No, I don't. Not at all. But if you *do* feel them, then they still have some value for you. And I don't think taboos should be broken just for the sake of breaking them! They should only be broken when they have no value for you any more."

"What value could a taboo *possibly* have?"

"What value? They're part of your soul, that's what value!"

"The soul has taboos?"

"Of course! Where *else* would they reside? Did you think a taboo was just something society imposed on us because it wanted us to have hangups? We *are* society. We *make* the taboos. And when they get broken, we're the ones who break them. And if enough of them get broken by enough individuals just like you, well then, what you've got is a new society, a new *ethos*. And for all I know that's precisely what you kids are busy carving for us. That's why I'm stymied. I've still got taboos coming out of my ears, and I've got to be awfully sure I'm not pushing them off onto others, especially you young people."

"What taboos have you got? I thought you were just fabulously free!"

"Obviously I'm not. When you told me who Hank was, I just about went through the ceiling."

"Right. But I understand that. After all, you're older! I don't mean you're *old*. But you *were* born in the dark ages. And it *is* all different now. Isn't it?"

"It's getting different awfully goddam fast, I'd say."

"Then you don't actually know of any reason, do you, why a woman shouldn't have an affair with her father? *Provided* she's on the pill—because naturally you wouldn't want children to be born."

"No, you would not want to conceive you father's child. Jesus, I'm glad *that* taboo's still operating."

"Right, but there aren't any other reasons, are there?"

"I can think of one offhand, can't you?"

I thought hard for a minute, but nothing ever happens when I think hard, so I said, "No, what?"

"You don't seem to be at all happy about it. Hadn't you noticed that?"

At about 8:30 the next morning, while I was in the kitchen finishing my coffee, Roy came in wearing his World War I Army coat. His face was all splotchy and his nose was running. He looked as if he'd been out walking in the cold. I asked him what he was doing up so early. He came over to the sink where I was rinsing out my cup and put his arms around me, resting his chin on top of my head.

"I haven't been to bed," he said.

"Is everything all right?"

"Yeah, but we've got to talk. Have you got time now?"

"Not really, but what is it?"

"I'll walk you to the subway."

314

Then, instead of letting go, he hugged me. "Witch, I've got a heavy decision to make."

"Join the club."

"You, too?"

"Me, too. But what's yours."

"You first."

I told him mine was too heavy to just blurt out like that.

"Really? What is it?"

I dried my hands and put them on his arms. Then I took a deep breath and said, "I'm thinking of having an affair with my father."

"Really?"

"Really."

"Very heavy. Very heavy."

"Do you have any spontaneous reaction to the idea?"

"It just seems really radical is all."

"You don't think I should?"

"I didn't say that."

"Let's talk on the way to the subway. I feel this absolutely urgent need to go to work today. Stability or something."

"What about Sally? Is she ready?"

"She's not working today. The moon's in Virgo."

"Let's go then."

We talked all the way down the stairs.

"What's *your* thing about?" I said.

"Splitting."

"What do you mean? To where?"

"Toronto."

"My God, that's *Canada!*"

"That's the point. Joshua's on the run, just like me. The whole Boulder family is going with him. They think I ought to come, too. Joshua says being underground really sucks. He's had a year of it. He split from the Marines in '68."

"You mean that beautiful man was actually in the Marines?"

"Yeah, and started out really gung-ho, too. Then one day he found himself running up and down a California mountain swinging a bayonet in 110-degree heat, hollering *kill kill*, and it freaked him out. He suddenly *saw*, you know? Anyway, he split."

"And now he's going to Canada?"

"He has to. They're on his ass. And you know why? His brother told them where he was. His own blood brother. Are you ready?"

"Fantastic."

"Weird. So anyway, they've been running all over the country in their bus saying good-bye. And when they're done, they head for the border."

"How soon will that be?"

"Maybe this weekend. They've got one more good-bye number to do in Baltimore. Lu's family. They figure it'll take a few days.

We were halfway to Broadway and I hadn't even realized we were outdoors yet.

"And you're going with them?"

"No, I'm just trying to decide. Would you come with us, Witch?"

"Oh, wow!"

"What's the matter?"

"I don't want the world to stop," I said. "But it could slow down a little. My brains are withering."

"Maybe you shouldn't go to work today."

"I've got to."

"Why?"

"I don't know. I think I'm trying to prove to the world that we take baths and are disciplined. Is that silly?"

"Only if it gets tense."

"It's getting tense. Oh, Roy, what'll I do?"

"Come to Canada."

"No, I mean about work."

"Fuck work."

"You're right." There was a coffee place across from the subway station. I said, "Let's go over there, I'll phone."

"Tell them it's your monthly."

"That's too gross. I'll tell the truth."

"Which truth? Canada, or your father?"

"Cool it, will you? You're making me nervous."

"Don't be nervous. Laugh instead."

"It is funny, isn't it? Look at us! Little John McFadden, and little Gloria Random. Remember when we were small, how we used to dream about being in the thick of it?"

"Yeah."

"Is it thick enough yet?"

"It can get thicker."

"You're right."

"I know."

Then I said, "John, I'm going to say something really awful."

"You called me John."

"No I didn't."

"Yes you did."

"All right, *Roy*. Roy, I'm going to say something pukingly female, only you've got to promise not to listen or I won't say it."

"I promise."

"If you go to Canada without me, I'll die."

"I didn't hear you."

"I knew I could count on you. What are we standing here for?"

We went across the street to this big brown Formica Fluorescent Kwik-Lunch horror. Roy ordered coffee while I

317

telephoned Mrs. Oggins at Capricorn Capers. She said it didn't matter whether I worked or not, there was nothing to do anyway. When I got back to the booth, Roy was half-way through a French cruller. That ought to be good for about six good fat pimples, I thought. But instead of saying anything about it, I ordered one myself. Thoroughly dunked, they're so terrific you tend to forget little details like the world's coming to an end.

Roy said, "You know, I just now got the full unadulterated blast of what you said before."

"What did I say?"

"About your father."

"What do you think?"

"I don't know. My head's still going *twaaannng!* You really dig him, huh?"

I nodded.

"I can see why."

"You can?"

"Sure. I dug him, too."

"Truly?"

"He could make me forget all about Steve McQueen."

"You really think he's that attractive?"

"I'm not sure how much I dig his head though."

"He's far from hopeless," I said. "Last night on the roof he talked about getting into some hash with Peter."

"Really? That's far out."

"His head is capable of change. Don't you think his head is capable of change?"

"Why not?"

"Okay, so what shall I do, Roy? Tell me."

"How can I?"

"*Think* about it. Say he was your father. Would you?"

"My head's going twaaaaanng all over again."

"Twaanng yes or twaanng no?"

"It means twaanng my mind is blown. I'm thinking about being in bed with Hank. And I dig it."

"Then you *would!*"

"Um, we're assuming no hangups, right? On either side? I mean, we both want to?"

"No hangups. Except for the bare fact that he's your father. Which in itself can't be a hangup, can it?"

"Not unless it bugs you."

"Say it didn't."

"Well then, I don't see what the problem is. Except that if you get into a big *thing* with him, you probably won't come to Canada with us. And that's a drag."

Later in the morning I went with Doris to the launderette and told her the whole story.

"I wouldn't go through with it," she said, "but then, I'm not you."

"Why wouldn't you though? Can you tell me why?"

"Easily. I couldn't handle it. I'm not that free and I know it."

"But if you were that free?"

"I'm not, sweetheart, so how can I know? I was born in 1923. Do you know what the world was like when I was growing up?"

"I sort of know. But tell me."

"Looking back on it now, it seems like a fairytale. Everything was so simple. Not easy, mind you, far from it. But simple it was. You knew what was right and what was wrong. Or you thought you did. And that's why it wasn't easy. You were always wanting to do the wrong things, and whether

319

you did them or not you felt guilty just the same. Frankly, I don't know how any of us got through it."

"What were some of the wrong things you wanted to do?"

"Sleep with boys."

"Did you do it?"

"At your age? Once. And I put us both through such hell as you wouldn't *believe!* He was sweet, too, and I'm sure he loved me, absolutely certain of it. But that didn't cut any ice. He still wanted something *bad.* And when I gave in—get that phrase?—that's what we called it, we called it *giving in!* Oh, God, let's not talk about it any more. No, I don't mean that, of course we'll talk about it. But I don't see how I can be much help to you."

The last rinse cycle was over, so we dumped everything into the dryer and sat down again.

"Witch," Doris said, "I just thought up some wisdom for you. Are you ready?"

"Let me guess. May I?"

"Sure."

"Whatever I do, it should make me feel good about being me. Is that it?"

She nodded. "Because there aren't any authorities any more, darling. Just the one, the one we carry inside."

"What if it gives us the wrong advice?"

"It won't."

I took a bath and washed my hair, and while I was drying it and think about what dress to wear—I felt it should definitely be a dress, not slacks—Sally came in to go to the john. When I offered to leave, she said, "You don't have to, it's only sugar water."

I said, "I knocked on your door a while ago because I

wanted to discuss something urgent with you. But it's not urgent any more."

"Well, if it's not urgent, we won't have to meditate first. What is it?"

"I want to have an affair with my father, and I wondered what your opinion would be."

"I thought so!"

"You knew?"

"No, just a hunch. Witch, you've got the prettiest toes."

"Do I? Thank you."

"Absolutely. Your entire *foot,* in fact. Um, why are you asking me?"

"About my father? Because I respect your head. You're the highest chick I ever met."

"Oh!"

"What's the matter?"

"You see what happened? Tears squirted out of my eyes the second you said that. Thank you, my adorable Witch, what a lovely thing to hear about oneself. But if I'm beautiful, it's just a reflection of you—because you're doing the seeing. Now I'm going to give you a present."

She ran down the hall and came back a few seconds later carrying a leather thong strung with turquoise donkey beads, and placed them around my neck. I looked in the mirror and praised the beads and thanked her.

"You really like them, don't you?" she said.

"Just look. They make my eyes go *zow!*"

She looked at me in the mirror. "Yes! They *do!*" Then I looked at her image and she was smiling at me. "Oh, Witch," she said, "I can't imagine you ever doing anything that wasn't beautiful. That's just an impossibility. You know that, don't you?"

"I think I know it now," I said. "Because I've made up my mind, and I'm very happy."

"You've made up your mind?"

"Mm-hm. But now I've got to decide what to wear, because I'm getting on the two-o'clock ferry."

I wanted to be in the parking lot, sitting in his station wagon, when Hank got off the boat.

———————

There were two minor flaws in my plan. One, all the doors were locked, so I had to sit on the hood waiting for him. And two, he wasn't alone. He had three people with him, two longhaired guys and a chick. One of the guys I recognized from class, a bright, tall, slightly fat kid named Terry. He and Hank were deep in conversation when I spotted them, the other couple was trailing along behind.

My first thought was *Get out of here, fast.* But by the time I picked up my notebook and got it into my bag, it was too late to escape. When Hank saw me he stood stock still and stared, mouth slightly ajar. And then he did something beautiful. He smiled at me. I was tremendously relieved. (Why did I expect to be humiliated?) I went to him and held out my hand. He shook it firmly, acting as if I were an old friend he was delighted and surprised to see, and introduced me to the others. The two I didn't know were called Cissy and Cosmo, a pair of Scorpios with far-out eyes. His were pale gray and hers were brown. Cosmo was tall and slender and blond, and full of high restless energy.

Hank said to me, "You come to cook for us?" But his eyes seemed to be saying, You come to make love with me? Whichever he meant, I felt that yes would cover it.

I'd never seen Hank happy before. All the way to the farm, whenever he looked at me, I felt he was seeing something that had been produced by a magic wand. After a mile or two I was completely over any disappointment I'd felt because he wasn't alone. Terry and Cissy and Cosmo seemed to be pretty good heads and I was glad it was all turning out as it was.

Conversation on the way home was full of excitement. Terry was expecting a big inheritance on his 21st birthday. I didn't hear the exact amount, but I guess it must have been in the millions, because he was hoping to buy a huge piece of land somewhere and start a new nation on it. Communes you hear about every day, but new nations are rare. And yet they all seemed to be dead serious about it. They were hoping some poor nation in South America would sell a piece of itself, or maybe one of the big countries would come up with an island somewhere and donate it just for the sake of getting rid of the longhairs. The new nation would be called New America, and it would be patterned after the U. S. as it was at the time of the first revolution. At first I thought Hank was just flattered at being consulted, but he kept asking more and more questions about Terry's ideas, his political philosophy, etc., and gradually it dawned on me he was really hooked on the idea.

When we got to the farm, Cosmo and Cissy lost all control. They were like a couple of wild things just let out of a box for the first time. They ran in and out of the barn, squealing and exclaiming and wow-ing. They rolled in fallen leaves and dropped them in one another's faces. They chased the chickens and quacked after the ducks and threw sticks for the golden retriever. Hank's face as he watched them kept filling up with emotion that caused his jaws to tighten. I began to feel that each present happiness of his life set off the memory of some past pain. And he didn't know how to handle it. All he could do was chew his own teeth and swallow his own heart and try as best he could to hold himself together.

I started getting the vegetables together and Hank and Terry went into the house for more talk.

Terry had a folder full of drawings to show Hank, plans for the architecture of New America. He'd been accumulating information on low-cost building techniques that were being developed by some of the communes out West. Someone from the Kingdom of Endor in Boulder knew how to build a Bucky Fuller-type dome house out of pentagram-shaped scraps of metal for less than $200. And someone else knew how to take trash and press it into building blocks ten times cheaper than concrete and twice as strong. Hank studied it all carefully and asked dozens of questions.

Terry's idea was to invite representatives of all the existing communes to a great convention to make plans for the new nation. I'd heard of some of them—the Hog Farm, the Brotherhood, Drop City, Endor, Mount Shasta, Strawberry Fields—but the list was two pages long. I had the feeling Terry was probably a reincarnation of some great empire builder of the past, one who'd worked off all his greed Karma and was ready now to dedicate his genius to mankind.

Hank said, "Where will the money come from? Your inheritance is not enough."

"It's enough to *start*. And all we *need's* a start. The rest will come when it's supposed to. Watch what happens when word gets around. Rich, powerful, turned-on people all over the world will want to help. And I don't mean just John Lennon either. There are people everywhere just aching for a chance to make something real and beautiful. Men with a genius for government who haven't been able to function because they're not corrupt, millionaires sitting on fortunes they don't know what to do with, guys with fantastic engineering skills who aren't interested in building another A & P

324

or patching up Chicago because they care too much about the future."

"You believe there are such men?" Hank said.

"I *know* there are! Some I've talked to myself, others I've heard about! They're everywhere!"

We heard a scream and went to the window to look. It was Cissy having a giggling fit. Cosmo was helping her climb a tree and must have touched her funny bone. They were as naked as Adam and Eve before the fall.

Hank said, "Is this what the new nation is for? Nudism?"

"No isms," Terry said. "No nudism. No clothesism. Just people living the way they want to."

"What happens to people who don't want to look at naked bodies?"

"Are there people like that?"

"Perhaps."

"I guess they'll have to—turn their heads."

"Or form their own little tribes," I said. "Couldn't they do that?"

"Sure," Terry said.

"All right," Hank said. "What do I do when the police come?"

"If there's a fine," Terry said, "I'll be glad to pay it."

"Paying the fine is easy. But I get fired, too. Then what?" At that moment Hank had a lightning quick change of heart. "Never mind. I don't care. I *like* to get fired. Let them play. They don't hurt nobody."

Hank sat down at the table again. "I wonder if I'm too old for new countries," he said.

"No, sir," Terry said. "I know you're not."

"How you know?"

"I just know."

"Okay. Maybe you're right. Let's smoke some marijuana. Maybe I get younger."

Terry broke out a joint and we smoked it.

A few seconds later Cissy chased Cosmo through the kitchen and they went flying up the stairs panting and squealing with joy.

Hank pointed after them with his thumb. "Who's that, the secretary of state?"

Terry laughed. "Cosmo's studying dentistry."

Hank nodded. "That's good. We need dentists."

"You said, 'we.' "

"I must be crazy." Hank began to stack the drawings and put them back in their folders. "Let's get this out of the way. My head's too full. I want to think."

"And I'd like to take a nap. Okay?"

Hank pointed to the stairway. "Go find a bed."

Terry went upstairs. And the minute he left the room, my heart went cold. Hank and I were alone together. And I was scared.

———

I concentrated as hard as I could on peeling the potatoes, grateful to have something to do. Hank was watching me and I knew it. For a long time neither of us spoke, and the longer the silence continued, the more careful I was with the potatoes. I longed to see his face, but something kept me from looking at him directly. I tried to think up some small talk, but I was afraid my voice would betray the panic I felt. What's wrong with you, Gloria? I asked myself. What's happening to you? But no answers came. Hank made some sound, but I couldn't interpret it without seeing his face. It was a kind of sigh, low and guttural and deep.

"What are you thinking about?" I said. I was surprised to find my voice functioning normally.

"You."

Oh, God! What am I doing here? What will happen to us?

"Me?"

"Your hair. It's like my mother's. Your hands, too."

Tell him why. Tell him why. Tell him why.

I put down the potato and the paring knife and looked at my hands.

"Come here," he said.

No! Don't go near him. Tell him who you are first.

But I didn't listen to myself. Instead, I picked up a dish towel and dried my hands. Then I walked over to him and stood in front of him, looking at him. There was so much going on in his face, I lost myself for a moment in wondering about him. He seemed to be straining after a key that would make his whole life come together in some true and comprehensible shape. And I knew he was hoping to find it in me.

He took hold of my wrists and studied my hands as if he'd never seen anything so strange and wonderful. Then he placed them against his face.

"Smooth, too," he said. "And cool."

The contact with his face set off some dreadful reaction deep in my stomach and my heart was beating so hard I had trouble breathing. I didn't know what was happening, but I longed for it to stop. It was like some ghastly sadness, but much worse. I remember once waking from a nightmare, I found my mother slapping me for all she was worth. I tried to explain to her some nameless grief I felt, but she went right on slapping me. The frustration was so frightful I thought it would kill me. And that's how I felt there with Hank, trying so hard to force the truth out of myself, but unable to. And the reality of what he'd suffer when I did kept slapping me and slapping me. But not hard enough to make me speak. And yet it kept getting worse.

With my hands still on his cheeks, held there by him, he raised his eyes and looked into mine.

"Who are you?" he said.

I had no voice left, but I managed to whisper, "Who am I?"

"All of you. Them, too." His eyes glanced briefly upward, indicating the second story of the house. "I don't understand," he said. "All these plans. All this young hope—*in my house.* I see it. With my eyes, I see it." He shook his head. "But I don't believe it."

Then he pressed his face against me, against my bosom. "I know the world," he said. "Good things don't happen. Not any more."

I said, "Yes they do, they happen all the time." But I don't know where that came from, because all I wanted to do was to scream and run.

Please tell him now, I begged myself. *Please, please, please. It's already too late, but tell him now before it's really too late.*

One of my hands was free. I touched the top of his head with it. "Hank, listen to me."

"Ssh ssh ssh! Dreams can't talk. You're a dream."

"No. No I'm not."

"Then why do I feel so good with you?"

"Do you really want to know?"

"Yes. Tell me."

"Because you're my father," I said.

I could only see the top of his head. For a moment he seemed awfully still, almost as if he'd stopped breathing.

Then he said, "Oh, I see. And you're my little girl. Is that it?"

He thought I'd been making up a lovers' game.

I knew I had to go on with it now. But not like this. Not with his head on my breast. I disentangled myself. "Excuse me, Hank." I walked over to the sink and picked up a peeled potato. There was a big eye in it and I found myself wanting to cut it out. Instead, I dropped the potato in the sink and looked out the window, forcing myself to speak.

"I'm Gloria," I said. Then I realized he wouldn't know that name, or if he had, once, he wouldn't remember it now. So I said, "You're Hank Glyczwycz. My mother is Irene O'Malley."

As soon as the words were out, I knew I'd done something dreadful to him, but it was such a relief to know they couldn't be taken back that for a moment I felt only pleasure. I just stood there and grabbed the edge of the sink as hard as I could. I felt his eyes on me, but I didn't know what was going on in them and I was afraid to look. Then I heard him say, "Detroit," and I said, "Yes."

There was a tremendous thump and crash behind me. I spun around and saw him standing with his fists clenched. He'd knocked over the table and one of the chairs, and seemed to want something else to smash. He was pure white, as if his blood was frozen with anguish deep inside of him.

My hands were pressed against my stomach, and he was staring at them. Then something changed in him. He cocked his head to one side and stood with his shoulders hunched, jaws clenched, and scanned me all over through narrow eyes. I still wasn't sure what was happening, but I knew I'd brought him pain and confusion so excruciating he could hardly endure it. At first he wasn't breathing at all, but then suddenly he began to take in short little gasps of air, letting them out with a rasping sound, almost a growl, like a badly damaged animal.

There were footsteps on the stairs. Then Terry and Cissy and Cosmo were standing in the kitchen doorway, looking, trying to understand what was happening. The water for the potatoes started to boil on the stove, and I thought, We'll be standing here, just like this, when all the water's boiled

away, and then the kettle will burn and still no one will move
or speak, and we'll go on standing here forever.

But Hank did speak, finally. He said, "Get away from here.
All of you. And take your New America with you."

Terry said, "Man, if you could just tell me what . . ."

Hank moved toward the dining room. They stepped aside
to let him through. He kept on going, and then we heard
him climbing the stairs. As soon as he was gone, I thought,
Now I can turn off the flame under the potato water. And
when I'd done it, I took the kettle and moved it to the side
of the stove. When the water stopped boiling, I started to
cry.

Cissy came over to me and put her arms around me. The
boys picked up the kitchen table and set the chair straight.
Then Cissy said, "Cosmo? Terry?" And the three of them
stood in a circle around me, holding me.

There was a gas station about a half a mile away. Terry
went inside and telephoned for a cab, and while we were
waiting for it to come, we sat on the curb and felt the sunset
and talked.

I didn't tell the story very well, but they asked questions
and I answered them as well as I could. Their questions
helped my head a lot, because I said some things I didn't
know I knew.

Cissy said, "Do you suppose it would've been better if
you'd told him who you were right from the start?"

And I said, "Yes, because then he wouldn't have had anything to do with me. He'd've thrown me out, like he did just
now. And I wouldn't have hurt him so terribly."

Cosmo said, "They're like that. They really are. They won't

let you tell them the truth. And if you tell them anyway, they clobber you."

"It's funny, though," Terry said. "If he liked you before, how come he didn't like you *better* when he found out who you were?"

"I guess it's the bed part," Cissy said. "He wanted to go to bed with you, and that must've messed up his head."

"That's it!" Cosmo said. "I'll bet *anything* that's it."

"Incest," Terry said. "They're scared shitless of incest."

"Poor man," Cissy said. "Imagine what he's putting himself through right now. Do you suppose there's something we could do? Why don't we go back and tell him we love him?"

Terry said, "I don't think we better, not right now."

"Why not?" Cissy said.

"I couldn't," I said. "I'd feel too ashamed."

"What's to be ashamed about?" Cosmo said.

"I deceived him."

"You *had* to."

"No, I didn't. I could have left him alone."

"You wanted to get to know your father," Cosmo said. "Is that some crime?"

"You know what I think it is?" Terry said. "I think it's life. I mean it's not always *us* that's wrong, you know. Sometimes it's just life that screws us up."

"Nah, it's *him*," Cosmo said. "They don't *have* to get that uptight. They just *let* themselves. I say fuck 'em."

Cissy put her hand on his. "Oh, Cosmo, you don't mean that. Do you?"

"No. I guess I don't actually. They can't help it."

Terry said, "This sky is fan*tas*tic!"

"It really is," Cissy said.

"The whole *planet* is," Terry said.

We looked at the sky for at least a full minute. Then Cosmo said, "I'll bet this is one of the best planets of all."

"You mean in this solar system?" Terry said.

"No, man, I don't mean in this solar system. I mean in any of 'em!"

"That's what I think," Terry said. "I really do. I really think Earth is really special."

"You bet your ass it's special. This isn't just some little leftover planet. It's got everything, for godsake. Can you name me a one thing it hasn't got?"

Cissy said, "Peace."

Terry said, "It's got *some* peace, hasn't it?"

Cissy said, "That's true."

When the cab came, Terry said he wanted to go back to the farm and see if Hank was all right. When we got there, the driver said he was sorry but he couldn't afford to wait for people. Terry promised him an extra dollar and that made it all right—so Cosmo and Cissy and I waited while Terry went inside.

He was in the house less than a minute. When he got back into the taxi, Terry told the driver we were ready to go to the ferry, but he didn't say anything about Hank.

By the time the cab got turned around and on the road again, I couldn't keep quiet any longer.

"Is he all right?"

Terry didn't look at me. "He's all right. He's got a bottle of whiskey."

"What's he doing though? Is he just drinking it?"

"Mm. He's already put away quite a bit of it."

"Did he say anything?"

"Not much. He wanted to be left alone."

"He did say *something* though, didn't he?"

"He wasn't too coherent."

"He said something ugly, didn't he?"

"You really want to hear it?"

"Yes, please. I have to."

"Well, like I said, he was very drunk."

"I know. But tell me."

"He said you were like your mother, that you'd like to have a—certain experience with a Polack, but . . ."

Cosmo said, "Come on, man, spell it out for her. She asked to hear it. It's *her* life, isn't it?"

Terry looked at Cosmo and nodded toward the driver. "I don't think it's cool to spell it out right now."

Cosmo said, "Oh. Okay, I'll shut up."

"He said *that*," Terry continued, "and then he said you wanted to make a fool of him. Only I'm not sure he wasn't talking about your mother. Like I said, he was drunk."

I asked if he'd said anything else.

"No, he just told me to get out. So I said, 'Okay, Mr. Gliss, but we still love you.' That got him really sore and he called us all some names. You know. The usual. So I left, and that was it."

We rode on in silence for a couple of minutes. Then Cissy said, "Why do they get so angry when you tell them you love them?"

"Maybe they think we're lying," Cosmo said.

"What about it, Terry?" Cissy said. "*Were* you lying? Or did you really mean it?"

"No, I wasn't lying. I think we *all* love him, don't we? I know *I* do."

"Me, too," Cosmo said. "He's a fantastic man. When he gets really tuned in, he'll be a giant."

"Truly," Cissy said.

"You agree?" Cosmo said.

"Oh, *truly* I do," Cissy said.

ORANGE—WILL'S GREENHOUSE, OCTOBER 31, 1969

Happy Halloween, dear journal, you gruesome, tender, relentless sonofabitch. Sally Sunflower has gifted me with a complete set of Magic Markers and Nyoom has comforted me with a small but superb chip of Lebanese Blond. And so tonight, for the first time, in honor of all the souls in hell, Ta-tum-te-ah-dah, ta-*taaaaa!* I scribble you in color, a lovely sweet orange to brighten this dark, moonless, high-flying night. Your mistress has ascended on her pure white broomstick to the rooftop, where she will pass the magic hour plying her wondrous crafts by candlelight. With the aid of one and a half tokes of Brother Nyoom's hash, I have achieved THE SUPERIOR ALTITUDE OF ALL TIME. And now, with Sister Sally's Magic Markers in my pointed hat, I will fly through time, coloring everything superpluperfectfantabulousMcWow!

Bright Green—Thanksgiving 1970

The greatest day in the history of the world! Blue sky, thrilling air, Indian summer sunshine! And *peace!*

Nixon got on TV last night and made a full confession. The war is over.

Amnesty has been declared for all draft refusers.

Also I have a lover.

I was sitting on the grass at the thank-in in Central Park this afternoon, playing my guitar and singing—

(Yes, I've taken up music. Not quite Judy Collins yet, but pleasing and true, and so much easier than diary-writing. Don't be offended, my love, but you are a down head, you know. You've always brought out the worst in me, forcing me to pick over my life like some ghastly deathbird that . . . Ah, but never mind, no recriminations!)

Um, where was I?

Ah, yes, the meeting with my new lover.

I was sitting on the grass at Bethesda Fountain, singing a John Sebastian song—

> *"I had a dream last night.*
> *What a lovely dream it was.*
> *I dreamed we were all all right,*
> *Happy in a land of Oz"*

—when suddenly I became aware of a dark, smoky voice in my ear, singing with me.

"What a lovely dream it was.
What a lovely dream it was."

His sound was a cool glade in a deep forest. Mine ran through it like a river of sunlight. At the end of the song, I turned to look at him.

It was Will, of course.

He was still wearing his black and white striped prison uniform. The second they opened the gates for him, he raced out to look for me, too eager even to stop and change clothes.

"Sally wrote me about you," he breathed.

"I know, I know," I said. "And your alcove under the stairs. If you knew how many nights—"

He silenced me with a kiss. Hand in hand, we walked together into the trees, where the rites of love took place on a high secluded knoll, accompanied by Hare Krishna chanters.

Later, walking down Broadway, bells and chimes ringing everywhere, still hand in hand, we were a breathtaking couple, I with my slim hips and Will with his statue-of-Prometheus build, tall and proud, receiving the adulation of the multitudes as people threw flowers from windows at the returning hero in his striped prison garb. Small children ran to—

Oh! But a woman in love has no time for a diary. Even as I write this, my lover is at my elbow, nibbling my ear, whispering . . .

Red—Christmas 1970

Enchantment continues. Nixon was so pleased by public response to his Thanksgiving show, he got on again last night and did a Christmas Eve number. He announced he was pulling the rug out from under every fascist dictator in the world. No more guns. The entire Pentagon has been turned into Third World headquarters, and all the $ is being spent on goodies.

Many surprise guests for dinner. Hank Glyczwycz with his terrific wife, newly returned from Pittsburgh with the two children, my half-siblings Andrew and Marie. Then there was Terry and Cissy and Cosmo, who said they'd given up their New America plans because Old America was getting so groovy. And Archie Fiesta, off dope forever, healthy and happy, and full of plans for getting his friends off their needles.

Robin's Egg Blue—Easter 1971

Now that spring is here, Will and I have moved into the greenhouse. It's heaven, but there are minor inconveniences. For instance, the smell of gardenias gets a bit heavy on warm days. And I suppose when the baby's born, we'll find it a little crowded.

Marijuana Green—Fourth of July 1971

Just got back from Washington. The smoke-in on the White House lawn was a fantastic success, thanks largely to Sally Sunflower. We haven't yet learned how she managed it, but in the middle of the afternoon she suddenly appeared on the podium with Julie and David Eisenhower in tow. The three of them stood there and lit up a red-white-and-blue joint, publicly challenging the police to arrest them. But they weren't into making busts today. Besides, while Sally was doing her thing with Julie and David, the police had their hands full trying to get J. Edgar back into his clothes. It seems the poor old thing can't handle Acapulco Gold unless he's naked. But he's terribly cute, and has dimples in the oddest places.

TURQUOISE—LABOR DAY 1971

Things are happening so fast I can hardly assimilate them. For instance, I had the baby this morning. On the roof. Will and I delivered him ourselves. We're calling him Free to make sure no one ever forgets who he is.

MAGENTA—NEW YEAR'S DAY 1972

Peter ran out of money. But it doesn't matter any more. We're all moving to Staten Island in the spring. Hank insisted. He feels Canal Street has become too crowded for us, and much too rickety. Besides, he wants his grandson to grow up in a country atmosphere.

Pink—Beautiful Spring Day 1972

Today we sail for Staten Island.

Later, on the ferry

There was no one to see us off on our voyage, because *everybody* came with us. However, departure was glorious. What a righteous-looking collection of riffraff we were, parading onto the boat. Joshua's VW bus, bursting at the seams. Sally riding on top of it with Nyoom and Mary. Hank's old station wagon, with beds tied to the roof. Jeanette, looking like she'd swallowed a basketball. Roy, the father-to-be, beaming with pride at her side. Doris, covered with pots and pans. Peter, carrying Percy the Cat. And all the others, marching along behind, carrying bags and sacks and cartons and baskets. Terry and Cissy and Cosmo of course, and Cary Colorado with Lu and Motherlove Ford. And bringing up the rear, Archie Fiesta, our beautiful minstrel, playing his guitar and singing even sweeter than Donovan.

And me. I'm writing it all down as fast as I can because not a moment of it can be lost!

Now where are Will and Free? The last time I saw them was back at the toll booth.

Oh! *There* they are! Will has Free in his arms and he's pointing out the Statue of Liberty.

340

PURE WHITE—THE FOURTH OF JULY, 1976

Dear oh dear. I've lost a few years, haven't I? Well, no matter! It won't take a second to bring it all up to date.

Obviously I've all but given up this nasty habit of writing. Much too busy living and grooving and being.

But I *must* make a few quick notes about what happened in Washington today. When the children grow up, they'll be asking how it all was.

First, I suppose I'd better do a little shorthand version of the last few years.

The Staten Island move was a fantastic success. The family grew and grew and then other families came to join us, and pretty soon there was a tribe, and everything worked out so perfectly that the next thing we knew we'd become a model for other tribes. Then the movement started spreading like wildflowers and, well, there's no use going into detail. Our history is common knowledge now. When the children begin to ask, we can take them to the U.U.N.N. Museum (Union of Utopian Non-Nations).

So! Back to Washington, and this afternoon.

Pat and Jeanette greeted us at the White House door. (They're close friends now, sisters really. Roy, as Secretary of Enjoyment, has to confer with Dick a dozen times a day, so he and Jeanette and the baby and Archie are living in the

341

Lincoln Suite. They miss the farm, but it's infinitely more convenient this way.)

The crowd was enormous. There were so many people I wanted to meet and didn't, but there'll be other occasions. Anyway, Will and I had a lovely chat with Mao Tse-tung. He's a real *alta cocker* and I thought Peter might enjoy meeting him, but I couldn't pull him away from Kosygin and Timothy Leary and Huey P. Newton. The four of them pow-wowed all afternoon, working out details of the World Peyote Congress that's planned for next spring.

I'm glad there were lots of movie cameras, because all the pencils and papers in the world couldn't capture the extravagant costumes. The Beatles, wearing George Washington wigs, played together for the first time in years:

> *All together now*
> *all together now*

And then the Big Moment arrived. Everyone went out on the White House lawn to watch the raising of the flag. And it was the most beautiful flag anyone had ever seen. Solid white. Even whiter than the whitest cloud. The pure white flag of surrender, and as it went gliding up the flagpole, a signal went out to the whole world by television and Telstar, and everyone alive who has a voice was wide awake and waiting for it.

Cary struck the note. "Om."

And then the sound of the universe was everywhere at once—

OOOOOM M M M MMMMMMMMMMMMMMMMMM MMMMMMM.

Later, when some of the excitement had died down, I felt it was time to find Roy and get him to introduce Free to the president. These things are still important to little boys. Besides, I was anxious to get a look at him myself.

On the way up to the Lincoln Suite, we bumped into Jeanette on the stairs. I asked her where Roy was, and she said he was in the Oval Office with Dick. So she took us by the hand and led us down the hall.

The door was open, so Jeanette walked right in, but naturally Free and I waited out in the hall. Then we heard her saying, "Hi, Dick. Hello, sweetheart. Heaven, wasn't it? Listen, Dick, I want you to meet a couple of old friends of ours. Got a minute? What *happened* to them? I thought they were right behind me. *Witch! Free!*"

Then Free and I walked into the president's office.

Roy was sitting on the edge of his desk, and the president was standing behind it. I suppose meeting any great leader could blow a woman's mind, but meeting America's first turned-on president did a permanent number on my eyes. He's gotten truly handsome in the past few years. His eyes have lost that awful beady look that used to frighten us all so, and his nose is much shorter than it is on TV. Also his hair, when you see it up close, has a lovely texture to it, and the length is perfect for him. It just *touches* the shoulders.

Black and White Again—Will's Greenhouse, October 31, 1969

Roy just paid me a visit. It was nice. He wanted to know if I was okay up here.

I said, "How would you like to read a capsule history of the entire world through 1976?" And I showed him my Magic Marker entry.

I thought it would make him laugh. But it didn't. It made him cry. Not a big boo-hoo number, but it put tears in his eyes. I asked him why, and he said, "I don't know, but I'd give my nuts if it could happen a tenth that good."

Monday we head for the border.

On Joshua's Bus, About 100 Miles East of Buffalo, November 3, 1969

Joshua's driving like there's no tomorrow. His shoulders are all hunched forward and he's leaning into the wheel like a racing driver. It doesn't do any good though. The bus has a top speed of about 65.

Nobody's talking much. We're all nervous about the border crossing. If Joshua gets caught and sent back, the Marines will put him in prison and torture him. It's hard to believe anyone could hurt such an obviously good and gentle person, but the whole idea of desertion turns them into sadistic maniacs. We've agreed not to think about this possibility, because if we think it, we'll bring it about. That's Motherlove's theory, and if it's valid, poor Joshua's had it.

Lu is in the passenger seat with his eyes closed. Roy and Motherlove Ford and I are riding in the back. It's like being in a covered wagon except that the pioneers didn't have Crosby, Stills, and Nash playing on the tape deck.

Motherlove is giving herself a Tarot reading. Roy is studying the map of Ontario. A few minutes ago he announced that as soon as we cross the Canadian border, his name will be John again. He says there's no point in moving to a free country if you can't be yourself.

As for me, I'm just sitting here, maintaining. I have a feeling I'm not supposed to be along on this trip. In fact, I know it.

Last night—my last night in Will's alcove!—I had a dream. The five of us are piling into Joshua's bus, but there isn't enough room. So we rent a little U-Haul trailer and hook it on the back. I insist upon being the one to ride in it. I forget why. I guess I felt it was my fault there wasn't enough room in the bus. Anyway, while we're driving along, the little trailer becomes unhooked. Nobody in the bus even notices. They just go driving off without me, and I'm left bumping along the highway with no motor and no steering wheel. End of dream.

This morning, like a dumb bunny, I went around asking everyone if they were sure the bus wouldn't be crowded. Naturally everyone said there'd be plenty of room. So here I am. And now that it's too late, I know exactly what the dream was trying to tell me.

I think I have every right to be a little bored by my own willfulness. Maybe with a little cunning, I could induce one of these peaceniks to kick my ass for me.

Oh well, there's nothing to do now but make the best of it.

———————

Ever since Roy decided to split for Canada, he's had this feeling he might never see Archie again. This thought kept bugging him more and more, so yesterday he asked me to walk over to Spring Street with him. We climbed the six flights to Archie's floor and then when we'd caught our breath, we walked down the hall to Archie's door.

Roy knocked and the door fell in.

Apparently it had been torn right off the hinges and was just sitting there propped against the doorframe. So we climbed over it and went inside. The whole place was a shambles. The kitchen window was wide open and the wind was blowing in, tearing at the window shade. Most of the furniture was upside down and broken. The mattress had been slashed open. The stuffing was coming out and there was blood all over it, dozens of big dried spots. At first I pretended—not only to Roy but to myself, too—that I hadn't noticed the blood. I just wouldn't let that word into my head. But then Roy looked at me in a certain way and I knew what he was thinking.

I said, "It may not be his, it may not be Archie's."

But we both knew it was.

I don't know which was most horrifying, the blood on the mattress, or the way the wind kept tearing at the window shade.

I said, "Shall we get the police?" But as soon as I'd said it, I knew how foolish the idea was. Obviously there was nothing to be done, nothing at all. So we closed the window and left.

Chances are, we'll never know what happened. And probably, for the rest of my life whenever I think of Archie I'll see his beautiful face in my mind and I'll hear that window shade flapping, flapping flapping . . .

After midnight

We're safe! We just crossed the bridge into Ontario. The Canadian customs men are beautiful. All they did was ask where we were born and wave us on through.

I could actually feel the place where the USA stopped and Canada began. For the last fifteen minutes leading up to it, the suspense was terrific. Hardly a word was spoken.

Then, at a certain point on the bridge, we all started talking at once.

Motherlove said, "Wow."

Roy, who is now John again, said, "Jesus, I'm a fucking Canadian!"

Lu said, "Man, we're out of it!"

Joshua said, "Nobody shit! Just think what powerful sphincter muscles we must have!"

Now he's sitting back easy for the first time since we left New York. Even his hair seems relaxed. It doesn't look nearly as electric as before.

Roy has his face pressed against the window, trying to dig his new landscape.

Motherlove says our success at the border didn't surprise her at all. The Tarot prophesied the whole thing.

———

Peter said one night that if Archie Fiesta didn't make it, we'd all go down the drain. He said we needed *everybody*. So, yesterday before we left New York, I reminded him of it. I asked him if he thought we wouldn't be able to create the golden age now, because Archie hadn't made it. And Peter said, "Oh, please, never pay any attention to the things I say. I must have been stoned. Of course we'll make it. Don't you know that?"

SPATAFORA STREET, YORKVILLE, NOVEMBER 4, 1969

The Toronto Anti-Draft Committee found this rooming house for us. We have an entire room, with a big bay window and everything included, for only $55 a month. We're not supposed to have more than two to a room, but nobody pays any attention. We share the kitchen with about twenty other freaks, but Motherlove doesn't mind. We weren't in here five minutes before she was down there doing her thing with the soup pot.

Roy's sitting on the floor next to me writing his father a letter. He could never write him from New York because he didn't trust him enough. He was afraid Dr. McFadden would give his address to the Army.

With fathers like that around, who needs the CIA?

————————————

Father. What a strange word. I've been sitting here tripping out on it. If you repeat a word often enough, it really goes through some changes. Now it's like a word I've never heard before. Our father who art in heaven. Hello, father.

349

The poor child had no father. Father's Day. God the father. G. W. was the father of our country. I haven't seen hide nor hair of my father for days and days. She had a falling out with her father. And now, my children, we have left the fatherland. Father father, quite contrary, how does your daughter grow? The father I go, the less I know.

I'm freaking out. Better take a walk.

The Zumburger Cafeteria on Bloor Street, later in the afternoon

Felt the need to be alone. But when I got about a block from the rooming house, I started feeling anxious again. I wonder if I'm getting neurotic?

Getting?

Ever since we got here, I've had the feeling that just south of us a few miles there's this enormous suffering animal, moaning and screaming with sadness and trouble, writhing and kicking and giving off smoke and dollar signs and poisonous gases and noise. And the name of the animal is America the Beautiful.

I wish I'd known it when it *was* beautiful. Maybe I did. In some other incarnation. Maybe a hundred years ago I crossed it in a covered wagon. Maybe I traveled then across the same country we passed last night, and with the same companions. None of us has changed much either. Mother-love even wears long dresses, just like she probably did in those days. No doubt Lu was our Indian amigo, turning us on with his peace pipe. And I'll bet Joshua drove the horses. I wonder what John and I were? Abandoned children they picked up along the way?

350

Just now, when I wrote about the sad suffering animal called America, I flashed on Hank, sitting in his lonesome kitchen on Staten Island, drinking his whiskey, thinking about me. I know what that means, too. It means that if there's suffering in America, I'm part of what caused it.

———————————

Canada is beautiful. The sky is enormous. And there's plenty of peace, space, time, air, freedom, everything a person could want. The streets are wide and clean, and nobody's mad at us.

There's only one little pocket of ugliness, a street called the Strip that's just like St. Mark's Place in New York. The same grimy-looking freaks sitting on doorsteps. I suppose they're on smack or speed just like the ones back home. The dumb shits. I had my usual schizoid reaction. Part of me wants to gather them up and help them—as if I'd know how! Part of me wants to spank their poor lost stupid little asses for them.

And a third part of me wants to grab a needle and join them.

Why am I so unhappy?

Spatafora Street, twilight

When I came back from my walk, I saw a note on the mailbox downstairs—

> SEWING—CHEAP
> buttons—5¢
> patches—10¢
> See
> Motherlove Ford
> Room 9

And there in the kitchen, right this minute, sits Mother-love, putting new elbows in some freak's fatigue jacket. Between stitches she stirs the soup pot.

If she's not a pioneer, the Pope's not Catholic.

Tonight I'm going to find some quiet corner and stay in it until I rot—or until I write a truthful letter to Hank Glyczwycz, my father who art in Staten Island. And if it's not truthful, really truthful, I will remain in outer darkness forever and ever amen.

Dear Hank,

If you'll just read this one letter with an open mind, I promise never to bother you again. After that awful day in your kitchen, I wrote you a letter from the ferry on the way home, but I didn't mail it, because what I wrote wasn't true. I said I hadn't told you I was your daughter because I was afraid you were so bitter about my mother you wouldn't have anything to do with me. *Not true.* I also didn't want you to think I was the kind of girl who'd lead a man on, etc. *But I am.* This is hard to admit, but I have to because it's true and I'm so sick of lying I just can't bear to do it any more. When I was 12 and they first told me about you being my father, I started having all sorts of dreams about you. They said you were an anarchist and an intellectual and all kinds of ugly things I wasn't supposed to like. But I did. In fact, all I could think about was finding you someday and getting close to you. And then when I did find you, something about you scared me I guess. So I tried to hate you. You seemed at first to be so bitter and tough I thought hating you would be really easy.

But still I couldn't keep away from you. I told myself it was because you were my father and I needed you. But now I know that wasn't true. The real reason I kept going to your class pretending to care about government and hanging around you all the time was because I knew you desired me as a woman and I enjoyed it. I didn't realize this at the time, but I do now. To help you understand this perversion of mine, I have to admit something else I've never admitted to anyone, not even my diary. Men don't often look at me the way you did. I've always gone around pretending they're all wild about me, but it's not true. I don't know if it's because of my hips or my personality or what, but I just don't turn men on the way some women do. (My mother, for instance.) Anyway, you're a super-attractive man, I guess you know that, and the way you look at a woman makes her feel pretty fabulous. Maybe you don't realize it, but women can get hung up on feeling like that. Even so, I had sense enough to know nothing could happen between us. I hardly ever thought about it even. But then on Moratorium Day night, when we were saying good night in the doorway at Canal Street, any sense I had left was shot. No man has ever come on so strong with me. And now I suppose you'll think this is the worst part of all, but I might as well admit it. When I went out to see you the next day, I still didn't intend to let you know who I was—not until after we'd become lovers. When it came down to it, though, I couldn't let the lie go that far. Something in me stopped it. In my opinion this indicates I'm not hopeless. I suppose it looks like I'm writing all this to justify myself. Maybe so. But I'm also trying to be honest for another reason that's more important. I got the feeling on Moratorium Day, and the day after, too, that you were beginning to like some of my brothers and sisters, especially Cosmo and Cissy and Terry, and I just can't have you thinking they're as messed up as I am. Because they're not. They're real people, true and honest, I swear they are, and besides, they love you, they really do. Also, they need you. No doubt there's a real credibility gap between us now, but if you could just *try* to believe me, I'd appreciate it TREMEND-OUSLY!

Love and peace,

Witch Gliz

P.S. When I left home this past summer, I changed my name. If you say it backwards, you'll know why.

A BENCH IN QUEEN'S PARK,
NOVEMBER 5, 1969

Three colossal pieces of news this morning.

1. Lu's got a job. He's going to be assistant mechanic for the limousine company that drives people to the airport.

2. I wrote the letter to Hank. Also, I *mailed* it.

3. John has a lover. He lives upstairs from us on Spatafora Street. They met in the kitchen and spent last night together. It must have worked out pretty well, too, because John's walking around pinching himself. The boy's name is Rio. He's dark and short, with big brown eyes like Dondi in the funny papers. He's a Mexican-Canadian, a student at the University, and he's a Taurus. This morning John's wearing a wooden love-cross Rio gave him. A love-cross, according to Rio, is just like a crucifix but it doesn't have any dead bodies hanging on it. It's supposed to remind you of love, which is what Jesus was all about.

John's never had anyone follow him around like a puppy before, and he's really digging it. Also it makes him walk differently. Overnight he's developed this kind of swagger guys get when they think they're pretty humpy dudes. And it's quite becoming. I've never seen him look so manly and handsome before.

This park is other-worldly. There are leaves of every color, even purple. The sky is so blue I can hardly look at it.

The sky's not the only thing I'm having trouble looking at.

Now that John has a lover, I can't pretend any longer that he needs me.

Oh, he needs me, of course. We all need each other. But what I mean is he doesn't *need* me.

And hasn't for a long time.

And won't for a while.

And that's that.

Wow.

It's Suzy Solo now.

Time to take a walk.

Another bench

This is weird. I've never felt so alone in my life, but I'm actually digging it. Refusing to face it got fairly heavy there for a while, but that's all over now, thank God.

Tomorrow I'm going back to New York.

Suzy Solo hits the road.

And she's feeling pretty fucking groovy about the whole thing.

SPATAFORA STREET, 7:30 a.m., NOVEMBER 6, 1969

Gorgeous, fantastic snowstorm. The whole city is covered in white and it's still coming down. Perfect for hitchhiking. I'll look like a waif and all the motorists will take pity on me.

Motherlove is cooking oatmeal for me. She calls it "a good hot meal for the road." After breakfast the entire family except Lu, who has to start work this morning, is taking me to the edge of town. We'll all climb into the back of the bus and have a Zap. Then I'll get out and stick out my thumb.

Last night they gave me a farewell party. Freaks from across the hall brought grass and everyone got stoned and gave me presents. Lu gave me a box of raisins. He says they're the best food for hitchhiking, lightweight and nourishing. Joshua gave me his jew's-harp roach clip, and Motherlove gave me the longest scarf I ever saw. It's a brown wool herringbone and you can wrap your entire head in it. I didn't like to take it at first, because her godmother knitted it for her a skillion years ago, but Motherlove said I had to, because when she first left home, she hitchhiked from Minneapolis to Chicago in it. Rides came along like magic. She says when the right moment comes along I'll pass it on to some other wintertime traveler who needs luck. Mother-love has a real feeling for tradition.

The present from John blew my mind even more. It's his love-cross from Rio. I started to put up a really big protest, but Rio was right there at his elbow, urging me to accept it.

Rio has this irresistible Taurus dearness. I felt sure that if I asked him for his *knees*, he'd start right in trying to figure out how to get them severed and delivered.

"You have to take it," he said, "you *have* to."

"But Rio, this cross is—*special*."

John said, "That's why you have to take it." He turned to Rio. "Right?"

"Jess!" That's Mexican for *yes!* His tone was so final I was afraid it might tip over into anger, so I kissed him and let him put the cross around my neck.

Then John said, "What time tomorrow?"

"I thought early'd be smart. What d'you think?"

He nodded.

"Saying good-bye is going to be a real super-bummer."

"Oh, c'mon," I said. "It'll be worse than *that*, won't it?"

"Yeah, right. It'll be superbummerscaryawful*McSadd*."

"Knew you could improve on it."

"Dig the McSadd?"

"Totally."

"Thought you would."

Then we both shut up and got into each other's arms. He whispered in my ear, "If you ever forget how beautiful you are, call me up and I'll tell you."

I promised I would.

The oatmeal's ready.

Later, in a very nice man's car

I am a peculiar girl.
I am not on my way to New York.
I am on my way to Belle Woods, Michigan!
Can't write more. Car or something making me nauseated.

Belle Woods, Michigan,
NOVEMBER 7, 1969

I feel as if my soul had grown about 24 years' worth in the past 24 hours. It turns out that for all my self-doubting and self-chastisement, I've been doing everything right, wonder of wonders.

For instance:

Going to Toronto was right.

Leaving there when I did was right.

Coming home was right.

Everything I've ever done in my life has been right. Life is guided. There aren't any mistakes. Not really. There's confusion and self-doubt, but there aren't any real mistakes. If I fuck up, it's because I'm supposed to—for growth. I have this perfect clarity about everything now, and oh, God, I pray I can hang on to it for a while. It's so beautiful to see things making sense for a change.

When Joshua and John and Motherlove took me to the highway on the outskirts of Toronto yesterday, we were all sublimely high. Not on grass or anything either. It was love. We parked the bus on the highway and got in the back and held hands together, all of us determined to feel a sense of rightness and peace before I got out and started hitchhiking. If we hadn't done that, who knows what would have happened? Anyway we did, and when the moment came for me to go, we all knew it was okay and that whatever happened would be good and beautiful.

And so of course the first car to come along was *my ride.* As soon as I saw it coming, I knew it would stop for me.

The driver was one of the sweetest people I've ever met, a baldheaded hardware salesman named Mr. Kaminski. When I told him I was going to New York he said that was fine, he'd be passing the New York turnoff on his way to Detroit and could drop me there. But the minute he said Detroit, something in my head went *clang!*

Pretty soon he started talking about this daughter of his who'd freaked out while she was at school in Kalamazoo and had to be sent to the Menninger Clinic, and how awful he felt because he knew a lot of her troubles had been caused by his own ignorance. I listened to the whole story and the next thing I knew I was *forgiving* him all over the place. As if I were his daughter or something. I told him mankind was going through the biggest social change it had come through since the days when we were swinging down from the trees 50,000 years ago, and nobody should blame himself too much for not knowing how to manage it. I'm not even sure where that thought came from. I must have read it somewhere recently. Anyway, I found all sorts of odds and ends in my head to comfort him with. I told him I didn't believe it was fair to lay *all* the hangups on one's parents. I said I was convinced that children are people with their own little trips going, and they're quite capable of doing some pretty fancy numbers on older people's heads, as well as the usual vice

361

versa. I have to admit I was brilliant. I was like Peter would have been. Peter said once that the best thing you can do for somebody is let them off the hook. Meaning, help them over their guilt so they won't be crippled by it and can be free to find ways to press on.

Anyway, Mr. Kaminski and I got really thick. He doesn't smoke pot, but he has a truly high grasp of things. He listens. He listens not just to the words but to where the talk is coming from. He sticks his ear right into your soul and digs it. I came right out and told him I wished I'd had a father like him, and I was sure that if his daughter had a freak-out, it was probably part of her Karma to have one. He didn't know what that was, so I explained the law of Karma to him, how each person, because of some past incarnation, was born to have certain difficult experiences that would foster his soul's growth. I said some really interesting things, stuff I'd heard from John and Sally Sunflower and Cary Colorado and God knows who else, all of which I sincerely believe but had never rapped to anyone else before.

I realize now that I've been doing a lot of sitting-at-the-feet-of this past couple of years, listening to all sorts of wise people and not doing much rapping of my own. And it's nice to be away from my beautiful teachers, off on my own, making use of the wisdom I've been gathering. (WARNING: Didn't I hear somewhere that only fools think of themselves as wise?)

Anyway, Mr. Kaminski needed to hear the things I told him. I'm sure he did. He went after every word like a pussycat lapping up spilled cream. Can it hurt to make a person feel good? Of course not! Besides, I was so high—and still am!—that I couldn't possibly have been *too* mistaken about anything.

So: We got along like—I was going to say gangbusters, but why not be accurate? I was like a priestess hearing his confession and giving absolution. But that's too cold. Priests are hidden in their little boxes and there's no warmth or humanness. I guess it'd be more accurate to say simply that we befriended one another. Yes, we got along like *friends.*

Anyway, about three miles before the New York turnoff, we stopped at this little roadside place and had a bowl of soup together. Barley soup. Hot and delicious. It made me think of all my faraway families in New York and Toronto, so I introduced Mr. Kaminski to the pre-meal Zap. Life is truly fantastic to think about. There I was, Gloria the Fuck-up Glyczwycz and a baldheaded traveling salesman holding hands in a Canadian roadhouse at high noon. What a dear good sweet man he was. And to think, wow! that an hour or so earlier I'd thought he was just a stranger.

And while we were having our soup, the roles got reversed. I made my confession and *he* forgave *me.*

I told him how I'd swindled mother that time at Western Union and how I must have made her suffer by doublecrossing her and not even writing to explain.

Mr. Kaminski was as brilliant in my behalf as I had been in his. He said he'd learned something from the Menninger people that might be of interest to me. They told him he wouldn't be allowed to visit his daughter for a few weeks because she needed, "for her mental health," an experience of separation from him. Parents and their young *need* such periods, he said. And perhaps cutting myself off from my mother for a while, cruel or not, was the healthiest thing I could have done.

Mr. Kaminski went on talking, maybe for a full five minutes, but I didn't hear much of what he said because my head tripped out on him.

Something had touched off my fantasy button. I started imagining things: Instead of going directly to New York, I drive on to Detroit with Mr. K. and check out the Belle Woods scene. My mind played out six or seven full-blown confronting-mother movies. In one of them, she's icy-cold and gives me the silent treatment. In another, she's super-civil and deftly hides her hurt to make damn sure I see it. In still another, she's genuinely loving and dear and everything's wonderful between us. In version #4, she just lets herself go and beats the shit out of me. Etc.

But I knew for certain the real meeting would be nothing like any of these. You can never ever guess how a thing is going to be. You just have to go and see.

Mr. Kaminski was delighted. Even though he himself was going to Dearborn, he offered to drive me all the way to Belle Woods, which would be roughly three million miles out of his darling sweet, generous way. Naturally I couldn't let him do it. The poor man looked tired enough to begin with, but by the time we got to the Ambassador Bridge, crossing over from Windsor, it was rush hour, the air was pure carbon monoxide, and I had flashes of Mr. K. having a full-fledged coronary right there in the front seat. So I told him I had scads of taxi money and could manage beautifully. Which wasn't strictly accurate. But I did have bus fare.

When we said good-bye, his eyes got wet. So I told him I'd always remember him. And it's true of course. I'll always remember Mr. Kaminski.

Detroit had some snow, too. Lots of it. The weather wasn't quite cold enough to keep it together, so the half-mile walk from the bus stop to home was pure slushville.

The sky was heavy as lead. No, it wasn't. It was dusky silver and quite beautiful. But it *felt* heavy as lead. And weird, too. Nothing, virtually *nothing*, looked the way it was supposed to. Everything had changed in sneaky surrealistic little ways that you weren't supposed to notice. The streets had gotten wider. Houses had changed shape. And color. And most mind-blowing of all, everything was *real*. I suppose I'd come to feel in the two months away (is that *all?*) that Belle Woods was just a remembered place, something that had dissolved along with my childhood. What a wild conceit! To be surprised that the old neighborhood had survived my departure from it!

Finally, trudging along through the slush, I rounded the bend where Warrington Drive meets Fisher Circle, and at that point I knew I'd arrived. I was a hundred yards from whatchacallit. The word, I believe, is *home*.

The house wasn't visible yet, but there was that preposterous stone arch, designed, I suppose, to make you think you were about to approach the Taj Mahal. I walked over and leaned on the hideous thing and looked up the driveway to the house.

Putty-colored stucco with black shutters. Just as big and handsome and chic and grim and grotesque as ever. And the grounds were like a sad, deserted park. Lots of gorgeous soft blue evergreens and vast snow-covered lawns. No gangs of screaming children. No dogshit, no litter, no old ladies with lumpy legs crowding together on benches. No homeless blacks sleeping on newspaper pillows. No fuck-yous scrawled on the pavement in chalk. Nothing had changed at all, it was just as useless as ever, a lovely, haunted wasteland presided over by Mother.

For a few minutes I was afraid I wouldn't be able to go through with it. In fact I actually heard myself saying so out loud. "I can't, I can't, I simply can't do it."

And then, *whoops! Who* can't do it?

I like myself, remember? I am beautiful. I can do anything that needs doing. I'm the girl that brought tears to Mr. Kaminski's eyes when he said good-bye. I have beloved families all over North America. I have a love-cross around my neck. This morning I was nourished by oatmeal cooked by a pioneer. I have friends to call up and think about and remember. And powerful Zaps coming at me all the time. John says if I ever forget who I am, I should call him up. Well, I don't have to. I remember me well. I'm one of the faces of God, that's who I am. I'm always futzing around with what to call myself, but it's very simple, really. I'm Gloria God. And now it's time to go ring the fucking bell.

Thus, with my motor all nicely revved up, I walked up the driveway, trying not to guess what would happen next. And it's just as well, because I couldn't have, not in a thousand years.

Maude Dangerfield opened the door. That meant there was a crisis in the house. How did I know? Very simple. She wouldn't be caught dead in a place where there wasn't one. (Scorpio, moon in Aries, I forget what rising.)

Mother, who has this fantastic faculty of turning friends into servants and making them like it, acquired Maude back in the days when they were both secretaries at Random Hogan Random and Hodge. But I don't think they got really thick until I turned up—in the form of a troublemaking little foetus. My hunch is that she tried to get Mother to abort me, but I have no real evidence. Also, I could be wrong about this. Let's face it, I'm *here*. But Maude is so efficient and sensible that she sometimes gives me the chills. Her natural habitat is funeral parlors (death really turns her on), but she can also be found in courtrooms, hospital corridors, and in homes where tragedy has struck. Her specialties are whispering, tiptoeing, administering dope and liquor, keeping her cool, knowing things nobody else knows, and seizing telephones on the first ring. I'm not putting her down for all these talents either. She's a fantastic woman. When I was small, she was kinder to me than anyone I can remember. And I suppose if I ever got busted or fell out of an airplane or something, I'd be really glad to have a Maude Dangerfield around to help get the pieces together.

What else do I know about her? She's 50, maybe 55, married but has no kids, lives in Palmer Woods, and has a husband who bores her so radically she gasps every time his name comes up. He's an executive at Detroit Edison, so of course he never gets busted or falls out of airplanes or anything, and I guess that's pretty rough on poor Maude.

So: There she is standing at the door in a flesh-colored jersey suit looking like a plucked grouse, with pearls.

"Well, my God in heaven, I do not believe this," she said. Her voice is a flat, utterly surpriseless drone. I suspect she knows this and cultivates it. It's the style she's taken on for her part in the movie.

She looks me over thoroughly, from muddy boots to unbrushed hair, clocking every detail. Then she purses her lips, smiling an eyes-only smile, and nods. "I told Irene she'd be hearing from you one of these days. Now get in here and take off those wet clothes. And whatever you do, don't make a sound."

"What's happening?" I sat on a bench in the foyer and pulled off my boots.

"What's happening, she asks. Nothing, girl, nothing at all. Oh, God. The irony. This is going to be really cute to handle."

"*What* is? Where's Mother?"

"Oh, she's fine. Irene is just fine. Everything is under control. Will you be here long? What are your plans? But never mind now, I've got to think what to do."

"About what?"

"About you. You're not supposed to be here. Nobody is. Irene's in hiding. She's had an operation, among other things, but it was nothing dreadful, so don't panic. She just doesn't want anyone to see her, I mean visit her, for a while. It's been ten days and somehow I've managed not to murder her in cold blood, isn't that amazing? No, it's not amazing at all, I love her to pieces and she's been good as pie. Are you confused? So am I. Listen, Gloria, you and I were always good buddies, weren't we? I think I'd better take you into my confidence. Promise not to betray me?"

"Of course."

"Good. Because I'm not sure how much of this she'd be telling you herself, so what I'm actually doing is taking one hell of a liberty. Are you ready, or do you want to get comfortable? I'm having a teensy in the sun room, what about you, will you join me? No, you won't. You prefer marijuana. I know all about it. Would you like to smoke some now?"

"I don't have any."

"Because I'm *not* opposed to it. I've smoked it myself once or twice, it doesn't do a thing for me, but you go ahead and light up. She'll never be able to smell it up there. Oh, but I don't know about her. Irene's got an uncanny nose. Better wait'll we get into the sun room with the door closed. I've got a gas log burning in there and it's terribly cheerful. How are you anyway? You haven't said a word."

I'd forgotten how pretty the sun room was, with its enormous windows opening on the woods, and several great fat ferns hanging from the rafters. Maude and I sat facing each other on bright yellow fireside chairs. Her cocktail was on the table between us, and just as she reached for it, a bell started ringing. It wasn't the phone and it wasn't the door.

"That's your mother. I brought her a bell last week. What a blunder. Excuse me, would you, I think I'll run up and smash it." On her way out of the room she said, "I assure you this won't take long. I'll be back in one minute. For godsake, don't make any noise. I'm not telling her you're here, do you understand? Not yet!"

One minute later she returned. "The television set was doing its little horizontal flip-flip-flip madness, but everything's peachy again. Why aren't you smoking your marijuana, sweetie?"

"I don't have any."

"Well, then for godsake have some brandy."

"No, thanks."

"No thanks in your own house? Don't be silly! Do *I* have to tell you to make yourself at home?"

I said, "No, but you said she'd had an operation, and I'd like to know—I mean, what was it?"

"Officially? A tumor. In cold fact? She's had her face lifted."

"*Face* lifted! You're *kidding!*"

"No I'm not kidding and I wish I were. Because we're none too certain how pleased we are with the results. The doctor told her not to even *look* for a month. It's been ten days and all she does is stare at the mirror and cry. I said, Irene, I'm sure the operation would be a dandy success if you'd just please refrain from crying yourself all out of shape. But she doesn't listen. Yesterday I took the mirrors away from her and made her promise faithfully not to look for at least another week. That lasted three hours. I'm going to be frank with you, Gloria, she's driving me up the wall. If I didn't have my little six-o'clock Manhattan, I'd be in a rest home by now. I'm not angry with her, I'm really not. She's been through absolute hell. As you can well imagine. After all, she had no warning whatever, not even a glimmer of suspicion, *nothing*. And whoppo, he's gone, like greased lightning."

"*Who?*"

"Your father, that's who! Oh, but of course you couldn't have known that. You haven't been in touch at all, have you, you naughty thing. Don't you know how to write a postcard? Oh, now don't be angry, I'm not chastising you. But you see, things *have* been *happening*. Glamour boy has flown the coop. Did you know he had a double life? Does that shock you? What am I saying? Of course it doesn't, nothing shocks you kids. And more power to you, I'm *right* behind you, every inch. Yes, a double life, sweetie, and quite an extensive one. I'm not *betraying* anything either, because I know you can handle a confidence just beautifully. Besides, he's your mother's husband and you have every *right*. Listen, do you want to hear the rest? The woman is only twenty-nine, and what's he, fifty? Which is all right, *of course*, May and September can be perfectly beautiful. But she's *very* lower class. I mean very-very. And that could be all right, too, I suppose, but my God, she looks like something the cat dragged in and she has three children. Oh! Did I mention she's Puerto Rican? Well, she is. And this, in my opinion, is what's *killing* Irene. Do you know what *she* says? She says Fred must have had some sort of sexual perversion he'd been hiding from her all these years. Isn't that touching? She's trying to justify things, you see. It's sweet, actually. Do you know, Gloria, I've always found your mother very appealing. It's true, I have. That's probably why I haven't murdered her. She's just a little bitty girl, that's all she is. She's about eight, I'd say. *Maybe* nine. And innocent? She wouldn't know life if it hit her in the face—and of course that's precisely where it's been hitting her! Oh, God, did you think I was making a pun? Because of the operation? Well, I'm not. I wouldn't joke about that. I *couldn't*. When something breaks my heart, I can't make jokes about it. And listen, now that we're talking about it, I may as well lay it on the line. A face lift is *major* surgery. She's got to be quiet and completely non-active. Any sudden movement could cause the stitches to pull and if that happens, the whole thing goes *flump*. Also there's some swelling and she's sort of black and blue. Or *was*. Now it's sort of green and yellow. And of course the bandages are still on, so naturally she isn't anxious to be seen. In fact, she made me swear on my eyes I wouldn't let a living soul come near her. And here *you* are. *Quel* dilemma. Any ideas?"

I didn't have any ideas about anything. I was too busy taking it all in.

I said, "Maude, please, what did she go and have her face lifted for? It didn't *need* it, did it?"

"No, not at all, she was pretty as a picture. Maybe a few crow's feet, but what's that?"

"Well then, why?"

"Very simple. Fred takes off with a woman of twenty-nine. So the next day she's looking up plastic surgeons. Perfect menopausal logic, don't you think?"

I didn't answer. And silence makes Maude uncomfortable.

"What's the matter?" she said.

"Nothing. I'm just thinking about it all. You said this woman is Puerto Rican?"

"*Or* Negro. I'm not sure which. The name is Spanish but she's involved in Black Power, so take your pick."

"Black Power! Wow! Where did he meet her?"

"At the office. She worked in the mail room, been there

for months apparently and Fred didn't even know her. Oh, he might've seen her at the water cooler, you know, just a face. And then somehow the word started going around that she was involved with Black Power and next thing you know there's a bomb threat coming in over the switchboard. Isn't this frightening? Anyway, this woman's *immediately* under suspicion. But nobody's got anything on her. So Fred takes her to lunch. *You* know—espionage. Lord knows what happened from there. I suppose he asked a few questions and she must have come up with some terribly beguiling answers, wouldn't you say?"

"And he's moved in with her?"

"Isn't it amazing? *Fred Random!* I didn't know he had it in him. Listen, I'm thawing some beef stroganoff. Why don't I go out there and double it up with a little rice or something. You must be famished."

"No! I couldn't eat."

"Why? What's wrong?"

"My stomach. It's upside down." I stood up. "Maude, Maude, listen. I'm leaving."

"Right this minute?"

"All I need is some dry stockings. I've got some in my bag."

"Where will you go?"

"Back to New York."

"Oh, Lord Jesus, what a situation!"

I walked over to the door and opened it just in time to see Mother scurrying through the front hall toward the stairs. It was like a scene from some spooky movie. Her head was all bandaged, except for some hair showing in the back, and she was wearing a gray chiffon wrapper that trailed behind her as she ran.

It was obvious she'd been listening at the door, and when

I'd said I was leaving, she must have decided to split. I guess I spoiled her getaway by opening the door too soon.

As she started up the stairs she glanced over her shoulder. We saw each other, and there was nothing to be done about it. What *could* I do? Become invisible?

She let out a little cry and kept running—right up the inside of her wrapper. And fell.

The fall wasn't violent. She'd reached out with her arms to break it, and it was obvious she hadn't been physically hurt. But of course Maude went right into action just the same. She tried to push past me, but I didn't let her. I said, "Maude, could you leave us alone?" And amazingly enough, she did.

Even though Mother hadn't injured herself, I knew there was something important about the fall. I knew it because she didn't get up. She didn't even try to. She just lay there on the stairs in a shapeless little heap, weeping gently. That's what wrecked me, the gentleness of it. She wasn't at all hysterical. Just defeated.

I went up and sat next to her, just close enough for her to know I was there. I was sort of afraid of crowding her, and yet I had the feeling she was going through something pretty heavy and could use some company. After a minute she stopped crying and one of her hands moved toward me. So I took it and held it. Then she cried some more, but not hard. Just soft. Soft and easy. It was as if the fall had caused some tiny leak way inside and now all the sadness of her life was flowing out of her as soft as breath. It must have been a fantastic relief for her. And I was enjoying it, too. It was really nice, being there with her like that. I think it was the first time she'd ever let me love her.

This morning—after lying awake half the night wondering what it would be like between us from now on—Mother and I struck a bargain. The miraculous thing is that no words were exchanged.

I went in to see her while she was having breakfast in bed. Maude was still busy raising blinds and arranging magazines and Mother was chattering. I didn't try to follow what she was saying. It was obvious she was just producing a lot of ladylike noise and stuffing up holes in the morning with it. ". . . I just told Maude if you spill coffee on crêpe de Chine you might as well drown yourself and it's the same at Bergdorf as it is at J. L. Hudson because what's money good for anyway if you can't get first class accommodations but I'm sure they sank the *Ile de France* didn't they not that anyone cares after all a hijacker couldn't care less about my comfort so let them put on security guards it's very simple everything is I know because I saw it explained on television it's just a matter of getting your pan good and hot and then. . . ."

I wasn't doing a very good job of listening, but I was seeing plenty. The bandages made her face look like a mask, and suddenly I saw her as a primitive woman, someone who had deliberately submitted to mutilation for the sake of adornment. I saw witch doctors slashing open her flesh and rearranging its form, and then sewing her up again with the guts of animals—or whatever it is they use for making stitches. There was something horrifying about it and deeply moving all at the same time. It was a tremendous insight to have, because it made me feel what it really meant to be the child of such a woman. Once a long time ago she had spread her legs and screamed with pain to give birth to me. I saw her life, and mine, too—and everyone else's, I suppose —as a long series of profoundly real animal events. We eat, we sleep, we make love, we give birth, we laugh, we cry, we hurt and sing and scream and dance and feel good and one

374

day we die. I'm tempted to rattle on here about how civilization is a costume we wear, a sort of false face to keep us from seeing what we're doing. But I haven't thought about it enough yet to make any real sense of it. Besides I don't want to lose my thread.

Finally the dangerous moment arrived. Maude sailed out of the room, leaving us alone together. And Mother ran out of words.

The silence only lasted around five seconds at the most but that's all we needed for saying what we had to say—and words would never have achieved such a breathtakingly simple pact; we agreed to give up on each other. That's all there was to it. She was going to go right on doing her living in the style of her choice, because she had to, she simply *had* to. And so was I, because I simply had to. And we were going to stop *influencing* each other. No more judgments were to be passed, no more fighting. We were going to allow each other to *be*.

Once that was settled, I went over and kissed her. Then I sat on the edge of the bed and we had what Mother always calls a good old-fashioned gab fest. She's fascinated by controversies like whether or not women over thirty-five can get away with wearing red, and I was surprised to discover that since I'd stopped passing judgments against her for being superficial, it was great fun to prattle like that. My dreadful seriousness as a child must have been an awful pain in the ass to her all those years, the poor darling.

In Mother's Room, Belle Woods, November 11, 1969

Delano said last night that maturity arrives at the moment you stop trying to guess what will happen next. You just know that whatever it is, you'll get through it somehow. I'm not sure he's right, but it's worth making a note of.

———————

I'm writing this at Mother's dressing table. She's reclining on her chaise, queen-style.

Now that Maude's gone, I'm doing the lady-in-waiting bit. What surprises me is that I'm grooving on it so much. I've always known I was the mother and she was the daughter, but now we've really gotten down to living it out. For instance she asks me whether or not I think she should go out and take a walk in the yard. And I say, "Well, Mother, you must feel up to it or the idea wouldn't have occurred to you. Why don't you try it? If it's tiring or too cold, you can always come back in." Then I remind her to bundle up good.

But I make sure the decisions are *hers*. I don't want her developing a dependency on me.

Delano wants me to go to work on the *U.S. Times*. I could have a column of my own and put anything I want to in it. I haven't said yes but it's fun to think about.

Maybe I could interview Fred Random and get his inside views on Black Power.

Interruption:

I guess I smiled or something. Mother just asked me what was so amusing. I started to lie, but caught myself in time. Instead I told her it was such a far-out thought I'd never be able to convey the humor of it to her.

Telling the truth is getting to be like some fabulous sport. I'm really digging it. So far I haven't lied to her once since I got here. Not even this morning when she asked me about Hank.

Interesting scene.

I brought in the breakfast tray (same as usual—scrambled eggs, crisp bacon, toast, marmalade, coffee with half-and-half) and sat it on the little table next to her bed.

She said, "God, what if I get *fat* waiting for this damn face to heal?"

And Little Mother Gloria responded, "Don't worry about it. You're young and healthy. If you gain a few pounds, you can always take them off."

"That's true," she said. "I *am* young. I keep forgetting that. D'you know, when I was a little girl in Corktown, we had this old woman living next door to us. I think she came from the hills of Ireland somewhere. She was fat and she didn't have a tooth in her head and she always went around in dime-store dresses spilling soup all over sick people. An absolute mess! But the point is everybody called her Gramaw because she was so *old*. Gloria, do you know how old that woman was? She was thirty-four! I nearly died when I found out." And without even pausing for a breath, she said, "Sweetheart, you haven't told me about Hank Glyczwycz. Did you find him in New York?"

If I were pressed to the wall with a bayonet pointed at my heart and they told me I had to explain how my mother's head works *or else*, it'd have to be or else. Maybe that's lucky. If I'd known in advance which question was on the way, I might have blown it. But coming at me out of left field like that, all I did was say yes.

"You've *seen* him!"

"Yes, I have."

"Why haven't you told me before?"

"You haven't asked."

"Well, I never dreamed," she said. "Tell me about it, for heaven sake."

"What do you want to know?"

"I want to know everything, naturally. What's become of him, what's happened to him? You know what I want to hear. Don't be maddening!"

So I sat on the end of the bed and filled her in on the bare facts. Teaching in Manhattan. Living in Staten Island. Wife, kids, separated, etc.

"What did you think of him?"

"I could see why you were attracted to him. I was, too. If he hadn't been my father, I'd have gone to bed with him."

Her mouth and eyes opened wide. Then she said, "*Gloria!*" as if I'd just announced I was taking up prostitution.

"You asked me what I thought of him. Didn't you want to know?"

"Yes, but what a perfectly tasteless . . ."

At that moment she stopped talking. I don't think she realized it though. Something truly captivating was going on inside of her and it was taking all of her attention. I wished she could share it with me, but I knew she couldn't. Even so, I said, "What are you thinking about, Mother?" But it didn't do any good.

Sometimes I feel Mother doesn't really have a voice. Her mind does of course, it chatters on and on, but *she* doesn't. Her real being is mute. I don't know why that is, or why I feel that way. But I truly believe reality is some kind of a wildcat to her, and it has her up a tree, too terrified to utter a sound.

In my room, Belle Woods,
NOVEMBER 13, 1969

I've got the Rotary Connection playing on the stereo. It's John's favorite, the one where they sing Amen Amen Amen about a hundred times.

Delano asked me to pass out leaflets with him at the Grosse Pointe shopping mall on Saturday. He says the revolution's coming faster than anybody anticipates. I asked him if he meant bang bang, death in the streets, etc. He does.

Mother won't be needing my company today. She's spending the afternoon on the phone with a lawyer, discussing her favorite subject, private property. Which means she's beginning to be herself again. Maude Dangerfield agrees. Maude stopped by last night and on her way out she said, "I think we'll have our little girl in dancing shoes and on stage again before you can say Jack Sprat."

There have been lots of signs. This morning she was trying on wigs over her bandages and working hell out of every mirror in the place.

When I first went into her room she was wearing a Rita Hayworth number and singing:

> *"I'm gonna change my way o' livin'*
> *And if that ain't enough*
> *I'm gonna change the way I strut my stuff."*

Then she got into a blond one and did a Lana Turner scene for me. I couldn't tell whether or not she knew the cameras were turning. Maybe she was just living the part. She stood in front of her dressing room mirror, hands on hips, looking herself over. It was obvious she liked what she saw. But there was something faintly creepy about it, as if she was *having* herself with her eyes. Then all of a sudden she said, "To hell with him."

I said, "Who, Mother?"

No answer. These old-timey stars know how to concentrate. She went right on with the scene.

"I'm getting a settlement," she said, still connecting with the mirror. "Oh boy oh boy oh *boy*, am I getting a settlement. Am *I* getting a *settlement!*" Then she winked at herself and changed into another wig.

A few minutes later, resting on her chaise between takes, so to speak, she said, "Gloria, don't you ever get the urge to doll up and knock people's eyes out?" And before I could answer, she said, "You know, I'd just love to know what goes through that mind of yours. What sort of thing do you think about anyway?"

"I don't know," I said. "The same things everyone thinks about, I suppose."

"Yes, but what mostly?" She moved over a little and made a place for me. "Come sit."

I got the feeling she was really ready to talk, so I sat next to her and looked at her.

"What do I think about?"

"Mm. But don't tell me if you think I'm prying. Because I'm not." She was being careful to speak without too much lip work, still cautious about the incisions in her scalp.

"I wonder a lot about what my life will be like," I said, "and what sort of people I'll be meeting. Also, I think a lot about how scary the world is. Every night I pray for a leader to come along to save us and—"

"For a *leader* to come?"

"Yes, a leader. You know, a great president or someone. Only he doesn't have to be political, he could even be from somewhere unexpected."

"I won't interrupt again," she said. "Go on."

"With what?"

"What else you think about."

"Oh. Okay. I think about the police and the government and the Army, and all the people getting killed. You know, in Vietnam and places like that. And all the ones in jails and prisons. And I worry about pollution, too, and the famine that's coming—"

"*Famine!* Did you say *famine?* I'm not interrupting. I just want to be sure I'm getting all these words."

"Yes, famine. Mass starvation everywhere. I worry about that. And the revolution that's coming, too, and all the suffering there'll be. And whether or not in the end it'll all get together. Also there's a—"

"Gloria, I'm sorry," she said, "I'm trying terribly hard to listen with an open mind. But we've got to be perfectly frank with each other. Aren't you being just a teensy bit pretentious?"

What I liked best about this moment was that I didn't

get angry. Not at all. I just said, "I don't think so, Mother. Does it sound pretentious to you?"

"No, of course not, I don't mean pretentious at all. So please don't take offense. I don't have your wonderful flair for words. But sweetheart! After all! Famines and revolutions! You simply *must* listen to yourself! Is this normal thinking for a lovely young girl who has *every advantage in the world?* Let me tell you what I think, may I? And I'm not being some kind of *mother* either, I swear. This is just person to person."

I said, "I know. And I'd really like to hear."

It was true, too. She wasn't just hassling me. She was truly concerned.

"Now listen hard, honey, the way I just did. Will you?" She didn't wait for an answer. She took my hand and held it tight. Her voice was soft and reasonable and full of affection. "Mother has an imagination, too," she said. "She knows what fun it is to have all these wonderfully dramatic notions and to talk about them with your young friends. And I adore your earnestness, honestly I do. That serious little face just breaks my heart. But please, honey, trust me when I tell you it's *not healthy.* Don't go on like this, I beg you."

Then she squeezed my hand hard and leaned in toward me, whispering for greater emphasis, "*I just know it's not going to make you a happy person.*"

Belle Woods, November 14, 1969

Beautiful afternoon. I'm out in the yard, sitting on the teeter-totter, feeling very young and very old, remembering some of the high dudes that used to sit on the other end of it, and wondering what will happen to us all.

The time has come for me to move along. I don't know when and I don't know where, but it'll be soon and it'll be somewhere. I can tell.

I just saw a squirrel I used to know, but I'm not sure he recognized me.